HIGH NOTE

CARDINAL SINS BOOK 3

HEATHER LONG

BLAKE BLESSING

Ingredients include: something pithy, probably a little dark, definitely sarcastic with a dash of burn it up spice. Shake. Serve at room temperature, be ready with ice. Warning: Please hydrate beforehand.

FOREWORD

Dear Reader,

What sounds better? "Eight Effective Ways to Dispose of a Body" or "10 Ways You Can Eliminate a Corpse"? We're totally asking for research.

Promise.

But that's probably not why you picked up High Note. Previously in Cardinal Sins, Fletcher and Rick let Cash out of the cell because they needed the former FBI agent's help to find Vienna who hadn't returned on schedule. When we last saw Vienna, she was bound to chair, with a hood over her head, having been taken prisoner   but by who?

Yes, we hear you loud and clear: "That's what we want to know ladies, can we get to the point?"

Sorry, we do like to entertain ourselves. The point, is that in Kill Song, we met a very lonely Vienna on the trail of her father's killer. Through happenstance and coincidence, she met Rick in a dark alley. While his name was Merrick then and he had his own issues, he brought something into her life she desperately needed: companionship, a friend, an ally, and eventually a lover.

Because she needed to get papers for Rick to help change

his identity, she ended up rescuing Fletcher from Dion, and he entered into their happy little circle of meting out justice and passion. Cash crashing into them all then, spending all of First Chorus in a cell while Vienna tried to sort out not only her feelings but what to do with someone who *wasn't* a criminal but clearly a threat, well, that was just meat on the bones.

Now these three unlikely allies, who aren't quite friends and are definitely not altogether trusting, have to work together to find the one thing they truly have in common.

The big question is what happens when they find her?

Or should I say that's *one* of the big questions.

We will warn you that as in previous books, this novel does contain graphic violence, depictions of human trafficking, sexual violence, as well as some scenes involving physical and psychological torture. This is very much a dark romance with emphasis on both the dark and the romance. We do try to inject some funny as well.

Please use caution and protect yourself.

Now for the short bit of business. This is a reverse harem which means the heroine is not going to have to choose at the end of the story.

Oh—and since this is a series, there will not necessarily be an HEA at the end of each book, but we do promise to sort out one by the end.

Probably.

Mostly.

Well, you know what? Just trust us!

xoxo

Blake & Heather

P.S. About those titles, we would love to hear which one you prefer. No pressure.

PROLOGUE

A FEW WEEKS AGO…

IT WAS EARLY when they left. The day had a watery gray kind of brightness to it. Not that the sun wasn't shining, it just seemed hazy. Maybe fires in the west. The light glinted off the window as they passed, but my proximity to the road didn't worry me.

The camouflage tucked my vehicle out of sight. I also didn't rush to follow. Today's vehicle had a tracker on it. A slap-and-track I'd placed myself. I took the time to finish my notes before putting away the laptop.

Five minutes later, I pulled out, following the red dot on my phone screen. She was too good not to pick up a tail. Spooking her wasn't the plan. I caught up to "them" at a gas station. Since a top-up wouldn't hurt me, I parked at the pump farthest away.

Pulling the card from my wallet, I skimmed my gaze over the name. Today I was… "Bruno." Humming to myself, I got the gas going and leaned back against the car. The angle from the windows of the little convenience store let me track their movements.

The hacker was with her today. I'd already pulled Fletcher Reed's background and added it to my notes. He seemed to be nursing a hangover—though the way he swayed a little when he walked suggested he might still be drunk.

Poor company.

Worse backup.

Suppressing the urge to curl my lip, I didn't linger after my gas tank was full. Leaving the station ahead of them. I parked one block east and one block south.

Then waited.

The gas station was a pit stop. When they started moving again, I fell in behind them at the same distance I'd maintained earlier. Her destination proved to be a storage facility. Curiosity pulled me from my vehicle, but I stayed downwind and out of sight.

Located in an isolated spot, the place just reeked of abandonment and disuse. The grass growing through the cracks in the pavement and blacktop pretty much cemented the local town's lack of interest in keeping up the maintenance in the area.

The address tickled something in the back of my mind. I'd check it out later. Low-glare binoculars gave a front-row seat as they opened the locker and went inside. It was empty—save for some file boxes. Standard. No guarantee of what they contained.

Tragedy crossed Vienna's face. The expression arrested me. While I would never label her as guarded, she'd always radiated a self-possessed air. Ethereal. Capable.

Talented.

A sigh half-escaped me, and I had to shake it off when the hacker kissed her.

It wasn't just a peck on the lips.

No, there was a ferociousness to that kiss that prickled over my skin. A possessiveness that had me curling my fingers into my palm. She allowed it.

Lucky for him, she returned it with equal fervor.

That move could have gotten him killed.

When they left the locker, they took the boxes and sealed them up. Even as I tracked their movements, I considered the storage facility. Once again, I let her leave ahead of me and just waited. If she turned in the direction of her home, I'd go investigate now. If she didn't—and it turned out she didn't—I'd make a point of returning later.

The next drive was nearly as long as the first, only we didn't go back to her place at all. We went to the port. Aware of exactly who owned the dockside warehouse, I parked a mile back. Any closer would really tip her off.

No one else was here.

The hacker was waiting in the car like a good pup. Amusement flared through me. Had she left the window open for him? Having been here more than a few times, I knew a couple of access points that would let me slip in undetected.

I made it just in time for the show. It *was* a show. Vienna worked with a kind of elegant efficiency few could ever hope to achieve. Captivated, I almost wished I'd brought a camera that would let me film her. She didn't play games, tease, or taunt.

She went straight to the questions. While I was too far away to catch all the words audibly, I could read lips. The last year had been very hard on her, not that you could see it in her professionalism. But the barest crack in her voice betrayed an ocean of agony.

It almost made me homicidal, an urge I kept in check. She didn't need me to take this from her. She had it.

While I soaked up and savored every moment of her work, someone else decided to interrupt. The bastard walked in, clapping. A sigh would have escaped me if I allowed it.

Rude.

He could have at least waited until she finished. Edging was fine. Taking one's time was fine. Interrupting her at the cusp of the orgasm in her work?

To… fanboy?

I was a heartbeat away from taking the decision away from both of them when the hacker appeared. He clocked the interloper with a tire iron.

I found myself almost… impressed.

Remained that way until he puked outside. However, the act only diminished my evaluation a little. He obeyed instructions. Like the professional she was, she cleaned the scene and removed the bodies—both the corpse and the prisoner.

What would she do with him?

A tingle shivered up my spine. I really wanted to know.

They took both cars after they were finished, including the removal of all the hard drives. I did a sweep of my own after their absence, confirming nothing remained that could trace back to her.

Speaking of tracing, I checked my tracker on the way back to the car. This late in the day, it didn't take me long to make up the miles separating us. I honestly didn't want to miss anything. She'd gone to a dump site, clearly. Well, a dump site for the stranger's car and Bailey's body.

Close enough to hear them this time, I appreciated her thoroughness in cleaning out the car before she put the hacker in the passenger seat and left. They were heading home.

I didn't follow. Instead, I waited for her cleaner. It didn't surprise me that Reuben showed up within the hour. He was the most logical choice.

Leaving the shadows, I approached him. His reaction didn't disappoint.

"Madre de Dios," he swore before he paled. "Why are *you* here?" Then he earned some serious points. "If you hurt Lily, you and I will not be friends." Lily was the pet name he used for Vienna. Cute.

"We're not friends now," I reminded him.

He swallowed, but his fist tightened until his knuckles

went white. Not backing down, despite the trickle of sweat rolling down his face. Loyalty. I respected it.

"We should talk, Reuben."

"About?" He didn't back down, nor did the suspicion in his gaze relax.

I smiled.

This time, Reuben retreated a step and cut his gaze away once before coming back to me. Solid survival instincts. Maybe we could be friends.

Probably not. But it might make him feel better if I let him think there was a chance.

"Let's start with this job," I instructed him. "Then we'll go from there."

RICK WAS NOT HANDLING this well.

I shot him an encouraging look as we trailed after the raging cyclone that was "Cash." He'd spent the last ten minutes circling the house checking cabinets, peeking under cushions and behind picture frames.

Every time Cash touched something new, leaving behind smudged fingerprints, Rick's right eye twitched. I was worried it was going to become a constant winky face if Cash didn't slow down.

I grabbed the cleaning wipes from under the sink and handed Rick one as I took one out for myself, and we started wiping down literally everything. Well, I wiped everything down, probably not to Rick's standards. The big guy periodically stopped to glare at Cash's back the longer he was out of the basement.

Goody. Ten minutes free, and he was already driving our big guy up the wall. I guessed I should consider myself lucky that I hadn't achieved this level of irritation from him.

"Where was the last place you saw her?" Cash asked almost absently, except his voice was too firm and assured for that.

"Here. She left for a job five days ago. She was only supposed to be gone seventy-two hours at most. A quick reconnaissance job," I rushed out before Rick could snap at him.

"You shouldn't be touching those things," Rick said, putting in his two cents anyway as Cash picked up a few knickknacks in the living room. I wasn't sure if they were things that had sentimental value to Vienna or if Rick just didn't like Cash's hands on her possessions.

Cash completely ignored him and headed to the study. "What was the job?"

"This is my space. Nothing of hers is in here." Whoa. Now it was me getting territorial.

The bastard shrugged as he put his dirty paws all over my beautiful setup. What? Was he looking for nudes stuffed between the servers?

"The job?"

I blew out a slow breath through my nose and wiped down the servers before the big guy got a chance to get that close to him.

"She was going to check out Sandra Jane. See if she could figure out what kind of information she has in combination with your dad's journals."

He paused. Maybe surprised that was who she was going to see? Especially since, you know, the reporter had his *dad's* journals. Something we'd have to get more information on now that we were all buddies.

"Sandra Jane is the investigative journalist?"

"Yes."

"Hmm." He continued making a giant fucking mess around my lair. "What was the job before that?"

This time, Rick beat me to the answer. I was just glad to see him snapping out of his earlier catatonic state. "It wasn't really a job, not yet. She met with a contact about a potential job. Why do you need to know all this?"

"Don't you know? Vienna should give you a list of shows to watch for educational purposes. Start with The First 48." He smirked at Rick, and his right eye twitched again. "Whenever someone is missing, you retrace their last known steps. Every single detail. Even when you think something won't be important, because those are usually the clues that lead to their discovery. That's what we're doing, we're retracing her footsteps. Now, who is this contact and what was the job." He made it a statement, not a question. Fucker.

Rick outlined as much as he knew as Cash finally left the study…and headed upstairs. The very first stop was Drew's bedroom. "Oh shit."

I ran the last few steps to get between Rick and Cash as he swung open the door to what I was sure Rick viewed as his current shrine to Drew. Good thing I did, because the dead eyes from the first time I'd met Rick made a reappearance. And I knew exactly what question would pop out, so I got there before he could say it.

"You can't kill him. Not yet." I pressed my palms against his pecs. If we weren't losing our minds with worry, I would have cracked a joke about how much he'd been working out. But I didn't. I didn't have the stomach for it at the moment.

"You can't kill me at all," Cash replied glibly as he took in the room. Did he just take a deep breath? I wasn't sure, it was too quick to tell.

Stepping away from Rick, I looked around the room from Cash's point of view. What did the Fed see, and what conclusions was he drawing from her space?

Sure, it was a nice room—clean, calming in neutral tones, and with all the typical bedroom furniture. But there was nothing here that screamed, *I'm a vigilante justice killer*! This looked like any other bedroom of a twenty-something woman. In fact, the entire house had a normal vibe that had really thrown me off at first.

I expected Cash to start flipping this room too. Instead, he sauntered over to the nightstand. Just to make sure he didn't do anything suspicious or creepy, I followed and stepped to the side to see exactly what he touched.

And…I was confused.

Because the biggest fucking grin spread across his face as he picked up a Rubik's cube I had watched Drew solve a few nights before she left. He touched it almost reverently, then gently set it back down on the center of the nightstand.

Clearing my throat, I pushed some stray hair behind my ears. "Fan of the Rubik's cube, huh?" Why was I trying to make conversation?

"You could say that." He opened the drawers and rifled through them as he asked another series of questions. Who did she normally associate with? How often did she leave on jobs? Did anyone else live in this house?

The questions went on and on. And the more he asked, the redder Big Guy's face got.

We answered because we needed him, though we kept it as vague as we could. I didn't know what was worse, that Vienna could really be in trouble and needs us right now when we had no fucking clue where she was, or that she could be on her way back to find we'd let out the Fed and given him her life story as we knew it. With a few exceptions, of course.

"Tell me about the frat boy." The demand in his words as he stepped into Drew's closet even made me twitch. The big guy shot a look at me. The vein throbbing in his forehead would give him a headache.

"You can't kill him," I said in a soft voice. "Not yet. We need him."

The 'not yet' seemed to settle the big guy.

For. Now.

I blew out a breath.

"Tell me about the frat boy," Cash repeated, appearing in the doorway with a shirt of hers in hand.

What.

The.

Fuck.

I beat Rick to him and yanked the shirt away. "Dude, you might be fifty different shades of fucked up, but there are lines. This is *her* shit. Ask questions, but keep your hands to yourself."

The Fed met my gaze without flinching. "Or what?"

You know…

I cut a look at Rick. "Maybe I was wrong. Maybe you can just go ahead and kill—"

The next words didn't make it out of my mouth cause Rick was just right there, and I found myself in the unenviable position of being the smashed meat in the Rick and Cash sandwich.

In any other situation, this might be hilarious. But frankly, when—not "if" 'cause clearly this was a *when*—Rick tore Cash apart, I truly didn't want to be anywhere in his way.

"Get out of her closet," Rick ordered. "Get out of her bedroom."

Icy menace wreathed every word. Yeah, I'd thought Rick was close to losing it earlier. I'd been wrong.

The big guy was *fuming* and the smoke coming out of his ears wasn't a fire but the vapor that a rocket released as it got ready to launch. I was way too close to the demolition zone.

Like—ground zero close…

Also… "Fuck, who stinks like that?" I curled my nose cause the body odor was just—repulsive.

Neither man said anything, the tense standoff escalating wildly out of control. Goddammit.

"Words, gentlemen, use your words."

I never wanted to be the reasonable one again. When we found Drew, I would file my complaint.

"I'm the hot fucking mess in this relationship." I slammed my elbow back into the Fed's gut and did not whimper at the jarring sensation that turned my hand numb. Then I gave Rick a shove.

What does one do when stuck between the immovable object and the unstoppable force?

Right.

Bring up the one thing they wanted.

"This is *not* helping *her.*"

Like someone thrust a blade into the ballooning tension, all the air seemed to whoosh out of the room.

Rick cut his gaze to me and the prickle of sensation on the back of my neck told me I had the Fed's attention. Then both men snapped their attention back to each other.

Time seemed to elongate. If they really decided to throw down right now, I was so fucked.

Worse, my sexy death angel might be, and that was unacceptable. Taking a deep breath, I gathered together every ounce of Reed arrogance. It was in the DNA. We were all royal fucking bastards right down to the marrow. The world fucking belonged to us. I'd been birthed and nursed on that. We owned it, and we could do whatever we wanted.

Fuck the consequences.

Even if those consequences… Nope.

Don't go there.

Not right now.

I needed to channel my inner asshole.

Right—just act like my father. He was a fucking master.

"Let me be clear," I said in a surprisingly strong voice, though I didn't waste time trying to marvel at it. Better to use it before I ran out of steam. "I will find her on my own if I have to. It'll take me a hot minute, but I will. And I already *saved* her once. I can do it again. So, get on board or get the fuck out of my way."

That went for the big guy too.

I needed him to see that. We were better working together, but this? This shit couldn't fly.

"Table this dick measuring contest until we have her back." Then I glanced at the Fed and met his hard, unyielding stare. "To be clear, the big guy will win, but my dick's pretty fucking spectacular cause I know how to use it. You? You're just a dick right now. A dick without a purpose."

Another endless moment of soul-crushing dead silence, then...

"The frat boy was a serial rapist who got off because of his family's money. We found him with another girl he was about to assault. We made it abundantly clear to him that those actions were unacceptable and offered to re-educate him. He chose poorly. Now, he won't hurt anyone else," Rick explained as he took the shirt from my hand and folded it over his arm. Withdrawing a single step, he let me out of the man cage of crazy.

Thank fuck. I knew the big guy had it in him. Escaping while I had the opportunity, I moved closer to the door out of the bedroom.

"After that," Rick continued. "We went to meet with another contact regarding an unrelated matter. After that, we returned home."

Cash nodded slowly. "The unrelated matter have anything to do with the reporter, the frat boy, or the pirate?"

Wait... "What pirate?"

Both men shot me looks. Right, shut up, Fletcher.

Got it.

"Bailey," Cash explained. "Did it have anything to do with him?"

In specific? Probably not. But...

"Yes and no," Rick answered in an obstinate, stiff tone. "It was a private discussion between business acquaintances."

With a less than patient sigh, Cash slid his hands into his pockets. He rocked back and forth on his heels as if considering our words. To look at him—besides the semi-rumpled clothes and disheveled hair, one would never know he'd been a prisoner.

Then again, Rick had fed him gourmet meals daily, brought him fresh clothes, allowed him to bathe, and even made sure he had plenty of water.

As imprisonments went, it was kind of like being at a five-star hotel—if it had bars and no access to a television or WI-FI.

"Would the man she had a private discussion with—as a business acquaintance—have a reason to come after her?" The question seemed almost reasonable.

"No," Rick answered bluntly. "He didn't want to piss her off."

A sudden smile spread across the Fed's face, this one damn near as delighted as the stupid ass grin he'd worn when he walked in on Drew at the docks. "He's afraid of her."

The big guy just shrugged. "He wasn't stupid."

Well, that was something, I guessed.

"Right. Did she give you the plans for approaching Sandra Jane?"

All he got out of Rick was a crisp nod.

"Care to share?"

"After you get out of her room and shower. Your stench is offending Fletcher."

Well, I wouldn't have said offending, but I sure as fuck wasn't going to contradict him.

"Fletcher needs to eat."

I wasn't especially hungry, but no fucking way was I arguing with the big guy. Nope.

"Shower. Clean clothes. Food." Rick ticked off the instructions in a rumbly growl that no longer held a lost note and the bleak look in his eyes had vanished.

For now.

"Then we find Vienna, and we bring her home."

Raking a hand through his hair, Cash cut me a look. Far from intimidated, he seemed bemused. "Is he for real?"

"Man, just go with it. Cooperate. Besides—he's not wrong. You stink, and you're way too close to her clothes."

A muscle ticked in Rick's jaw. Yeah, he'd noticed.

"Fine," Cash agreed, and I wasn't sure who was more surprised, me, Rick, or the Fed. He made a beeline for her bathroom.

Rick cut him off. "We have bathrooms for guests."

There went all my hard work. The Fed was gonna be an asshole, Rick was gonna tear him apart, and I'd have to learn how to get blood out of the carpet.

Bile climbed my throat. I didn't want to learn that.

Shockingly, Cash actually backed up a step. "Then point me toward a shower, and let's get this shit over with. I also want to get my shit from my car."

Oh.

His car.

Right.

We'd have to deal with that later.

"You shower too," Rick told me, some of the command in his voice wavering.

Don't worry, Big Guy, I told him mentally. I got you. "On it." I needed a break from this testosterone-choked fest as it was. "I'll be downstairs in fifteen."

Rick still held her shirt, but he pointed Cash out of her room. Usually, I'd have just gone to use my own shower. The longing for Drew crashed through me, though. When I headed for hers, Cash made some grumble of objection.

Whatever Rick told him shut him up, then the door to Drew's room closed and I sagged against the doorframe to her bathroom.

Where are you, Drew?

The thought circled in my head like a nightmare waiting to drag me into Hell. Straightening, I stripped—folded my clothes neatly and did not leave them in a heap—then stepped into an ice-cold shower.

It made my teeth chatter and my balls want to shrivel, but it also shocked some clarity back into me.

Hang on, Drew. We're gonna come get you.

I promise.

CASH

I CRACKED my neck as we entered the old, two-story cookie cutter on the end of a cul de sac. Half a day's drive was killer on my back and neck, especially when I started the damn trip in the trunk.

Again.

"Is picking locks part of the FBI training?" Fletcher whispered as he entered the house behind me. We'd already handed our shoes to Rick, who was taking his off.

"Sure," I sighed. Fletcher Reed was a talker. Luckily, he'd saved me from that version of himself when I'd been in the basement. But damn, he drank an entire energy drink and practically bounced in his seat the rest of the ride.

That was then. It was work time now.

And I was finally out of that fucking basement. It was hard not to grin as I took in the living room and kitchen. We'd entered through the back after Fletcher confirmed she was in another city for a guest appearance. Having a hacker at your fingertips was handy. Something I'd taken for granted when I was with the bureau.

I scanned the room as Rick arranged our shoes in the plastic bag he brought, then shut the door behind him. That man was like a neat freak MacGyver, with his Sani-wipes, roll of plastic baggies, plastic gloves, and lint roller. Probably why Vienna had picked him up in the first place. He was a serial killer's wet dream as far as it came to cleaning up DNA. Next thing you know, he'd start carrying around the booties real estate agents used and hair nets from the beauty salon.

Actually, I turned to Rick. "You need to get shoe covers for our shoes, so you don't have to mess with the bag and we don't waste time taking off and putting on our shoes. You can either buy those online or at any hardware store. You need hair caps too. Also available for online ordering or from any beauty supply store."

His gaze jerked to mine, and he studied me for a fraction of a second before nodding. See? I wasn't such a bad guy.

On the way, I'd listened to as many of the interviews Sandra Jane had given as I could, starting with the ones since I'd been acquired…

Her house was exactly as I pictured it. Neat, staged, and bland. If she had hired a decorator to puke up every fashion trend in suburbia, this would be it. At least there was a reason Vienna's place was as generic as it was. If someone stumbled across it, she wouldn't want them to have any knowledge about who she was or her patterns.

But I still caught the few items no one else would think meant anything. My favorite was my Rubik's cube on her nightstand. It had been a testament to my willpower that I didn't pop a goddamn boner right there.

"Why are you smiling?" Fletcher frowned as he stepped up beside me. At least he had pulled his hair up into a tight bun with hair gel slicking down any stray pieces.

I shrugged and continued my first pass.

Sandra Jane was young but accomplished. A social climber, but more in the academic sense rather than high society. Just from watching her mannerisms in her interviews—from the way she leaned forward when she spoke, the subconscious softening of her mouth that threatened to turn into a smile at any second—she operated with a single-minded focus toward her goals, and that was currently finding the real identity of the Judge. And she got off on it.

Not all that unusual for an up-and-coming overachiever who had never failed.

Her comments about Pops' journals were interesting, although she never came out and said what was in them. Of course, she wouldn't. She'd want to hold any unique information to herself until she had a concrete trail or even the identity of the Judge.

I wasn't that concerned about them. I'd read all of his journals and everything that led me to Vienna, I'd discovered after Pops' death.

Now, *how* she got them? That was something I was extremely interested in. I'd be giving my bitch mother a call sometime soon.

I adjusted the gloves and started combing the space, checking for hidden papers, cubbies, or false drawers. Anything that offered her a hidey-hole or place to camouflage her secrets.

"Give me the run down again. Everything you can remember," I ordered Fletcher as I started in the living room.

"Okay, first, please and thank you go a long way. And second, how come you're not spinning around this place like you did Vienna's?" he asked with a huff of indignation, even as he pulled his phone out.

I didn't bother giving him my full attention since I was already focused on the task at hand. "Because Sandra Jane can't know we were here, can she?"

A brief pause of silence. "Good call. So, according to my handy-dandy memo pad, here's what I have. Sandra Jane, age twenty-four, investigative journalist for two years. Had two cold cases solved that put her on the radar for bigger and better things. One was a missing person's case, and the other was a murder case. Working on the Judge is a larger and more infamous fish, which is probably why she's focused on this particular cold case…Or cold *cases*. Graduated from Stanford, almost at the top of her class. Two people beat her out." He paused. "I bet that really chapped her ass," he said lightly. "She—"

"Give me her personal details. Relationship status, hobbies. Family history." I finished up the living room and went to the kitchen next. As I had suspected, nothing out of the ordinary. She also seemed like she had a bit of a cleaning OCD problem. Normally, there was dust on the shelves and lint under the couches and couch cushions.

None of that was present. Everything was as squeaky clean as if she'd moved in yesterday.

"Father died when she was eleven. He was a criminal defense attorney. Mother's still alive, remarried, and living in Boca. It doesn't appear they have a relationship, based on phone and email records. No boyfriend since sophomore year of college and no recent dating history. I couldn't find her registered on any dating apps. No pe—"

"Trends on her social media? Friends she talks to often? Places she checks in at?" The kitchen was clean. Of course.

Sandra Jane was most likely not our person, but we needed to start here to cover our bases. The more I thought about it, the more I wanted to pick their brains about her associates. Rick had been far too vague about the last errand he'd run with her. And when people held onto secrets, there was usually a good, and damning, reason.

"Would you stop interrupting me?" Fletcher tossed his hands up. "We went over this in the car already."

"Yes, but I was too busy picking apart Sandra Jane's interviews, and you were talking too much and saying too little. You really ought to think about cutting back on the caffeine."

His face darkened as I slipped past him to head toward the front of the house. I caught the lip twitch on Rick before I passed him too.

I see you and know you agree even if you won't admit it.

The house was a bust. The longer we were there, the clearer it became. Still, I did a thorough search. Every cupboard. Every drawer. Behind items in the pantry. If there were appliances on the counter, I picked them up.

Whatever she had, it wasn't here. Fletcher stared at me when I opened the woman's underwear drawer, but I ignored him. Silent Rick just followed as he did the same thing I was. Checked everything with a kind of methodical precision. Open, examine, search, and leave everything where it went.

"This isn't her home," I said after I finished in the bathroom. It couldn't be more plain. This place had zero personality.

At all.

Rick exited her closet with an expression set in stone, and Fletcher glared at the walls like they'd personally done something to offend him. They were as different as night and day.

"What do you mean?" The first real words the silent giant had spoken directly to me since ordering me into a shower.

See, I can share.

"She might sleep here. She might even pause long enough to unpack her overnight bag and repack it. But she doesn't *live* here." I motioned to the room. "Eliminate everything else, the monotonous art where there is any, the plain decorations, the lack of personal pictures or even scattered beauty items on the counter. What else is missing?"

"She's a neat freak," Fletcher said with a shrug. "The big guy is, too, that doesn't mean anything."

I cut him a look. "Even Vienna has a handful of cosmetics and hair items on her counter."

Nothing that actually touched her or could contain DNA. No brushes or makeup applicators. No actual combs or sponges or washcloths. What linens were in her bathroom were all freshly laundered. If I were a betting man, I'd say even the bottles and cosmetic cases had been wiped down.

Still—they were there.

Sandra Jane lacked even the most cursory of personal hygiene products, which were all stored in a container *beneath* the sink.

The pair glanced at each other, then scanned the room. It came as no surprise that Rick detected it first. The guy had an eye for details.

"It smells empty."

Pointing my index finger and thumb in his direction like I'd cocked a gun, I nodded. "Exactly."

Fletcher wrinkled his nose. "It doesn't—smell like anything." He cut a look at Rick. "How is that empty?"

"Vienna's room smells like hope and peace." Bleakness stamped its way across the guy's face. Her absence was seriously fucking him up. Even Fletcher's expression tightened at the loss in his voice. "This place smells like…"

"Nothing. The lack of dust says she has house cleaners. Everything is wiped down and shiny. If she has ever cooked anything on that stove, I'd be shocked. She probably does takeout, but there was nothing in the fridge—not even *milk*—that's gone bad. It has some general condiments, a case of water, and two bottles of wine."

They were the most personal things I'd found. But they were generic, store-bought wines. Cheap and easy to obtain, and she probably drank it because she was on a budget.

"The clothes in the closet," I said, motioning to it. "They're knockoffs and mid-labels. Every single item has also had its inner tags removed. Inexpensive. Sure. She's probably on a budget, but she wants to look like she has expensive taste. There's also a retro nature to some of them. I'd bet she picked them up at a second or third-hand store."

Especially the pair of evening gowns.

"What about Drew's closet?" Fletcher asked as he ducked into the closet to look. The Reeds were loaded. He'd recognize the knockoffs like I would bad beer. It was just how it was.

"Classy, tasteful. Some of it is downright dirty. But what looks like a label *is* a label. What doesn't…" I spread my hands because I had to admire art, and she was a goddamn work of art. "Isn't supposed to. I can imagine whatever role she plays, whatever she wears, she fits in. No one would ever see her as out of place. Anywhere."

A brilliant chameleon who outshone even those born into the life, but at the same time, earthy, provocative, and everything I'd ever imagined my perfect woman to be.

Not that I'd focused on that, and I had to get my mind off seeing her in one of those outfits, or better, out of them. My dick twitched at the thought and the hunger I'd had for her in the beginning, had nothing on the ravenous need I'd developed since finally meeting her.

"She's not here," Rick said with finality. "She hasn't been here."

"Nope."

If she had come after Sandra Jane, it hadn't been here.

"Fuck." Fletcher emerged from the closet. Though the sudden suppression of his manic behavior proved far more unsettling than his bouncing off the walls. "What do we do now?"

Not waiting for an answer, he stalked out of the bedroom with his phone in his hand. Without much to offer, I headed to the front door with Rick following in my wake.

Nothing was spoken until we were outside and back at the car. Fletcher reset her outside cameras. A little power surge had "knocked" them offline. It would take the system a bit to reboot.

By then, we would be long gone.

"We have a job to do," Rick said when we got to the car.

"Can we do it without her?" Fletcher asked.

Rick nodded. "Vienna said we'd be there. So that's where we'll be." Then he glanced at me.

"I'd rather keep looking for her. You guys feel free to do whatever. Just give me a number I can—"

"No."

I sighed.

"What the big guy is saying is," Fletcher jumped in, "we're not separating. You're only out of the cell to help us, so that means you stay with us."

Right.

"So where we go, you go."

Rubbing the back of my neck, I stared at them. "This wastes resources and time. I'm more effective hunting for her. As you stated earlier, I was the guy who found her."

I also had contacts I could pull in. To do that, though, I needed a phone. My car wouldn't hurt, but they'd remained mute on the subject.

The flat-eyed look swept through Rick's gaze again. Right.

"Fine, I'll drive. What's the job?"

Fletcher might be malleable, but the big guy definitely wasn't. "Backseat with Fletcher," Rick ordered as he opened the driver's side door.

Fuck me. "Seriously?"

"You prefer the trunk?" The barest hint of a thin smile creased his lips.

"No, I don't prefer the fucking trunk." They'd made me ride in the damn thing for over an hour before letting me out.

"Come on, Fed. We'll do road trip games," Fletcher said with a fleeting grin that didn't touch his eyes. Not that he looked at me long. His attention was back on his phone.

"You know," I said as I slid into the backseat, behind the empty front passenger seat rather than the driver's. I'd give Rick credit. He refused to give me an inch, and he wasn't taking chances. "I'm good. You play on your phone. If you give me one, I can make some calls."

That just got me a bland look from both of them.

Right.

"Fine—what's the job we're doing?"

That got me another look, though at least Rick answered this time.

"You'll see."

Sure. That was so helpful.

VIENNA

A HARD, open-handed slap sent my head snapping to the left. I groaned in pain when I really wanted to laugh. But if I made it seem like she was doing some damage, I might be able to pump up her ego enough for her to get lazy.

As with anyone, laziness bred carelessness. With carelessness often came opportunities to escape.

"Don't think I'm stupid," she spit.

Oh, I don't think you're stupid. A little weak in your arm, but not stupid.

I was actually kicking myself for not paying better attention when I pulled up to her place. Daddy would be livid with me. I couldn't even use the excuse of approaching a civilian, especially one with no history of violence, martial arts, or any kind of tactical background.

The ghost of his disappointment was a living thing pressing ice down my neck and shoulders. He would have taken her as a real threat for the simple reason she had the journals of an FBI agent assigned to find the Judge. He wouldn't have hurt her, but he would have approached using the same level of caution.

And I had failed. Spectacularly. The burn of bitter anger at myself did little to combat the ice, but it helped.

Rick and Fletcher were probably losing their minds. Especially my sweet Rick. I hoped Fletcher was helping him while I was away. If I was lucky, his hyper-happy energy would keep Rick grounded rather than send him into an irritated rage.

I…missed them.

I took in a calming, stuttering breath. That was something I couldn't do anything about for the moment. What I could do was figure out why this bitch, Sandra Jane, had decided to abduct me.

The obvious answer was that she saw me around her house, although I canvased the place for people and cameras before I approached. I stayed in the blind spots. So that couldn't have been it. She hadn't even *jumped* me there.

"Why did you take me from the gas station?" I croaked. My throat was dry and she'd been stingy with the water.

She'd actually used some foresight and waited until I was almost ready to leave the gas station before ambushing me. Lucky her, the bathrooms were porta-potties around the back of the property. It had been dark and empty, with no one to see her or me.

Clever girl.

I preferred that anyway.

She paced around the small basement, ironically like a caged animal. This was a girl who had always achieved whatever goal she'd set out for herself. Tenacious was the perfect epithet for her. Even the most untrained person could see that.

I'd watched her interviews, and I'd taken the time to study her. But the one thing that hadn't come across through the television was the dark light in her eyes.

Which meant it probably burned her pride that she'd had me here for five days and collected zero answers.

Using the time to study my environment once again just in

case I missed something the first two hundred times, I glanced around the space.

We were in a cabin of some sort. Specifically, in the basement. One that could double as a guest room from the size of it. Furniture, including a large armoire, is stacked up against the back wall, blocking the one small window near the ceiling. When she left me locked in here, dull light filtered between the cracks of the furniture so I wasn't in pitch darkness. Not that the hood let me make out much, but when I moved my head, I could look down.

Sandra Jane was definitely an amateur.

She was dressed in a pair of trim black slacks and a tucked-in white blouse. Each time she'd come to "interrogate" me, she'd been dressed similarly.

Fletcher had outlined her schedule before I left. That meant we had to be close to an airport or a big city for her to keep her speaking engagements.

"The better question is, how are you connected to the Judge? I have my suspicions, but I'd rather you confirm them for me." She grabbed an old kitchen chair she'd set by the door and moved it directly across from me.

With grace and poise that only came with a wealthy upbringing, she sat down. Her light brown hair was clipped at the back of her neck and the loose waves tumbled over one shoulder. She clasped her hands over her knees as she quietly watched me.

I knew this game.

She thought the attention would hike up my nerves—a solid thought process when her light torture hadn't done the trick.

Funny that she went straight into violence. Sandra Jane must have had a lot of pent-up aggression to get out. But I recognized that with minimal training, she would have been a great career criminal. Maybe even doing the kind of work I did.

She had a fire for what she thought was "righting" wrongs. Her perception was just a little skewed.

After ten minutes of us watching one another, her patience started to wane. Her lids lowered, her nostrils slightly flared, and the thumb of her right hand dug into the inside of her thigh.

This was a dance we'd done several times over the last few days. She cycled, watching for signs that something got to me. But this time, she drew in a deep breath, and after she let it out, her posture relaxed from its rigid stance.

"Let's try this a different way. Maybe you don't know all the facts. I mean, how could you?" One shoulder lifted a fraction of an inch. "Let me tell you a story about my father."

Tell me whatever you want, I encouraged her mentally. Though I kept my words to myself. She wanted me to talk. Somehow, some way, she'd linked me to the Judge. It didn't make sense on any level. So, I needed more information.

This was an awkward method of interrogation. It was better than the first few days she'd left me to sit here. Despite my best efforts, I'd still pissed myself. Course, the fact she had to clean it up had kind of made up for that.

I tried to flex my hands against the zip-ties, but they were too damn tight. The chill in the basement, coupled with the restraints, kept turning my hands and feet numb. My ass had long since stopped caring about the hard chair, and I couldn't feel it.

"My father was a criminal defense attorney." Her gaze went distant, her lips compressed. He was also dead; the pain was something with which I had an intimate familiarity. Not that I offered her any kind of sympathy. Clearing her throat, she refocused on me. "He was a good man."

After several heartbeats, it became abundantly clear she wanted a response from me. "Okay."

Two syllables were all I'd spare her. My throat hurt. I was a prisoner. I still wasn't entirely sure *why* I was a prisoner. She clearly wanted information from me on the Judge. But the *why* remained elusive.

Crossing her arms, she leaned back in the chair. She still had one leg crossed over the other. Everything about her screamed defensive posture, as if our positions were very much reversed. Not that I had much choice in my posture. I was literally lashed to the chair.

"He was a good man," she repeated. "Dedicated to his job. He took pro bono cases. He helped out the poor and the indigent. The accused are entitled to a defense. It's a cornerstone of our justice system."

Frustration edged her voice. That was new. Though I had to wonder who she was trying to convince, me or herself?

"I was only eleven when he died." None of this was new information. "He was really good at his job, used to tell me stories when he came home from work. I mean, he obviously couldn't talk about his cases."

Oh, sure, obviously.

"But he believed in the legal system. He believed that the burden of proof was on the prosecution. His job was only to debunk their proof or to offer compelling evidence to defend against it."

Chin lifting, she squared her shoulders. "Almost thirty years ago, several boys from a prestigious…" Thus began her recitation of the Weston Prep case up to her father's death following the trial fifteen years earlier.

While I listened, I focused more on her pupil response, the way her breathing shifted, and how her knuckles would whiten. Three times she tried to relax her posture from the folded arms, and three times she failed.

No matter how much she strove for dispassion, she couldn't quite get there. This wasn't some exciting news story or passion project. This was about her father. Clearly, she still grieved for him.

"I need to know," she said, finally. "I need to know *why* the Judge targeted him."

Except… "Didn't you say he died in a car accident?"

Heat bloomed in her eyes, almost a veritable explosion of emotion. It gave her away before she could mask it. "Not all the Judge's kills appear to be what they are."

I didn't have to pretend to be confused by that sentence. She couldn't know that for certain, so she was basing it off of what? The information in Morgan's father's journals?

"You have to see it," she persisted, leaning forward. "You have to *know.*"

I did the best facsimile of a shrug I could manage. While the zip-tie on my right wrist moved a fraction, I kept my attention on her. "I see you," I said. "You don't seem well."

Four little words rocketed her out of the chair, and she slapped me. My ears rang from the force and my face lit up. Something stung along my cheek, sharper. Had she scratched me? Probably.

"You little bitch. You know what happened. You know what he did."

When in doubt, a little truth wouldn't hurt. Well, actually, it would probably hurt. Her, more than me.

I hoped.

Turning my head to face her again, I tilted my head back. It wasn't my favorite position, baring my throat and craning my head so I could see her. But since she wanted to relate more as people… "Fifteen years ago, I was almost nine years old. How would I know?"

She wasn't all that much older than me.

"Were you there?"

"No," she snapped in an impatient tone. "I wasn't there. But my father was involved in the Weston Prep case. Everyone involved in it—the boys, witnesses, the actual trial judge—even members of the jury—were all executed. By the Judge."

"So you keep saying. What does that have to do with me?"

"I've been looking for him since I was old enough to understand what he'd done. Revealing that I had those journals was my play—I needed to lure him out."

Wait…

Head tilted, I studied her and didn't even try to hide my frown of confusion. Intelligent. Driven. Failure was not an option for her.

"What?" she demanded when I said nothing.

"You wanted to lure out someone you claim is a serial killer?" I compressed my lips. Talking was getting harder, and I needed to generate more spit in my mouth. "Doesn't seem very bright."

Now a smirk curved her lips. "It brought you to me." For a second, a manic flicker of glee crossed her face. "I know that *you* aren't the Judge. But he could have sent you…so what are you? His protege? His lover?" That was disgusting. "His secretary?"

Secretary?

Laughter bubbled up inside of me. "Secretary?" It came out a hoarse kind of squeak. Then I laughed harder.

"Stop it," she ordered, but I let the humor out. The rush of endorphins helped with the soreness in my limbs and the lack of feeling in my hands.

Another slip of the zip-tie and the vaguest sensation of pins and needles. That was something.

"Stop it," she yelled, this time slapping me again. My cheek alternately stung and throbbed. When I looked at her, she backhanded the other side of my face.

That was going to get old.

When she drew her fist back like she planned to punch me, she didn't actually let it fly. Instead, she just screamed. Then pivoted and stormed away from me.

Only to storm back and drag the hood over my head

again. A minute later, the sound of her shoes hitting the stairs told me she intended to flee the rest of the conversation.

"Are we done then?" I called, running my tongue over the blood in my mouth. My whole face hurt now. The footsteps continued to climb the wooden steps. "Maybe bring some water next time," I croaked. "You're gonna need some towels if you don't let me go to the bathroom."

The door slammed with a resounding thud that carried all the way down to vibrate through me where I sat. Dropping my head, I let out some of the pain I'd been holding back. The coppery flavor in my mouth wasn't ideal, but it was moisture, and I needed it.

Taking mental inventory, I began to move my hand slowly. Where the zip-tie had some give, I started to work on it. Meanwhile, I turned over the information she'd revealed.

The journals had been bait in a trap to bring the Judge to her. Even if Daddy would have considered her a threat, she'd done nothing wrong. Just being the child of the attorney didn't make her a criminal.

All he would have done was take the journals. It was what I'd planned to do.

What I still *needed* to do.

My bladder protested. The lack of food and the bare minimum of water had been good for something, but I still needed to pee. I'd rather not piss myself again.

Still…needs must.

The thought of food made me think of Rick, and that in turn brought Fletcher to mind.

I really missed them.

RICK

"IS THIS TRULY NECESSARY?" Cash grumbled from behind the grate.

I glanced over my shoulder as Cash pressed his face closer to the panel. One turquoise eye glared at me through the punch hole.

"Yes," I confirmed, then turned back around.

After leaving Sandra Jane's house, we headed to one of Vienna's storage units. One of the perks of doing so much work for her was that I had access to her property, vehicles, storage units, and accounts database.

She'd told me enough about this job for a woman named Mart, that I knew the car would never work. We needed something bigger. Like the first time we were doing a job without her, we would be representing her brand to her associates. The last thing we wanted to do was embarrass her.

Luckily, on the way to the address Mart had provided, Vienna had a work van stashed in a storage unit.

Unlucky for our new friend, there were only two seats up front, and the back was separated by a panel with holes punched through it. The back was empty except for Cash, but this time he had room to move, and he could see us and talk to us. He should be happy with the upgrade.

At least he got to stretch out to sleep through the night. I'd driven the whole way, and Fletcher had tried valiantly to keep me company, but I'd needed some quiet to process my thoughts. The next time we stopped for gas, I'd handed off a bottle of prepped water to him and one to Cash for good measure. They both were knocked out within thirty minutes.

"Mart Abernathy," Fletcher mused as he tapped away on his laptop. Before we'd left the house, he'd made sure to pack it. Anything that got us closer to Vienna. "I think I know her. Or at least, met her in passing on occasion." More tapping. "Yep, yep. She used to be married to my uncle's arch-nemesis. Huh, I wonder what happened. Oh…." he drew out. "They divorced seven years ago, and she won quite the settlement. Interesting." A few more keystrokes. "He had a series of unfortunate business deals that bankrupted him. Oh, that's too bad. The old bastard died of heat stroke in Bermuda before the year was out. He was the only one who ever made my uncle cry. Pity."

"Does he always have full conversations with himself?" Cash snapped, but we didn't pay attention to him. He served no purpose on this job, and we needed to focus.

"Five minutes, and we'll be there," I warned Fletcher. Without a word, he started shutting down his laptop and stuffed it in his bag, then shoved it under his seat.

We pulled up to a sprawling mansion on equally impressive grounds. The lawn was emerald green in the early morning light; the way lawns were when they were only watered every day. No HOA regulations here.

When we reached the wrought iron gate, it started to swing open before I had a chance to hit the call button.

"She's expecting us," Fletcher murmured.

"No shit? You did say the job was supposed to be

completed today, right?" Cash tried to insert himself into the conversation one more time. At some point since we took the work van, his attitude had started to deteriorate. It was fine for him to be grumpy, as long as he didn't screw this up for us.

I got it. I'd hate being in the trunk and stuffed in the back of the work van too, but we had to think about our safety, and finding Vienna, first and foremost.

If there were grounds keepers, they had the day off. No one was in the gatehouse, and no cars or people littered the lawn. But there was a small, polished woman standing on the steps as we passed the fountain in the middle of the circular drive.

She was a timeless beauty, even when scowling at us as we climbed out.

Because I was trying to stay on friendly-*ish* terms with Cash, I opened the back, and he hopped out. Now that I'd had time to think about it, I agreed, grudgingly, with Fletcher. Cash was our best bet.

Mart's gaze roved over the three of us. Her dark brown eyes pinched at the corners and her full mouth turned down. She wasn't happy to see us. That was okay, I realized she expected to see Vienna. But we'd make her understand we were loyal and capable.

"Who are you, darling, and why are you here?" She addressed me in a sugary southern voice.

My chest swelled. I could be the person in charge of Vienna. She'd be proud of me. "Vienna sent us. She said you have a transport job," I answered and nodded in greeting.

"Mm-hm. And just who are you? I've known Vienna since she was a child, and I've never seen her in anyone else's company. Especially for work." She eyed each of us carefully. Her gaze snagged on Cash the longest before flitting over to Fletcher.

For once, he wasn't fidgeting and bouncing around like he

stuck a wet finger in a light socket. He stood tall and had put his hair into a neat bun, so it didn't fly around his face like it normally did.

He understood we represented Vienna too.

"We're good friends and associates of hers," Fletcher chimed in with a deep nod of his own. "You could say we've decided to pool our resources and go into business together."

"Where are the goods you'd like to be divested of?" I stepped toward the massive front doors, but no one followed me. When I glanced back, a defiant Mart had her chin tilted up while Cash stood with his feet apart and his arms crossed while staring her down.

Or attempting to, anyway.

"Mart Abernathy?" Cash asked as more of a statement.

"Oh honey, I would hope you'd know my name if you're truly working for Vienna. Otherwise, she might as well cut her losses and find better eye candy. Like that one," she said as she nodded over her shoulder at me.

Cash was undeterred.

"I just like to make sure she's safe. How long did you say you've known Vienna?"

"Longer than I care to explain to you."

Cash raised his head to survey the mansion. "Nice place you have here. Just why are you asking for a large transport?"

"Honey, Vienna knows all she needs to for this job. If you don't know the answers, that means she doesn't trust you enough. Which makes me wonder why you're here in the first place." Mart stepped forward. Not threatening, or intimidating. She couldn't come across that way if she tried with her five-foot-two frame. But danger came in small packages, as Vienna had taught us.

My heart skipped a beat in my chest as I pictured her beautiful face. I wasn't sure how I was functioning without knowing she was okay, but doing this job for her helped.

We were keeping her word, and that would be important to her.

The sound of Cash grinding his teeth made my ears hurt. "I'll pass your concern on to Vienna, and you can take it up with her." Fletcher's head snapped toward Cash. "But she's my first priority. I'll ask a different question, because I know just how well Vienna likes to isolate herself. Why are you using *her* specifically, when there are a hundred other transporters available with cheaper prices and more muscle?"

Mart's abrupt laugh was high and full-bodied. "Ask Vienna your questions if you really want answers. If I had to guess, she's not going to take it very kindly that you're interrogating her colleagues. It screams that you don't trust her, and," she raised her shoulders in a delicate shrug, "that means I won't have to deal with you again. For now, I have a better question for you," she said as she turned to meet my gaze. "What are you doing with the missing FBI agent?"

"I'm standing right here," Cash said in a crisp, near dismissive tone. "And I'll be the one asking the questions."

"Hey," Fletcher said. "New Guy, you're the one who's going to shut his mouth and let the adults talk."

That was damn near laughable coming from Fletcher, but it had an interesting effect on Cash. His expression darkened though his lips twitched.

Once.

But they twitched.

"Please," I said to Mart. "Point us at what we're transporting, and we'll get to work."

That would probably save us all some grief.

"New Guy?" Cash demanded, and Fletcher just gave him a cool look. The arrogance and the disdain rolling off of him was a new one. His normal flirty nature seemed completely absent.

"Yeah, New Guy, as in expendable and unnecessary.

Hush." Without missing a beat, Fletcher gave Mart an apologetic grin. "The big guy is right, we're here to do a job. The sooner we get it done, the sooner we're out of your hair and back to *other* tasks."

Fletcher had a point, but before I could say a word, Mart smiled—it was almost a fond, sweet smile. A moment later, Cash was on the ground, hands over his groin as all the air whooshed out of him in a pained groan.

I winced.

"There, he's out of our hair, sugar," she told Fletcher before patting his arm. Fletcher gawked, then shot me a look. "Let's go." With a saucy little wink, she was marching off.

With a shrug, I glanced at Cash. "Get up and be useful with your mouth shut, or I'll tape it closed and put you in the van. We don't have time for this."

"What the big guy said," Fletcher declared before circling the guy and hurrying after Mart. Probably a good idea for one of us to keep her in sight at all times.

The *former* FBI agent grunted a very unnatural sound. He was pale and sweating but pushed himself to his feet and obeyed. Taking a note of his shallow, agonized breathing, I planned to avoid being anywhere near Mart's vicious little knee.

Without wasting any more time, because *she* didn't have time for us to spend, we found Mart inside. The items she had marked out for us ranged from works of art to pieces of furniture to little knick-knacks.

There were even rugs.

Fletcher did a full sweep of each one, muttering to himself. I only caught a sentence here or there.

Cash hadn't said a word. He also hadn't touched anything to help us move it. He and Mart kept a wary eye on each other. By the time we'd finished—including emptying half of a wine cellar into the van—there was barely any room for Cash in the back.

I ignored his glare and shut him in.

I needed to make him some more water, the man was giving me a headache.

"Anything else?" I asked Mart, because we'd been at this for a little over ninety minutes.

"Where's my Vienna-baby?" She studied me, the piercing assessment in those eyes demanding an answer.

"I don't know." It was the most honest answer I could come up with. "But she gave her word this job would be done, and that's why we're here. Doing the job."

Not one dishonest syllable.

She sighed. "You know where you're going?"

"Yes, ma'am."

"Hmm." She dipped a hand into her pocket and pulled out a single white business card. After studying me for another moment, she handed me the card. "For when you arrive. Also, so you can reach me if there are any issues."

"There won't be."

"I appreciate the confidence." She cut her gaze to the van and then to where Fletcher waited. He'd stuffed his hands in his pocket and seemed to be concentrating on being as unobtrusive as possible.

He was almost good at it.

"Still, any issues, you call Vienna, but then you call me."

I would give my right kidney to call her right now.

"And you be careful with that Fed." That was already my plan. "I don't know what is going on with him, but there's more than one alert out seeking him and asking for anyone with knowledge about him or his whereabouts to call in."

She removed an imaginary speck of dirt from her shirt.

"Make sure Vienna-baby knows that, will you?"

"Absolutely." Right after I made sure *she* was all right. "We'll keep him out of sight."

"You're a good boy." The warmth in her smile had my shoulders straightening. "Talk to you soon."

It wasn't until she returned to the house and closed the door that I managed to take a full breath. The ache in my chest had gotten tighter and tighter the longer we stood there. Every single mention of Vienna was a razor blade over my soul.

For once, neither of the other two men said anything once Fletcher and I were back in the van. I checked the address where we needed to deliver everything in the truck, except for one painting. Mart insisted we keep that one for Vienna.

It was a beautiful scene, and I agreed with the diminutive woman—Vienna would love it.

The vise around my heart seemed to tighten, making drawing in air harder and harder. We were almost to the highway when Fletcher said, "I liked her. Is that weird? I mean, that's roughly eight hundred thousand in goods back there, based on fair market value. And I couldn't really get a read on her. You?"

I glanced at him. "No, but I didn't try to. And I liked her too."

Especially after she put Cash on the ground, I definitely understood why Vienna liked her.

"I don't," came the strained response from Cash. "If anybody cares."

"We don't," I said in near unison with Fletcher. A beat later, a laugh worked free. It wasn't much and it didn't last long. What humor could survive in her absence? Still, I appreciated it.

We needed to find her.

We'd needed to find her five days earlier before she went missing.

Never again, I promised silently. Never again would I let her face any mission alone. One of us *needed* to be there, even if all we did was wait.

At least then, we could have done something.

"How long until we get there?" Cash called.

"When we do," I answered, ignoring his muttered deprecation in response. Especially since every hour we spent on this, was an hour we weren't looking for her. The job, however, would be done.

That would make Vienna happy, I hoped.

VIENNA

"ARE YOU HUNGRY?" Sandra Jane had called in a near chirpy voice when she opened the basement door earlier. Over the past two days, after her violent episode, she'd been beyond bubbly. Kind even. Except for the calculating glint in her eye.

Did she honestly believe that I couldn't read right through her? She had *enjoyed* inflicting pain a little too much for me to believe that was a fluke in her plans.

"Yes," I rasped, then coughed to clear my throat. Even held hostage, I understood the value of keeping your strength up. When the opportunity presented itself, and it would, she was too much of an amateur for it not to. I needed to be ready to take it.

Sandra Jane had at least brought me one or two meals a day with water. It wasn't the excellent level of care Rick provided to Mr. Morgan, but it was enough.

"I also need to pee again." I opened my mouth as she lifted a forkful of brown rice to my face. Poison wasn't a concern. Not yet. Sandra Jane needed too many answers for that.

"Fine," she said as some of the forced pleasantness left her expression.

When I'd pissed myself before, she'd ended up pacing around the small space for about fifteen minutes, trying to figure out how to take care of it. I was grateful she was just as put off by the stale scent of urine as I was.

At least when it was on my person.

Finally, she'd decided handcuffs would be the better option. After an hour-long absence, she came back with a handgun and a pair of cuffs. Once she cut the zip ties, she held the gun on me, with no safety, as she watched me strip, shower, and redress. Then she moved my chair to the far wall of the room and had me cuff my hands with the chain looped behind one slat.

It was uneventful, and her hand had remained steady for the most part. She seemed peeved I wasn't more worked up, but I was exhausted.

I used all my energy to watch her cues, pick apart her patterns, and constantly scan my surroundings for the smallest change. Who gave a fuck if I showed her a reaction to boost her ego?

After I swallowed the bite, she gave me another, this one with a smaller piece of grilled chicken. Barely above room temperature, she was most likely giving me her leftovers.

Every few bites, she held the water bottle up to my lips. Then the food was gone. She unlocked the cuffs and stepped back with the gun raised. My body screamed as I stood, my joints angry at me for staying in the same position for such an extended period. I moved as much as I could, but the range of motion wasn't there.

"My body is sore, and I need to stretch," I warned her before slowly twisting left then right. I pushed my hands to the ceiling then hugged my knees to my chest one at a time. That would have to do for now.

Like before, she followed me as I hobbled to the small

bathroom outside this room, and her gun hand never wavered. Even after stretching, the numbness in some of my limbs promised punishing pins and needles. At this point, if I ever felt my ass again, I had a feeling I would hate it.

Pissing had never felt so good. Once I was back in the seat, with the cuffs latched over my wrists, she pulled the spare chair over and sat across from me. Crossing one leg, she locked her hands over her knees and leaned toward me.

"I'm not trying to be a bitch here, okay? I don't know who you are or what your name is, but you have to have a life you want to get back to, right?"

I didn't answer.

"Listen, all I'm trying to do is avenge my father. He was my biggest supporter, my best friend. He meant everything to me." She looked at her hands open on her thighs as her voice took on a manic quality. "I've done the research, followed every possible trail, and interviewed every connected person. The few who have been left alive," she added as an afterthought. "Doesn't that mean anything to you?"

For the first time since I'd been in this basement, her anger and self-righteousness cracked, and real human emotion leaked through.

My chest squeezed.

That did mean something to me. And she would never know how much.

Ever.

It was like looking in a mirror as far as motivation went.

My father had been everything to me too. To the point that I would not rest until I found his killer, and their blood painted whatever room I found them in. Avenging the one person you didn't want to live without was a driver with which I had become very acquainted.

As much as I sympathized, she was not my friend.

"Why won't you even answer the most basic of questions?" Frustration edged her words again.

My face was still sore. The bathroom had no mirror. It barely had a toilet. I'd used worse. But the inflammation and stiffness told me she'd bruised me. Not that I cared. The swelling beneath my right eye had diminished.

Good, I'd prefer not to have my vision compromised.

She stomped one foot, and I flicked my gaze upward. I hadn't missed a single nuance of her aggravation as it danced in and out of her expression. "Is it too much to ask?"

"What?" I coughed the word, more than said it. Despite the water, my throat was still dry. The basement was cold and drafty. It was definitely not constructed for long-term guests.

"What's your name?" It was the first direct inquiry regarding my name that she'd made.

Huh.

"Why do you care?" I almost laughed, so I covered it with a cough. Not that it required that much effort. "You tased me, drugged me, dragged me to god knows where—and you've starved me, left me chained down here, ranted, raved, and beaten me."

With every single crime I ticked off, a muscle at the corner of her eye began to twitch.

"You didn't need my name for that."

Her lips compressed into a flat line, all the color bleeding from them. Nostrils flaring, she glared at me as she flexed her fingers. I braced for the hit, but it didn't come.

"Fine," she admitted with a grating laugh that warbled up then down again. "You're right. I've been a terrible host."

Well, on that, we agreed. I shifted my weight in the chair like I needed to stretch my legs. Not smelling my own stench was a perk, though it meant the cloying nature of her gardenia-based perfume was unavoidable.

I flexed each butt cheek slowly. I needed to alleviate some of the numbness. My shoes had come off when I changed, and she hadn't returned them. So I had a good view of my swollen feet.

Not pretty.

"But you were in my house," she continued in that same conversational tone. "My neighbors have street cams, they gave me the code once when they were out of town, and then they never changed them. So I could check on my house even during random power outages."

Huh.

"That sounds entitled," was all I said.

She shrugged. "If you give someone your password, you shouldn't be surprised when they use it. But I saw you watching my house."

"I could have been a saleswoman," I pointed out. It was a cover I'd used once.

"Maybe," she agreed. "But then why didn't you go to any of the other houses? No, you watched mine. Then you went inside. Only when I tried to see what you were doing, my cameras were off."

Head cocked, she assessed me with a small smile playing over her lips like this was the most entertaining of conversations. The trouble with her expression was that she'd never learned how to let it touch her eyes.

"Water?" She held out the bottle again, all smiles.

"Please."

I had several long drinks this time—more than just wetting my mouth and throat. With the food in my stomach, I needed hydration too. Plus, none of the earlier sips proved to have any effect, so I was still going with she still needed me alive.

"There, see," she offered as she settled back and put the bottle down on the floor. "I can be nice."

Yeah, I skipped responding to that.

One leg crossed over the other, and she clasped her hands around her knee. I shifted again, adding a touch of squirm so I could stretch my legs and flex my ass. Yeah, it wasn't doing much for the feeling, but I needed to do whatever I could.

The cold metal of the cuffs didn't register, but then they wouldn't after warming to my body temperature. Or maybe I'd just cooled that much. I flexed my fingers, not reacting to the fact the cuffs weren't locked right on my skin.

At least not on my left hand.

Huh.

"Where were we," she said as though asking a question we both knew she wasn't. "Oh, right. My house. So, you were in my house, and the cameras were off. Why were you in my house…?"

Anger flashed in her eyes when I didn't answer, but the syrupy sweetness returned almost as swiftly. It was kind of nauseating that she thought this tactic of alternating bitchiness with a sugary tone would have any effect.

Then again, it had probably netted her something in the past. Why else use it?

"My father," she said, seemingly switching tactics. "Finding the person who killed him, it's all I want to do. I don't want to hurt you. I don't like holding you here."

Uh-huh, I believed that last line. She definitely didn't want to be caught holding someone hostage. The rest was bullshit.

"I could show you a picture of him, tell you about him—I mean, I mentioned he'd worked many cases. Some of them pro bono." The grief on display was also real. "I researched those too, you know. The cases he worked on and the results. What happened to his clients… The Weston Prep case, it was controversial at the time."

A very real sigh escaped her.

"It'd probably be controversial now, especially after the 'me too' movement, but Dad—Dad believed everyone deserved a fair trial. He won that case, fair and square. The prosecution failed to prove their case… I would like to have talked to the girl involved in the case."

The girl involved in the case. "You mean the victim?"

Because that was what that poor girl had been. A victim. A

victim to a ruthless bunch of selfish, entitled pricks who'd never been denied a damn thing.

It was Sandra Jane's turn to look uncomfortable. "The alleged victim."

"Whatever helps you sleep at night."

"So you knew her?" She narrowed her eyes.

I gave her a bland look.

Then she sighed. "Well, you seem so certain…"

"I saw pictures," I told her. "She also killed herself."

There it was. The twitch again.

"Two days after being destroyed on the stand by the defense attorney."

"He was doing his job." But her control wavered, and she glanced away from me. "Clearly, the woman was mentally unstable. I tried to speak to her parents, but they'd moved, and the neighbors wanted nothing to do with me."

"Why would you even go to talk to them?" I studied her, she wasn't manufacturing her unease. This was the part of the story she didn't want to focus on. "She was dead long before the case was done, so… why would they even be a focus?"

"Because the boys who were accused—the Judge killed them. One by one. Horrific deaths. One died from ingesting tree nuts—he was allergic to them. He suffocated to death in his own room, just a foot away from others, and no one heard him."

Too bad.

"Another died from exposure. He'd broken his leg on a hike and must have been there for days. More followed. One after another. Everyone involved in the case—I told you this —died. Every single one of them. Including my father."

"Who died in a car accident," I commented. "I remember."

Leaning forward, she stared at me as her breathing grew more shallow and erratic. "The Judge killed him. Just like he killed all those other boys."

"Allegedly."

She blinked. "What?"

"You said the Judge killed them all. The legal term you forgot was, *allegedly.*"

Genuine anger flashed in her eyes and she stood up abruptly. I tracked her movements, leaning back a little and stretching again as I flexed my hands.

"You think this is funny?"

"No," I told her. "That's the very last thing I think it is."

"But you don't believe me..." Suspicion marred her expression.

"I absolutely believe you. I believe you believe every single word you're saying." I also believed Daddy would never have let it stand. Not after those boys damn near killed that girl, then Sandra's father all but finished the job.

"Then you agree—the Judge killed my father."

"Probably. From the sounds of it—he deserved it."

All the air seemed to evacuate from the room as her pupils constricted and her nostrils flared. She lashed out with a hand, but it never touched my face. I caught it with the hand I'd pulled free. Yeah, I'd left skin behind, and there was blood leaking from my abraded skin.

But I was free.

She wasn't hitting me again.

No. We were done with that part.

I was past done.

"I'M GOING to need access to a phone at some point," I drawled as I spread my arms over the back of the sofa.

Fletcher paced back and forth in front of me, wearing out a narrow strip of the clean yet unremarkable neutral rug. There wasn't even a pattern in the fabric. I actually had to admire how thoughtful the decorator was. I bet it was my dark saint. I couldn't imagine she'd let anyone else in to measure the rooms and memorize the layout.

Rick had his arms crossed as he watched our exhausting exchange from the doorway.

"I don't trust you yet," Fletcher said as he whirled around to point a finger at me. The guy never stood still. How did Rick keep the house clean of DNA when he fluttered about shedding hair all over the place?

Oh yeah, he had a handy dandy fanny pack on steroids, all for cleaning. That was how. I smirked, and Fletcher's ears started to turn red. Poor guy, he probably thought I was antagonizing him.

Wiping it away, I settled on an imploring yet reasonable expression. I hoped.

"I searched Sandra Jane's place; I went on the job and was

a good little boy. I even tried to extract information from that crazy-ass woman while you two were concentrating on getting in and out. Didn't you hear me when I said we had to retrace her steps?" I tossed my hands up. This whole adventure was like training intelligent half-wit newbs. They knew enough to make them dangerous but had no idea how to apply the knowledge to real-world situations.

That was a pretty reckless way to operate. If they hadn't let me out of the cell, who knew what would have happened to them. I would have starved to death when they didn't come back. Hyperbole? Maybe. Then again, they were not handling all of this well.

"He has kept his word so far," the friendly giant rumbled. His whole demeanor was really a study in psychology. His height—which almost matched mine—and build, radiated menace. But he cleaned and cooked like the happiest little housewife, and I'd bet he melted for Vienna. I hadn't seen it, but I could just tell by the way his morose eyes softened any time we mentioned her.

"Thank you," I said, trying to hold the exasperation from my voice.

"Who are you going to call? In case you missed the memo, there's a missing report out for you. The police, and I'm sure the FBI, are looking for you. Anyone you contact could alert authorities, and then where would we be?" He fell in the chair and scratched at his scalp. "We'd still be without Vienna and constantly looking over our shoulders, afraid someone found us. If that happens, we're screwed." He dropped his hands to cup his knees. "Listen, New Guy, I like you. Kinda. Even though you're a bit of an inflated ass at times, you've not caused us much trouble. But there's literally no reason for you to contact anyone."

I raised an eyebrow. "How exactly did you expect me to help you find Vienna? Use my epic power of deduction based on limited and flawed information to guess her whereabouts?

That's like playing a game of Clue with a quarter of the board missing as well as half the pieces. It doesn't work that way." I held up my hand when he opened his mouth. "I don't need to actually talk to anyone. I have an answering service I use for all of my informants. There could be something of value there, but regardless, it's a good starting point."

"Why would your informants have any information on Drew?" Suspicion dripped from Fletcher's words. "You said you *lucked* into finding her at the warehouse."

I took in a deep breath through my nose and tried for patience. "I did. But prior to my termination, finding the Judge was my *job* and my passion. So much, that I continued it even once I went solo. My informants are still mine, and they call in periodically. Some tips are helpful, most aren't, but we won't know unless I call and check any messages."

Fletcher held his breath while his mind turned over possible scenarios of how this might help or hinder them. It was fascinating to see his hacker brain analyzing this situation. He'd give in. In a few minutes, he'd realize we were out of options if they wanted to continue the search for Vienna.

"No comments from you?" I glanced over at Rick. I didn't believe for a second that Fletcher ran the house, but Rick seemed content to let him lead most conversations. He just sent me warning looks on occasion if he thought I was pushing Fletcher too much.

"No."

Okay, then.

"Give me the number. I'm going to run a search on it and confirm it's an answering service. Once I'm satisfied it's not a trick, I'll dial it. The phone will be on speakerphone." Fletcher's chin jutted out as if daring me to argue.

"Fine. Hand me a notepad and a pen." I held out my hand.

"You're agreeing? Just like that?"

I shrugged. "I'm all about working smarter, not harder. I'll get any information much quicker if you do your checks rather than arguing in circles about my intentions." I paused. "Even *if* I've proven myself."

Shaking his head, Fletcher walked to the door, hopefully, to get some paper. "You have to earn privileges. No one gets a gold star just for following simple directions. And we can agree that you struggled with that, given Mart's nice kick to the boys, hm?" He ended up yelling the last few words as he disappeared down the hall.

Huffing out a breath, I readjusted into a more comfortable position. I really couldn't complain. Between being cramped in the trunk and crammed behind priceless artwork, my sore muscles were killing me. Sleeping on the lumpy cot in the basement would have made it worse. Instead, they'd given me a spare room.

They didn't say anything, but from the sounds I heard outside the bedroom door, they most likely took shifts to make sure I didn't run away.

Kind of them. Especially when it would have been so much easier just to lock me up. I eyed Rick. He was probably the one behind that decision. Hospitality seemed ingrained in his bones.

Was his family southern? I'd have to ask sometime.

The nervous hacker? Reed would have happily tossed my ass behind the bars until he had another way for me to be helpful. Not that I believed it would have been malicious. He was too on edge to relax properly when I was out. Based on what I knew about his family? That fit.

Hell, I wouldn't have blamed them.

"Here," Fletcher said as he waltzed back in with a sheet of notebook paper and pen in hand.

I scribbled the number out and handed it back. He was gone in a blink to check it out. It wouldn't take him long. The number was well known for a popular and discreet service— all legit.

"So, Rick. How did you meet our lovely lady? I can't imagine you growing up in the life, but you fit in so well."

His chest puffed out with his next inhale. He enjoyed hearing how neatly he complimented Vienna. And then his words contradicted everything I read about him in the last two seconds.

"Mind your own fucking business," he growled.

I chuckled. "You're a funny guy," I said before reaching for the cup of coffee I had sitting on a coaster. A choice, certainly, but it had scored points with the "gentle" giant earlier. Not that they'd done me much good.

"It's clean," Fletcher announced as he strode back into the room. "It's an answering service. Messages only. Even when he dials in, he can only pick up, save, and delete messages."

Biting back the urge to say, "I told you so," took a measure of effort, but I was nothing if not accomplished. Fletcher glanced at Rick, and the man just shrugged. "Give him a phone. If it helps us find Vienna, then do it."

"Thank you," I said and held out my hand. While not wholly convinced, Fletcher didn't hand me the phone immediately, instead, he dialed the number and put it on speaker.

"This is Morgan. You know the drill," my own voice responded after two rings.

"Star-seven-six-four one-one-triple zero-eight-four-three-two-one." The thirteen-digit pin code earned me a slow whistle, but Fletcher punched it in.

"You have forty-four messages," the computer recited and I blew out a breath. Rick pivoted and left the room as Fletcher dropped onto the sofa to my left.

The first dozen or so messages were tips of so-called sightings, I still had the pad and the pen, so I jotted down notes. These were not sources I gave much credit to, but if I'd been bored—well yeah, I would have checked them out.

Sometimes the best clues were obscured, and you had to

be willing to dig into the bullshit. The thirteenth message came from an informant I hadn't heard from in months.

"Call me."

He didn't waste time with pleasantries, platitudes, or even trying to tell me how exciting his information was. Another seven messages, and he came up again.

The time and date stamp indicated the first call came in on the day Vienna left.

Interesting.

Then three days later, when I was still in the cell.

Krystle left me three messages in rapid succession.

"Where the fuck are you? I didn't tell you about the task force to have you fall off the face of the earth. Call me."

Hours later. "Seriously, where are you?"

"Goddammit, Cash. Are you really trying to sabotage the task force before it even fully forms? How did that reporter get your dad's journals?"

Fletcher grimaced. "Remind me not to piss her off."

Eh, Krystle was just dedicated to her job. Rick reappeared with fresh coffee—he refilled my cup, and when Fletcher reached for his mug, he froze under Rick's cool stare and took the water instead.

"Killjoy," he muttered, but Rick ignored him. Sandwiches were next. My stomach growled at seeing them, but I just nodded my thanks.

My informant popped up again. "It's unusual for you to not have reached out to me by now. Should I presume my services are no longer required?"

That could be a problem. I took a bite of one of the sandwiches. It was good—whatever it was, but I was too focused on sorting the messages to pay much attention. It was fuel. Damn good fuel, but fuel.

When he called for a fourth time and this one just hours earlier, I straightened.

"If I do not hear from you within twelve hours, I will

assume our association is at an end. Based on our history and your current focus, it would be in your best interest to return the call before I terminate this number."

"I need to call him," I said before punching the star to end the messages without deleting them. Some I wanted to keep for later.

"Who is he?" Rick asked before Fletcher could say a word. "Your current focus was Vienna, right?"

"*Is* Vienna," I corrected him. "He's an informant. Been working with him on and off for years. He never brings me anything that isn't actionable. He's not an excitable man. His business is numbers, but he has a lot of less than savory clients, let's call them. They trust him because he's a vault. But because he is in and out of their places, he hears things, and whatever he reports to me—it's stuff I need to hear."

"That still doesn't tell me who he is," Rick said.

"Or why he's so insistent on talking to you right now…if his information is important, why not just leave it in a message?" Fletcher jumped in. "Then again, anyone listening to that message who isn't you wouldn't even know who he is, what he knows, or why he called, much less how to get back in touch with him."

Well, his talking to himself proved useful.

"That's actually smart. If he works for people who might take offense to him talking to a federal agent…"

"Former federal agent," Rick connected. "If he knows something about Vienna. Call him."

While Fletcher might still be waging some internal dialogue war, Rick wasn't. I finished my sandwich and reached for the phone again.

"On speaker," I said around the last bite of the sandwich before I washed it down with coffee. The constant need to debate every single move in committee had grown old before "Mart" slammed her knees into my balls.

They were still sore.

"Lennon," the man answered in a crisp, professional tone.

"Ratio," I greeted him. "I'm returning your calls."

"Agent Morgan," he said after a long moment. "I was beginning to believe our relationship had been terminated."

"Just busy. What do you have for me?"

"Information. This is time-sensitive, though. I'm also leaving tomorrow. Can you meet me this afternoon?"

Pinching the bridge of my nose, I ignored the pointed stare from Fletcher. Rick's face, however, was expressionless. "Where?"

"I'd say the usual place, but I'm actually out of town. You'll have to come to me." He rattled off an address, and since that was hours away, I sighed.

"It could take me a bit to get there."

"Then I suggest you hurry," Ratio countered. "I will only wait thirty minutes."

Then the call disconnected.

"Call him back," Rick said. "We need more information than that."

"It won't do any good," I told him. "Ratio won't say anything over an open line. Anything can be trapped and traced. So, he keeps contact to a minimum and says only what needs to be said. The fact he even gave me an address is because it's not our usual meet-up."

"I don't like it," Fletcher said.

"I don't either," I agreed with him as I stood. "But we don't have a choice. Ratio knows I'm hunting the Judge. It's not a mystery. If he's calling me right now and the way he has been, he has something I can—we—can use. Make a decision, boys, because one way or another, I'm going to that meeting."

They didn't say anything as I picked up my mug and plate, then carried them back to the kitchen.

Finally, Rick said, "Do you really think he has something about where Vienna is?"

"Yes." I wouldn't offer platitudes or explanations. Ratio

was a clever guy and he knew a lot of people. Even if he'd only heard a rumor of a rumor, he wouldn't have called me unless he'd confirmed it. His intelligence was always solid.

"Pack," Rick told Fletcher. "I'll prep a cooler. That's a drive and we will be cutting it close to make it."

The same thought occurred to me. I didn't even argue about the trunk this time, but Rick skipped the car and brought an SUV back to the house instead.

How many cars did my dark saint have tucked away?

Without a word, I dragged the bag over my head and rolled into the back. At least the back of the SUV wasn't anywhere near as uncomfortable. They also let me climb into the backseat with Fletcher within forty-five minutes instead of an hour.

Look at that... progress.

Still, the energy in the car crackled. Even after Fletcher passed out cold in his seat. I closed his laptop at Rick's request and eyed him from where I sat behind the passenger seat. "You drugged him."

"Melatonin," Rick answered without looking at me. "He needs more rest than he's getting. Vienna doesn't like it when he's strung out."

Yeah, I could see that.

"If you need help driving —"

"I won't."

Right.

Still, I didn't sleep. I kept turning the information I'd acquired over in my head. The fact we were heading back to where we'd been just a couple of days prior hadn't been lost on me. Highways, pushing the speed limit, pausing only long enough to refill the tank and empty bladders, then back on the road again.

We made it to a diner on Route 7 just north of Leesburg, Virginia, with barely five minutes to spare and I wasn't the only one who needed to take a leak.

Ratio waited for us, sipping a drink from a to-go cup while leaning against a rather nondescript, mid-level sedan that suited his rather mundane job as an accountant.

"Ratio," I greeted him, extending a hand. Like I'd told the guys, he was a lean-built man wearing a sharp, if not expensive, suit. Always put together, he didn't waste much time or money on being more than functional. His dark brown hair was a little spiked like he'd had a recent haircut, his face clean-shaven, and the only thing angular about him at all was his jaw.

"Morgan," he responded, clasping mine before glancing at my companions. "Friends?" He had one of those everyman faces, though it wouldn't kill him to smile more.

"For the moment."

He nodded before he pulled off his sunglasses. Yeah, we were not here for a social call. This was business.

"Fuck," Fletcher muttered almost under his breath behind me. "Why does he have to have blue eyes?"

Whatever the fuck that meant.

"You have something for me?"

"More like someone," Ratio said. "A woman…"

VIENNA

SANDRA JANE LOOKED from her wrist clutched in my free hand to my face, then back again. The horror slowly crept into her eyes as she realized what this meant.

She was no longer in charge. No longer able to smack me when she felt like it when I didn't spout the validation she seemingly needed for what *she'd* done to *me*.

An innocent as far as she knew.

The moment she realized she had to do something other than gape at me, her top lip lifted in a sneer, and she tried to rotate her hand to grip my forearm.

I let her.

Her hand holding the gun started to rise, and she was going to aim straight for my face. I could read the intentions in her manic eyes.

Using my weight, I propelled her backward, giving me enough room to stand up. Then I twisted my cuffed hand to grip the slat of the old wooden chair and swung it around to smash the legs against her head and arm. My muscles screamed in protest. Inactivity to abrupt activity was gonna leave me hurting more.

But I'd be alive to hurt. Win-win.

It wasn't a perfect move. There was too much incoordination, and I was too weak to really knock her out, but it had enough oomph to disorient her. The gun flew from her hand and skidded across the floor close to the pile of boxes.

Good. She couldn't shoot me. And from everything I learned about her, she would try if it was me or her.

"You fucking bitch!" she screeched and tried to claw my face. I was too quick, bringing the chair up between us. Her arm bounced off the seat and she backed up to avoid being stabbed in the legs.

This wasn't going to work. I needed the chair off of my wrist. Now.

Moving the chair to the side, I planted my hand in her chest and shoved her backwards. While she was reeling, I slammed the chair on the concrete as hard as possible. It broke the legs, but the seat was still intact.

Shit. This was one of those old sturdy kitchen chairs.

Sandra Jane rushed me and I tried to aim for her head again, but the bitch turned and covered it. She stumbled forward and the chair still hadn't broken. Damn it.

I beat it against the floor while she gathered herself, and *finally*, the seat broke off and the handcuff slid from around the slats.

Squaring my shoulders toward her, I huffed from the exertion as she slowly turned around to face me. Her heavy breathing offered vindication. But I was half-starved, numb, stiff, and dehydrated.

Her blouse was ripped at the collar and the left side of her cheek was red and starting to swell. There even seemed to be a slight plumping of her bottom lip. Good. The more hits she took, the quicker she'd wear down.

No one had taught Sandra Jane how to fight or how to endure pain. And it showed, especially with the rage darkening her face.

She glanced to the side where the gun had slid—we both dove for it, except I was faster.

Using the butt of the gun, I brought it down on her temple, but she was too close to have any real power behind it.

Then she was gone, grabbing the old metal chair she'd been sitting on. I rolled to my feet, but she caught my hip.

Snarling at her, I stepped forward, but she stepped back, holding the chair as a barricade between us.

"You're not getting out of here until I have some answers," her voice slightly trembled, but I had a feeling it was from exertion rather than actual fear. She was too obsessed with finding her father's killer to see me for who I really was.

I understood that.

Damn, if I didn't understand exactly how it felt.

But it didn't matter. Not when I had Fletcher and Rick counting on me. And my own killer to find.

She backed up until she blocked the stairs, still holding the chair with the legs facing me.

"I don't want to hurt you." She braced her legs apart as if expecting me to tackle her. I wouldn't use that move, not with the way she held the chair.

"Don't you?" I stepped forward, raising the gun to her chest. Unlike her, I kept the safety on.

Why was I leaving it on? She wasn't going to back down. I'd have to at least incapacitate her.

But something inside me wouldn't let me outright shoot her. I saw too much of myself in her even if we were not the same.

Could I kill her for loving her father so much, that she

made it her mission to find the person she believed was responsible?

I studied her as she returned the favor. No stress lines around her eyes, no rigid brackets around her mouth. There was so much light in her eyes, it was blinding. All the signs of someone who grew up in a toxic environment or in an abusive home were missing.

She'd had a good childhood. I would wager her father's death was probably the one dark spot in the fabric of her life.

Maybe he'd been a good father. She acted like he had adored her. She'd said as much when she admitted he was her best friend and biggest supporter. But that was the funny thing about people.

The good didn't outweigh the bad.

When he decided to help the Weston Prep boys walk away from any type of judgment or punishment, he signed his own death warrant. A right to a trial didn't mean a right to perpetrate another crime.

How could he have done that with a precious little girl at home, knowing she could be their next victim? I knew. He thought he was untouchable. His status and profession probably gave him a lot of notoriety. He might have thought no one would dare touch his little girl, knowing they might one day need his services.

The bigger question was, how could she love a monster who freed rapists?

At least I knew Daddy was a good man, ridding the world of the monsters so women and children would be safe. Or safer once they were no longer able to target anyone else.

That was the difference between us.

I loved a hero, and she loved a monster.

But sometimes, their ghosts only let you remember the good, which was clearly what Sandra Jane had decided to hold onto.

"What if your dad really helped rapists go free? Have you

thought about that?" This was my last-ditch effort to determine if Sandra Jane was redeemable.

"My father did his job," she countered. "Their guilt or innocence wasn't the issue."

I raised my brows. She couldn't possibly believe that.

"It wasn't." She swallowed, her grip on the chair wavering. Adrenaline was a fantastic resource. It gave you strength and speed when you desperately needed it. But it also crashed if you lingered too long…

Or if you let yourself relax.

"His job was to provide them with the best defense. He did that. He owed no responsibility to the prosecution or anyone else." There—right at the very end of that sentence, she wobbled. "My father wasn't perfect."

"No one is." No one. Rather than waste my energy keeping the gun trained on her, I lowered my hand, but I kept my grip firm. "That doesn't answer my question."

"He did his job," she repeated. Who was she trying to convince at this point?

"His job freed several rapists. Did you ever wonder how many more they raped *before* they died?"

"Alleged rapists." Sweat dotted her forehead, and she took an uneven step forward. The whites of her eyes were on full display as she gave a violent shake of her head. "And don't you mean before the Judge *murdered* them?"

"Allegedly." My thin smile wasn't for her but for the ridiculous politics of language. Discourse could be a weapon in and of itself. One only needed to know how to wield the words.

The chair lowered a fraction and the trembling in her arms increased. It was funny how even holding up a light weight over time could prove stressful.

"You are such a bitch," she finally spat out like she almost hated using the word, and I had to laugh.

"Because I won't cooperate?" I shrugged. "I think our last

week together speaks for itself. We're just on more even footing now."

She slammed the chair down. "Then tell me who you are."

"No."

"Why not?"

Another shrug. "Because who I am doesn't matter. Who you *thought* I was might, but the rest of it is window dressing and noise."

"I have to find the person who killed my father."

Yes. I understood that. Still, I said nothing as we stared at each other. Her panting slowed, but her breaths remained shallow. Projecting an image was something she'd practiced. The panic, however, was real.

"So, it changes nothing for you if your father chose to betray you by freeing rapists while victimizing a girl who'd already been destroyed?" By the time everything went to trial, though? And when it came to the sentencing?

Daddy's anger had been real. So had the disappointment.

"Would it matter to you?" Sandra Jane challenged. "What if someone told you that your father was the—" Everything in her expression changed. "Your father." Her mouth formed a little "o."

I kept my emotions in check. I needed to be dispassionate here. Sandra Jane was, in her own way, a victim. A victim of a father who cared more about a career than he did his family. A victim of a man who freed criminals without a thought for the girls they would hurt in the future.

Without understanding—or maybe just without caring, I couldn't judge him—how his actions would affect her. Still, here we were.

"He's your father," she exhaled on a note of damn near breathless wonder. "That's why you came. Your father is the Judge."

"If he was, do you really think you'd have held onto me

for over a week?" I'd tracked the days, but it blurred a little. Brows raised, I dared her to dispute it.

"No—but then—I covered my tracks." She sounded almost proud of that last one. "You didn't find anything at my home because I didn't want anyone to find something there. This place—I don't own it in my name *or* my mother's. It's set back from the road, with lots of trees, no neighbors. It's quiet. Doesn't even have a street address."

A smirk hardened the lines of her face.

"No one to hear you even if you shouted and screamed. Which you never did." It was her turn to shrug. "Researching the Judge taught me a lot. I've talked to criminalists, investigators, psychologists, and even other killers."

The last sounded like she wanted to tempt me with uncovering what she'd figured out. I didn't care about that part so much. The civilized veneer peeled away from her, roughed off by life choices dictated by a selfish man's actions.

"You're proud of yourself." It wasn't a question.

"I'm an investigative journalist," she declared, chin lifting. "I'm looking at a prime headline, a story that will break open a hundred different cases. I know I'm right, though—my instincts are solid. You're his daughter. You know where he is…"

I wished I didn't.

"What was your exit strategy?" I already knew the answer. Did she?

Confusion clouded her expression. "What exit strategy?"

"You sanitized your home, set it up as a trap, but only as a lure. This place—this place is where you planned to bring *whomever*. Their identity didn't matter, only your belief in who they were."

"I have the right to know." A bead of sweat slid from her temple down along her nose to fall into the crease of her cheek like a tear.

"What do you do with the person you bring here—

whether they admit to what you want to hear or not? Kidnapping, after all, is a crime."

Hesitation marred her expression. It didn't linger for long, but long enough to pull the curtain loose. The person she brought here would never leave.

"I've treated you well…"

"No," I told her. "You haven't." She could fool herself if she wanted to; she couldn't fool me.

"I fed you!"

"That was hardly an act of compassion." No, every single move had been calculated to get me talking. She wanted to foster a dependency in me. I understood the moves. "You made a choice when you brought me here and locked me to that chair."

We all made choices.

Only one of us had ever been leaving this basement. Turning the situation over in my head, I looked for any possible exit that allowed her to survive. Seeing me had been bad enough, but that concerned me less than what she would do with the information.

Who else would she hurt on her quest for justice? Or had she already hurt some? Was I the first she'd brought to this cabin? She had everything set up; too many questions and not enough answers.

The trail of bodies in my wake all had names, a list of crimes, and evidence—well-researched and documented—to prove their complicity. The ones where the evidence had been thin or circumstantial where Daddy was concerned? Well, their other crimes had not.

"Well, you made a choice, going to my house." She took a step toward me as her voice pitched higher. "What were you going to do? Kill me?"

In a move I half-expected and yet still managed to be disappointed by, she swung the chair at me. I twisted away from the blow, taking most of it to my right side. The time standing there had restored feeling to my limbs, not that I enjoyed the agony of movement on abused muscles.

I caught her in the chin with my elbow. The shock of the blow raced up my arm to my free hand as blood spouted from her mouth. Even as I avoided her next blow and used the flat of the gun to slam against her back in a low kidney shot, my mind raced.

No solution presented itself.

Sandra Jane wouldn't stop.

I caught her next blow and twisted her arm. The bones in her wrist ground together, and she let out a wail of sound. "I hate you," she screamed while scrambling for the gun.

This fight ended only one way.

I got the gun away from her, then struck as she twisted. The blow crashed into her cheek and part of her nose. Blood fountained. The crunch of bone echoed inside of me. We went down to the floor, my hand on her throat, my knees pinning her arms. She tried to buck but didn't have the leverage she needed.

When I pressed the gun to her temple, she stilled. Flexing my fingers, I studied her eyes. The light in them was still too bright, too out of control…

"Let this go," I told her. "Your life is not worth his crimes. Don't let your father destroy you too."

Could I let her go? Did I dare?

"No," she spat the word, as blood and saliva struck my cheek. "I have to find him—I have to make him pay." Her eyes narrowed as she bucked again but hadn't mastered flattening her feet to the floor to get better leverage. "I will *never* stop…"

That made my decision for me.

Strangling a person took time and energy. It also took strength I didn't possess in my current state. Snapping the neck required far more torque than I would even be able to manage at the moment.

The scorpion and the frog. How I hated the fable. It came up in everything. A scorpion would always be a scorpion, and the frog was a fool to believe otherwise. It didn't matter if, in the end, it killed them both.

Releasing her, I stood, and she stared up at me. My legs protested even those movements. Sandra Jane pushed herself up on her elbows.

"Tell me—who is he?"

Pointing the gun at her, I eased off the safety in the same smooth motion. "No."

"You know, I can't let this go."

I did. "That's the most unfortunate part of it all." I squeezed the trigger.

At this range, I couldn't miss. The sound exploded through the basement and my ears rang.

Everyone made choices.

This was mine.

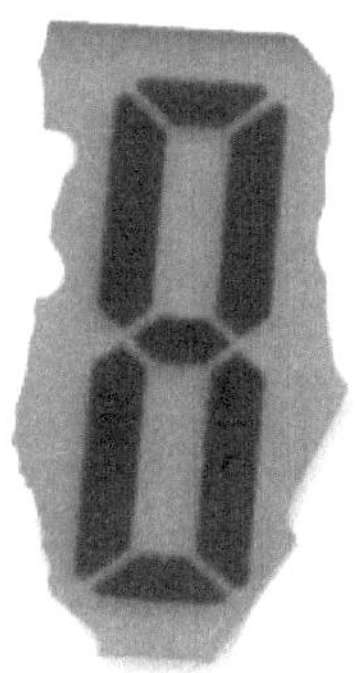

VIENNA

I PLACED the safety back on the gun and bent down, a soft groan escaping from the effort. I was going to pay for this fight later. If Rick wasn't too upset with me for staying gone so long, maybe I could talk him into a nice long bubble bath. Fletcher too. I'd just have to take his caffeine away first. No one wanted to feel like their relaxing, fragrant water was an angry tide out to get you.

Choking out a laugh, I buried my eyes in the crook of my gun arm.

Damn, I missed them so fucking much.

I hoped Fletcher had kept his word and taken care of Rick. With his attachment issues... He was probably in a constant state of catatonia. One time, he explained why he had such a hard time with people leaving him. The pain he experienced after their departure felt like his soul was being ripped apart with self-doubt and worry. His mind was a constant whirl-wind of thoughts and feelings he struggled to process.

Did he do something wrong?

Did they not love him anymore?

How could he take care of them when he wasn't there with them?

Rick was the most caring, gentle man. It angered me that people refused to see the real man underneath, to not understand his needs were just a little different than most. Then, I reminded myself that if someone else had found a way to appreciate him, I wouldn't have him. Neither would Fletcher. Not having him was not okay with me.

All his internal questions broke my heart. I never wanted Rick to feel that way with us, and I'd gone out of my way to reassure him in healthy ways. I hadn't wanted to cripple him and indulge his issues, but I wanted him to be comfortable in our relationship.

If he was able, Rick was doing his best to take care of Fletcher. The ridiculous man would never admit it, but he loved being taken care of in the only way Rick knew how. They were good for each other.

My boys were everything to me too.

Damn, Rueben.

If he wasn't taking a temporary hiatus, he could have done my body disposal for me. Instead, I'd have to clean up this bloody mess and do my own disposal before I could go home to my guys.

The light in Sandra Jane's manic eyes had already extinguished, leaving behind a softer version I'd never seen while she breathed. Doing something I'd never done before, I reached down and closed her eyelids.

My targets were worse than scum. The dregs of society. They didn't deserve any type of respect.

But Sandra Jane? I hadn't wanted it to come to this. She left me no other rational choice. Not one that would let me protect Fletcher and Rick. Not one that would let me go back to them.

Even now, with her dead at my feet, I still felt backed into a corner.

She wasn't perfect, she was damn near on the edge of insanity, but outside of taking me, she hadn't toppled over it. And what had she done that I wouldn't in order to avenge my father?

Only the ones I took and questioned had blaring stains on their soul. Torturing innocents for information was never a level I would lower myself to. I needed to hold onto that piece of information the next time Sandra Jane popped into my thoughts unwelcome.

Surveying the scene, a decent collection of blood had already pooled under her head, and light blood splatter dotted her face and shoulders. Glancing down, I caught a few spots on my free arm, the underside of my gun arm, and my legs.

I needed to shower to scrub off as much DNA as possible before I started cleaning the basement. It would waste my fucking time if I continued to just spread it around by not being clean myself.

The hot spray of water would help my aching muscles anyway.

Sandra Jane most likely didn't have the right supplies to get rid of a body. I'd need to catalog the cabin and see what she did have. Worse case, I'd clean up as best as I could, then run to get supplies to bring back.

And I needed to find those fucking files.

She was too obsessed to leave them anywhere other than within reach of her person. That was fortunate.

Pushing to my feet, I stumbled out of the basement and to that tiny, almost finished bathroom. It had enough to be functional but seemed like was then forgotten in the construction phase. It didn't matter, it would get the job done.

The water pressure left much to be desired, but the steam helped clear my head. I played over the checklist as I indulged myself in the shower for a few minutes, checking and triple checking what I needed to do to get out of here.

Unplanned kills were a pain, and I avoided them at all costs.

Except for this time, I'd been too cocky. Hadn't seen a civilian as a real threat. I'd *never* make that mistake again.

Pink water sluiced down the drain as I scrubbed my body. A small amount was my own blood. She'd gotten in a few good shots, sadly. But that was to be expected when I'd been kept in a basement and tied to a chair for a week with minimal food and water.

After I stepped out of the shower, I wrung out my hair, finger combing it into a ponytail and slicking back any loose pieces, then knotted it. That would at least take care of loose hair.

I padded up the stairs naked so I could snag one of her outfits. Peeking through the doorway, I stepped out after I confirmed all of the blinds were closed tight.

Sandra Jane hadn't wanted to take a chance that anyone would be able to see inside. Good. All the locks on the doors and windows were engaged too.

The upstairs surprised me. It was feminine. Very feminine, with delicate lines to the furniture and splashes of pinks and purples over everything. The decorations reminded me of something a preteen girl would have in her room.

Oh, shit.

Sandra Jane was more off her rocker than I'd given her credit for. This property might not have been in her name, but it was definitely hers. And she'd built a shrine to who she was when her father had been alive. It was only an assumption, but my gut told me I was right.

Fletcher would need to search out the title and make this property a non-issue, which might not be so hard if she'd gone to such lengths for it to be untraceable.

In the master bedroom, I picked a simple outfit of sleep shorts and a tank out of her suitcase that was neatly open beside the canopy bed. She must have been too paranoid to unpack her clothes here, even though this was clearly her safe haven.

Ideally, I would have picked something that wouldn't be looked at twice during the daytime, but she was too thin. Her jeans and slacks wouldn't fit me, and she probably burned the outfit I'd pissed in.

I would have.

After I was dressed, I grabbed food and water out of the kitchen to keep my energy up. Then I set about the task of cleaning the entire cabin from top to bottom. This was going to be a fun few hours.

I drained two bottles of water in quick succession. Was it too much all at once? Probably. But the world wavered a little. Dehydration and exhaustion were the enemy.

A quick inventory of the cleaning supplies she kept under the sink in the kitchen netted me two-gallon bottles of bleach, some scrubbing bubbles, and what looked like a homemade organic cleaner in a spray bottle.

Ammonia touched my nose as I opened it and then checked the contents. Probably some kind of glass cleaner. That would work to wipe down prints. There were also a pair of thick yellow rubber gloves and sponges.

No bucket, though.

Setting what I needed on the counter, I began an inventory. She had a medicine cabinet in the tiny pocket powder room near the front door. A glance outside showed me she really didn't have any visible neighbors. It was also getting later in the day.

The lack of a landline didn't bother me. She had to have a cell phone, all I needed to do was make sure I unlocked it before I wrapped her.

Wrapped her…

No large garbage bags were in the kitchen or pantry. I opened the doors until I found a garage. My car was parked next to another. I'd never been so relieved to see a vehicle.

The bag in the backseat and the one in the trunk were missing, and so was my phone, purse, and wallet.

Right.

Clean up the scene, then inventory the house. I chewed methodically through the two protein bars I'd gotten from the kitchen. Then washed those down with more water. I did find a bucket and a shovel in the garage, along with a tarp and plastic wrap. Interestingly enough, she also had a supply of hydrogen peroxide.

She might not have realized it, but Sandra Jane had set herself up with everything she would need to dispose of a body. Maybe she'd gotten ahead of herself. Maybe it all spiraled out of control.

Or maybe, just maybe, she planned to do what I had to do now.

Shaking my head, I dismissed that particular train of thought. It wasn't productive, and I had a *lot* of work to do. Gathering the supplies, I went back down to the basement. The blood pool beneath her head had already begun to spread.

Death had never really bothered me. I refused to let it get to me now. Gloves on, I went to work. I checked all her pockets for ID or phone. She had nothing on her.

Fine.

Then I got her wrapped in plastic bags. It wasn't the cleanest job, but it would prevent more blood from spreading. Securing her for now, I spent the next hour sanitizing the floor.

Blood on porous concrete was not my favorite, but the hydrogen peroxide would break it down, and then bleach across the whole floor would suffice to destroy any genetic material. Sweat stung my eyes along with the fumes, but I just kept moving.

Anything I'd touched, or that had touched me, got a thorough wipe down. I took the time to finish breaking down the chair and getting the handcuffs off it. While I could sanitize them, I didn't want to leave evidence of my presence.

While the peroxide worked, I walked back up the stairs for more water and to splash my face. I began my search in her bedroom, checking every drawer, every inch of closet space, including the floor. Five boards over from her bed, there was give in the wood.

Using a butter knife from the kitchen, I popped the board up and studied the stash. I reclaimed my phone and my wallet. The ID inside of it didn't name me Vienna Drew. However, it was one of my newer aliases.

Burned now.

Pictures. A couple of envelopes, inside each, was about three thousand in cash.

Clean money. Smart.

My bags had been stored in a utility closet. They'd been rifled, probably emptied and tossed, because everything had been shoved back in haphazard.

I didn't care; I just stripped out of her clothes and pulled on my own. Knife and gun were gone. They'd been stored separately. She had another stash under a floorboard in the living room. The cabin, with all its pretty pastels and throw-back furniture, seemed more like a time capsule than anything else.

A place for her to bottle her obsession with that point in her life. Hiding evidence of the present in the floorboards was also clever. It was at hand but out of sight. Who was going to take the time to test each and every board for the ones that creaked?

The files were in a burn-proof sack beneath two bricks on the edge of the fireplace. Her phone was there, as well as her purse and her ID.

Taking the time to separate out her items and store them in different hidey holes took a certain mindset. Peeling open the burn-proof sack, I checked the files.

Eight of them.

Some thin, three thicker.

They had the smell of age on them and yellowing to some of the paper. I stuffed them back inside along with the other items. I'd add them to my growing stack to take with me. I still needed to finish the cleanup then decide on the best method to dispose of the body.

That meant I also needed a better idea of where I was. The world swayed a little when I rose to my feet. Exhaustion wore at me. Too many days of sitting in the chair, catching what sleep I could. Bags gathered, I did one more sweep of the place before turning on my phone.

Only, it was dead.

Perfect.

Fine, I'd charge it in the car. In the garage, I repacked my car. The keys were in a toolbox. As meticulous as Sandra Jane had been, I had a feel for her and how she thought. Uncommon hiding places, but also easily accessible.

Hitting the button to open the garage door, I took a deep breath of the cooler air as it rushed in. The whole time I'd been cleaning, I concentrated only on the next task. I'd ignored the throb in my face, the aches in my muscles, and the bruises on my flesh.

Real fresh air had been absent for days, and I hadn't realized how much I missed it until—a car's engine had me moving for the gun I'd already stored in the vehicle.

Sandra Jane said we were far from neighbors and no one came here. A lie? Or was this just some unfortunate luck? Braced, I wasn't prepared for the familiar vehicle that skidded to a halt or the precious faces of Rick and Fletcher as they all but lunged out of the car.

The joy flooding me made it hard to even take a breath. That fierce emotion tanked when two more men emerged from the vehicle.

Morgan.

He was out of his cell.

The second man… How did they find *him*? Apprehension curled through me.

"Why are you here?" I demanded, my attention shifting focus back to Morgan, who looked far too pleased. Not only was he out of his cell, but he was also *with* Rick and Fletcher. He could have… I couldn't even contemplate what he could have done. The weight of the gun in my palm was a comfort I didn't even know I needed, even if my hands were still behind my back.

But the fourth man with them gave me more pause than the former FBI agent being out of his cell. Why was *he* with them?

Then Rick filled my vision, blocking the others, and I cast a smile up at him. "Sorry I'm late…"

9

"SORRY, I'm….. Sorry, I'm fucking late!" I stuttered and tossed my hands up as I rushed up to Rick's side. I glared at Drew. What the actual fuck? She was sorry she was late? Sorry some psycho took her prisoner? What the fuck was she *sorry* about?

Apparently, Drew needed the adult-and-responsible Fletcher, too, goddamn it. I didn't like this. I didn't like this at all. Especially when Drew looked like she went on a triple date with Pennywise and his buddies Freddy and Mike, then decided to hang out in the sewers for a couple of hours.

She winced as Rick wrapped her up in those big tree trunk arms of his. A sharp gasp escaped her and he immediately loosened his grip. Not much, but enough so that she wasn't breathing hard. Or heavy. Or fuck, I didn't know. Just less strained.

"I missed you, so fucking much. Please don't leave us again. Not alone," Rick mumbled. His voice lowered to a whisper, obscuring the rest of what he said.

And Drew, like the champ she was, rubbed his back and

let him hold her. Meanwhile, I was left flapping my arms to the side like a damn rooster.

Where was my love? I was about to make this a group sandwich with Drew in the middle.

What was I thinking? Fuck it. We'd done the threesome thing.

I fitted myself against her back, not liking how slender she felt against me but sighing in relief when I gathered them up in my arms. Her ass rubbed against my cock, and I realized just how genuine my concern had been and *was,* when my happy man didn't even twitch.

Drew tipped her head back and kissed the underside of my jaw.

"I hit a few snags, and it took me longer than I'd anticipated to work through them." Her voice rasped as if she'd either drank very little water over the last several days or screamed her head off.

If it was the screaming… God help us. Rick would go ballistic.

Who was I kidding? I was on the teetering edge myself.

"I'd say," Cash drawled, crossing his arms as he studied Drew with a gleeful glint in his eyes.

If he hadn't led us right to her, with the help of his informant, I wouldn't trust him. Hell, I still didn't trust him.

Drew turned her head to Cash, and he continued like he had a death wish.

"You look like hell."

I gasped, and Rick stiffened.

Even Horatio, our quirky—and coming from me, that was saying something—number-obsessed accountant, shot him a narrow-eyed look.

No, no. I didn't like the steady way Horatio watched Drew when he turned back to her.

Letting Cash's insult roll off her back, Drew said, "Some jobs require a little elbow grease." She lightly pressed against

Rick's chest. "Are you okay?" she asked softly as her hands trailed up his chest to cup the sides of his neck.

Big Guy didn't even blink. Just drank her in.

Then he slammed his lips down on hers, devouring our little death angel as he gingerly wrapped her back up in his arms.

That was okay. It wasn't like I didn't want my own hug and kiss anyway. We all knew Rick had the hardest time with her absence. I was the strong one. The responsible one.

It didn't hurt at all—

She stepped away from Rick and turned to face me. When she slid her arms around me and tipped her face up, I took my own kiss from her luscious lips, sipping like I could refill the hole she'd created when she hadn't come home.

With her in my arms, wrapped around me, I could admit it. I might have struggled with her absence too. I just handled it better than the big guy, on the outside.

After what seemed like seconds, but was probably closer to minutes, she stepped back, right into Rick who let us have our moment while still crowding her. He probably wasn't going to let her out of touching distance for the next year or until he forgot how the last seven days felt.

Actually, a year wasn't long enough. I'd say the next decade.

Rick's hands flew to her waist to steady her, and blow me, she needed the help. That was it. We needed to go get her a burger. Rick would want to cook for her, but she needed nourishment quicker than that.

"What happened?" Rick asked. "We waited for you…"

Okay, even I melted a little at that quiet admission.

Drew turned and patted his chest right over his heart and left her hand there, as if she realized he just needed physical touch. "I'll explain all that later. What's most important right now is why he," she pointed at Cash, who grinned like the devil he was, "is with you. And how you found him." She pointed to the blue-eyed fucker staring intently at Drew.

Yeah, I didn't like him at all.

We still hadn't discovered how he was able to bring us here.

Rick didn't seem inclined to throw himself in the naughty circle, so I explained the easiest of the two. "We couldn't find you," I started.

Fuck, I sounded just as pitiful as Rick.

"I knew something was wrong, and I exhausted all of my resources and skills and still couldn't find you." I sucked in a deep breath for courage. "Because we were desperate, we let him out to help us find you." Tossing an arm out at Cash, I almost yelled, "And look! It worked! Because he has a spidey-network of people on your trail. You should be upset with him, not us."

Drew should be proud. I incorporated one of her 5 Ds. Deflect. I was deflecting the blame onto the ex-Fed.

Cash shrugged, all nonchalant. "I got us here. And you look like you could use the help, even if you got out on your own." The fucker looked so proud I wanted to punch him in the face. But from over here.

She turned to Horatio, not even acknowledging Cash. "And you?"

He stepped forward, still drinking her in. Had he even blinked?

I was on to his game. The fucker wanted her to notice his blue fucking eyes.

Rick hugged her waist from behind when she lifted a foot to get closer to Horatio.

I studied him through new eyes, trying to see what Drew saw. She obviously knew him, and that irked me.

He wasn't the stunner Rick was, or even Cash. He was maybe half an inch shorter than me and just a little broader. Standard brown hair. No distinguishing features except for those fucking *blue eyes* he didn't even try to hide beneath round frame glasses.

"When you didn't surface for a few days, I thought you might need some help. And these knuckleheads didn't know their asses from a hole in the ground. So, I…assisted." One side of his mouth kicked up in a crooked grin, transforming him into a somewhat attractive man. I guessed. If you squinted and tilted your head sideways.

Yup, still hated him.

Drew's brows dropped and her lips pinched. "How did you know where I was?"

His grin grew. "Ah, that's information. We could say you already owe me for getting your boys here."

"How much?" She shot back.

"Dinner?"

"I'm not going on a date with you," Drew said as I shouted, "Hell no!"

Rick just growled. Good. We could intimidate the accountant with our psycho puppy. To him, Rick would look like a rabid rottie.

"A family dinner is fine."

"Nope! No. Hell to the fucking no." This man was not invited into the house. "No more." I stopped and pointed at Horatio. "We already have enough foxes."

He crinkled up his nose as he watched me resume my pacing behind Drew and Rick. "Excuse me?"

"No more blue-eyed fucking foxes in the hen house!" I shouted, then pressed up behind Rick's back like he was holding me back from raining destruction on Horatio's head. "We have enough, thank you fucking much."

While *Horatio* didn't so much as glance in my direction, Drew did. At her quirked brows, I frowned and then flushed.

"Well," I continued in more of a mumble. "We do."

"You never mentioned *knowing* her," Cash said into the silence, his tone less arrogant and much more broody. I damn near smirked. Oh, look at that. Mr. I-Fucking-Know-Everything didn't know something.

"You never asked," Horatio told him without a sideways glance, then nodded to Drew. "Do you require medical assistance?"

With one question, he flipped my attention back to Drew. She really did look like death warmed over. Our death angel was still there, bruised and battered, but very much alive. Rick rumbled a sound, but she just rubbed a circle against his chest.

"I do not," she answered. "We can discuss a family dinner later." Then she flicked a look at Cash. Some of his smugness had drained away as he studied her in return, then eyed Horatio. "We will also discuss the releasing of dangerous individuals when they could be a threat to the two of you."

Could be. Not was.

That actually made my chest puff out a little.

"Since you're here, someone manage him. I need to get some more supplies."

"What do you need?" Rick was ready to open a vein if necessary. Me too, if it came to that, despite the fact I'd prefer to never see blood again.

"Besides a steak, a hot bath, and perhaps a very large glass of wine," I tacked on for him. There was no mistaking the faint gurgling noise that came from her stomach.

"I need to wash up," she said, choosing her words carefully. Our accountant "friend"—okay, not our friend, but clearly he wanted to be Drew's, the blue-eyed bastard—nodded.

"You also require rest," he said. "If you have no objections, I'll take care of closing the cabin. Probably better for you to get home."

"Wait a fucking minute," Cash said abruptly. "Wash—where's Sandra Jane? Is that what you need help with? She should be arrested—" He stopped abruptly, and I stared at him.

Was *he* for fucking real, now? Did they all take stupid pills this morning? We couldn't hand her over. I had no idea what she knew or didn't know, but that wasn't the point. She *hurt* Drew. That was unacceptable.

Period.

"Ignore the former federal officer," Horatio said. "Some habits are almost impossible to break. He is, however, not an idiot. I also assume the two of you need to have a conversation. Those two would be better somewhere else, with you secure."

If by somewhere secure, he meant home, and without him, I was down with it.

"And you?" Drew asked, ignoring Cash as easily as Horatio did. That was almost funny, because a vein throbbed in his forehead as he cut his glare back and forth between the two of them.

"I am a patient man. You're safe. As for the rest, we can call it a favor…"

Before any of us could object, Drew merely shook her head. "We don't deal in favors."

"True," he said with a faint smile. "But that, too, is an old habit."

"One, I'm not interested in breaking."

"Heard," he acknowledged. "Then add, allowing me to bring a dessert or a bottle of wine to the family dinner for the cost."

A troubled look passed over her face. The fact Drew let me see her feelings in her expressions at all was a gift, but this, I didn't think was so much about allowing any of us. She sure as hell wasn't allowing Cash. No, there was a weariness to her, a kind of strung too tightly. Now that I'd noticed it, I couldn't unsee it.

Rick didn't offer any objections. I expected the Big Guy to

just shut this down, but he didn't. Instead, he let himself be lulled by the contact with her. Yeah, that I got. I didn't want to focus on them at all, just on her.

"If that means we can get you out of here," I said. "Then let's go. I can handle dinner with the numbers guy, as long as we don't have to talk math all night." Then again… "We could do group rounds of Sudoku. Pretty sure I can kick his ass."

That pulled a smile from Drew, and she chuckled. "I think we'll be fine. Dinner, and you may bring the wine after Rick decides what we're having. I'll message you the details."

"Accepted." Horatio turned to go back to the car, pausing only when Cash grabbed him.

Oh, was someone about to get their ass kicked?

"Ratio, you didn't tell me you knew her."

Yeah, we established that.

"No, I didn't. Nor will I ever confirm it for you. The lady is tired. Try not to be too much of an ass." Then he glanced back at Drew once more. "Unless this is another issue you need cleaned up?"

It was probably the most civilized and scary fucking threat I'd ever heard. The man was an *accountant,* but you'd have to be an idiot to miss the actual menace underscoring those perfectly polite words. Like said idiot, who released him with a laugh.

The Fed was definitely out there. "I'm starting to think there's something really wrong with him," I told the Big Guy quietly. Drew definitely heard me, but she didn't look away from the other pair. I could imagine she weighed all the pros and cons in an instant. It seemed a very *her* thing to do.

"No," she said, finally. "Thank you for offering."

"Of course." He shook off Cash, or maybe the Fed just released him. Either way, he returned to the car and retrieved a bag. "Good afternoon, gentlemen," he said as he returned and headed toward the house. "Vienna."

She summoned something close to a smile for him, and then he entered the house via the garage she had just exited. Her car sat there too. We'd need to get that out of here.

"Want me to take your car?" I offered. "That way, you can ride with the Big Guy?" I suppose I could take the Fed.

"No," she said after a moment, and I tried not to let my relief out. She clasped my hand briefly, squeezing it and my rabbiting pulse settled down to a more tortoise-like pace. "That'll be part of the cleanup. It all needs to go. I just need to get my things out of the back."

"'I'm sorry," I offered. "I'll get them."

"I can." Rick gave her hips a squeeze then gave me a look. It was the first true animation since he'd kissed the hell out of her. I interpreted the look as a pair of commands: *stay with her* and *don't let her out of sight*.

Happy to accommodate. When I brushed her hand again, she slid her fingers between mine. Elation from a single touch swelled within me. It outstripped pretty much everything. It was better than when Diana McAdams, in the seventh grade, had given me her bubblegum for the first time by kissing me.

"Are you all right?" The question reminded me that Cash was still with us. Rude.

"What is your next play?" Rather than answer him, she offered up her own question.

"Get you home. Make sure you get some rest. Then talk to you."

Well, that was straightforward enough.

"Why?"

Rick passed us on his way to the vehicle with Drew's bags. I recognized both of them from when she packed at the house. He didn't slow as he passed Cash nor glance at him.

"Because we just got you back."

We. I almost scoffed but managed to resist. Instead, I just traced my thumb up and down the side of her hand.

Touching her made it real. She was right here after what had been *endless* days.

Rick loomed up behind him, but Drew just gave the barest shake of her head. Cash twisted, snapping around as if he'd just realized the threat. The Big Guy just met Cash's stare with an implacable one of his own.

"Get in the car. Shut up. Let her rest." He ticked off the items. There was no mistaking the warning in his tone. Cash got in the car willingly, or Rick put him in there. Good times. "Fletcher…"

"In the back with Cash, on it." But I didn't move until Drew did. Cash scowled, then glanced back at the house.

"Guys," she said, and all three of us froze. "Can you give me a moment with Cash?"

Rick frowned.

"It can wait," I offered, but she shook her head.

"Better to do this now before we get on the road." She squeezed my hand.

Yeah, he had a thousand questions, but not today. No, sir, today we were taking Drew home. Hell yes.

Win for Team Frick.

A laugh escaped me, and Drew gave me a startled look, but then she smiled and I grinned.

"I'll explain later," I promised.

"I'm looking forward to it." Then she brushed another kiss to my lips before motioning to Cash. "Shall we?"

DAMN, I'd missed my guys. It was almost hard to stop smiling as I led Cash a few steps away so we'd have a modicum of privacy.

Except, Fletcher did a very poor job of busying himself around the car with one ear pointed our way. Rick didn't even hide the intense scowl he aimed at Mr. Morgan. I laughed under my breath. They both looked good. Really good. A bit frazzled, but that could be expected if they'd been searching for me this past week.

I hated that I did that to them. But hopefully, now that they could see and touch me, they would forget about the stress of me being gone. I was already losing some of my own anxiousness. Who knew having them within touching distance would settle some of my frayed nerves?

Suddenly, with the accountant taking care of the house, and the files in my possession, exhaustion was doing its best to pull me under.

But I was too well trained to give in to the pull.

I glanced back at the house. Could an accountant take care of cleaning up a scene?

Shaking my head, I pushed the doubt from my head. I never worked with him, but he was one of Daddy's associates, and on the rare occasion when he did talk about him, his words had been tinged with respect. The accountant could handle it, or he wouldn't have offered.

Then Mr. Morgan stepped into my line of sight, completely blocking out the guys, and I found it wasn't hard to lose my smile at all.

He was so tall, that he nearly obliterated the sun. Standing this close to him, when I wasn't sitting down or he wasn't on the other side of cell bars, he gave off an overwhelming vibe. The hairs on the back of my neck stood at attention as he shifted his body closer.

Mr. Morgan was dangerous. I just needed to know if he was a danger to me and mine. If he was…he wouldn't be for very long.

I would never allow Rick and Fletcher to come to any harm. Ever. "Mr. Morg—"

"Cash. I go by Cash." The cocky grin that had clung to his face a few short minutes ago was still absent as he kept glancing back toward the house. "How do you know Ratio?" He asked as he ground his teeth.

"No, Cash. I ask the questions." I gave him an appropriate amount of time to argue. He didn't. Good. I didn't have the energy to fight with him just yet. "I hope you understand, you've placed me in a very unfortunate situation."

A ghost of his smile returned as he tipped his head down, his light turquoise eyes threatening to swallow me up. "Not the kind of position you and I would enjoy, I imagine."

"No." I frowned. "You're an ex-FBI agent with too much knowledge about me and my family." His nose twitched when I referred to the guys as family, but it felt good to make the declaration. Right. "Now, I have to decide what to do with yo—"

He stepped closer, and Rick started to march toward us, but Fletcher jumped in his path.

"I'm coming back with you."

"No." However, that was the only real option available to us. Whether he went back to the cell or not…

"Yes." Here was the argument I'd been waiting on. And the brain power I didn't think I had surfaced with a vengeance.

"Why? Why would an ex-officer of the law want to come home with me? I don't trust you. There is no reason that I would believe anything you said. Even if you gave me your word that you had no ill intentions toward us. Turning us in could get you back in with the Bureau, and I can't ignore that."

"I think you forgot they canned me. There's no love lost between me and that team. You're also forgetting another important fact…" He trailed off as if he wanted me to bite. I kept my lips clamped shut.

He sighed. "My one goal in life was to track down the Judge. And I found you. You could say finding you holds sentimental value to me. I know you can't be the Judge, not really, with your age. But you're part of the Judge somehow. You're connected in a way that fascinates me. You think I'd share that with the fucking FBI? After they fired me? Please." Cash raised his hand and ran a finger down my arm.

His touch burned as his tone tried to soothe some of my suspicions. Luckily, I wasn't taken in by deep voices and handsome faces. Daddy taught me better than that.

"And when you have all the answers?"

The manic grin he'd sported earlier came back twofold. "Well, Vienna," he let my name roll off his tongue. I stiffened. He had gotten a lot closer to the boys than I had initially thought. "By then, I'll be so ingrained in your operation, you'll never be able to let me go. Even if you did, the FBI would see me as an accomplice."

I squinted, ignoring the tightness of my skin where Sandra Jane had bruised my face. "Do you really think I'm ignorant of undercover agents?"

"But I'm not one. I don't expect you to believe that. In fact, I expect that you wouldn't. But believe this. Fletcher and Rick let me out of the basement. At any time, I could have over-powered them and turned them in—"

"No, you couldn't have!" Fletcher mock-yelled as he stood in the open back door of the car they arrived in.

Cash's nose twitched again, but he kept going. "I didn't do that. I haven't called my family. I haven't called the FBI or the local police. What I did do, was assist them in searching for you. I completed a job with them. And," he drew out the word. "One of my informants led me straight to you, where we would have saved you by any means necessary, if you hadn't already saved yourself." A note of pride entered his words.

Ignoring the warmth threatening to flood my body under his praise, I turned to the guys. He could have hurt them, that wasn't a lie. As much as I had worked with Rick on self-defense and Fletcher, who participated under duress, both Cash and I knew he was the superior fighter. Anyone could see that if they spent a few minutes watching the way he moved and controlled his body.

"I still don't see what's in this for you. Why do you want to be on this side of the law when you've worked on the other side your entire life?" Both Rick and Fletcher studied us with undisguised interest.

Rick's gaze was steady, as if to tell me what Cash said was true. Fletcher fidgeted with his bun, wearing a similar expression on his face. He really had been invaluable in helping them find me.

"I told you why. This is a wet dream for me. If you were a psychopath who killed indiscriminately, then maybe I'd have an issue, but coming from that side, I understand exactly how the system is broken. You won't have any issues out of me." His gaze roamed my face, likely committing every detail to memory now that he could see me so clearly under the light of day.

Glancing at the guys again, Rick nodded, and Fletcher, who had watched Rick nod, turned back and shrugged as if to say *my call*. I had a feeling my flirty hacker wouldn't miss the Fed too much if we decided to leave him behind somehow.

But that wasn't an option either. We couldn't let him go, so taking him with us was the only option. Before sharing that, I needed to address something else.

"What job did you do?"

What job had *any* of them done?

"Some hauling art job for a lady named Mart. Little piece of fluff with a lot of attitude." The last he delivered in a dry, almost sardonic tone. "I thought your attachment to Reed was a little strange."

If he was fishing for a reaction from me, he wasn't going to get one. The job for Mart…

I'd remembered the work I'd agreed to before I left, but the last few days had turned that into a blur. "How did that go?"

The plan had been that once we'd cleaned out the target's collection, she would be absenting herself and making herself visible elsewhere while I took care of him myself. Sandra Jane had cost me several days, and I could only hope it hadn't cost any other girls in the interim.

"Well, she kicked him in the balls when he wouldn't stop interrogating her," Fletcher supplied helpfully, and Cash bared his teeth for a moment before he laughed.

"She definitely nailed me in the nutsack. She has excellent aim."

I didn't doubt it. But I was almost not laughing. Their appearance at Mart's job without me meant questions. My phone needed to finish charging, but I had a suspicion that there would be messages on my other phones at home.

As if noticing my lack of reaction, Cash sobered then met my gaze evenly. "We picked up a white panel van from a secure facility a few hours from here, *after* we searched Sandra Jane's place. The idea being she was your last target, but there was nothing there to indicate this level of socio-pathic behavior. That said, the utter lack of personality in that place was also a clue—but I needed more context for it."

I shrugged that off. "You weren't the one she ambushed. Nor the only one she fooled."

Why was I comforting him?

"Get back to the job."

"You're a tough audience." The barest hint of a smile kicked up the corner of his mouth. He'd continued to trace a finger up and down my arm but finally dropped it away. "Right, the three of us arrived at the location. Big Guy over there had all the details. She met us and let us in to begin the load. Everything was clearly marked from the Remingtons down to the Manets. There were a couple of more modern pieces that I wouldn't call art, but then I don't work in White Collar either. Once we packed it all in—it was a tight fit—we transported it to another storage place where we picked up a key, emptied everything into the assigned locker, then he mailed the key off before we left."

I cocked my head. Each detail he related included some-thing specific for one of our jobs. A clearing house would pick up the artwork from the storage facility, and it would then be fenced and cleaned. Eventually, the money would make its way back to The Accountant, and he would handle the disbursements, including my transportation fee.

While Rick had some idea of the system, he had executed the steps with perfection. I couldn't be prouder of him.

"The only thing I couldn't figure out was why you'd be involved in any kind of B and E." Cash shrugged. "I can't imagine this is some kind of justice play and the job wasn't only for you. So, that makes me want to ask more questions about…"

"Don't."

He paused. "Don't?"

"Don't ask questions. You did a job, you followed instructions, and that's all you need to know."

"Well, on that, Beautiful, we're going to have to agree to disagree." The fact that he hesitated on the word beautiful and still managed to make it sound like a compliment might have amused me. Today, it only served to highlight my point. "I ask questions. I take things apart. I put them back together. You have to see the whole picture…"

"You're right," I stated, and surprise actually flickered over his face. "*I* have to see the whole picture. You don't."

"That's not how partners work."

I laughed. "You're right, but we're not partners."

"Yet."

I snorted.

"That's not a no, Vienna." Now his grin turned almost playful. "I know I have to win you over. I looked after your boys. I didn't do anything to them. I let them set the rules—I even cooperated when they put me in the trunk."

I quirked an eyebrow at that last one and glanced toward Rick, who gave me a small smile and a shrug. He didn't like me lingering here, but he also had no apologies about the trunk.

"They're not so bad," Cash continued as I faced him again. "I think if you give me a chance… you'll find out I'm not so bad either."

I didn't laugh in his face because that would be rude. "So just like that, you walk away from your life and into mine."

"Yes."

"What happens when you wake up one morning and decide that you can't anymore? Do you just turn us in and take off? You had a hell of a career before they 'fired' you."

Yes, I did air quotes when I said fired because he might be presenting honest and earnest, but who just walked away from their lives because they had a hard-on for someone they'd pursued for years?

"I can't convince you with words," Cash answered. "I wouldn't believe me either. I can only prove it with my actions. If you want me to climb in that damn trunk right now, I will. It's a bit of a hike back to your place, so I'd rather not until I absolutely had to, though."

Such a strange man. I tilted my head to the left, watching him from beneath my lashes. Did I want to believe him because the guys did? Or because I couldn't stomach killing someone who was technically innocent? But was he…

"How dirty have you gotten before now?" Because that was a question we'd never fully addressed.

"I don't break the law if I don't have to." It was the most direct answer he'd ever given me. "But I will bend it if the ends justify the means. The justice system is flawed. Every-thing I know about the Judge tells me he—and by extension, you—only go after the people who truly deserve it. There is never collateral. More often than not, they are also people who would never have been stopped any other way."

"You sound certain." It was uncomfortable how on the nose he'd come. Daddy's rules were very specific.

"I am. It might take a year, sometimes ten years, but the truth always comes out. Every single victim we can attribute to the Judge—and the few I'm pretty sure were also his—they all have one nasty habit or another in common. The world is better for their absence."

When I continued to say nothing, he spread his hands.

"What else can I do?"

The weird thing was, I believed him. Yet, I couldn't quite put a finger on why I hesitated. Something about Cash Morgan was *off,* and I couldn't identify what it was exactly.

That left me more than a little wary.

Instincts, as Daddy would say, were honed for a reason.

"You come back with us, you follow my rules."

"All right."

"That means no questions."

He grimaced.

"That means you listen and do as you're told. If I say something doesn't concern you, it doesn't concern you."

"I'm an investigator by nature, Vienna. Asking me to not ask questions… to not investigate."

I gave a little shrug. "Those are my terms. You will follow my rules. You will not ask questions. What I say goes. Take it. Or leave it."

"Can I reserve the right to renegotiate at some future time when we've earned some trust between us?"

Again, with the partner language. "You're going to try to do it anyway, aren't you?"

"I'm a determined man."

That was part of the problem.

One way or another, he was going back with us because I needed to know he wasn't out there waiting to threaten Rick or Fletcher.

Exhaustion weighed down every muscle in my body. He put a hand on my arm to steady me, and I locked my legs. I'd been swaying.

"You're tired. We need to get you home. If the only way I get to come is to agree, then I agree. For now." The last two words he added in a huff of breath.

It would have to do.

"Don't disappoint me," I told him as I folded my arms and gave Sandra Jane's cabin one last look as I walked back toward Fletcher and Rick. Cash fell into step with me swiftly.

"I won't," he promised.

You better not, I told him silently. "Good," I continued aloud. "I don't want to have to kill you too."

WHEN WE PULLED into the garage, my brain operated on less than ten percent. Rick did all the driving over the day, allowing me to rest, but that hadn't really been an option either.

While traveling, I always watched the roads, scanned faces, and cataloged anything remotely out of the ordinary.

Luckily, nothing smelled suspicious, which was a boon after the past week. We needed a day or two without any additional surprises. Although, I wasn't sure what was more shocking—realizing a civilian could get the jump on me when I wasn't careful or getting free only to find my guys with unwelcome reinforcements skidding to a halt outside the cabin.

No, I'd think about that later. Tonight, I just needed to be close to my guys.

But this nostalgic feeling of coming home that lapped at my chest now that we were in the house I'd shared with them over the last few months...I'd never experienced this before.

Every property had a purpose. When one house was no longer a safe option, we destroyed it and moved on. No sentimental attachments, no second thoughts, no looking back as we walked away for good.

I glanced over at Rick as he put the car in park. When he met my gaze, he smiled like just being next to me was his most favorite thing.

Daddy wouldn't approve. He would say this was too careless, left too much room for error. But Rick's smiles and Fletcher's quiet snores in the backseat that Rick induced with melatonin filled me with a love so encompassing, this couldn't be wrong.

It was absolutely right.

Although, I should probably talk to Rick about how often he was giving Fletcher sleep aids, natural or not. Then again, Fletcher would hardly sleep without Rick's interference.

Opening my door, my legs shook when I put weight on them. I stretched my calves and hugged my knees to dispel some of the stiffness, but a hot bath and a good night's sleep with the guys would go a long way to restoring my physical and mental health back to normal.

I gently shook Fletcher's shoulder as Rick popped the trunk.

"Goddamn," Cash groaned as he unfolded his long, lean frame from the small space. It *was* cramped back there, especially for a man of his size. "Okay, I understand your need to lock me away, but I'm the biggest man here. If this is going to be our thing, we need to invest in a larger vehicle, so the trunk doesn't feel like I'm playing Tetris with my limbs." He moaned as he rotated his shoulders and a series of cracks accompanied the movement. "That felt good."

Fletcher stumbled out of the car, rubbing sleep from his eyes. He dropped a kiss to my temple and an arm around my shoulders as we walked toward the laundry room door. "I don't know, man. That's a big investment. I don't think it would be wise to waste money on a bigger vehicle just so you're comfortable for two hours of our road trips. It's not like you spend the entire ride back there."

"Right, because that would kill me. And that's rich,

coming from a Reed." Cash frowned at Fletcher. The expression was more of a grumpy inconvenience than actual fear. If at any point Cash became disposable, we could get him in the trunk under the ruse of going home, then drive until the exhaust did, in fact, kill him. He had to have known that.

He must not believe we'd actually do it…

"At this rate," Cash said as he followed behind us, leaving Rick to bring up the rear. "I'll cash in my 401k to purchase a vehicle with a trunk of my choice. I'd prefer to just earn your trust, but that takes time. I get it."

"You're very strange, Cash Morgan." I kicked my shoes off and lined them up on the rack in the laundry room. The guys all followed suit, even Cash. Then we were left staring at each other.

"Cash. Calling me Cash Morgan or Mr. Morgan makes me feel like I'm still a stranger, or you're an android. I'd expect that from the hacker, but I would prefer you just call me Cash," he said through a grin, like he hadn't been complaining two seconds ago.

Yes, something was definitely off with him. Until I figured out if his quirks were in our favor or not, he was here to stay.

I glanced toward the secret door to the basement. With very little fuel left, I would crash soon. I could already feel the fatigue crowding in at the edges of my mind. For me to really rest like I needed to, Cash needed to be secured.

"No." Cash crossed his arms, glaring mutinously at me. Ah, so not only did they let him out, but they also let him explore the house to know where the door to the basement originated.

"I need rest," I sighed, swaying into Fletcher's side. He tightened his grip on my body.

"Absolutely. I'm sure you didn't sleep on the drive, and I know you didn't when I was in the backseat with the sandman here." He nodded at a still groggy Fletcher. "But I'm not going back to the cell. I'll get in the trunk so you can pretend I'm less of a threat by not knowing the exact location of this house, but I've earned the right to stay out of the basement."

"Says you," I snapped. Cash must have thought we were past polite negotiations to be making demands. That wouldn't end well for him.

"Says Rick and Fletcher," he fired back. When I glanced at the guys, Rick gave Cash a sharp side-eye while Fletcher widened his eyes in a mock innocent expression. "The entire time you were gone, I slept in the guest room. I'll continue to sleep there, and lock me in if you have to. Just no basement. That's a hard stop for me."

"Or what?" I growled, stepping forward, ignoring the way my body protested as my muscles tensed.

"This do—"

"Stop," Rick barked. "Vienna just went through a week of torture from Sandra Jane and that has to be taking a mental toll on her. We can all see the physical toll. What she needs is a nice glass of wine, which I will get for her. A hot bath, and sleep."

And sex. Nothing relaxed a body like a good fucking. But I'd convince one of the guys to indulge me when Cash wasn't within earshot.

"She also needs to not worry about you. If she needs you in the cell to relax, you'll go in the cell." Rick squared up to Cash, and their heated glares raised the temperature in the small laundry room.

The room wasn't actually that small, but with all four of us crammed in this space, it felt like a tin can.

I stepped forward to put a stop to their posturing, but Fletcher tugged me back.

"I have a solution. I think." He mumbled under his breath about being the responsible one, but I was too tired to laugh or even react at all. "Rick, grab her wine and take her upstairs. You need the time with her just as much as she needs it with you." He glanced at me, his cobalt blue eyes lighting up as we locked gazes. "Drew, as much as it pains me to admit, I do trust him. A little bit. Not enough to run free and have all the electronic access, but enough to not sleep in the basement. I saw the cot. It's terrible. So," he took a deep breath like he was making the gravest of sacrifices. "I'll watch him. I just had a good long nap, so I won't be going to bed anytime soon. And I know where Rick stashed my energy drinks if I need them."

Rick snorted but remained quiet.

All three men watched me, waiting for what I wanted to do.

Slowly, I nodded. "You can stay with Fletcher. But Cash, don't forget what I said. He's very important to me." Which translated to, you hurt him, you die.

Cash jerked his chin down once in understanding as his posture lost some of its rigidity. "I have no ill intentions toward him. As long as he stays out of the caffeine stash."

"Fletcher," I murmured, and he followed me into the main part of the house. I didn't go far, but I wanted some semblance of privacy. "You don't have to watch him." I touched a hand to this chest. I needed the grounding just to remind myself we were both here.

"You need time," Fletcher answered in a similarly low voice. He cut his gaze to the left, then moved to shield me from both Cash and Rick. "The Big Guy needs it, too."

I needed them both. "What do you need?"

"To do this for you," he said, the corners of his mouth quirking into a smile. "Though being responsible and in charge could go to my head, so you might have to spank me later."

Adoration filled me. Rising on careful, if bruised toes, I pressed a kiss to his mouth. He met the kiss with one as gentle as mine, and we just held there, breathing each other in.

"Go on," he whispered. "I'll be here. I promise."

I followed his gaze to where Rick cast me a look of longing as he uncorked a bottle. What he needed right now was to be close to me. I rubbed Fletcher's chest gently, grateful for him. I waited at the island until he handed me the glass of wine, then we walked toward the stairs together.

Soft sounds from the TV and light chatter were already coming from the living room.

"They'll be okay," Rick whispered as he placed a hand on the small of my back.

"You trust him not to hurt Fletcher?" I asked just as quietly.

"Yes." He didn't even hesitate, and that further relaxed me. I trusted Rick, and, even though he hadn't grown up in this kind of life, I trusted his judgment. He was very protective of me *and* Fletcher. He wouldn't dismiss any real threat to him.

"Then what do you say you join me for that nice hot bath?" I leaned in and brushed my nose against the column of his neck once we reached my door. Anticipation of being alone and naked with Rick zinging up my spine, pushing most of the exhaustion away.

"I'm not going anywhere," he promised as he opened the door. The interior of the room was cool, the blinds were closed and it was a cozy kind of darkness. Everything was in pristine order and there was no scent of emptiness. Even the bathroom carried a hint of my shampoo in the air, likely from the last time someone showered. An odd pang went through me.

"You guys stayed in here while I was gone?" I walked into the bathroom and took a swallow of the wine before setting it on the counter. I didn't want too much. Rick had tried to coax me to eat food on the way home, but I just wasn't interested in fast food options. I had a salad.

"Yes," Rick told me with a smile, his gaze firm on me in

the mirror. The worry in his eyes tugged at me. "We wanted to be close and Fletcher couldn't sleep."

A sigh escaped me. "Thank you for looking after him."

"He looked after me," Rick offered up, then gave a puzzled little smile, like he still didn't know what to make of it. "But you were right, he did good."

"You both did."

The grave concern in his eyes was unwavering despite my compliment. Refusing another sigh, I glanced at myself in the mirror. My cheek was definitely bruised and swollen. So was my eye. I barely even felt that. It had a variety of colors, from greenish-yellow at the edges to more mottled bluish-black near the center. It could be worse, I suppose.

Better to get this out of the way, I'd done an inspection at the house, but Rick needed to see and I needed him to *know* I was all right. It wasn't just his concern but the emotion behind the concern. The open affection and pleasure he took just in my company. I actually hated that I'd let him down in any way.

As I shed my clothes, Rick turned to the bathtub and got the water running. He didn't put the stopper in until steam began to rise from the water. Then he added a couple of the bath bombs I liked. Besides their name, I loved the colors they transformed the water into and how soft they were. The scent was beautiful and clean, with elements of citrus and vanilla.

Closing my eyes, I took a deep breath and just filled my lungs with the scent of being home. Of Rick...

A half-step of movement alerted me a split second before he said, "Vienna."

"I'm here," I promised. "You can look at every mark and bruise. You can make notes, and I'll let you treat anything that needs to be treated. Then you get in that bath with me and we're going to soak away the last few days and just be together."

The brush of his lips to my shoulder sent a shiver through

me. "I missed you," he admitted, and I raised a hand to cup his cheek while I opened my eyes to meet his gaze in the mirror.

"I missed you too."

He cradled me and we stood there as the tub filled. With a hint of reluctance, he finally let me go then turned off the water. Straightening, he focused on me again as he squared his shoulders.

"Come here," he murmured and it wasn't a request. "Let me look at all of you."

My heart squeezed at that command, but another knot of tension loosened in my system. I liked it when Rick took over. He needed to take care of me, and right now…

Right now, I needed *him*. I needed to be taken care of.

THE QUIET NEED in her tawny eyes had been the last lance I needed to bleed away the turbulence of her absence. She hadn't stayed away willingly. Far from it. The week I'd endured had been nothing compared to the suffering she had faced. If only we had found her sooner. But I could either nurture that anger, or I could look after her. I couldn't do both.

Right now, she needed me.

While the bath waited, I ran my hands over her lightly. As much as my body always leapt to her nearness, it wasn't my cock or my desire that she triggered at the moment. Bruises scattered over her skin, the worst of which seemed along her side, especially her hip. I knelt to inspect it, looking for any abraded skin beneath the discolored striations.

"What did she hit you with?" I had to ask.

"A chair." The admission fanned the anger fisting in my gut. "It probably looks worse than it feels. Though admittedly, it doesn't feel great."

Pressing another kiss to her shoulder, I continued my inspection—small burn marks on her back.

"Taser," she murmured.

Bruises and scrapes turned her wrists into a riot of colors.

"Zip ties and handcuffs."

Those were the worst, save for the way her ribs jutted a little. She'd lost weight during her time there. Impatient with my own need to check every inch of her, I caught her hand and guided her over to the bath.

"Are you going to join me?" she asked even as she stepped into the hot water. A hiss of pleasure escaped her as she began to lower herself into the fragrant water. I held her hand until she settled. I didn't think she needed the assistance, but she indulged me and I adored her for it.

"Yes," I promised. "Just wanted to get you in the water first." I carried her wine glass over where she could reach it. "Do you want me to get you some food?" Not that I was in any rush to leave her. "I could put together a charcuterie board. Something to nibble?"

She'd enjoyed the one at Fletcher's apartment.

"Maybe later… I'm really not hungry."

Some of my skepticism must have shown, because the corners of her mouth tilted up into a gentle smile.

"Rick, really, all I want or need right now is you. If Fletcher could be up here with us, that would be great."

"But he needs to be where he is." Settled, I pushed the door to the bedroom closed to keep the air warm. As I stripped out of my clothes, Vienna shifted in the large tub of hers and watched me. I didn't need to puff out my chest or show off. She liked me just as I was.

Clothes folded and set aside, I moved over to slide into the tub behind her. Stretching out my legs, I lifted her up to sit on my lap. The water was more than deep enough to keep her submerged. My dick stirred at the first brush of her ass, but I ignored it as I stretched over to grab the hairbrush she kept in a basket near the tub. We always stripped it of hair when she was done, so it was perfectly clean.

As I began to brush her hair, she let out a low groan and settled more firmly against my chest before taking another sip of the wine. All the tension of the past week began to drain out of me as I worked the brush through her hair. It was soft, but it lacked the sheen it normally possessed.

She'd showered before we got there, that much she'd mentioned.

Only in as much as she hadn't been able to bathe or clean up much at all. All of her nails were broken. She'd filed those on the drive. There were bruises around her fingertips—from fighting or from getting out of her restraints.

I needed to stop the spiral of thoughts. Positive things. Refocus on the moment. All at once, the lessons from my program surfaced. I hadn't been able to find a single one in her absence, but now? Now they were there.

"Fletcher did well on the job. Mart had no complaints about him or me," I offered. "She seemed charming, but I didn't assume she was helpless."

Vienna let out a throaty laugh and tilted her head back to look up at me. "No, she's not helpless. Though very few often notice that."

"Well," I said, with a grin of my own. It felt almost alien on my face. "I have some experience with delicate packages harboring a great deal more than most people see."

"Thank you, Rick."

"My pleasure," I murmured after making sure there wasn't a single snarl in her hair. It may lack the shine of health and vitality in the immediate aftermath, but we would get that back. Setting the brush aside to clean off when we were done, I reached for one of the loofas and spread a generous amount of the soap she enjoyed.

Like her bath bombs, it held elements of fresh citrus with just a hint of sweetness. It always refreshed me when she used it. Made me think of orange juice on a bright sunny morning, like some ridiculous commercial where the whole body jolted in reaction.

Then again, every day with Vienna was a full-body jolt I'd grown used to and craved. With care, I lifted her free arm and began to run the loofa up and down her arm, spreading the soap with care. Taking my time, I let her finish another sip of wine before she set the glass aside then I went to work on her other arm. When she leaned her head back against my shoulder, I smiled down at her.

"Better?"

"Yes," she murmured, stretching to press her toes to the edge of the tub. The move arched her back, lifting her breasts from the water. Accepting the invitation, I moved the soap over her chest. Bringing my free hand into the action, I massaged her breasts, teasing the nipples as they beaded tight.

The soft exhalation of a breathy moan made my smile grow. My dick twitched. The need to lick, nip, and kiss every inch of her grew more fierce. When I cupped one breast, spreading my hand out and letting her fill my palm and then tweaked the opposite breast's nipple with a twist and pinch at the pressure she liked, her low moan extended.

"More?" I asked. She'd invited me into the tub, but that could have been for contact and comfort. I would be more than happy to—

She twisted in the tub, not quite turning but arching and lifting her face toward mine. The part of her lips was an invitation I couldn't resist. I claimed her lips and her tongue twined with mine the moment we made contact. Kissing Vienna was like dancing in the rain too close to where the lightning struck.

The hairs on my body seemed to stand on end and electricity sizzled along my nerve endings. The loofa drifted away as I ran my hands over her torso, alternating between massaging her breasts and tormenting her nipples. Every single touch seemed to draw a soft sound from her. The throatier ones that encouraged and the strained notes that demanded more.

My dick stiffened as her ass rubbed against me and when I delved my fingers between her thighs, she released a long moan that sounded a lot like my name. Delving my fingers along the seam of her pussy, I sucked on her lower lip as she strained toward me.

I kept one arm locked around her so she couldn't twist fully. Now that I had her back and she was in my arms, I wanted to give her all the pleasure I could wring out of her. I wanted her to feel nothing that wasn't me, wasn't the rapture she pulled from me every single fucking time she let me play with her body.

The water agitated as she thrashed and then rolled her hips as I found her clit. The silkiness of the water and the hints of essential oils gave me all the lubrication I needed to begin circling it with my fingers. She bucked her hips up and then back.

"Fuck," she whispered against my mouth, and I pinched her clit in response. That pulled the most delicious sound out of her. I wanted to do it again. Too late, I realized she'd also settled her ass far more securely against my dick.

Every single clench of her ass squeezed my rapidly hardening cock as all the blood in my body fled southward. Firmer, swifter strokes of her clit had her breath coming in sharper gasps. "That's it," I encouraged her in between kisses. "Fall apart for me, Vienna. Come on my fingers. Then I'm going to take you out of this tub, and you're going to come on my mouth."

A low keening note broke free, and I kissed her as the scream built. Twisting one nipple almost painfully as I teased her clit, I savored the detonation as she came. The sob of sound, a gasp against my lips as she kissed me with a kind of desperation I'd never experienced.

Trapped between her ass cheeks as she clamped down on my cock, I let out a little growl of my own. "I want to fuck your ass tonight," I told her. "I want to feel you split apart as I pound my cock into you."

I wanted every fucking inch of her.

"Yes," she whispered, almost feverish as she shuddered

and quaked in my arms. I was still stroking her clit and there were tears dampening her cheeks. "Too much. Oh, fuck—I'm going to come again."

Not once did she say stop, so I thrummed that little swollen nub until the scream she released was full-throated and drenched in pleasure. Then and only then, did I surge upward with her out of the water. We dripped as I put her on her feet. But I kept an arm around her. She was shaking badly and swaying.

With a few quick swipes of the towel, I got most of the moisture off us before I lifted her in my arms and carried her into the bedroom. She wrapped her legs around my hips, soaking my cock with every step. I nipped her lips and kissed her as she trailed a kiss from my ear to my mouth. On the bed, I set her down, intimately aware of every single bruise on her.

Dropping to my knees, I pulled her right to the end of the bed and hooked her thighs over my shoulders. Lifting my gaze, I found her sitting up on her elbows and staring at me. Blowing a teasing breath across her pussy, I paused to take in a deep breath of her. So fucking sweet and all mine.

"Take me…" she ordered. "Take control."

I already had, but I understood what she wanted. What she needed. Spreading one hand against her chest, I pushed her back to the bed even as I pressed my face right into her pussy. Spearing her on my tongue, I used my nose to tease that little bundle of nerves as she clenched her thighs. The pressure was delicious but nowhere near as delightful as her.

I sucked, nipped, licked, and devoured her as I feasted on every drop of pleasure she released. The rush of it seemed to fill my mouth and I couldn't get enough. She arched her hips, answering the rhythm of my tongue until she let out another lust-filled cry as she stiffened. Aware of her orgasm, I shifted my attention to her clit and sucked it hard against my teeth.

Only the press of my hand kept her in place as I thrashed

her clit, drawing on it over and over until another rush of dampness escaped her, and then I lapped up the treasure. The hammer of her heart and the raggedness of her breathing was a reward all its own. When my face was soaked with her release, I lifted my head and sucked a kiss right against the inside of her thigh that had her shuddering.

Even tracing my fingers over her skin sent shivers over her skin and goosebumps rippling. My cock was so fucking stiff, that I eased her thighs apart as I stood. Not letting go of her, I reached up to snag a pillow from the head of the bed then dragged it down to fit under her hips. It shifted the angle and gave me more room.

"Rick…" The sound of my name on her lips was everything.

"Hold on, my sweet queen, I am far from done with worshiping you. You're going to come again," I informed her as I thrust my cock into her. It was always such a gloriously tight fit, but she could take me. She always did. The rush of her breath as I gave her no warning, the thrust relentless until I bottomed out. "You're going to come on my cock."

I locked her legs against my chest, her feet against my shoulders as I began to pound into her. Every slam of my dick into her provoked another arched body response. Sweat gleamed on her skin and she'd flushed this beautiful pink. Her eyes were huge and the tawny, golden light fierce.

"My Vienna," I whispered as I set the pace she liked, the furious, demanding pace that gave no quarter. When her inner walls began to clamp and spasm around me, I teased her clit with just a brush of my thumb and then she came hard, and the sobs were the most sensual high note I'd ever heard.

Far from done, I fisted my cock as I pulled out and she let out a low note. "I'm not done," I promised her and helped her to turn over. She was almost boneless, and at the same time, there was a wild smile on her lips. Fletcher kept the lube in the nightstand drawer. After I got her propped with the pillow, I retrieved it.

In no time, I had two fingers stretching her and my dick thoroughly lubed up. "I'll try to be gentle," I promised her.

"Don't," she informed me over her shoulder, her eyes incandescent. "Just take control, Rick. Fuck me hard."

I landed a slap against one ass cheek, the crack of it echoing through the room. "Don't tell me to hurt you."

She opened her mouth then shut it again. At her nod, I caressed the heat from the stinging slap.

"Never tell me to hurt you," I added a third finger and she pounded her fist against the bed.

"You aren't," she swore. "It feels so fucking good..."

Something in me just snapped then, the control I'd been exerting ceding the very primal need to mark her in every single way. I replaced my fingers with my dick, and while I was a little more careful than when I'd fucked her pussy, I didn't let her tightness keep me out of her ass.

"Let me in," I ordered and she relaxed, spreading, and then I was in so deep and so tight, my world flexed with every squeeze of her sweet ass. "Hold on," I murmured as I dropped down to press my hands on either side of her and then kissed along the back of her neck. When I bit down and thrust, she bucked. Fucking the ass took a little different rhythm, but Vienna met my every push, her ass gripping me and pumping my dick every single time I sank into her.

The white-hot heat dancing along my spine went molten and my balls were so tight they were going to explode. But I wanted her to come again, and even as it was a fight to keep from losing it right there, I got one hand under her and all I did was graze her clit and she orgasmed in a rush of soundless little cries and fisting the covers until her knuckles were white. She clamped down on my dick and everything rushed out of me.

Dropping over her, I kept my full weight from smothering

her as we trembled and shook together. The kisses I pressed to her cheek and her hair were a litany of all the words I couldn't find the voice for right now.

She was home.

With me.

With us.

Where she belonged.

CASH

TWO DAYS HAD PASSED since we arrived back at the house with our beautiful, deadly Vienna. My dark saint had definitely lived up to my expectations when we found her.

From the moment Fletcher and Rick let me out of the basement, I hadn't been concerned. She was too well trained not to survive. Then finding her walking out of that hunting cabin banged to shit but alive and strong... I had to focus on anything other than her resourcefulness, or I'd have been fighting to hide my erection.

I didn't care if Rick or Fletcher saw. But something about the way Ratio watched her hadn't sat well with me. Before too long, I didn't have to force my thoughts away from Vienna. They became stuck on Ratio.

"We're having lamb tagine." Rick carried in a large serving platter of rich yellow rice smothered with meat and sauce. The aromatic scent of the spices had my mouth watering.

Damn. Vienna knew what she was doing when she brought Rick into her inner circle. I'd only had tagine once and it didn't look or smell half as good as this.

"Moroccan?" Fletcher leaned forward and took in a big whiff of the food, then groaned. "Big Guy, I think you've outdone yourself with this one."

"It looks fantastic, Rick," Vienna said softly as she followed behind him with a pitcher of lemonade. She wore a pair of black lounge pants that hugged the curve of her hips, leaving just enough to the imagination. The oversized t-shirt hanging off one shoulder said she was relaxed and content. The bruises had faded, but they were still there. Her hand lightly grazed Rick's back before reaching up to kiss his cheek.

The blank, somewhat cold expression melted from Rick's face to be replaced with preening warmth. The entire exchange was fascinating.

I sat up in my seat to study them better.

When she walked behind Fletcher, he tipped his face up and puckered his lips even as he fought a smile. They all laughed, and I joined in because it was a fucking ridiculous face. Still, Vienna gave him a kiss too.

Over the last two days, that was what had caught my attention the most. They were clearly a threesome. Fletcher and Rick weren't together as far as I could tell, but from their comfort with each other, they had definitely engaged in sexual play with Vienna.

I tugged my pants down into a more comfortable position over my growing cock. Apparently, all I had to do was have a passing thought about her and I got hard.

She took a seat between Fletcher's chair and mine. I was tempted to lean over and pucker up to see if I'd get my own kiss too.

That would go over as well as a botched crime scene.

Rick served each of us, and I dug in right away. No sense waiting when my stomach growled. Immediately, I moaned. "This really is good, Rick. Where'd you learn to cook like this?"

Fletcher and Vienna both murmured their own praises with their first bites.

"Practice. Cooking Channel."

I nearly smirked. Rick was a man of few words most of the time. In that regard, he complimented Fletcher well. It seemed like that man never shut his mouth. I'd know, with him being my shadow for the last two days.

Not that I wasn't grateful to be kept out of the cell, but his and Rick's vouching for me hadn't been enough with Vienna. She'd needed extra insurance that Fletcher had reluctantly provided.

Hell, I was willing to get an ankle monitor at this point just to have some time to myself.

Conversation stalled like it always did when we were all together. Most people probably wouldn't think anything of it, seeing it as an easy silence between friends. But with the way Fletcher kept darting his gaze between Vienna and me and her subtle attention to my every word and body tick, gave away just how different they were when I was locked up.

Well, too fucking bad. They'd have to get used to me being here. Eventually, the three of them would settle, and I'd earn their trust. I had earned Rick's and Fletcher's. Only they seemed to take cues from Vienna when she was in the room.

"Vienna." I wiped my mouth with the cloth napkin that had been folded over my place setting before Rick served me. "You never shared how Sandra Jane got the drop on you."

In the time since we found her, I'd been minding my manners so they wouldn't feel like I was about to turn them in. I'd also avoided the hard questions. If she'd filled them in at all, it was when I wasn't around. Which meant she wouldn't have talked to the two of them together.

Even though my curiosity was eating a hole through my stomach, I'd held my tongue. Mainly, because as much of a turn-on as it was that she saved herself, she really had looked like death warmed over.

I'd bided my time, waiting for her to share, but two days was my limit. I needed answers to assuage at least a few of my questions. The most important was the journals. I caught a glimpse of them when we got back here, but she'd stored them somewhere. Most likely her bedroom.

Why was she hiding them from me?

I could tell her so much about which journals she had. After Pops died, I'd scoured each one looking for clues to the Judge's identity. Not that she would have a ton of answers from the journals. Everything that helped me find her came after his death.

But Sandra Jane had to have found something in them interesting. She might have even figured out something I had missed. Otherwise, how else would she have known to take Vienna?

Too many possibilities swirled inside my head, disrupting my sleep. I needed at least a couple of answers, but I could work up to the journals.

Vienna snared me with those tawny eyes as she met my gaze. Her cheeks pinkened, and her eyes flashed. Damn, she was gorgeous when she seemed cornered.

Using the back of her hand, she swiped a few loose tendrils that had come free from the messy knot on top of her head.

The heat of Fletcher's gaze touched me every few seconds, but I kept my attention all on Vienna, enjoying the building tension between us.

Come on, my dark saint. Let me in. Just a little. I won't tell your secrets, and maybe I'll give you one of mine.

"I didn't," she finally said as her right eye narrowed.

Taking another bite, I chewed slowly, playing through the different ways this conversation could go. I didn't expect Rick to jump in, and I sure as hell didn't expect him to be on my side.

"Vienna, you should talk about it. I know you aren't happy with the way things went down, but it helps you move past the trauma when you get it off your chest." He reached across the table and tucked his fingers around hers. "You did nothing wrong."

Clearly, she talked about her experience with Rick. That was fucking great. From the blank expression Fletcher was sporting, we were at least in the same boat.

She scoffed and shook her head. "This isn't group therapy," she said gently, swiping her thumb across the back of his hand. Her lips tilted up, softening her gaze and her words.

"I don't know, Big Guy." Fletcher scratched above his ear. "I'm curious what happened too, but…" he flicked his gaze to me. "Maybe she shouldn't share all the details with Cash when it's not necessary."

Scowling at Fletcher, I pressed my stomach into the table to tell him the truth was absolutely necessary when Rick spoke again.

"Cash isn't going to betray us, are you?" He glared at me as if daring me to contradict him.

I had zero intentions of that, and I had little doubt he was doing this for Vienna rather than me. I turned my attention back to Vienna. "Look at this from all angles. You've kidnapped me. I watched you leave the scene of a crime, and I know you're the Judge…or some integral piece of the Judge. Now, I also helped these two find you, I assisted in completing a job for you, and I'm still here. *Not* trying to leave or contact authorities." I needed to drive that last point home. Each decision I'd deliberately made while here was to gain their trust

Her trust.

At some point, she'd see I wasn't going to betray her. She was all I'd thought about and obsessed over for far too long. My life's work was sitting in this room. Nothing could force me to lose access to her.

I'd call in all my favors to keep her off the government's radar. Rightly, she wouldn't believe me on that just yet. But soon.

"If you don't want to talk about how she took you, tell me about how she got the journals." I lowered my voice as I leaned toward her. Not close enough to be a threat, but enough that it soothed some of the craving to be near her.

Of everything I'd learned from Ratio, the one thing that irked me the most about Sandra Jane was how she'd have access to something that should have been locked up in my house.

"She didn't tell me," she said, sparing me a look before taking a long drink from her lemonade. The motion of her throat as she swallowed was nearly as captivating as her eyes.

Nearly.

This close, it was difficult to ignore the shadows beneath her eyes. The smudges of tiredness that showed even beneath the layer of yellow and green bruise stretched from her cheek to her eye and almost down to her chin.

She'd taken repeated blows there.

Open hand would be my guess because of the even distribution of the bruises.

"Obsession," she continued before I had to prod her, "can lead to unhealthy choices."

"Sure," I agreed. "It can. So can drive, determination, and grit." All of which my dark saint possessed.

She snorted and shook her head before returning her attention to the food. I gave her a couple of bites, taking one of my own. Not a hardship, considering I got to sit with her and eat the food.

The weight of two men boring their gazes into my skull didn't faze me in the slightest. Rick wanted her to talk. So that was two against one. Fletcher wanted the same thing, but he was also offering her an out. Maybe they couldn't run the tough love gambit with her.

I had no such problems.

"Being obsessed or having determination does not immediately equal a bad outcome, or a bad person for that matter."

She flicked a look at me, eyebrows quirked. I held that gaze as she took a bite and mirrored the action. "You sound very certain," she offered as her only comment.

"The whole problem with the world," I quoted, "is that fools and fanatics are always certain of themselves, and wiser people so full of doubts."

Surprise flickered in her eyes. "Bertrand Russell."

I grinned and picked up my glass to toast her. "You are neither a fool nor a fanatic."

She didn't smile in response. If anything, she looked more thoughtful, and I left it there. For now. We finished the meal in relative quiet, though more than once, her gaze came to rest on me. I had to fight the urge to respond.

The last couple of days she hadn't spent as much time out of her bedroom as in it. Then, she was often shut away with Rick. The soft cries of pleasure were hard enough to drown out when they were happening, even with movies or whatever other crap Fletcher put on.

He controlled the remote, and I was supposed to shut up and just watch. It was fine. But it was hard to ignore replaying those sounds in my head when it was quiet and wondering just what she looked like when she came apart.

Fuck. I wanted to know so much.

When the meal ended, she rose and brushed her fingers over Fletcher's shoulder before walking away. He rose with a hurried excuse and followed. Rick stared after them for a long minute before he, too, stood.

Helping him clear the table, I carried the dishes into the kitchen. "At the risk of pissing you off, has she talked to you about what happened?"

Rick spared me a look as he moved about the kitchen, packing away the leftovers.

"If she hasn't," I said, probably pressing my luck, but what the hell. "You need to get her to talk. Something is troubling her, and before you say it, it's more than just me."

When he continued to be silent, I nodded.

"Good talk, Big Guy. I need to take a leak. So, I'll go upstairs, piss, wash up, and come back. Good?" I didn't wait for his nonverbal response, I just walked away like I didn't need his permission. "Good."

The water didn't cut off, nor did I catch the sound of his steps on the stairs. I went straight to my room and into my bathroom. I really did need to take a leak. I also needed five minutes without an audience.

As soon as I'd finished, I washed my hands, then retrieved the phone from behind the mirror where I'd hidden it. I'd been careful to move it each day. The chances they searched my room were high, and I'd only managed to get this from Fletcher the day I called to get my messages.

Then I'd just kept it.

Fletcher never asked for it back. I needed to get a feel for what was going on outside of our bubble. If I wanted to continue being useful to her, I needed information to trade-in. Calling Krystle was an option. She was on the new task force, but she'd already compromised herself to give me the info in the first place.

No.

Ratio was another possibility, but the minute I thought of him, the way he watched Vienna snapped into my head. I had a lot of questions for him, but I recognized his interest and Vienna definitely interested Ratio.

No, better to keep him away for now.

That left… yeah, fuck it. I dialed Lescheva's number from memory. To my surprise, he answered on the second ring. "Who is this?"

The gruff response almost made me laugh. Then again, if I were some scam caller, I'd probably think twice about fucking with him.

Which meant… "Well, I was calling to discuss your auto warranty with you…"

"Cash?" Surprise exploded through his voice. "Where are you?"

"Following a lead," and keeping it vague. "Wanted to check in since—"

"Since the FBI put out feelers looking for you?"

What? "Well, you know what they say…"

"What did you do?" Lescheva's brusque tone cracked so much like Pops' that it made my spine straighten. Unfortunately for him, even if I responded physically to the cues, Pops hadn't been able to order me around in a long time.

"Good question. What are they bitching about this time?" I kept my tone light. Lescheva knew damn good, and well I'd been suspended and then summarily exiled step by step until they could terminate me for "mental health" concerns.

At least it came with my pension intact.

"They are looking for you in connection to the disappearance of that reporter—Sandra Jane."

Of all the things it could have been, *that* hadn't even hit my radar.

"Your mother was questioned, she indicated she'd given the journals to the reporter. She's been using them to make a lot of hay—you have to have seen it?"

"I heard some of it," I admitted, still unwilling to confirm anything. "Just that she had a hard-on for the Judge and a lot of unspecific promises to out him. She's missing?"

"Yeah. Tell me where you are, and I'll come back you up. Probably better to talk to Quantico sooner rather than later…"

"Thanks for the offer, but I'm not coming up for air yet." I opened the door to the bathroom and came face to face with Vienna. Her expression was cool and unreadable.

Fuck. Me.

"Speaking of which, gotta go. I'll be in touch." I ended the call and erased the call history with two clicks.

"Who were you talking to?" Before I could even debate

the answer to that, she continued, "And who gave you a phone?"

Unwilling to surrender that phone just yet, I shoved it in my pocket. "I was getting some information—"

"Fletcher." She exhaled, then closed her eyes for a moment before shaking her head. "How did you convince him to give you a phone?"

"Because we were looking for you. I needed to reach out to Ratio. He'd called and left a tip. Speaking of which," I said, taking a step toward her and enjoying the fact she didn't back away at all. "How do you know him?"

"Who were you talking to on the phone?"

"Just a contact. I have a lot of them. See…" I offered. "I can cooperate. I'll answer your questions. You answer mine."

Giving in to the temptation, I brushed my fingers down her bare shoulder. A second later, I slammed face-first into the wall and my arm was twisted up behind me. The strain definitely didn't feel good, but…

"Fuck, that's hot," I admitted. "I love a woman who knows how to take care of herself."

"Who were you talking to?" The press of her right against my back was everything I'd ever imagined, and my dick threatened to snap into two behind my zipper.

"I told you." I kept it light. "A contact. I was going to call my mother next." Before I said it, I hadn't realized that, yes, that was precisely what I needed to do.

"Why?"

"Because she gave those journals to Sandra Jane. Journals you retrieved but haven't asked me about." Come on, Dark Saint. Look at me cooperating with you. "Granted, my mother's a bitch, and we're not close, but I wanted to know why she gave them to her."

The grip on my hand loosened a fraction, easing the pull on my shoulder.

"If it's any consolation," I continued. "I'm apparently on

the FBI's radar. They want to talk to me in connection to Sandra Jane's 'disappearance.'"

Dead. She was definitely dead. Since she'd taken Vienna and clearly tortured her, I was fine with that. The law was a little too black and white on these subjects anyway.

She wasn't quite leaning into me anymore and I missed the press of her breasts to my back, so I made as if to pull my hand away. Her grip tightened, and my shoulder jerked again as she leaned into me.

Fuck, that felt good.

"Any more questions?" Please have more questions.

VIENNA

"YOU HAVE ALL THE DETAILS?" I bent over the back of Fletcher's chair as he typed away on his computer.

Cash sat in Rick's seat in the corner as he watched us, an excited expression plastered over his face that made absolutely no sense. I tried not to pay attention to him, but his presence was a physical energy pressing against me. To ignore Cash Morgan was akin to trying to hold your breath. You could do it for a short period, but you were always aware you weren't breathing. Then when you couldn't take it anymore, it slammed into your chest with a vengeance.

No, Cash Morgan wasn't a man you could forget or ignore.

"Yes, yes, and yes." He punctuated each word with a hard keystroke. "Everything you'd ever want to know about Levi Ross." Papers started rapidly spitting out of his printer, and he wheeled over, grabbing an empty folder at the same time as he snatched the papers from the tray.

He spun back around and laid them out over the opened folder. "Twenty-eight. Definition of entitled trust fund baby. Multiple allegations of sexual abuse, including those from underage minors. However, with bribes and what I'm guesstimating to be blackmail, he's managed to push them under the rug. No charges were ever officially filed." He sneered.

"That I knew," I said, crouching to get a closer look at the papers he'd printed out. "A list of his properties?" I moved one page over to the side.

"Yes. Along with a detailed report on his known associates. You're in luck today. His credit card was just charged at Casa Del Grande. Which means, he's at the marina and will most likely be on his boat all day."

"I'm familiar with that area." Mart had a boat docked at the same marina. The river wasn't so much a river but a series of channels where some branched off into dead ends, so much of it was blocked in by high cliffs. During this time of year, the waterfalls would be in full force from various points on the rocks creating a serene, almost tropical landscape.

It had been about five years since I'd been there, but the wealthy used to love to dock under the falls while still in plain view of the main route. See and be seen in that circle.

"What was the charge?"

"Breakfast, and from the amount, for at least three people."

Mart's words traveled back to me. He had a thing for older women, especially those with underage daughters. I glanced over his list of associates, and of the three, two were nowhere near the marina right now. That could mean he was with the other man, or a woman and potentially her daughter.

Sighing, I pulled the last page into full view. It was inconvenient when there were potential witnesses, although given who he was and how he typically operated, we'd be hard-pressed to find him completely alone. Everything I read said Levi Ross was an insecure man who craved attention.

"What kind of boat does he have?"

"2020 Absolute Pilothouse yacht. Two bedrooms, sleeps four. For ocean sailing mainly, but this river does connect to the ocean. Eventually." He pulled up layout plans on his screen.

"Crew?" I asked as Cash scooted to the edge of his seat. He was most likely itching to come closer and peer at the screen, but he attempted to stay in his corner.

Good. After yesterday, I didn't have time to deal with him. After I took care of Levi Ross, then we'd have a conversation about his long list of contacts. I'd confiscated his phone, but he'd been too quick to delete the call log. And apparently, he dialed another number while in his pocket. It went to the time and date line. Asshole. On a burner phone, there wasn't much else I could do to figure out who he'd been speaking to.

I took him at his word that it hadn't been a malicious call, but I still had one eye constantly on the door.

"There are two employed by Ross. Although, if he's like most of the rich pricks I know, he wouldn't have them aboard when he's out leisurely. They'd stay on land until he's docked. Then they'd take care of meals and cleaning."

That might take a little finessing to double-check, but shouldn't be too hard.

"Thanks, Fletcher." I kissed his lips when he turned his face up, then gathered the papers in the folder. "Given the distance to this marina, I should be back within twenty-four hours." Mutiny clouded his beautiful blues. He started to stand, but I placed a hand on his shoulder. "I'll—"

"Take me with you."

Fletcher whipped his head around to Cash. My reaction was a little slower. When I straightened and turned, he stood on the other side of the desk, his gaze burning into me.

"You shouldn't go alone."

"What he said." Fletcher pushed out of the chair, pointing at Cash.

"I'll go with you."

"Not that, though." Fletcher shook his head.

"Why would I take you on a job with me?" I asked, more curious what his reasoning would be than actually entertaining the idea.

"They don't want you to be alone, and I can tell from the way you look at them, you don't want to put them in danger, not so soon after your scare with Sandra Jane. But I know how to handle myself. I can be your backup."

I smiled. It amused me that he actually thought I would trust him. And interestingly, he presumed to know what I was feeling. "What kind of backup would you provide?"

"Lookout, getaway driver, you name it. I'm willing."

My smile died. "That's not a good idea." I didn't need to voice all the ways this could go wrong if he betrayed me.

In three quick strides, he was around the desk, his fingers lightly touching my arm. The man really could not keep his hands to himself.

"Hey, hey, now. No touchy." Fletcher forced his way between us. Cash ignored him and kept his unblinking gaze locked on me.

"Think about this then—I'll do the job. I have no skin in the game. This is your chance to make a true accomplice out of me. Then, you'd have to trust me."

I shook my head. He still thought I was so ignorant of undercover agents and the lengths they would go to in order to catch the bigger fish. Although, murder was a bit of a stretch. They could walk the walk, but committing a full felony was generally a no-no.

We had let him see too much already. Know too much about who we were. Maybe if he had enough rope to hang himself…

"What are your hard stops? What aren't you willing to do?"

He glanced down at the report Fletcher had put together. "For a piece of shit that assaults young girls? I have no hard stops."

"You're not really considering this, are you?" Fletcher asked quietly as he glanced over his shoulder at me.

"I helped you find her. I thought you at least knew I

wouldn't do anything to jeopardize you all at this point." A note of exasperation coated his words.

Fletcher faced him. "I trust you not to jeopardize Rick and me. I also trust you not to run or try to slit our throats in our sleep. But Drew is a different matter entirely. I don't trust you with Drew." He crossed his arms.

Cash rolled his eyes. "This is where I want to be. I can shout it over and over again until I'm blue in the face, and it still doesn't change anything. This is my opportunity to prove it to you. Give me that chance. I trust you when you say he's scum. I heard your report. Over the past couple of days, I've also been your little shadow the entire time you researched him. I know you did a thorough job based on your mumblings when you found something nasty in his past."

He moved closer, bringing his heated stare back to me.

"Give me a chance. I'm offering myself up on a platter here." He stopped when his chest bumped against Fletcher's.

Then, Rick appeared in the doorway to the study.

The posturing wasn't lost on me, nor on Rick, for that matter.

"Back up," he ordered. The whip-crack of command in his voice sent a pulse of liquid heat right through me. "Now."

Cash actually cut his gaze from me to Rick, then back to Fletcher.

"You heard the Big Guy," Fletcher said, his tone sharp. "Back up."

Even with the distraction of Rick's presence inflaming my senses, I kept my attention on Cash. No fear flashed in his eyes. In fact, he seemed utterly unconcerned by the implicit threat present in Rick's attitude and words.

If anything, he seemed—amused?

Nothing about this Fed, former or not, lined up the way it should. He enjoyed it when I slammed him into the wall. Instead of being offended when Fletcher said he didn't trust him with me, Cash just rolled his eyes. Then he offered to kill a man—granted, Levi Ross needed killing—but he wanted to prove himself.

To me.

With another harsh sigh and a gaze sent skyward, like he couldn't believe we were wasting time on this, he backed off. Not far, but he did it. Arms folded, he stared first at Fletcher, then Rick, and finally back to me.

"Better?" The question held more than a little sarcasm.

"Why are you causing trouble?" Rick asked. "You said you wanted to be here. That's not wanting to be here."

My lips twitched when Cash's gaze shot back to Rick. "I'm not causing trouble. I'm telling Vienna that I'll go with her on this job."

"You're leaving already?" Rick shifted his weight and his attention. "You shouldn't go alone."

"Thank you," Cash said, smug grin in place. "That's three against one. I think we hold the vote."

"I think there's a cell downstairs, and I can still put you back in it."

That wiped the smirk off his face. Ignoring him for the moment, I turned to Rick. "I shouldn't be gone longer than twenty-four hours."

"And I'll go with her." Cash offering his opinion was one annoying thing. His declaration was something else entirely. "I'll even do the job for her. That's what you walked in on. Fletcher doesn't want her going alone either."

"Vienna," Rick said in a softer tone. "Can we speak for a moment?"

"Yes," I said, then pointed at a chair. "Mr. Morgan, take a seat."

"I told you to call me Cash," he argued.

"And she told you to sit down," Rick stated. "Now, take a seat before I put you in the chair."

With all the grace of a two-year-old on their way to a

tantrum, Cash stalked over to the chair he'd occupied earlier and sat down.

"Good boy," I told him. "Now stay."

His lips compressed. Not so fun to be told what to do, was it? Keeping that thought to myself, however, I linked Fletcher's fingers with mine to usher him out to the hall with Rick and me.

Rick positioned himself nearest the door where he could see Cash, and I appreciated that. Fletcher interlocked his fingers with mine.

"I know I fucked up with the phone," Fletcher began in a soft voice, but I shook my head.

"That's done. You had other things on your mind." I could only be glad that it hadn't hurt him. "This is not about that."

He nodded. "I know, but I'm still sorry."

I squeezed his hand, then lifted it and pressed a kiss against his knuckles. Some of the tension eased away from his expression, and he looked almost tickled at the contact. Fletcher had been on Cash duty almost non-stop. Rick and I had been… well, Rick had been looking after me and I needed the time.

I needed the sensual exhaustion he worked me up into each time I seemed to recover some energy. When I got back, I needed to make time for Fletcher too. I hadn't only missed Rick.

"When are you leaving?" Rick asked when I glanced at him. Like Fletcher, he'd pitched his voice lower.

"I thought I'd leave tonight. I need to scout. I can wait until morning, and Fletcher can check on his location again." If he remained at the marina, though, tonight was the better option.

"I can go with you," Rick said. "Fletcher is right. You shouldn't go alone."

"Hey, I say let the Fed go too," Fletcher said with a great deal more calm than his usual hyperactive self displayed.

"Let him be an accomplice, or better yet, let him do the deed. It gives us leverage, and he wants to prove himself so badly, I say let him."

"No," Rick countered. "I disagree. Sending him with Vienna is a bad idea. He has his own agenda where you are concerned." The last he said to me, almost as an apology. "He was eager to help us find you and he's cooperating right now."

But it didn't sound like Rick believed that would be the case forever. I didn't disagree with him.

"Then take them both," Fletcher said. "I can track you all from here, work on getting into any systems at the marina and on his boat. I can be your backup."

"Rick, why do you think he won't be cooperating in the future?"

He shook his head. "I don't know that he won't," he said slowly, then spared a look in the room. Whatever Cash was doing seemed to satisfy him. "He wants you."

"Oh, yeah, Big Guy. We all see that." Fletcher scratched at his jaw, then returned the favor of kissing my hand like I had his earlier. "Can't fault his taste, you are pretty perfect."

That was sweet. They were both being sweet. Except... "Yes or no, do you trust him?"

"Yes," Fletcher said, with Rick only half a step behind him.

But Rick added, "Within reason."

"We define that as being within Rick's line of sight," Fletcher offered with a quick grin and I smiled. Closing my eyes, I turned the whole problem over in my head.

They waited me out. Tucking the folder under my arm, I leaned into Fletcher, then held a hand out to Rick. He wrapped his arms around both of us, and I savored being sandwiched between them.

This was what I'd longed for that whole week in Sandra Jane's base. This familiarity. This safety.

Them.

They were worth everything. I needed to know if Cash was worthy of them. If I could trust him because right now, I did not. If they did, that was another potential threat to them.

Decision made, I readied myself for the next possible hurdle.

"Rick," I said, leaning my head back so I could look up at him. "You won't like this...but I need you to stay here with Fletcher."

Objection filled his expression.

"You have to trust me," I told him.

"I trust you," he said firmly. "But you just—"

"I know," I promised him. I absolutely knew. What happened with Sandra Jane I would never forget. It was why I couldn't give Cash the opportunity to ambush me as she had.

Or worse, ambush them.

"I got myself out too. I know it took time, and I know I'm asking for a lot..."

Rick cupped my face and gave me a fierce look. "You can ask me for anything, and if I have it, it will be yours. I just don't want to risk you so soon."

"It won't be any easier in a few days," I told him. "This is my life."

"Our life," Fletcher said, though there was a strange tension in his voice. Clearing his throat, he added, "For what it's worth, I'm not a fan of you taking him on your own."

"Well, he might not be coming back and that's a decision I have to make."

Understanding flared in Rick's eyes and Fletcher blew out a breath. Would they fight me on this, or would they accept it?

"Alright," Rick said after a long moment. "You should eat before you go, and I'll pack some water for both of you—in case you need it."

"Oh boy," Fletcher said, then gave me a squeeze. "He's gonna be insufferable when he finds out."

He was going to be something. But I needed to get to the bottom of who Cash was and what I was going to do with him.

Fletcher wasn't wrong, though. As soon as I stepped back into the study, Cash's grin grew wide and fierce. Rising, he said, "Finally. When do we leave?"

THE LONG STRETCH of road yawned ahead of us, but I didn't give a shit about that, except that I was ecstatic this job was more than a quick trip into town.

Vienna had let me out of the trunk about thirty minutes earlier, after she felt confident I wouldn't know how to find their house on my own. She even went the extra mile and took a few right and left turns before stopping to open the trunk.

I loved the methodical way her brain worked. Pops would have liked her too. He wouldn't have approved of her methods for cleaning up the justice system, but he'd have liked her strong morals that she never deviated from. Ever.

To Pops, hesitation was what got someone killed. Before going on a job, a search, a hunt, anything remotely danger-ous, he said you should take a good long look at your beliefs and what you were willing to live with. That was how you stayed safe. Alive.

Yeah, Pops would have flipped his switch if he'd seen her escaping that lunatic reporter all on her own after days of torture and starvation.

He'd threaten to steal her away if I didn't claim her for myself.

No worries there, Pops. She doesn't know it yet, but she's mine.

In the light of day, even with her fading bruises, she was so young. Just a few years into adulthood. Twenty-two or twenty-three tops. The somber look on her face as she prepared herself for this next job smoothed out any lines on her face. Not that she had wrinkles. Not at all, actually, but she did have a little line between her eyebrows when she was deep in thought.

She was beautiful and sexy but somewhat sheltered. Dangerous, but compassionate. Focused, but craved attention from Rick and Fletcher. Her contradictions drew me in, fascinating me more than my lifelong hunt for the Judge ever had.

I couldn't wait until she told me all her secrets.

"What are you staring at?" she asked without taking her gaze from the road.

Grinning, I twisted my shoulders to face her. "At the ultimate puzzle."

She snorted, a delicate yet disbelieving sound. See? Contradictory.

"I doubt I'm that fascinating to most."

"I disagree." Then because she was talking to me, and I couldn't pass up an opportunity… "Tell me how you know Ratio?"

Any humor fled from her expression. "I'm sorry, Mr. Morgan. That's privileged information that you don't get to have."

"Yet."

That little furrow between her brows appeared again. "You're very full of yourself, aren't you?"

What I wasn't hearing was a denial. She'd tell me. One day. Along with all her other delicious secrets, and I'd delight in discovering every single one of them.

"I wouldn't say that. What I am, is seasoned. Experienced. Capable." My lips twitched as I tried to suppress my grin.

She sighed.

My dark saint could hem and haw all she wanted, but there was a crackling electricity zapping between us anytime we were in the same vicinity. Vienna felt it, just like I did.

Hell, I would bet Fletcher and Rick felt it too. Why else would Fletcher's panties have been up in a twist anytime I got close to her? Rick...well, Rick had a death stare for everyone who wasn't Vienna, so I wasn't taking that personally.

"Okay, if you're not ready to talk about Ratio, let's talk about the journals. Have you read them?" Because she damn sure hadn't shown them to me. Although, if she told me the dates of each one, I would know exactly what she had in her possession.

"Have you?"

"I've read all Pops' journals. So, yes. The question is, what information did Sandra Jane really have, and who could she possibly have shared it with?"

The fingers of one hand fluttered against the steering wheel for a few seconds. "I did read them. There isn't anything that would concern me, even if she did share it."

That was the case with most of the journals, but Vienna wouldn't know that.

"I'm more interested in knowing how she came to be in possession of your father's notes." Her statement wasn't quite an accusation, but it was close. Narrowing my gaze on her profile, I mentally went over what Lescheva had told me. Only I couldn't share that with her, not yet. She didn't trust me, and alerting her to the fact I spoke to someone even mildly connected with law enforcement would set her on edge, making it harder to accomplish a more permanent status within her inner circle.

"I have my suspicions, but I'd need the phone back."

"No." Quick, succinct. No hesitation in denying me access to a tool of communication.

"I had that phone in my possession for days. If I wanted to fuck you over, I would have done it by now," I huffed through my irritation. I needed to take this kill from her. Otherwise, it was just as I'd said before. I could shout from the rooftops my intentions a thousand different ways, and it wouldn't make a damn difference. She needed proof that I was on her side and her side only.

My dark saint was pushing me into a corner, but that was fine. I worked well under pressure. Some would say those were the moments I did my best work. I certainly found *her* when I shouldn't have.

"That's irrelevant."

"Not exactly. Would you like to hear all the ways it's a valid reason to trust me, at least on a surface level?"

She shot me an irritated look, her tawny eyes flashing. My dick started to harden. Vienna was beautiful, and shapely, but it was her fire that really did it for me. I'd have to keep that to myself, otherwise, she'd change her reactions just to spite me. I laughed.

That tiny furrow appeared for a brief second, probably because she was confused about why I would suddenly laugh. Oh well, I wasn't about to clue her in. Let her think I was crazy.

"You do have surface-level trust. You haven't been put back in the basement, and I allowed you to come on this job with me. That's as much trust as you can have at this particular moment."

Those were all very good points. But it wasn't enough for me. I wanted more. I wanted *everything*.

I traced a finger down the length of her biceps, causing her to stiffen. Fine, I'd take the hint, for now.

"Fair," I agreed. Because if this job went my way, soon, I'd earn that higher level of trust.

"What we should be talking about is the job. None of your other questions are important." I started to argue, but she continued, "You were serious about not having any hard stops? I need to make sure before we waltz onto his yacht, assuming that's where he is when we get to the marina."

"He'll be there. I read over every detail Fletcher amassed

about this guy, and his habits say he'll spend another two days there at least before returning to the city." I had to hand it to Reed, as quirky as he was, he was damn good at his job.

"You didn't answer my question, Mr. Morgan. Are you having second thoughts?"

I chuckled under my breath. "Sorry, I didn't realize that was a real question. If I had any doubts about what I was willing to do for a job, I'd have been killed a long time ago. So yes, I'm serious. Whatever you need, I'll do."

"Do you have any questions about Levi Ross? I know a man of your…background probably needs more than our word that he's an abusive pedophile before going through with a felony crime."

"Murder, Vienna. Why don't we just call it what it is. Murder. And no. As I also said, I watched Fletcher put the entire file together. I saw the sources, the articles, and all the minute details that painted a picture of just how crooked and depraved this man really is. I'm good."

Her lips pressed together. "I didn't realize Fletcher let you sit close enough to see what he was working on."

"Don't worry," I said, reaching up with my right hand to cup the headrest. "It wasn't by design. He was in the zone and didn't even notice I'd gotten so close. He goes into almost a trancelike state when he's deep in research. He also talks to himself, if you weren't aware."

"I'm aware," she said quietly, in a softer tone than anything she'd ever used with me. Then back to her normal voice, she said, "That still doesn't change the fact that you were able to see everything he did."

It wasn't hard to guess what she was thinking. If I saw that, what else had he been working on that could now be compromised? That was what I'd be thinking.

"Let's pick that particular conversation up on the way home. For now, tell me what your plan is. I'm dying to hear how you approach a job when so many factors are unknown." I rolled my head to face her as a small thrill slid up my spine when her cheeks heated.

Vienna wasn't used to being questioned. That was almost cute. But with me covering her back, I needed to know all the steps, contingencies, and possible exits. She'd eventually learn to work in a team.

She said nothing for another mile, then tilted her head a fraction as if she'd come to some internal decision. Not that she shared whatever the decision was, not immediately. Somehow, I rather doubted I'd be privy to it anytime soon.

"The plan," she said finally, "is to get his attention." She spared me a look then gave me a once over. "Your clothes will do, but we'll need to get you a better jacket. Maybe add a hat to distract from your face."

"Okay. You have a role for me to play." That wasn't hard to figure out.

"Yes." The corner of her mouth kicked up and lust punched me square in the gut. "Ross has a thing for underage girls. His approach is through their mothers—whether they are single, divorced, or married—it's all about getting access to what he really wants."

That made a lot of sense. "At the same time, he milks them for money while going after their kids." Disgusting piece of shit.

"There's no reason in the world to believe his targets are only the children of his female marks."

I let that sit with me for a minute and turned it over. As distasteful as it was, I couldn't find fault with the theory. It was definitely plausible. "Agreed."

"The easiest way to get on board is if he invites us. The easiest way to get an invite is if he's dealing with his own kind—"

Disgusting, but also plausible.

"Or," she continued, the corner of her mouth kicking a little higher. "Someone he thinks he can take advantage of. I can pass for younger if I have to, so it won't be a stretch for me to look like I'm a teenager. The bruises can help here too, though. I can cover those up." She spared herself a glance in the rearview mirror.

"Fuck me, you want me to sell you to him."

"Close," she said, her expression far too serene for this discussion. "You can just be the uncaring father who doesn't care what happens to his daughter as long as you can get your dick wet."

Everything inside of me rebelled at the concept. She wanted me to let that piece of filth put his hands on her and get her alone? This is right after she got away from the reporter.

No wonder she hadn't wanted her boys on this trip. I swallowed my immediate rejection of the plan, however, and just settled for, "I'm thirty-two."

"So?" So much arch challenge in that one word.

"Not old enough to be your father." Lover. Yes. Father? Fuck no.

She chuckled. The rich, heady sound of her amusement was the single best aphrodisiac I'd ever experienced. She needed to laugh more. Even if it did threaten to cut off all blood supply to my brain.

"If you started at sixteen? Sure, you are." Then she patted my leg like I was some errant child. "Besides, when I'm done, I won't look a day over fourteen. I was an early bloomer. I know just what that kind of man likes."

"Tell me whatever man confirmed that information for you is dead, or give me his name."

That earned me an enigmatic look but no answers. I didn't punch the dashboard. That wouldn't get me what I wanted. My dark saint was going to trust me if I had to die for the effort.

Three hours later, I debated all the ways I could kill Levi Ross in the most efficient manner. If I had a rifle, I could do it from a thousand yards and just be done with it. But no, we were heading to the marina—with me driving—in a car we'd picked up at a storage place.

I was in a light jacket and a hat, perfect for a day out on the river. She was dressed in shorts that barely covered her ass, a tank top that had to be spray-painted on, and no way she wore a bra with. Fuck, I was pretty sure she was commando under those shorts, and it kept me hard as a stone until I'd gotten a look at her hair and her face.

The cosmetics were almost untraceable, even if I'd sat there and watched her do it. She looked five years younger, easily. Painfully young. She'd pulled her hair up into a pair of plaited braids that fell into pigtails. Not quite little girl with a bow on her head, but as disgustingly close as you could get to it in a teenager.

"Stop choking the steering wheel." The crisp instruction wrenched me back to the present. The stop at the storage place had also earned me several minutes on my own while she was out of sight and changing. She hadn't said a word, just nodded at me when she'd found me waiting right where she left me.

The black sedan we were in was expensive but not flashy. Favored by many attorneys at the Justice Department. Also suitable for my role—the attorney with his teenage "daughter" out for a day of indolent fun and hedonistic pursuits.

Cause, that was what dads did, they took their children out to pimp them for their own fun.

"Stop glaring out the windshield. If you can't do this, say it now, and I'll change the plan."

That doused my temper as effectively as her looking so fucking young had done to my dick. There couldn't be more than a decade between us, but not right now.

"I can handle it," I told her. "I don't have to like it."

She appeared to consider that. "Acceptable."

I waited until I parked to cut a look at her. "Did you just agree with me?"

What I could only describe as a smirk with a lick of evil kissing each corner of it touched her lips. "Nope." She slid a piece of gum into her mouth and smacked it for effect. "Let's go, old man. You promised I'd get to have some fun today."

She was out of the car and strolling across the sunny lot toward the restaurant, bar, and shop that served as a kind of club for the wealthier who kept their boats here. The sway of her ass seemed even more emphasized in those cut-off black shorts.

"Maria," I shouted as I slammed out of the car. She jerked around at the yell and glared at me. Well, sunglasses hid those wild golden-brown eyes, but my dark saint did not look happy. Too bad, no real names, and we were playing it fast and loose. I was Mark, and she was Maria.

When she said "Mark," she'd worn this private little grin. Yes, I got it, she meant mark like target. Whatever.

"Don't you walk away from me," I continued, embracing the role and slamming the door shut before I stalked after her. My longer legs ate up the ground between us and I didn't slow when I got to her. Instead, I just gripped her elbow far gentler than it looked.

"Oh, get real," she complained in the most obnoxious voice. I would bet money she rolled her eyes at me. "I'm just going inside."

"We'll go in when I say we go in," I continued, changing our direction from the club to the marina.

She dragged her feet in the little wedge sandals she wore that didn't do much for her height. If anything, they just emphasized her legs and how delicate she was. If you weren't paying attention to the smooth muscles that rippled with every step.

This close, I couldn't miss the faint gap in her shirt or the greenish-yellow bruise on her side. How badly had she been hurt? None of them talked about it around me. I'd seen her move, though, and I'd seen her face.

Mouth tightening, I stuffed that irritation away for now. Her *father*—what a piece of shit—wouldn't give a damn about a few bruises. She huffed along with me but yanked her arm away as we got to the gate leading to the marina proper. When I gave her a *look*, she defiantly rolled her eyes and held up her hands in a mock surrender before she folded her arms and ever so slightly hunched her shoulders.

Fuck, she was a goddess at this.

For the next thirty minutes, we made our way along the wooden dock, checking out the different vessels. Most of them were expensive yachts, whether they were sexy little clipper types or the far too fucking wealthy for my blood.

The whole time, she kept up the bored act. I nodded to people like I had every fucking right to be here, and most of them nodded back. It was a lot like walking into a crime scene, act like you belonged and they would defer to you.

I'd spotted Ross' vessel toward the end of the pier. The "man" himself was out on the deck, smoking a cigarette and drinking a beer. That was convenient. He was also watching "us."

More specifically, he had his eyes on my dark saint.

That was not working for me.

"Levi Ross," I called as we neared, raising a hand. "Damn good to see you, man."

He gave a little start and peered at me. An almost sardonic smile quirked his lips. "Is it?"

The question managed to be both arrogant and cautious.

"Are you really going to just go hang out with one of your loser friends?" Vienna piped up in a voice that bordered on nails on a chalkboard. "I need to pee."

Above us, Levi chuckled. "Bored, little girl?"

"You have no idea," she commented, then gave the appearance of a little double-take as she glanced back at him.

"Are you sure you're one of the old man's friends? You don't look that old."

I scowled, but Levi just laughed. "Got yourself a handful there…" He glanced at me.

"Mark," I supplied.

"Right, Mark. It has been a while. Didn't know you had a kid."

"Some days, I wish I didn't."

"Yeah, you aren't the only one," she made another huffing noise and rubbed her thighs together like she really did have to pee. With her arms folded, it thrust her breasts up a little higher and Levi was definitely paying attention. "Look, you talk or whatever, I'm gonna go find a bathroom…"

"Hang on, sweetheart," Levi said in a smooth voice. "Come on up, you can use the facilities in the main cabin."

She just gave him a look. "I don't take offers from strangers."

"Your dad and I are friends, right, Mark?" He grinned at me like we were in on the secret together. What a fucking idiot. "Come on, long walk back to the club."

That seemed to decide it for her, and she glanced around like she had no idea how to get aboard, but he motioned her around to the other side. I followed my gaze on him and not the very fine, firm ass shaking in front of me as she climbed up the ramp.

As sexy as she was, there was nothing about the "pubes-cent girl" look that was doing it for me. Dealing with Ross, though, gained in appeal. Especially when he held out a hand to her when she reached the top and helped her on board.

"You sure you're his daughter?" Levi asked with a hint of a slur. "You're almost too pretty to be his."

"Almost?" She sniffed. "I look like my mom. He just looks like an asshole."

With a flounce, she headed toward the door as Levi chuckled and put his beer down. "Hang on," he said. "I'll show you around. Have a seat, Mark, have a beer. There are some party favors in the cooler if that's what you're here for. Don't worry, we've got privacy."

The asshole didn't even wait for me to say anything before he followed her right into the boat. I stayed on the deck for less than two minutes, only long enough to make sure we were indeed *alone* and no one else was on the deck.

Vienna had a plan.

I was aware of the plan.

She was also belowdecks with a guy who had at least seventy-five pounds on her. Even if he was drunk and she was capable, that didn't sit well with me.

Downstairs, I found them in the first cabin. He had his hands on her hips and one arm around her chest, as he held her from behind. She laughed—the sound just barely carrying a hint of nervousness.

"Hey, Levi," I said, and he jerked away from her like a scalded cat. It was almost funny. I didn't give him any time to react before I seized him from behind and did a chokehold. I was a fit guy. I knew how to apply the right pressure in the wrong places.

Vienna stared at me, and I locked my gaze on hers as I squeezed the life out of this fucker. Then as he sagged, I twisted hard. Necks didn't snap *that* easily, but the right amount of pressure could herniate the discs, cutting off the feeling and paralyzing him. He was dead from the pressure on his jugular and carotid arteries before I released him on the ground.

A vicious kind of pleasure threaded through me.

"What the fuck are you doing?" she demanded as I straightened. Gone was the girlish demeanor and fire burned in her eyes as she glared at me.

There was my dark saint, all wicked fire and heat. I closed that distance between us, and with the same hands I'd just wrenched the life out of Levi with, I cupped her face and dipped my head. I wanted one taste of that fire. The first brush of my lips on hers was like kissing that living flame, it burned through me.

Then her knee slammed into my too-hard dick and I jerked my head back as all the air exploded out of me. Some distant part of my blood-deprived brain saw the fist coming and I didn't have the time to dodge.

The blow sent pain exploding through my eye and face. A second blow to the center of my chest forced out what air I'd managed to suck back in. A third, this time delivered by her foot, caught me in the back of my knees and I hit the ground right next to the dead fucker I just killed for her.

"Who gave you permission to touch me?" The ice sheathing her question didn't do a damn thing to quiet the lust and joy rioting in my system.

"Worth it," I told her. "Totally fucking worth it."

I laughed. Killed for her and then kissed her.

It was a great fucking day. The best.

"You're so fucking beautiful," I told her. "He's dead, and that's what counts."

Standing over me, she stared at me like I'd sprouted some second head. "What is *wrong* with you?"

I laughed. Cause, not a goddamn thing. This was living my best life, whether my dick agreed or not.

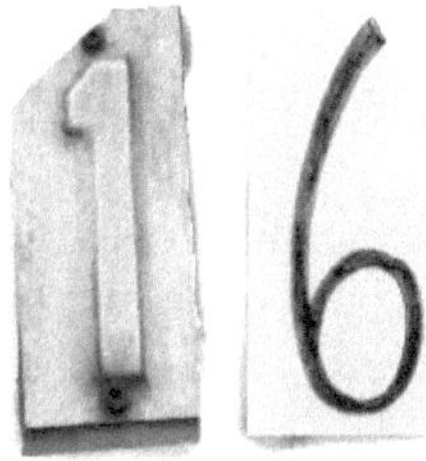

"THEY'RE BACK," Rick said with as much animation as the big guy ever had as he turned from the window. It wasn't like he stood there the entire time she was gone, but the closer and closer it got to when she was expected back, he'd find a reason to pass by it and the later it got, the more he'd linger.

Today was especially bad, though. It *was* Drew's first job away since that beady-eyed reporter abducted her. And she had the ex-Fed with her to boot.

Yes, he was again the ex-Fed in my book. The fucker lost his name privileges when he wedged his way into doing the job with her, leaving Rick and me, the ones who actually had her back, at home.

"That's early, isn't it?" I glanced at the clock on my phone as I joined him. The sun was barely starting to set, but Drew made me think she wouldn't be back until after nightfall.

"Good," was all he grunted, as he pushed past me toward the garage.

Not one to be left out, I followed behind him too. As we crowded the doorway while she backed in, I snorted. I couldn't see her reflection in the rearview, but she had to see us waiting for her like good little puppies ready for some love and attention.

Oh, how the mighty had fallen.

Once she parked, she unfurled out of the front seat, her shapely legs drawing my eye first. Then I glanced at the empty passenger side.

Holy shit. Did she actually get rid of Cash? Of course, he would have done something to piss her off. That was his MO. He liked to needle people while studying them, figuring out what made them tick.

The funny thing was, while he'd been watching me over the last few days, I'd also been watching him.

Uno reverse card, mother fucker.

I pressed my hand against Rick's back to steady myself as I peered over his shoulder, because he was taking up the entire fucking doorway.

"She did it. I think he's gone," I whispered. I wasn't sure how I felt about that. Sure, he was irritating, but he was the first person I'd actually spent any time with before he purposefully met his demise. And by purposefully, I meant from our sexy death angel.

Damn.

"Do you—" I started, then Vienna leaned back in the car to pop the trunk. "Oh." I laughed, and it sounded awkward, even to my ears. Why was my heart suddenly racing now that I realized he was still with us?

Just in the trunk. *Duh, Fletcher.*

She wouldn't trust him from one job. Although...I'd known the location of her house from the beginning. It was hard to keep the smugness out of my thoughts, but I managed. Barely.

She used her hip to shut the door, and completely ignored the groaning ex-Fed climbing out of the trunk. Even when he started to laugh periodically between stretching noises.

The look on her face though, as she approached…

Damn, she wasn't happy *at all*. Rick and I both stepped

back as she climbed the stairs. Different from when she left, her hair was tossed in a bun on top of her head, and she was beautifully barefaced. Had she stopped for a shower somewhere?

I knew that marina. It was a secret "be seen" destination. She would have wanted to fit in with the fake and overdone women.

"Everything go okay?" Rick murmured as he cupped her elbows, drawing her close to his chest.

Drew let out a breath, like she was trying to force all her irritation away with that small action. It didn't work that way, but I commended her on her effort to put Rick at ease.

Pushing up to her toes, she kissed his chin, then stopped next to me, brushing a kiss along my jaw as her fingers grazed my side. This…this was nice. Being included in the welcome home, even if the tension radiating off her, wired the air between us.

She slid off her shoes, tucking them neatly under the bench, then moved further into the house as Rick followed right on her heels.

I stayed behind. One, to make sure Cash didn't do any funny stuff. Two, to make sure he hadn't fucked up. But the shit-eating grin on his face, and the pinched frown on hers, meant he absolutely had fucked up.

Cash slammed the trunk shut with his forearm, then rubbed his jaw as he approached. At first, I almost didn't notice it, then he stepped right into the light of the laundry room.

Dark bruises covered the area under his left eye and across his cheekbone. Wait, his right, my left—whatever, it didn't matter. His nose was also a little swollen. Not broken, but he'd definitely taken a brutal hit to the face. Maybe even a couple. The bruises were new, maybe just a couple of hours old, which made sense. They'd left yesterday when his face was as fresh as a daisy.

"What the fuck happened to your face?" I ground out, closing and locking the door to the garage.

He shrugged and started to stroll off into the kitchen.

"Hey! Hey," I whisper-shouted. "Ignoring me is not the way this works, buddy. Especially when I've pretty much been the only one in your corner."

"Do you want to have this conversation here?" He pointed at the floor. "Or in there, where the object of our attention is currently pouring wine?"

Ha! That showed what he knew. Rick would be pouring the wine.

"No, not cool. Didn't you hear me when I said there were too many foxes in the hen house?" He was already gone. I doubted the bastard even heard the words tumbling from my lips.

Throwing my hands up, I stalked after them and pulled up as soon as everyone came in sight. Hell, the insufferable heat bouncing back and forth between Drew and Cash threatened to push me out. I didn't think I could take another step into the kitchen if I wanted to.

Rick clearly had no qualms as he capped off the wine with the fancy stopper to suck the air out and checked the casserole he had baking in the oven. Drew took a sip, closing her eyes as Cash leaned against the counter behind her, his gaze never leaving her ass.

Wonder how her knuckles got scraped. And swollen.

I narrowed a look on the ex-Fed.

"I didn't know you'd be home so early, or I would have made something nicer, with larger portions. Maybe a roasted beet salad." Rick frowned, glancing over at Drew, lightly chastising her for not giving us a heads up.

Hell, I didn't care about the call since she, you know, she actually came back, and early too. You gotta pick your battles. Rick still hadn't been able to let go of the fact that one time she nearly didn't come home.

If I was honest, I hadn't let go of it either, I just operated under stress better than he did. With copious amounts of caffeine.

"This is fine, Rick. You don't have to do anything special for me. In fact, how long before it's done?" She watched him poke a knife in the tartiflette.

I saw how it was. It was okay to bog me down with lots of cheese and potatoes and clog my arteries, but not for Drew. Whatever, it smelled delicious.

"It's done now."

"Will it keep?"

Rick froze, and I also perked up a little bit. Could it be, that she needed to work off a little stress like last time? Rick got time with her first after she came home from Sandra Jane's, maybe this would be my turn.

"I can put it in the microwave." He used the potholders to pull the casserole out and set it on the stovetop as he turned off the oven. "If I leave it in the oven, it will still continue to cook."

"Good. I need a workout—" I stepped forward. "And you all could use a refresher on self-defense." She glanced at the gym shorts and t-shirts we were both wearing, because apparently, we didn't bother getting out of our pajamas when she wasn't here. "I need to change. Then we can head over to the gym."

God dammit. I hated working out, although if this was like that one gym session…

"Perfect. I need to see what we're working with." Cash clapped his hands together as a dark gleam slithered through his terrible blue eyes.

Nope, it wasn't going to be one of those gym sessions with the ex-Fed going. Damn it.

I thought Drew might reject Cash joining us, but instead, she didn't even look at him as she headed for the stairs— wine glass in hand. Frowning, I tracked her progress until she disappeared up the stairs then focused on the grinning idiot.

"You're way too happy," I commented. Rick said nothing while he took care of storing the food in the microwave. Unsurprisingly, he also set up the dough to rise. I'd forgotten he'd even been working on that earlier, but he pulled it out and put it next to the stove—not on it.

"We had a successful trip," Cash said, then grinned even wider. I really didn't like that smile. Not at all. A part of me wanted to ask—a lot of questions—beginning with what the hell happened and ending with, why was he so happy.

"Get changed." His attention on Cash, Rick cut into the conversation before I could say anything. "Fletcher, go turn on everything in the gym."

Go turn on everything? Even with an argument on the tip of my tongue, I spared Rick a glance. His expression invited no arguments. "We're going to need water." By the gallon, if I was supposed to let Rick or Drew kick my ass.

"I'll take care of it." With that enigmatic response, Rick patted me on the shoulder. Right. Whatever that meant.

Throwing up my hands, I stalked out of the kitchen and grabbed my shoes on the way out the side door. The house next door wasn't that far, but I still stuffed my feet into the shoes before I crossed over to let myself in.

I had the access code and everything. I knew where we were, I could find it blindfolded with one hand tied behind my back and I *belonged* in Drew's bed. So why was Mr. "Call-Me-Cash" dancing on air?

Why was it bugging me so much?

Descending the stairs, I flipped on the light switch. The interior was already cool. Somewhere the generator rolled over and fired up as the fans kicked on. At the base of the stairs, I pushed the door open and headed for the cabinet where they kept the towels.

Honestly, the whole space was spotless. Rick and I had

come down here *after* they left, and he'd used the weights while I ran on the treadmill. I would have walked, but Rick reminded me Drew worried about me, so running it was.

Gag.

Still, it kept Rick from bench pressing me, so I'd take it. I'd just finished setting out the towels when the sound of the door opening and closing above reached me. The air conditioning turned on at the same time. The cooler air would quickly be circulating.

Drew appeared first. Dressed in shorts, a razorback workout tank that left her arms and her bra free since it had the built-in, she moved with a predatory grace I'd always admired in my sexy death angel.

Rick was behind her, keeping Cash from being right on her ass. Good man. Straightening, I took a deeper breath as some of the vise-like pressure on my chest vanished with her arrival. She didn't pause at any of the equipment as she headed straight for me.

"You're stretching with me," she said as she looped her arms around my neck, and I fell quite willingly into her kiss. The brush of her lips against my chin was an afterthought— except I hadn't shaved and was definitely on the bristly side.

Not that it slowed her down as she tightened her hug and I slid my hands under her ass to lift her up so our heads could be even. The silky slide of her tongue against mine was both a relief and a temptation. A relief, because she was here and she still wanted me. More, she sought me out.

Temptation because my dick was one hundred percent on board. Then again, maybe this was all cognitive therapy designed to make me horny every fucking time I came down to the gym. She cupped my nape as I lifted her a little higher, then I was drowning in her kiss as she locked those legs around my hips.

"Yeah, that looks like a workout."

Fucking. Ex. Fed.

Drew's only indication she'd even heard him was to deepen the kiss. It shut down my higher cognitive functions as I sucked on her tongue while she played with my piercing.

"My little pincushion," she murmured as she lifted her head. Granted, my breaths were coming in sharp, little explosive pants, but she sounded pretty reluctant to me.

"I missed you too," I confessed, not even remotely ashamed of it. I'd been stuck with Cash for days, and I could handle it because she needed me too. But it was really fucking nice to be wanted.

She massaged my nape even as she cupped my cheek. "I'm going to shave you later, okay?"

"Anything you want," I told her.

Her smile lit her up, making those tawny eyes glow. "Anything?"

Fuck. It. "Anything. Just—don't bruise me so much I can't be of service post-game."

Laughter bubbled out of her; it was the first time she'd sounded like *her* in days. I caught Rick's approving nod before he pointed Cash away from us. Yep, thanks, Big Guy. You can be on Fed-sitting duty.

She swiped her tongue over her lower lip, leaving it perfect, pink, and plump. "Stretches first, then we'll work on holds. I want you to put me in them, okay?"

"Sure." Seriously, it was either blood deprivation because my cock was so hard there was no way she could miss it where it rested against her cunt—shorts notwithstanding—or I really had lost all capacity for higher brain function.

Fifteen minutes, and a lot of stretches, later where I got a front-row seat to enjoy just how flexible our sexy death angel was, I groaned as she slithered out from a hold before I could even close it.

"You are made out of rubber, I swear," I complained.

She grinned. "I've just had lots of practice." Being under

the full weight of her attention was like magic. I kept forgetting we had company until…

"You need a better partner," Cash said.

Until *that*.

I cut him a look. "Yeah, you saying it over and over again isn't like Beetlejuice. Just cause you say it doesn't mean it's gonna happen."

He had barely worked up a sweat and he'd been pacing Rick on machine after machine. They were definitely lifting the same amounts.

Fuck. No.

Then again, Rick didn't look that overheated either. What he was doing, was staring laser beams through the Fed's head.

Pushing to my feet, I held a hand out and Drew let me pull her to her feet too.

"Reed isn't a fighter," Cash continued.

"No one asked you," I countered. "And I seem to recall I took your ass down, so maybe a little less yapping and a lot more working out before I invite you back into a cell."

"Like you could," Cash said, barely giving me a dismissive look before he crossed the mat toward Drew. That—*irritated* me.

Like, really.

I was just about to step in front of her when I caught Rick's shake of his head. Pausing, I frowned at him. Was he really… yep, he really was looking at me and he shook his head before he nodded toward our sexy death angel.

Cash was just in her space. One minute, he was on his feet, and the next, he was down. Then I had to scramble the hell out of the way because he didn't stay down. He had a hold of her shirt and her shorts as they rolled.

The speed of movement between them had me torn. But the big guy was right next to me, and for the first time that I could recall, he really did put an arm up to push me back behind him.

A grunt escaped Cash as he slammed against the mat, but then he caught Drew and flipped her whole body. She hit without a sound but rolled right to her feet and away.

Sinuous, graceful, and deadly, she climbed Cash like he was a damn pole, and then he was hitting the mat. Instead of her getting him in a lock, though, he threw her off—literally tossed her and she hit the ground, rolling on her shoulder and back to her feet.

Pivoting, she faced him, hands open and ready to strike.

Cash stood there, not closing the distance between them. "You need a *partner*—not a liability."

Oh, fuck you, buddy.

I didn't get to say it, Rick's fist crashed into Cash's face so hard, that he went down and did not get up.

"Yes!" I fist pumped, and Rick spared me a small smile before we both looked at Drew. It had been *her* workout, after all.

"YOU NEED A HAND?" I crossed my arms, fully prepared to help out, but it seemed like Rick had a good handle on it.

"No," he grunted, and he grabbed Cash's arm and leg, hoisting him up in a fireman's carry. The muscles in his legs popped as he strained to stand up. Drew eyed him appreciatively as he turned toward the door.

I got it; I was impressed as hell too. I'd just have to find other ways to impress her, because weights weren't my thing. Now my piercings, she got a lot of enjoyment out of those.

"Here, I'll grab the door." I jogged around him and held it open.

"Don't worry about cleaning up, I'll come back over and take care of it," Rick said as he passed me.

"Really?" That was kind of him. Although I wasn't all fired up to be on Cash duty again. The mother fucker burned my biscuit a little too much today. If he couldn't play nice in the sandbox, he didn't deserve to play at all.

"Really. You can go with Vienna to get washed up."

Now that…I could get behind that plan one hundred percent. "I'd love to." I glanced down at Drew as she sidled up next to me. "Is that good with you?"

Her skin was flushed from the exertion she'd just

expended kicking Cash's ass, and I'd never seen her more beautiful. She brushed damp ringlets away from her face and nodded. "That sounds perfect," her voice rasped and my dick twitched.

It had been too long since I'd heard that deliciously sultry voice in my ear.

We walked out together, but I ran ahead to open the door to our house for Rick. Cash started groaning, but he hadn't woken up yet.

I frowned.

"How are you going to clean up over there if I'm with Drew?" Otherwise, why not just leave Cash in the gym to sleep it off?

"He's getting a time-out. Cash doesn't get to challenge Vienna like that and get away with it."

"That's a solid thought process," I said, clapping him on the back. I'd tried to help Cash, giving him the benefit of the doubt since he had helped us find Drew. But railroading everyone to get closer to Drew? Not cool.

And that was exactly what he wanted. There wasn't a doubt in my mind now that he wanted to be here for his own selfish reasons. The way he chose to go about it wouldn't win him any friends with anyone in the house.

Did Rick and Drew see that?

I opened the trap door in the laundry room for him to descend the steps. A nasty little smile formed on my lips as Rick descended into the basement, bumping Cash's head on the wall. The way he glanced over, noting the spot for clean-up, had me thinking he'd done it on purpose.

"Should we go down with him?" I asked as Drew closed the main door, then shook my head. "Nah, Rick's got it."

We waited until I heard the telltale signs of the cell door sliding into place, then we moved deeper into the house. Her fingers wove through mine as we reached the bottom of the stairs. I stopped and glanced down.

Our hands looked right intertwined like that. Almost as fantastic as we looked wrapped around each other, naked.

Heading up to her room, we didn't speak. At least not until we were tucked away in her private space. I moved to the bathroom and turned the shower on, letting it warm up while we undressed.

I tracked her every movement, enjoying each inch of flesh she exposed. Once we were completely naked, she moved into me, looping her arms around my neck as she kissed me.

Never one to turn down any type of affection from Drew, I leaned into her, wrapping my own hands around the dip in her waist. When she tried to go further, I stopped her.

Pulling back, her brows wrinkled.

"I want you. So much. But you've been gone on a job. Let me wash you in the shower. Then worship you in bed. Okay?" My words were quiet.

Did she know I'd never paid this kind of attention to a woman before? I knew I wasn't her first with this kind of intimacy. I'd bank my left nut on Rick already filling that role. There was something about that crazy fucker that just called on someone to take care of him, even as he constantly took care of you.

And I was okay with that. He deserved it, and so did Drew. But now it was my turn. I wanted to show her in my own way that she was important to me. More than just a quick fuck or a warm body.

She smiled with her eyes as she opened the door to the shower and stepped in. I had one foot inside when I realized I hadn't grabbed a washcloth or a towel. Shit, I was bad at this already.

"Hold on." I held up a finger, then grabbed two towels and a couple of washcloths from under the sink.

She laughed when I joined, probably because I was a dork. That was okay, I owned it. At least with Drew.

I swooped down, stealing a kiss before I turned her under

the spray to wet her hair. Then I grabbed the shampoo and worked it into her scalp while keeping her lower half under the hot water. I was only barely shivering, but I wanted her to be comfortable.

See? I was a thoughtful gentleman when I wanted to be.

Although, I'd be lying if I wasn't making a note in the back of my head to invest in a shower with multiple sprays.

My cock, which had been half-hard, was completely erect by the time I rinsed her hair. But I didn't pay any attention to it, nor did she as I soaped up the washcloth and ran it over every inch of her body, paying special but clinical attention to her pussy and ass. I was only a man, after all.

Getting to know every inch of her body was a thrill all on its own. Now I knew every single spot and crevice, and no one could take that knowledge away from me.

"My turn," she said as she moved me under the spray.

If I enjoyed taking care of Drew, but it was torture having her take care of me. She was gentle but firm, touching everywhere but the place I wanted her hands the most.

Fuck, I'd never been so horny in my life.

She slid the washcloth down the crack of my ass and my eyes popped open. I hadn't even realized I'd closed them; I'd just been in that deep of a pleasured haze. But this ass crack stuff, it put a whole new light on when I washed her. Maybe I'd let her wash her own ass next time because this was weird.

"Poor Fletcher," she murmured, as she pressed her wet, soft body against my front.

My poor dick was at least a little happy at the secondhand attention.

"Why poor me?" I wheezed, as she tossed the cloth in the corner and moved her hands over my slick skin, washing away the soap.

"You've been so good, taking care of me. Letting me take care of you, when what you really wanted was for me to touch you here, hmm?" Her small hand closed around my dick and I groaned. She gave a twist as she stroked me and my eyes rolled back in my head.

Fuck, I might have just come a little. But not much. Nothing that would stop me from worshiping her in the bedroom with every inch of my body.

Drew had other plans.

The slow caress of her hand combined with the added pressure as she stroked me from base to tip had me bracing a hand on the tiled wall. "Drew…"

"I'm here, my sweet little pincushion."

Sweet. A laugh worked its way out of me. I didn't think anyone would ever refer to me as *sweet*. Not even my mother. Right, I shoved her the fuck out of my head. The teasing roll of Drew's thumb over my piercing dragged me right back to the present.

The shower continued to rain down on my back as she slid around to kneel at my feet. "Dammit, Drew," I groaned when she sucked the tip right between those perfect lips. "I'm supposed to be taking care of you."

Despite my protest, my hips gave a little jerk, and I swore her eyes smiled at me when I pressed all the way to her throat. She swallowed, the feeling was so fucking erotic as she pulled me deeper.

The image of fucking her mouth had my balls tightening almost painfully. When she dug her fingers into my ass, I gave another thrust and then her mouth relaxed around me as if giving me freedom.

"You're a bad girl," I growled, sliding a hand down to grip her damp hair. "Do you want me to fuck your mouth, Drew? Is that what you need?" Did my sexy death angel need this from me?

The thought, coupled with my view of her lips stretching around my cock, flipped a switch inside me. Droplets of water skated down her cheeks, but they didn't distract me from the hint of tears in her eyes.

"Whatever you want," I promised her and tightened my hand in her hair. The rocking motion pulled me out to the tip and then I thrust back in. She swallowed around me, tracing her tongue along the underside of my dick like an erotic allure.

With slick hands, she massaged my ass and then my thighs. I kept one hand on the wall and the other on her. The pace I set was brutal for both of us and my balls dragged up tighter and tighter.

The endless days sprawling out between our shower and when she'd left for Sandra Jane's seemed to come sharply into focus. Tugging her hair, I thrust in so deep, that the flexing of her throat around me damn near made me come.

Holding off lasted only a few seconds though, because she dug her nails into my thighs. "Fuck, Drew…"

The light in here gave her eyes this wild amber glow, I pulled back as my orgasm detonated. She tilted her head so I could watch as I came all over her tongue.

It dribbled from the corner of her mouth, but she swallowed, and that just tightened the need inside of me all over again. Another jet escaped and it splattered against her chest. It was kind of filthy, even with the water slanting against my back cause I shielded her.

Fuck.

Panting, I dragged her upward, or maybe she just pushed up from the floor, but her mouth fused to mine. The bitter saltiness of *me* lingered on her tongue and I chased after it like I'd take it from her. The rake of her nails, no matter how blunted they were now—after—lit up my back.

I yanked us both under the water to rinse us off, then she turned off the water. Not once did I let up on the kiss and she swallowed against my tongue the way she had my cock. With roaming hands, she stroked my sides, then my nipples. The flick of my piercings had me groaning, even as rubbing against her slick skin had my dick rallying.

Sorry, Big Guy, I apologized mentally as I lifted her up and carried her out of the shower. We were both soaking wet. Somehow, she snagged a towel and it hit the bed along with us. We'd have to change the sheets later, but I was a man on a mission.

The strength of her grip in my hair kept me in place, kissing her as I rolled her nipples and then gave them a sharp pinch. That gasp freed my tongue and I mouthed kisses down the column of her throat, descending her body to worship like I promised.

One of the best things about her loving my piercings was her reaction when I rolled her nipple with my tongue while pinching the other. Pain and pleasure. She bucked against my weight, but I didn't have to worry if it was too much.

My sexy death angel could toss my ass easily. If she let me manhandle and edge her, it was because she wanted it.

Wanted me.

Powerful thighs squeezed against my chest as I paid particular attention to her breasts. The motion rocked my dick against the comforter. The fabric, both soft and rough, just added another layer of stimulation.

She turned me into a teenager again, and half-hard went to fully erect by the time I pressed her thighs wide with my hands and bared her pussy to my view. It gleamed, glistening with dampness, and she went slicker when I rolled my tongue around her clit.

The nub engorged, shrugging out of its hood. Watching her from between her thighs, I loosened my grip on her legs and they closed around my head. My life was in her grip, even as I pursued her pleasure with a relentlessness. I wanted —no, I fucking *needed*—to have her fall apart and come on my tongue.

The light played over the gleaming inches of wet skin as she ground her pussy to my mouth. I claimed every fucking inch, licking, sucking, and teasing until the first spurt of wetness escaped her. She fisted the covers as her whole body bowed.

When her back arched, thrusting her perfect breasts toward the ceiling, I ran a hand up to pinch the nipple and she let out a soundless scream as she came. I lapped at her pleasure and then pried my way free. I wanted in her cunt while she was spasming.

She must have had the same thought, because she rose, colliding with me. I half-picked her up as I twisted to sit and then I brought her down on my lap. The heated glove of her pussy enveloped me as she sank down on me.

Swearing, I wrapped her up as her breasts teased my chest and she fused her lips to mine. Her muscles trembled, and her cunt flexed around me, pumping me as I thrust up and she slammed downward.

It was a frenetic pace, and we barely parted our lips to breathe before she gave another little scream against my lips as I slammed home on a final few stuttering thrusts. The hot wash of release turned my whole body to jelly.

We clung to each other, panting. The dribble of cum escaping her slicked on my thighs, but I kept her in place. I didn't want to even think about moving. Connected to Drew was the best thing ever, if I could live in her cunt I would.

Might not be comfortable when Rick was railing her, but it definitely wasn't a deterrent. The thought made me laugh and she dragged her head up to look at me. Kiss-swollen lips, red eyes, damp face, and a flush that turned her this gorgeous shade of pink had my dick stirring again.

"Again?" Breathless, she stared at me.

"I hope so," I swore, mentally crossing my fingers. "I need to see you come again."

"Pincushion," she whispered, and I hesitated at the raw emotion in her voice. "Thank you."

"For what?" First, she called me sweet, and now she thanked me.

"For being you," she admitted. The kiss she gave me this time turned me inside fucking out. Open, accepting, and tender, she offered as much as she took.

"Anything," I promised her, cradling her to me as the most unusual sensation unfurled in my chest. "Everything."

Then she flexed around me and we fell back on the bed. Kissing Drew needed no words.

VIENNA

HARSH MOVEMENT to my right abruptly ended my sleep.

I was a light sleeper anyway, but this was out of the ordinary. I took a few seconds to focus on the sounds in the room before I opened my eyes. On the off chance someone broke into our house, I didn't want them to know I was awake until I had an idea what was happening.

Daddy taught me to always keep the upper hand.

"Shit," Fletcher cursed, shooting out of bed, panting.

He was already out of the room and heading down the stairs when I sat up. I placed my hand on his side of the bed, smoothing over the damp, warm sheets.

He'd had a nightmare. That was the only explanation for why he'd fled the bedroom so quickly. It could have been caused by our separation when I was with Sandra Jane, but he hadn't had any nightmares since I'd come home. Even when he'd been on Cash-duty, I'd been aware of him. Rick and I both checked on him, if only to reassure ourselves he was still okay.

I'd give him a few minutes, an opportunity to sort himself out. But if he didn't come back to bed soon, I would hunt him down. Give him whatever comfort I could from the demons that plagued him.

Rick turned over, sliding an arm around my waist, and I settled back down in the bed. Not closing my eyes, just waiting as Rick snuggled closer.

My sweet Rick. He'd come to bed much later than normal, probably giving Fletcher time with me alone. And watching over Cash, although I was surprised he even came to bed with Cash free in the house. Or maybe he put him back in the cell.

After Fletcher and I had gone a few rounds, we'd headed downstairs to find Rick in the kitchen with a full spread on the island. The potato casserole was there, alongside a whole baked chicken and a beet and orange salad.

"I see how it is, Big Guy. I get potatoes, and Drew gets the full food pyramid," Fletcher had said, slapping Rick on the shoulder.

My pincushion had been in an effervescent mood the entire evening, and I smiled to see Rick and Fletcher interacting with such ease. They needed each other as much as I needed them.

We'd enjoyed an easy banter until Rick had sighed, looked at the clock, then back to me. "We should probably let Cash out. He's had enough time to cool off and might be hungry."

Fletcher had scoffed. "He definitely doesn't deserve this kind of meal. Take a stale peanut butter sandwich down... with tap water to drink."

Rick had whipped his head around so fast, giving Fletcher a comically shocked look. We had a good laugh and, in the end, we let Cash out. He'd apologized under Rick's warning glare, but it wasn't heartfelt. Not even a little.

He didn't see anything wrong with the way he tried to bulldoze everything and everyone to get his way.

The entire experience of the previous day had just left a sour taste in my mouth.

Minutes had gone by, at least fifteen. Fletcher still hadn't come back to bed. Gently slipping out from underneath Rick's hold, I padded quietly out of the room.

We usually slept with the door closed, but in Fletcher's rush to escape, he'd left it wide open.

Creeping down the stairs, I followed the soft light spilling from the living room. What surprised me was the soft voices inside. More than just Fletcher's.

At the bottom of the stairs, I took a seat. I could see into most of the living room, and cast in shadows, they wouldn't be able to see me, not unless they were looking directly at me.

Fletcher sat on the couch, his elbows on his knees and his hands cradling his face. Only the top of Cash's head was visible where he lounged in the oversized chair facing Fletcher.

"I take it these nightmares happen often?" Cash's deep voice rumbled, roughened from recent sleep.

"Not as often anymore. But before...Before I came to stay with Drew, they happened almost every night." Fletcher's words were slightly muffled as he talked through his hands. That could be why he hated sleep so much, choosing to over-load himself with caffeine nearly every hour of the day. My chest ached for him.

Scrubbing his palms over his face, he sat back against the couch. Threw himself back, really, like he needed the extra bit of violence at that moment.

"Why'd they stop?"

"I have no fucking clue, man." Fletcher closed his eyes, just seeming drained.

"Then what triggered this one?" The soft note of curiosity was odd from Cash. It wasn't quite clinical, but it wasn't really concern driven either.

"Does it need a trigger? This shit lives in the back of my head rent-free. I guess I should just be grateful they're fewer and farther between here."

"It could be the sense of safety and inclusion you feel with

Vienna and Rick. You all seem to fit perfectly together, like a complex puzzle." Cash reached a hand up to scratch his head.

"You and your puzzles. You're off your rocker, you know that?"

Cash laughed softly. "What can I say? You three fascinate me."

"You mean Drew. *She* fascinates you," Fletcher shot back, some of his personality bleeding back into his voice.

Shrugging, Cash settled deeper into the chair so I almost couldn't see him anymore. "Yes, but she comes with you two. I can recognize a package deal." They fell into a long pause, and then Cash picked the conversation back up again. "What happened to give you nightmares like that? When you ran down the stairs, you looked like you were being chased by a serial killer."

They both snickered.

Silence descended once more, and Fletcher peered up at the ceiling. The stillness of his body as he was lost in thought was unusual for him. I wasn't sure I was a fan. His overactive excitement grated on Rick's nerves from time to time, but to me, it was just him. His natural energy brought life into this house that had sat quiet for too long before they came.

He sat up, rubbing his palms up and down his legs, then pinned Cash to the chair with his gaze. "I survived a shooting when I was in high school," he blurted out.

If he thought he'd get shock value from Cash, he was wrong.

"I know. I researched you after I found your torched apartment." Something about that statement pulled at a thread in my memory, but I discarded it, preferring to focus on the conversation at hand.

"You know I was present. What you don't know is that I made it possible. That's what plagues my sleep and most of my wakeful thoughts."

"Did you fire the guns?" Cash's voice had lost its sleepiness now.

"No, of course not." Fletcher jerked back, affronted.

"Did you talk them into shooting up the school? Tell them it was a good idea?"

"Fuck no," he said as his top lip curled.

"Then it's not your fault. Everyone makes choices that affect everyone else. It's a ripple effect. If that's the game you want to play, you could blame their parents or their jobs for supplying the cash to buy the guns. You could blame their gym teachers for embarrassing them in class. You could find a hundred different people who touched those two fuckheads and made it possible for them to go through with something that was tragic and heartbreaking. But the blame game is useless and a complete waste of mind, space, and energy." Leaning forward, he cupped the back of Fletcher's neck, bringing their foreheads closer together. "It's not your fault."

Fletcher sucked in a trembling breath before pulling back and releasing it.

My eyes widened at their entire exchange. I hadn't realized they had developed this kind of relationship. Not after the way Cash put him down in the gym. But that hadn't really been about Fletcher, more about needing a partner to challenge me. His methods were just unwelcome.

Nodding, Fletcher curled his fingers into a fist where they rested on his thighs. "Maybe you're right."

But I couldn't fault that he connected with Fletcher in a way that reached my pincushion. And for that, I'd always be grateful to him.

"I know I'm right."

And *there* was the arrogant man I'd gotten to know.

Then Fletcher turned his head barely an inch and made eye contact with me. So, my little pincushion did know I was here. He was getting better at paying attention to his surroundings. "I should sit Drew and Rick down. Share my past with them. They deserve to know what happened now that they've welcomed me into their lives."

"Good idea," Cash grunted, clearly done with his heart to heart.

One side of Fletcher's mouth kicked up into a wry smile, and I grinned, shaking my head.

He was okay. He was going to be okay.

Getting to my feet, I headed back up to my room, leaving Fletcher with Cash. He'd tell me in his own time, or not. I didn't require all of his secrets to know he belonged here with us.

It was another hour or so before Fletcher climbed into bed, wrapping me up in his arms. I'd already been dozing, but now that I had them both in bed with me, I could sink into that deep, restful sleep I needed after a job.

The last thought before sleep ultimately dragged me under was how Cash was proving more complex than I'd initially realized. He was more than black and white. He had to be if he wanted to stay here with us, if that was truly his goal. And the more I was around him, the more I believed him.

I still didn't fully trust him, but I was starting to believe him.

Tomorrow I'd have to watch him a little closer around Rick and Fletcher, see what else I missed.

———

When morning came, Fletcher and Rick were both up before me. Fletcher's absence was unusual enough for me to consider it. The dream the night before had unsettled him. Now he was up before me. The past few days, sleep had been as exhausting as waking. This was the first real sleep I felt actually *rested* from since escaping the basement.

Since killing Sandra Jane.

The scene replayed in my mind. Every word. Every action. The obsession and madness infecting her would have been a noose around our necks. Still, if there had been a way to not kill her…

Pushing out of the bed, I tried to shrug off those bleak thoughts in the shower before I dressed. As with Sandra Jane, I had a problem with Cash. Allowing him to stay threatened to be as dangerous as letting him go. Impulsive. Bull-headed. Stubborn.

The arrogant certainty in his own rightness.

Everything about him was a fly in the ointment. He would kick a door in rather than finesse it open. He killed—yes, he killed someone who deserved it—but their death was so quick it was almost merciful. He overstepped in every area and then the night before…

He'd been *kind* to Fletcher. Kind and direct. Maybe Fletcher wouldn't have believed those words from anyone else, but Cash offered him an absolution. One I wasn't even sure he would take from me, though I tended to agree with our Mr. Morgan.

I descended the stairs, following the scents of coffee, bacon, and banana bread? Or muffins? Something smelled sweet and inviting. I also followed the murmur of male voices. Cash was already in place at the table with Fletcher. They had coffee but no food, even though the place settings had been put out.

"Good morning, Drew," Fletcher said, his whole demeanor brightening as I entered. He rose, and I gave him a gentle kiss in greeting. Rick sailed out of the kitchen with my favorite coffee mug in hand. His good morning kiss was as warm and gentle as Fletcher's had been.

What surprised me, though, was that Mr. Morgan rose as Fletcher did, but he made no move to touch me or kiss me.

Well, maybe he could learn.

Maybe.

When Rick pulled out my chair, I took a seat and it wasn't long before we had huge plates of food in front of us. The conversation resumed with Cash complimenting Rick's cooking, then asking how he planned out each day's meals because there was always plenty of food.

Fletcher laughed, teasing Rick that he had been a butler or maybe a house chef in a previous life, because he could do everything. While Rick didn't rise to any of the bait, there was no mistaking the quiet pleasure radiating off him. When he stole a glance at me, I smiled and added my own thanks to theirs.

It wasn't until we were almost finished and Rick prepared to clean the table that Fletcher brought up the night before. "I need to tell you guys something," he said, flicking a look to me. I nodded. He knew I'd heard, but he still wanted to tell us—including Rick.

The story came out slowly, in pieces, as he described the shooting right up until the moment the boys had shot each other. Like some macabre dance with death, they hadn't suicided precisely, but they may as well have.

Guilt draped Fletcher like a shroud, and I reached over to take his hand when his leg began to bounce mid-story. "Then—it was over. The cops, paramedics, parents—it was a whole shit show and all over the news. My family paid a lot of money to clean up my links to them, but...they wouldn't have had weapons if I hadn't gotten them the IDs. That was how they were able to buy them. I was already a master of fake IDs then, and it didn't occur to me anyone was gonna do anything other than buy beer, but..."

"It wasn't your fault," Cash said, having sat through the whole story without interrupting him. "How many kids get fake IDs? How many at an expensive prep school? At the end of the day, did you make a mistake? Sure. Did you make a choice? Yes. But your choice didn't hurt anyone."

"I agree with Mr. Morgan," I said softly, and that jerked

his head in my direction, but I ignored him. "Fletcher, you are not a violent or thoughtless person. You also wouldn't be blaming yourself now if you had truly meant anyone harm. I understand that choices can be difficult, but he's right—this wasn't your fault."

Fletcher tightened his grip on my hand. "I don't want you to just forgive me."

"I'm not," I told him.

"It's not ours to forgive," Rick said finally, and I smiled at him. He'd taken his time, considered everything before he responded. "You need to forgive yourself. That's not something we can do for you. I agree with Vienna and Cash, it wasn't your fault. I think you were a kid and kids make dumb choices sometimes." He shrugged. "Thank you for trusting us."

Mouth open, he glanced at each of us before blowing a breath. "I don't know if I know how to forgive myself."

"It takes time," Rick said as he stood. "We can talk more. It's good to talk. But you'll forgive yourself when you're ready." After gathering up plates, he headed toward the kitchen.

"Wait—" Fletcher scooped up his and Cash's plates before he followed Rick, leaving me alone with Cash.

He met my gaze without the normal cockiness. That was different. "Thank you," I said.

He blinked. "For telling him the truth?"

"Yes." I picked up my coffee cup and took a sip. "You could have fed his insecurities. You could have tried to manipulate him. You did neither. You even reinforced it now."

"He was a kid. Like your man said, kids make stupid mistakes."

"Yes," I agreed. "They do." Cash didn't want my thanks for this. If anything, it seemed to make him uncomfortable.

Which—intrigued me. Brash and bold, definitely not humble —and yet he would rather skip past gratitude.

"I think we're going to do something different today…"

"Oh?"

"Yes," I said as I stood. "We're going to have a family day, watch movies, relax—get to know each other."

When he eyed me, I waited, and then he slowly stood up to face me. "What changed?"

"A very good question, but Rick left you alone last night, and he slept."

Which he wouldn't have done if Cash hadn't earned his trust on some level. Fletcher's too. We might still have a ways to go, but maybe—just maybe—we could start.

"Well, not going to say no, Vienna," he told me, and there was that cocky grin of his. "I've been dying to get to know you more for a while."

Hmmm… maybe we should both be careful what we wish for, then.

But I kept that thought to myself.

For now.

VIENNA

"WHAT DID you say the name of this was again?" Cash asked as I selected the movie. Rick had quietly slipped out, probably to make us popcorn. I was excited to see what flare he'd add to it to make it extra delicious.

Fletcher was the only one who seemed to appreciate my choice.

"Frailty, man. It's an underrated Matthew McConaughey movie from 2001. Much more well done than his rom-com movies." Fletcher pulled a face.

"What's it about?" Cash persisted.

He wasn't a very good movie watcher. I should stick him and Fletcher on the same couch so they could ask each other questions. But alas, Fletcher snagged the seat next to me. Cash was in the chair I loved so much, leaving the cushion on the other end of Fletcher free for Rick.

"You'll see," I answered cryptically with a secret smile that Fletcher caught. He gave me a wink, as amused as I was with the choice.

We'd already gotten the blankets out and closed the blinds to cut down on any glare on the screen. The lazy day yawning before us thrilled me.

How long since I'd relaxed like this? Never?

Daddy and I had watched some movies, a few shows, and news channels, but that was more to stay current with what the general population consumed. It was hard to blend in if you could never keep up a conversation about what was trending.

"Mr. Morgan, while we wait for Rick, what were you doing before you found me?" I smoothed the soft blanket over my crossed legs, then moved my attention to him.

The crumpled look of concentration he'd had while asking about the movie smoothed out as a grin overtook his lips. His bottom was fuller than the top, adding a bit of boyish charm.

Anyone else might believe that made him look less dangerous, but I saw the intelligence and determination in his gaze that would never allow me to make that mistake.

"I was searching for you. Or the Judge." I thought he was going to leave it there, but he must be taking me seriously on getting to know one another. "I'd love to tell you I had a slew of interesting hobbies and how I worked on self-care and my mental health in my downtime, but there was none. Pops, my dad, who you already know was a career agent just like I was, taught me to take breaks with activities that still fed the mind."

"You're hurting my head, man. Just simple answers. You like donuts and fishing, don't you?" Fletcher shook his head.

Cash snorted. "Hardly. The body is your temple, and I never knew when I'd need speed or force to take down my target. And fishing is too slow for me. A mind number. Pops taught me to work puzzles. Rubik's Cube is my favorite." His gaze flashed to mine and I flushed.

Had he seen his on my nightstand?

"And when I wasn't working on solving that, I watched educational documentaries, read books. Things like that." He shrugged like he was like any other man, when he was decidedly *not*. "What about you, Vienna? What do *you* do for fun?"

His unblinking gaze tried to snare me, and I admit, I was losing the battle not to fall into their turquoise depths, but then Rick appeared. Walking right between us with three bowls of mouth-watering popcorn.

"Popcorn seasoned with a mixture of cheese, salt, and chives." He handed one bowl to Cash, one to me, and then Fletcher. He was gone again, and I thought about answering, but Rick appeared much quicker with a tray of glasses of his homemade lemonade and his own snack bowl.

Everyone's gaze was momentarily on Rick as he got everyone ready and settled himself on the couch. Reaching across Fletcher's lap, I caught Rick's hand and smiled. "Thank you."

Turning back to Cash as I picked up the remote, I said, "Much like you, everything I do has had a purpose. But I also enjoy reading, and more recently, spending time with Rick and Fletcher is an important stress reliever for me."

Then I hit play.

The movie unfolded, and before long, the plot was teased through different scenes.

Predictably, Rick was quiet, studiously waiting to get answers to his own questions rather than voicing them. Fletcher, my little pincushion, gave us a nice commentary until Rick shot him a threatening glare, pulling a laugh from him as he held up a hand in apology.

Cash, though, every time I snuck a glance his way, he bore that same intense look of concentration he'd had earlier. He was probably wondering why I picked this movie out, if it was a message, a joke, or a test.

It was actually a combination of all three.

At some point, once the popcorn bowls were empty, Fletcher wrapped an arm around me, tugging me against his chest. The simple affection was soothing as we had just spent the afternoon watching a movie.

Once the credits rolled, Cash started clapping. That must have been his thing when he was impressed.

"Great choice," he applauded. "I wasn't sure where that

was going, but I loved the surprise ending. Not many things surprise me."

"It was Daddy's favorite movie. He was never into religion or the supernatural, but he could understand the reasons the father did what he did."

Cash's gaze sharpened on my face.

Shit. I just gave away a very vital piece of information in my relaxed state that he hadn't had. He didn't need to ask me for confirmation or clarification. The subtle satisfaction dripping from his expression said it all.

"My turn to pick the next movie," Fletcher said as he grabbed the remote.

"Then it's my turn to sit next to Vienna," Rick rumbled as he stood to give Fletcher room to take his spot.

Throughout the entire exchange, Cash never pulled his gaze from me. Time would tell if it would come back to bite me in the ass.

"Blindfold him," I said to Fletcher when we were heading out to the cars the next morning. Rick, Cash, and Fletcher all paused to stare at me. Rick frowned, but he only glanced from Cash—who was already *next* to the back of the SUV ready to climb in—back to me with a faint quirk of his eyebrows.

Fletcher wasn't quite so *relaxed* in his reaction. "Did he drug you?" He didn't wait for my response, just rounded on Cash. "Did you drug her?"

For his part, Cash barely glanced at Fletcher. Like the day before, when he spent the entirety of the second film studying me, he seemed riveted and trying to find answers in my expression. This was a change—a huge one. A gamble, but not really. As irritating as Cash could be, he'd also shown his cards again and again.

If I chose to extend a measure of trust to him in allowing him to stay, then I needed to extend that trust to all things. We would work up to the location, but he didn't have to ride in the back.

"Blindfold him," Rick echoed as I climbed into the driver's seat of the car.

I left the three alone but observed via the rearview mirror. Fletcher looked like he wanted to protest, and Rick appeared concerned, but it was Cash's reaction that interested me at the moment.

He was neither smug, as he had been other times when he got his way, nor was he displaying any obstinance. If anything, he seemed more confused than anything else. I waited them out. Cash liked puzzles, obsessed over them.

I could almost see the way his mind went to work on this —what was the trap? Was there a trap? What hidden meaning did he parse from my statement? I hadn't brought it up at all today while we relaxed.

Rick had been right about us needing the time. We'd all needed it.

Me. Rick. Fletcher. Cash.

The door behind me opened, and a hint of Cash's shampoo filled the car. He bathed rather thoroughly and somewhat frequently—a note Rick had made. Probably directly impacted by his time in the cell.

Or maybe it was just a quirk of the field agent who showered when it was available. Another piece of the puzzle to fit into place.

"Are we sure that's secure?" Fletcher asked as he opened the front passenger door. A worried look crept into his eyes as he glanced at me. I let my expression relax and I smiled at him.

Trust me, I told him silently and he gave Cash a wary look but nodded to me. Touching two fingers to his lips, he stretched his hand over to touch mine. In turn, I kissed them.

Relief eased across his face and he nodded as he slid into the car and buckled his seat belt. A moment later, Rick slid into the back passenger seat. He'd also secured Cash's seat belt for him. When I quirked my eyebrows at him, Rick gave me a relaxed nod.

"I'll make sure he doesn't take it off."

Enormous warmth swept through me. No question. No hesitation. But he would also make sure Cash didn't take advantage of his newly acquired freedom.

"I'd give you guys my word," Cash said almost idly, "but I've figured out that you need actions to prove my agreement. Frankly, I much prefer sitting upright than being crammed into the storage area under a blanket."

Accepting him at his word and trusting Rick to verify it, I started the SUV and opened the garage. I didn't pull away immediately. I let the garage door close as I scanned the area before sliding my sunglasses into place.

Fletcher stretched a hand over and brushed the side of my thigh with his fingers. I nudged his hand with my leg, and he turned his palm over to just rest there. It was—different.

I liked it.

Accelerating, I headed out of our little slice of hidden suburbia and headed toward the club that Mart preferred. It was a risk to take Cash there, minimally. Mart would be moving on from this particular persona any time now. It wasn't that unusual for her to migrate between wealthy "hot spots."

She'd been at this one for the last couple of years. It had been nice, especially after Daddy, to have her close. At the same time, if she lingered too long—it was a risk for her. I wouldn't begrudge her safety in her cultivated hunting grounds.

Ten miles from the house, I flicked a look to the rearview mirror. "He can take the blindfold off now."

Cash wasted no time taking it off, then pulled out a pair of sunglasses from inside his jacket pocket.

"You really look like a Fed," Fletcher said over his shoulder. "You should think about changing your style."

"You should consider a haircut," Cash retorted. "But let's not quibble."

"My hair is a part of my personality. It says, fun, flirty, and downright sexy." He gave my thigh a gentle squeeze. "That suit and no tie look says stern, boring, and infinitely square."

"Thanks for sharing your opinion. Do you mind if I ask Vienna where we're going?"

"Yes," Rick said without offering up an explanation.

"What he said," Fletcher added, and I had to bite the inside corner of my mouth to keep from smiling.

"Fine." With that, Cash let it go.

It was my turn to flick a look at him in the rearview mirror. Surprise, surprise, guess who was looking at me? The next time I glanced at him, he winked. A smile escaped me before I could slam the brakes on it.

The man was relentless.

Determined.

Stubborn.

I almost liked him.

I just wished I knew for sure I could trust him.

Thankfully, they didn't seem to need to fill the car with idle chatter on the way. Or maybe they were preoccupied. The lazy day before had led to a lazy evening, then an even lazier night. If not for needing to see Mart myself, I might have voted for another down day.

Rick gave a surveying look when I pulled into the lot near the club. The SUV, while not as expensive as the sports car, still fell in line with acceptable income for the venue. Fletcher made a face. "Ugh, they are either going to have great food but shitty portions or terrible food and all you can eat."

I didn't laugh, but it was funny.

Cash was out of the vehicle before all of us, he even opened my door, his smirk having been rediscovered.

"Behave," I told him as I climbed out. The purse strap I slid over my shoulder was thin, but the bucket bag it held was light. It was all about appearances. When Cash offered his arm, I debated ignoring it.

Then just took my own advice and threaded my arm through his. Rick and Fletcher fell in just behind and next to us as we made our way toward the building.

"Doll baby!" Mart said as she sauntered out the doors, all smiles, and cool beauty. I released Cash as she swept me into a quick hug then brushed kisses to each of my cheeks. "I've missed you, you bad girl. Sending these boys to do a job but not coming along to tell me all the details."

She tsked, curling her arm through mine, and I chuckled. Mart was in a mood, from her manicured hands to her thousand-dollar shoes and the breezy outfit she'd dressed in. She wasn't dressed to kill, but there was no doubt she would get attention from everywhere.

"I was unavoidably detained," I told her. "You know that some jobs cannot wait."

"Yes," she said with a huffed sigh. "I'm aware, but I do have to question the company you've been keeping." The last she delivered in a lower tone and her lips barely moved. I rather doubted anyone not us would hear her. "Thank you, John," she said, raising her voice a bit as the waiter ahead of us opened a private room.

We'd eaten in here before, away from prying eyes and ears. My stomach plummeted when Mart ushered us all inside.

"John, bring mimosas and coffee for everyone, but give us a few minutes before you come back, darling. Thank you."

The moment we were alone, she pivoted to face me. "I tried to call your father and he hasn't responded. At all." It wasn't a question or an accusation.

It was fear.

I sighed. The guys were all there, aware of our conversation, all the while Rick was stoic, true sympathy shimmered in his and Fletcher's eyes. I didn't look at Cash. For now, if this fed his speculation, so be it.

Mart was too good a friend and had been for so long.

"I should have told you," I said, because there was a small flare of guilt, particularly in light of her genuine concern. "Daddy… Daddy died."

Shock rippled across Mart's expression and Cash's, but Rick turned abruptly and gave us his back. It took me a moment to even process what he and Fletcher were both doing. They were crowding Cash away, giving Mart and me privacy as I told her about his death.

"A year?" Mart said softly, tears welling in her eyes. One slipped free and smudged some of her perfect eye makeup. "He's been gone a year, Doll baby, and you didn't say anything?"

"I didn't—I didn't know what to say. I've been focused on finding the people, or person, who killed him and…" And if I didn't say anything, then maybe he wasn't dead. Maybe I could pretend for a little while.

Mart hugged me; the fierce grip of her arms around me almost cracked the reservoir of the tears I'd kept at bay for so long. I didn't know how long we stood like that, but I found myself hugging her back.

Rick and Fletcher had both offered me comfort in their ways, but Mart had known Daddy. Unlike Uncle David, her comfort and reaction were closer to mine than his. She'd *liked* Daddy. When he paid attention, he'd liked Mart too.

Thankfully, I hadn't done my cosmetics artfully, so when she let me go, I dabbed away the tears. She gave an indelicate sniffle, then looked at me.

"Sweet baby, I am so sorry. I know how much you loved

him—and more, I know just how much he loved you. You were his whole world."

He'd been mine too—then I met Rick, Fletcher, and now Cash. The last name snuck in there, stealthily, like a thief before the door closed.

Pulling out a handkerchief from her purse, Mart blew her nose and then shook her head. "I need to go to the ladies…"

"Mart," I said, sorrow for her vying with my own grief. Grief, that was a little easier than it had ever been in this moment.

"Don't worry about me, Doll baby. I'm just going to splash a little water on my cheeks and then fix my makeup. You never know when you're going to meet your next husband."

She flung a look at the guys.

"Or maybe you do…" The last she said almost voicelessly, then winked a reddened eye before she strolled out of the room.

I swallowed around the lump in my throat and turned to find all three of them staring at me; none looked happy.

"What?"

None of them said a word, then Cash threw up his hands. "If they won't comment, I will. Your *next* husband?"

Oh.

A laugh escaped me. A real one that rolled up from my toes and vibrated through me like a storm unleashing a soft, spring rain rather than a tempest.

They were still staring at me as I laughed when our mimosas and coffee arrived.

RICK

FEELING IN A VERY...ASIAN mood, I had pulled out ingredients to make adobo for dinner. It wasn't long before the savory yet tangy scents started to fill the air, drawing both Cash and Fletcher into the kitchen.

Vienna had gone up to take a shower after we'd gotten back. I couldn't say I wasn't happy to see some space between her and Cash. He studied her too closely.

I doubted there was a breath she took that he didn't catalog.

"Smells fantastic, Rick," Cash complimented as he came close to bend over the pot. He took a long inhale as if he could smell it any better. He couldn't. It was a strong, delicious aroma, but he was getting steam on his face.

"What is this?" Fletcher popped a grape from the cheese and fruit tray I had laid out as soon as we got back in case anyone needed a snack. "I've never seen you really go with this type of cuisine before. What is it, Filipino?"

Nodding, I used the slotted spoon to stir the pot. "Yes, a pork dish over white rice."

"Well, whatever it is, I'm excited. And famished," Cash sighed and rubbed a large hand over his stomach. "So, what's on the agenda for the rest of the day? We have a few hours before bedtime, at least."

I cut my gaze to him. Whatever we'd be doing, it wouldn't be with him. I wanted to spend some quality time with Vienna. Fletcher was welcome, although if he was with us, we'd have to find somewhere to put Cash until we could watch him.

When I told Vienna I trusted him, within reason, I hadn't been lying. But the way he tracked her every movement with his heated gaze didn't sit well with me at all. Not after the way he dedicated his entire focus to her today.

I slid my gaze toward the laundry room. We could always send him back to the cell for a few hours. I wouldn't mind the break.

"I think what the Big Guy is trying to say is, you talk too much," Fletcher slapped Cash on the back as he plucked an imported cheese slice off the board.

"Please," Cash scoffed, his head rearing back. "I think you hold that title all on your own."

Fletcher shrugged as he refilled his wine glass that he'd carried in with him. "Let me rephrase. You say too much that he doesn't want to hear. He doesn't mind my rambling most of the time. I have this soothing quality to my voice. It's easy for him to zone out."

I chuckled under my breath as I added a little more vinegar to the pot and checked the rice. It was almost done. Maybe another five minutes for both. I was really impressed whenever I could time my dishes so perfectly.

Except for the ones that needed rest. I always tried to build in an extra ten minutes for those.

"Hm, that's not something I'd brag about." Cash stepped away from the stove as he pulled the bottle of scotch from the top of the fridge.

"Irrelevant. Rick loves me, don't you, Big Guy?"

I grunted in response. I did enjoy Fletcher's company. Mainly because I completely trusted him. Cash was a wild card. I wanted to trust him, but there was something too possessive in his gaze when he watched Vienna. Which was any time she was in the room.

I didn't like it.

"So, Cash," Fletcher started casually, "what are you planning to do about your potential debut on the side of a milk carton?"

"With this ban on electronics you all have placed me on? Avoidance is the only course forward," Cash replied drily with one brow quirked.

Fletcher scowled.

"I don't like the situation any more than you do, but if I'm going to clear anything up, I'm going to need access to a phone and or a computer. That's the only way I'll be able to take care of anything."

He had a point. But I didn't see how he could clear it up at all. The FBI was a powerful organization. I couldn't imagine he could reach out, let them know he wasn't really missing, and the entire situation would just disappear.

Life didn't work that way. Especially after the news stations had started playing his picture and tying it to the missing report on Sandra Jane. The conspiracy theorists were probably having a field day with this.

It had to be playing on Vienna's mind. It would be mine. It *was*.

I had no idea how to help her keep her stress levels down except for what I was already doing: massages, good food, great wine.

"What are we talking about?" Vienna asked as she breezed into the kitchen. Fletcher immediately grabbed a wine glass, filling it with her favorite wine I started stocking just for her.

"Cash is complaining about his lack of access to electronics," Fletcher filled her in as he handed her the glass with a kiss to the temple.

Because I needed my own connection to her, I circled the side of the island, slipping a hand around the curve of her hip and pressing my lips to the top of her head.

When I stepped back, Cash's normally turquoise gaze had darkened with one corner of his mouth tipping up. He crossed his arms as he slowly smiled, never once pulling his gaze from her.

He wasn't this intense when it had been the three of us. From his nonchalant attitude tinged with excitement the whole time we were looking for her, I'd had the niggling thought that he really would turn us in. I just hadn't allowed myself to think about it too much.

But once we'd had her with us, his entire demeanor flipped. Now he had a clear goal he was working towards, and he didn't hide the fact that his endgame was Vienna from anyone. Least of all, Vienna.

Vienna raised her brows as if daring Cash to complain to her. He just grinned, and I wanted to smash my fist through his face.

I cast a glance at Fletcher to see his brows scrunched up as he examined Cash. He saw it too.

"He asked what my plan was. His first mistake when I have had zero control over anything. I merely pointed out that I can't actually fix anything until I have access to the outside world. Otherwise, we're just treading water with no forward momentum."

"Even if you were able to reach out to someone, the Bureau isn't just going to take your word for it. I wouldn't, I'd want to interrogate you and the mysterious circumstances you disappeared under, and I don't even have any law enforcement training." I turned off the burners and pushed the pots off the heat. "Dinner's ready."

"It smells wonderful, Rick," Vienna murmured softly as

she scooted the bowls I'd gotten down closer to the stove. The soft roll of her voice fell over my shoulders like a warm blanket. I loved pleasing her. It was, without a doubt, my favorite thing.

"You underestimate my connections with my last team. And you also don't realize how often I went off-grid for the sake of a job."

"But you're not on the job anymore, period," Vienna said sharply before taking a sip of her wine. The way her tawny gaze dared him to contradict everything he'd told us went straight to my cock.

With a long, excruciatingly slow exhale of breath, Cash met her stare without flinching. "Sweetheart, you're going to have to find a way to trust me, or this isn't going to work."

"Trust takes time," she replied without raising her voice or hesitating. "You're here. You stay here. You want access to electronics? Don't challenge every single decision. I let you go with only a blindfold today—perhaps that was a mistake." Taking another sip of wine, she glanced at me. "Can I do anything to help?"

Did she want me to defuse the situation, provide a distraction, or just knock his ass out so we could have a quiet meal? Unfortunately, I wasn't quite getting a definitive choice from any of my idealized checklists. "Go take a seat," I suggested. "Let me bring this out to you." I didn't glance at Cash, merely cut my gaze to him briefly. It was more a way of asking for permission than anything else.

At the very slight shake of her head, I fought my own need to sigh. Very well. I couldn't stuff him in the cell yet. Maybe I could shove him in a closet—unconscious. The day was young.

"Come on, Drew," Fletcher said, holding out a hand. "Let me seat you, then I'll come back and help Rick bring out the meal." He bowed with a hint of gallantry and then winked at her. It summoned a genuine laugh from her, a sound that had been lacking since she'd told Mart about the death of her father.

Mart's very real grief had circled them both through the rest of the meal. Later, it seemed to follow their conversation —one none of us had been privy to—as they'd walked a long circuit around the club's lake with us following at a discreet distance.

When Cash started forward as Fletcher led her away, I stopped him with one hand to his chest.

"Are we about to have a problem, Rick?" The way he delivered the question made me wonder if he'd enjoy an affirmative answer.

Honestly, I wasn't even sure what my response would be as I studied him. "Leave her alone this evening," was what I finally landed on.

"I'm not trying—"

I cut him off with a shake of my head. "You want her. You can't take your gaze off her, and you can't seem to stop challenging her. Leave. Her. Alone. You want to resume your games tomorrow, I won't stop you, but for tonight—leave her be."

With that, I released him and returned to preparing the meal. Instead of laughing or offering some other inappropriate response as had become his custom, Cash stood there, a silent observer, while I prepared the plates.

Fletcher sailed in as I put the last portion in place. He glanced from me to Cash, then back again. "I'll get the wine, since you two are having a moment."

At the comment, I spared Fletcher a look, but he nodded toward Cash before taking the wine bottle and returning to Vienna.

Meeting Cash's stare, I considered him before saying, "If you want to say something before we join them, now would be the time. I do not want the food to get cold."

"Okay."

That was it.

"Okay?"

"Okay, I'll leave her alone—for the evening. She's obviously still grieving and… I have a feeling that answers some of my questions. Questions I don't intend to continue pursuing tonight."

That seemed almost too reasonable.

"You don't like me," Cash said.

"I don't not like you," I corrected him. "I don't trust you. I don't trust your intentions. I definitely don't trust how fiercely you want her."

Surprise flared in his eyes. "You aren't jealous, though."

"I trust her."

The silence between us swelled as he favored me with the same penetrating stare he'd used with Vienna—thankfully, it was not as heated or as lust-filled.

"Then let's have dinner, because it smells fantastic. Do you mind if I have a beer with it instead of the wine?"

"Not at all."

"Thank you." He opened the fridge, retrieving a bottle of beer then picked up two of the plates, balancing them easily.

"You're welcome." I lifted the other two and then nodded to the door. "After you."

Without a word, he headed out to the table, and he served Vienna, then Fletcher before he took a seat—opposite her, leaving the chair next to her for me.

It wasn't until I'd joined them and Vienna smiled at me, as did Fletcher, that I let myself relax. They refilled their wine, Cash opened his beer, and then he asked Fletcher about his game.

That led to an hour of humor-filled stories as Fletcher explained everything. Vienna laughed and seemed almost indulgent. When she brushed my foot with hers, I caught her questioning look.

But I smiled because nothing was wrong. Nothing at all.

Cash engaged her, as well as Fletcher and myself. The conversation stayed firmly away from all uncomfortable topics, and more than once, I caught her laughing at something Cash said or smiling at him. Maybe not as often as she did at Fletcher, but she was.

What had just happened?

FLETCHER

I YAWNED, scratching my chest as I sat down on the mats. Rick shot me a stern look, but I quickly reached for my toes and raised my brows.

See? I'm stretching.

His stern look fell away, leaving mild exasperation behind. I grinned. He really was too easy to rile up. He took a seat next to me and started going through the stretch routine Drew taught us when she started making gym time a part of our living requirement.

Then, there was the fucking happy clown in the corner doing a series of push-ups, high knees, or whatever else ridiculousness to get ready for the upcoming workout, while Drew connected her phone to the stereo system.

Why had we invited him?

I safely spoke for everyone when I said the last sparring session had been a disaster. And ended with Cash in the cell.

Although, that might not be such a bad idea. Let him continue to get himself in trouble. I wouldn't mind Mr. Blue Eyes getting tossed in time out as often as possible.

Last night was a fluke. Rick must have said something to him, because he was on his best behavior the entire time we were all together. But I caught his sneaky little glances at Drew any time she walked by him.

I guess that was a step up from when he stared unabashedly at her all the damn time.

"After we're warmed up, we're going to start with some light sparring, do a review of what you've learned so far, and then work on a few new things. Fletcher, I want you to work on getting out of holds again today. How do you feel your progress has gone?" Drew asked as she started going through her own stretches. She was naturally more flexible than us, and her routine was different because of it.

And I loved watching it.

Discreetly, of course. Because she took working out seriously, and as a byproduct, so did Rick. Then Drew reached over to touch her toes, and Rick's gaze tracked the curve of her ass, just like mine would have done if I wasn't watching him.

I see you, Big Guy. You're as horny as me, you just hide it better.

Cash went the exact opposite direction. The fucker had changed his position so that as he did his next round of push-ups, he locked all of his attention on her.

It was like Cash wanted her to know he desired her. Taunted her with it even.

"Why don't you let me work with Fletcher today? He could benefit from a different teaching style." Cash dropped to his ass as he draped one arm over his bent knee.

Oh, *hell* no.

Except, Drew studied him a little too much like she was going to give in. *Don't do it. Don't do it, Drew.* I chanted in my head.

"Okay. But I call the shots. You do nothing that will permanently damage Fletcher, and when I say stop, you stop." She gripped her elbow and stretched it behind her head.

"Hold the fuck up, Drew. You can't seriously want me to

spar with him?" I waved my hand in the Fed's direction. He looked entirely too happy at the prospect of sparring with me.

"Your growth is limited if you only have one teacher and one sparring partner. As talented as Vienna is, and knowing she probably switches up her approach with you, you'd still plateau at some point." Cash hopped up to his feet like he was a gymnast in his youth or some shit. How did a man as large as he was, and as broad as he was, move so quick?

"I'm not at my plateau yet, so your argument is null." I wrinkled my nose as he walked toward me. Rick, the traitor, left me to go to the weights. He was going to be no help now that Drew had made her decision.

"Come on, stand up." Cash had lost his shit-eating grin. He had his hand out to help me up. I didn't want to do this. At all. But if I backed out now, he'd think I was afraid of him.

I wasn't. But I appreciated the size and strength of his muscles. That respect didn't mean I wanted him to wipe the floor with my ass.

With only a little visible reluctance, I let him help me up. Drew stood off to the side with her arms crossed, as if she were an auditor, waiting for Cash to screw up. Or maybe that was me projecting.

"Vienna is strong. Arguably as strong as most men who don't work out regularly. But she doesn't have the size advantage I do. Whenever you're trying to escape a hold, the size of your attacker makes a difference. It changes the way you have to strategize your moves." Cash was all business, walking around me, shoving my shoulders back, pushing against the back of my knees, correcting my position.

"Don't lock up. Keep your body loose but strong. Ready." Then without any warning, he grabbed me in a chokehold. I'd gained a little stamina since the first time Drew showed me how to fight. As soon as he cut off my air, I dug my fingers into his arm, looking for that trigger point that was supposed to work like magic and release. Except Cash didn't fucking have one.

I ended up giving him weak kicks as I hung in his hold. Right before I passed out, he released me, gripping my shoulders. "Not bad. I saw what you were going for. You were off on the location of the pressure point, though. My arms are bigger, longer. It's not going to be the same." Cash held out his arm and showed the points that I should have been aiming for. The red marks from my fingers were about an inch off.

"Again." And the mother fucker charged me before I caught my breath.

Over and over, he ran me through drills. I was sad to admit I didn't escape once. But the fucker was a great teacher. He showed me my mistakes every time and talked me through my options if one way didn't work.

"You have to make these decisions in a split second. If you try one and it doesn't work, go on to the next best choice. And you keep going and going until you get free. If you stay stuck on the same pressure point without changing it up, you'll either pass out, die, or have a broken bone. None of which are great options," he instructed as he walked around me again, lulling me into a false sense of safety.

Silly me, I thought we were done with our sparring session when he attacked me again, this time, taking me to the floor in an arm bar.

"Uncle," I gasped, tapping his thigh when my bones began to protest. Any second, they were going to snap under the flux of his hips.

"That's enough," Drew said as she stepped closer. He released me immediately, rolling away to bounce up to his feet. Fucking ninja.

I flopped onto my back. I thought one of them would reach down and pluck me from the ground, but nope. They engaged in a discussion over my progress.

Wait. What was this look Drew was giving him?

Cash was now shirtless, having removed it at some point, though hell if I knew when. I was too busy fighting for my life. And even though he wasn't the least bit winded, he sported a nice sheen of sweat over his perfect muscles.

And *Drew*? Not only was she looking at him with something akin to respect, but her gaze snaked down his torso every few words. The smug twitch of lips said Cash knew exactly what his sweaty muscles were doing to her.

She glanced back up, and he ducked his head just a little to entrance her with his blue fucking eyes.

"Our turn now," he grinned.

"Yeah, I bet you want a turn," I muttered under my breath, but there was the barest hint of a smile on Drew's face. Was she amused by me? Or by *him?*

Not gonna lie, my heart kind of sank when she slid off her shoes and backed up a couple of paces. "Rules?"

Cash all but radiated joy. It was fucking painful to be in the presence of that much glee. The man was a fucking lunatic.

"No face or groin. Slap hits," Cash said firmly. "No closed fist."

When she stretched her arms above her head, it arched her back and lifted those perfectly curved, sweet breasts of hers. I wasn't the only one riveted, though. Admittedly, I glanced to see what Cash was doing before I looked back.

The man licked his lips.

I shot a look around for Rick, but he was still on the weights. He pumped his legs steadily, but his gaze was on Drew and Cash. Okay, cool. Big Guy knew the score.

"Slap fight?" Drew chuckled. "Taps for head or face, no groin *hits*. Anything else?"

"Acceptable adjustment. I'm good." Cash rolled his shoulders and it had the effect of rippling motion across all his muscles. How had I not noticed he was built like some golden

Adonis with blue fucking eyes that captivated Drew like the Trojan Horse?

Wait, that would be a Hell to the no on a Trojan Horse. If we're going for Trojan metaphors, that would make Drew Helen and all of us the various generals—I just didn't want to have to wage war.

Let Rick take him on. I mean, I'd knocked him on his ass once, but Rick had done it a couple of times and didn't need a weapon.

"You have any rules before we get—hands-on, Vienna?"

Really? I made a gagging noise and Cash flipped me off casually like he did it every day.

Drew *laughed* again. Kill me.

"Put up or shut up, G-man," Drew taunted in that sexy, come-hither voice. "We're sparring, not debating. A bloody nose has never killed anyone."

Wait…

Rick sat up abruptly as Cash's grin grew.

She still had some bruises from her time with the reporter, and I knew damn well her ribs ached from time to time, and she wanted to take the gloves off.

"To three?" Cash asked.

"Tired?" Oh, the taunt was there in her voice, all daring invitation. "Don't worry, G-man, we'll make sure you get a nap if we're wearing you out." She canted her head. What had she said about fight training? It was as much psychological as it was physical.

Fuck knew she had both down like an art.

Before I could say a word though, to object to whatever they were about to do, Cash rushed. Full-on fucking charged. She didn't evade him, or even try, she just swiveled on her feet like it was a dance move and spun away before he could get his hands on her.

Cash's grin went feral, and he was in pursuit. They never left the mats, and while the former Fed might be stronger than her, she was blazingly fast. Just as swiftly as she'd danced away from him, she shifted direction and went after Cash.

He was no longer the predator, but the prey. Spots danced in front of my eyes as she sent him backpedaling across the mat. I exhaled and sucked in a noisy breath. I couldn't hold my breath through the whole thing.

The sting of her slap against Cash's bare back echoed through the gym, and it definitely left a mark right over the guy's kidney. That probably stung like a bitch.

Better him than me. Folding my arms, I dug my fingers into my biceps as she danced away from his retaliatory strike and ducked beneath his arm.

Cash threw his head back and laughed like a maniac. Rick came to stand next to me as the pair ducked, parried, evaded, and pursued all over the mat. It was a dance of her avoiding then striking. He feinted and tried to catch her going for the obvious target, only she just rolled under him and then kicked the back of his knee.

It was kind of beautiful, but when she left the ground entirely, climbing the guy like he was a tree and got her thighs around his neck—well, almost, because Cash jammed his shoulder up to break the hold and slapped her hip at the same time.

She hissed as he all but tossed her. Not that I should have worried cause she just rolled to her feet and caught his follow-up blow. When she put a foot on his knee and climbed him again like she was gonna knee him in the face, I braced for the sound of a broken bone.

Instead, all she did was flip over him and slap his ear so hard mine fucking rang. Sweat gleamed on both of them, but there was a fierce kind of focus on Drew's face as she darted in and out, striking, taking hits, retreating, then coming for him again.

At some point, this was going to come down to pure

endurance—who could outlast who. The whole tempo of the fight changed though as she came at him in a flurry of kicks and slaps.

Unfortunately, he got an arm around her and flipped her toward the floor like he would body slam her. But he didn't. Instead he went down with her and tried to body pin her to the mat. Three slaps between them, and then she peeled out of his grip like she was smoke.

Blow. Block. Twist. Block again. She fucking bent over backwards—literally bending away from one of his hits. It was like we were in the matrix. They were all over each other, and I lost count until Rick murmured, "Nine-nine."

Holy shit. "What do we do?"

"We wait," Rick said, never taking his eyes off the duo. The pair went down again. This time, Cash did have her on the mat, his hand around her throat. Their slaps landed in the same breath—a tie.

"All I have to do is squeeze," Cash said, his voice giddy with a kind of wildness even as he panted out the words.

"And all I have to do is twist," she retorted, and that was when I realized where her other hand was. She had a grip on his junk.

"Sweetheart," Cash whispered as his face hovered spare centimeters above hers. "You can do anything you want to me."

Drew did the very last thing I expected—again.

She laughed, then locked her legs around him and flipped him onto his back, where she stared down at him with an amused expression.

"Who says I want to do anything with you?" The moment the dare left her lips, it hit me.

Cash was in.

The fucker had figured it out.

"Things are going to change," I said in a low voice that I hoped didn't carry.

Rick clapped a hand on my shoulder. "They already have."

VIENNA

I PRESSED my palm against my forehead. It was a sad attempt to stop the budding headache from staring at a screen for too long. Hours I'd been in this spot scouring my notes.

Now that we'd been paid for the art transport job, I could breathe a little easier and make finding Daddy's killer my priority again. Except I was no closer than I was months ago. I managed to mark a few people off the list and clean up some of the corrupt members of the network, but as far as actually figuring out who killed Daddy, I was at a dead end.

"What about the Vanisher?" Rick asked softly, shifting on the pillows beside me.

Fletcher had been in the study all day, working on some projects he'd committed to, so Rick and I had camped out on the couch. Cash went back and forth between us and Fletcher, and surprisingly, Fletcher hadn't kicked him out. Otherwise, there would have been creative yelling any time his door opened.

For the last twenty minutes, Cash had sat in the chair fiddling with the new Rubik's Cube Rick had ordered for him. I'd tried to give him the one I'd completed one night, and he took it, but he refused to mess it up.

He didn't admit it, but that cube held some kind of sentimental value for him. I understood that. I hadn't touched the room Daddy had used here. Rick didn't even open the door.

Daddy wouldn't have been attached to anything in there, but it was the last place he'd slept, and I couldn't bring myself to clear it out.

"He's on the list as a potential suspect, but I haven't found a lead on his identity yet." I clicked on the Vanisher's file.

I knew two facts about the Vanisher. He was in the work of body disposal. Occasional kills, but from what Daddy had said, he was like us; he wasn't a killer for hire. And secondly, he always left a photograph behind when he finished.

Hypothetically, I knew he had to have a vast personal network to make his marks essentially vanish outside of the photograph. Still, for all the connections he must have, no one had any information on how to get in touch with him.

Daddy had always spoken of him with respect, until he'd done something to piss him off. He never told me, but he stopped talking about the Vanisher. Which made him a prime suspect, if I could figure out *who* he was.

Cash stopped twisting the Rubik's Cube as he glanced up. "Tell me about what you're trying to do." It wasn't a question.

Since the day we sparred in the gym, everything had changed between us. The sizzling awareness that had always been there had ramped up tenfold, and what had been distrust on my part, slowly bled into small touches, looks, and light verbal jabs—a kind of thrilling foreplay.

The more we circled, the closer we came together. Before long, we'd collide. I just didn't know when, and Cash seemed content not to push it. If anything, he appeared to enjoy the dance as much as I did.

Fletcher and Rick had also stepped back from their harsh treatment of him. Somehow, over the course of the past ten days, they'd created this casual friendship. Cash didn't bond with them the way they had bonded to each other, but he wasn't necessarily on the outside anymore.

So subtly, I couldn't pinpoint the exact moment Cash had

become a part of us. But that didn't mean I was willing to share the details of my personal mission.

When I remained silent, he rolled his eyes.

"Let me put this together." He scooted to the end of the seat, propping his elbows on his knees. "Your father is the Judge. True or false?" The deep turquoise of his eyes nearly disappeared as his pupils expanded.

"True." I couldn't deny it. He'd heard too much, seen too much.

"He was murdered. True or false?" This time his voice softened.

"True," I confirmed, my own voice losing its strength.

"You're searching for his murderer. True or false?" The steel returned to his words as he continued to hold my stare.

"True."

He stood, motioning for Rick to get up. Shockingly, he did.

"I need to get started on dinner anyway." He shot me, then Cash a curious look before he dipped out of the living room.

Cash slid into Rick's spot, his side brushing mine as he laid an arm over the back of the couch to see my screen better.

My first instinct was to shut the computer down. Rick and Fletcher were the only two I'd ever trusted with this information, but Cash had earned the right to have an opinion.

"Fill me in. I might be able to offer a fresh perspective." He nodded to the screen. It was a DOS-like system. I doubted he'd understand it without training, but I gave him the details he asked for.

"A little over a year ago, Daddy left on a job, and he didn't come back. It was a few days later that I'd found out he died. I—"

"Did you revisit the last place he was at?"

"Yes. He was supposed to be taking care of a job, and I cleared that lead. It wasn't a trap. The man he was after didn't even know he was a target." I blew out a breath, clicking out of the Vanisher's file.

"How did you clear that lead?"

I gave him a dry stare. "I finished the job."

He nodded, dropping his gaze to the keyboard. "How did you find out he was missing?"

"He didn't come home." I barely had the last word out before he fired another question at me.

"Body?"

Tensing, I curled my fingers around the lap desk to keep from slapping him. "Uncle David took care of it so I wouldn't have to."

He tilted his head, lips pursing. "Uncle David?"

"Yes, literally the only friend Daddy ha—"

"And he took care of the body?"

"Stop interrupting me, Mr. Morgan, or this conversation is over." I tried to rein in my temper, but he was pushing all the wrong buttons with his insensitive questions and ridiculous needling.

"This friend, he took care of the body?" He persisted.

"Yes! How many times do I have to repeat myself?" I breathed through my nose to keep the threatening tears from filling my eyes. The way he asked that, *the body*, was so impersonal.

We killed for justice. I understood the irony. But it hurt to think of Daddy as just a body, and everything that once made him, *him* just…gone.

"Why are you angry?" Actual confusion crossed his face.

"Because I wanted to say goodbye! Uncle David didn't want that to be my last memory of him, so he took care of it for me." Bitterness soured my tongue as Cash unintentionally opened an old wound.

"I should interview your Uncle David. You're too close to—"

"Hell no." I shut my computer and set the desk on the side table. I faced him. "Uncle David taught me most of what I know. He's the reason Daddy and I were as safe as we were. He never asked for favors in return, he never asked for payment, and he always looked out for us, as much as Daddy would let anyone. You're not treating him like a criminal. And before you ask the next question on the tip of your tongue, if he were still alive, he would have come back to me. He would never have abandoned me. He wouldn't have run away. Daddy wouldn't have done that." My chest rose and fell with each labored breath.

"Then what have you been doing?" Cash angled his body toward me. "From the outside looking in, you're spinning your wheels, Vienna. Clearly, you're doing something wrong if you aren't making any progress. The first rule of investigation is everyone is a susp—"

He didn't get another word out before my fist crashed into his cheek.

I rarely, if ever, horrified myself. Punching his face was like punching concrete. My knuckles screamed, but my heart raged even louder.

Almost instantly, I could hear Daddy snapping at me; *act, Vienna. Do not react. Reacting means you aren't thinking.*

Pain splintered through me. To my surprise, Cash said nothing, even as he rotated his jaw a little. I—needed to get out of here.

I didn't make it two steps before he caught my arm and hauled me backwards. This time when my fist flew, he caught it and locked his hand around my fist. Shock traveled up my arm.

"The first rule of an investigation, my sweet dark saint," he said in a voice far steadier than I felt, "is everyone is a suspect."

I peeled his fingers off me even as I twisted. He'd either break my arm or let me go. To my surprise, he did neither.

Instead of releasing me, he flung me onto the sofa and invaded my space again.

"You can get as pissed at me as you like, Dark Saint," he continued like this was some normal conversation. The red mark on his face seemed to barely even faze him, while my hand throbbed. I knew better than to do a closed fist hit at the bone. "But *this*—finding killers. It's what I do. You need me."

The last three words raked across my soul, and I planted my bare foot on his chest and shoved. He staggered back a couple of steps and then crashed into the coffee table. It broke, but I was already over the back of the sofa.

"Go to Hell," I said and then headed for the stairs before I killed him. How *dare* he…

Three steps from the top, I felt more than saw him coming after me. Whirling, I glared at him. No amount of schooling would put my temper back in a box. I'd already lost this fight when I let my anger have control.

"What do you want?" I demanded.

"You." He paused one step below mine, and I swore his whole body invaded my space. "I want you to stop running. I want you to let me help. I want you to trust me."

"Being flippant about my father's death does not make me want to trust you." The tears burning in my eyes clogged my throat. I didn't want to have this conversation. I hated talking about him like—

Cash wrapped an arm around me and lifted me right off the ground, then slammed me back into a wall after he climbed the last few steps. I barely felt it, his arm absorbed most of the shock and I braced to keep my head still so it wouldn't snap back.

A picture frame fell and crashed into the carpet, but neither of us looked at it.

"I wasn't being flippant," he growled, the heat of his breath feathering over my cheek. "I was doing my *job*. You want to know why you're getting nowhere? Because you don't want to know—the minute you find out, the minute you accept that he's truly dead, you're going to feel like your heart has been ripped out of your chest, and the only reason you're breathing is because you don't know what else to do."

"Shut up," I ordered.

"No," he snapped back. Then his mouth fused with mine. He tasted like danger, edged in pure fire. If I wasn't careful, I was going to get burned. I fisted his hair and yanked. He bit my lower lip, and I swore I tasted blood as he *let* me pull his head back.

"My sweet dark saint," he whispered in this raw voice. "I know what it feels like to lose the man who raised you, the man who was your partner, and set you on your path in life. You want to scream, but you can't. You want to destroy everything, but you don't dare. You need to break something so you won't break—so use me. Beat me. Bite me. Claw me up. I can take it, and fuck knows I want you."

I lifted my legs reflexively, my thighs clamping to his hips and the heavy weight of his erection ground against my cunt. The thin pajama pants were no barrier, even if his jeans were.

"Why?" I asked.

"Because you need me," he repeated that earlier phrase without any of the earlier arrogance. "Your boys know it too."

What? Then the music floated up from downstairs. A symphony came from the kitchen, the volume cranked up and my heart fisted. Rick…

"If he thought I was a threat," Cash said, dragging my attention back to him. "Do you think he'd be down there prepping dinner to Mozart?"

No. "I hate you."

"That's okay," he whispered before he kissed me again. The pressure of his lips was a hot demand that would not be ignored. I dug my fingers into his back even as I raked my free hand down his scalp to his neck.

Hissing against my lips, he bit me again, and this time I

did taste blood, so I bit him back and his laughter vibrated through me.

He gripped my ass, massaging it as he squeezed, forcing my hips to tilt so he could grind against me more effectively. Fuck if the roughness of the denim and his zipper against my clit wasn't intoxicating.

My nipples beaded up tight and the anger and grief twinning in my blood turned to fire. The thrust of his tongue swept across mine, an invader seeking conquest and refusing to be denied. I raked my teeth over his tongue and he only laughed as he gripped my hair.

The hot pull against my scalp lit me up as he abandoned my lips to spread hot kisses down my jaw, but not once did he release me. I could probably have gotten away.

Probably.

But a groan spilled out of me and I arched my hips to rub myself against him, chasing the pleasure his jeans offered.

"Tell me if this is too much," he ordered before biting my throat. There was nothing gentle in the way he sank his teeth into me like I was a delectable morsel. The suction pulled the crackling desire in my belly taut, teasing my cunt until I was writhing against him.

"Fuck me," I whispered, both in awe of how he laved at the bruise he'd surely left before he ripped my top to leave a similar one at the top of my breast. I bucked, needing more and digging my nails into his nape, but that only seemed to encourage him.

Then he lifted his head to gaze at me, his eyes glowed despite the darkness of his pupils. Heat swept over me as he raked my face, studying me. "Is that an invitation or permission?"

My inner walls clenched at nothingness. In some ways, this was like my dirty hookups in the bars. Fierce, fiery, determined to scratch an itch that I needed and free because I would never see them again.

· Only Cash lived here now. Cash, who had pursued me until I let him in, if I did this…

"Vienna?" He'd gone still, his dark expression foreboding, and his cock was still hard enough it seemed to try and fuck me through his denim.

If only it could.

"It's an invitation and permission," I told him. "Fuck me, G-Man. Make me see stars."

I didn't get another word in. He yanked me from the wall, and in the space of three heartbeats, we were in his room—the room he'd been using anyway, the door was closed, and he practically ripped my clothes off.

"Do I need a condom?" he asked even as he stripped his own clothes off after he'd tossed me on the bed. I lifted up onto my elbows to admire the way his muscles stretched and pulled with every motion.

The man's physique was fucking impressive. There were scars too, and a smattering of fine gold hairs on his chest. His nipples were taut and there was a tattoo on his side that I couldn't read.

I'd noticed it before but said nothing because he took too much enjoyment when he caught me looking. His dick jutted out like a lance extended for a joust, thick, uncut, and the tip red where it escaped the hood.

My mouth watered a little. Like Rick, he was generously endowed, but it was a heavy length, like it was too weighted to point upwards.

"Vienna." Cash's voice cracked against me, and I lifted my gaze to where he watched me with fire in his eyes. "Do I need a condom?"

"I have an IUD," I informed him, running a hand against my breast and toying with the nipple. He was taking too long and I fucking *needed*. "Rick and Fletcher are both clean."

"I haven't fucked a woman in a year, and I've never had an STD," he informed me as he surged onto the bed and over me. He had my hands pinned above my head and his knees on the bed between my thighs, forcing them apart. "Don't touch yourself when I'm here," he snapped. "I get to fuck you, not you."

"Then do it," I ordered, my teeth clicking together as though I threatened to bite him.

"Yes, ma'am." He didn't give me any more time to think or plan, he just gripped my hips, lifted them and slammed into me. Even as slick as my cunt had grown, the stretch burned, and he didn't give me any time to get used to it as he pulled out to drive into me again.

When I asked him to make me see stars, he apparently took it seriously. He put his thumb against my clit and as he settled into a brutal rhythm that appeared half-determined to tear me apart.

I fucking loved it.

The first orgasm crashed over me and I swallowed my screams. That just pissed him off, and I gloried at the anger in his eyes a split second before he dipped his head to suck almost my whole breast into his mouth.

Pain edged the pleasure as his teeth found purchase on my nipple. He released it with a pop and kissed me, thrusting his tongue in time with his dick before he yanked back. Then he pulled my legs up to his shoulders and pressed me back onto my own, damn near bending me in half as he fucked into me like a man on a mission.

I writhed as he seemed to slam into that spot inside of me so hard it actually hurt. But I wanted that pain, cause the pain exploded the pleasure. I reached out only to have his hands fist mine.

"You're going to come on my cock, Vienna. Come and scream my name... do you hear me? Scream. My. Fucking. Name."

I glared at him, but the air came back up into my lungs as he redoubled his pace and it felt like he swelled more inside of me. Was he a fucking grower, or was he so goddamn deep, that I could feel him everywhere?

"Scream," he hissed, his teeth clenched as a vein throbbed in his forehead. He was magnificent. The heat splintered inside of me, spiraling out faster and faster.

He pushed his thumb into my ass even as he pinched my clit, the world truly detonated and took me with it. The first rush of his release lit me up, and he kept thrusting like he was determined to get every fucking drop inside of me.

I screamed.

But not his name.

My heart raced, sweat beading over my skin as I floated back into my body. He pulled me up, rolling over, so I was on top of him, but his dick was still semi-hard and twitching inside me.

The world softened a little. The jagged pain inside of me was blunting. I toyed with the little sprigs of golden hair, studying them even as my body throbbed.

"This can only be a one-time thing," I warned him, finally finding my voice. "It should be. I didn't talk to Fletcher or to Rick…if they aren't on board…" I would never hurt them.

Even if they seemed to have been content to let me have this.

"Fine," Cash growled. "I'll get them on board. Now, are you ready to tell me everything, or do I need to fuck the edge right off you until you trust me?"

I lifted my head, almost bemused. "I just said it was a one-time thing…"

He thrust upward, and I shuddered. "My cock is still in you, so we're still on our one time." He fisted my hair and dragged my mouth to his. The kiss threatened to pull my soul out of me, even as he began to rock upward and I couldn't help the gentle roll of my hips.

Could he get hard enough to fuck me like that again? I

jerked my head back and stared down at him. "This is insane."

"So they tell me. But crazy is my specialty, if you haven't noticed."

Hot and funny.

Impulsive.

Pushy.

Asshole.

"Yes," I whispered, and I didn't need anything else. He kissed me until it seemed all we had was the oxygen between us, and in a very short time, his dick thickened in me again and he pulled out, flipped me over, dragged my ass up and the thrust into my cunt again so fast, I didn't even have time to respond.

"Hold on, Dark Saint," he taunted in a sexy fucking growl. "I'm about to fuck every single edge off."

The bed slammed against the wall and another picture fell. I was pretty sure I had bruises inside and out, but the orgasm tearing through me loosened my tears and the grief digging into me.

Then he fucked me again.

CASH

"WHY ARE YOU WHISTLING?" Fletcher scowled at me as I jogged down the stairs.

I grinned. I was pretty sure it had been permanently glued to my face since I had Vienna's sweet, hot body underneath me the day before.

Hours, we stayed in my bed. I hadn't spent time like that with a woman since…

Hell, my early twenties, at least. I'd always been focused on the job, and women tended to get real clingy quick. Some loved the size of my dick. Others the sheen on the badge. And a few were just bat shit crazy over the combination.

I'd get them off; then I'd get off, and then I'd get out.

Not necessarily your wham bam, thank you ma'am, but I definitely never spent the night.

My dark saint hadn't spent the night with me after our hours of brutal, no holds bar sex. Oh, she gave me what I was sure she thought was a nice post-coital snuggle, then she slipped away back to Rick and Fletcher.

That wouldn't last for long. I wanted everything. But I'd start with a full night of her delectable scent in my nose and her silky hair spread across my chest.

She had said this was a one-time thing.

Unless… And this was the kicker.

Rick and Fletcher were onboard.

It was cute that she thought I would just accept that without taking things into my own hands to get the results I wanted. Naive of her, given how much of my background she knew.

Fletcher probably had my entire history tied up with a bow in his study.

"I didn't realize I was whistling." Still grinning. And now that it was pissing him off, it was more fun. But I tempered it. As much as I liked to needle Reed, I did need him on my side.

"You were." He frowned. "What was that? Ring of Fire?"

I shrugged. Pops always had a thing for the original country. I wasn't much of a music man myself except for background noise, but I retained a lot of memories with those songs.

"Pops was a hardcore Johnny Cash fan." I took the seat next to him at the dining table. A foil-covered plate was left on the table, which I assumed was mine. Rick really was a master in the kitchen.

It wasn't a hardship at all to have him around.

"Mine?"

Fletcher grunted as he gulped half of his coffee like it was a shooter. Then he promptly began filling it up again.

Removing the foil, heat rose from the plate along with the smell of bacon and eggs—a simple but delicious breakfast. Rick had even started preparing the eggs the way I liked them.

Not wasting time on either front, I dug in. "Where's Vienna?"

"Errand," he said before shoveling a huge bit of fluffy eggs in his mouth.

I huffed a laugh and promptly cleared my own plate. It was obvious Fletcher wasn't the kind of man to hold a civil conversation before he'd been properly caffeinated.

Once we were finished, I grabbed his plate to stack on my

own. He narrowed his gaze on my actions, and surprise, I grinned again.

"Where's Rick? He go with Vienna?"

On his third cup of coffee, it actually looked like he had two brain cells to rub together now.

"Nah. He's prepping the cleaning supplies. It's cleaning day." He grimaced.

"Cleaning day?" A smile threatened to break free. We must have had a hiatus from cleaning days while Dark Saint was missing.

"Don't tell me you haven't noticed how sparkling clean this place is? Rick cleans everything. *Everything.* I'm pretty sure when I have to take a piss, he sneaks into the study and cleans the skin grease from the mouse and keyboard. You know it's suspicious when the grease spot is missing from the space bar."

I chuckled. This guy was ridiculous. "If the skin grease is gone, that's a good indication he went behind you and cleaned up. He's only doing that to protect you."

He quirked a brow. "I can see that. DNA and all, especially since he gave me a tutorial on how to clean the shower after I got out." He gasped with way too much excitement just as Rick entered the room with a feather duster and a bucket of cleaning supplies.

It was hard not to laugh at this deadly Rottweiler of a man carrying a dainty feather dusty.

"Rick! Big Guy. Have you given Cash the lecture on bathroom cleanliness?" Fletcher slapped the table.

Rick's eyes widened. "Shit. No. When we were looking for Vienna, I did all the cleaning because it calmed me. Let's go ahead and start there." He picked up all of our dishes, which admittedly wasn't that much, and took them to the kitchen. He was back in a blink of an eye.

"Let's go check out your bathroom." Rick picked the feather duster and bucket back up, nodding to the stairs.

"This is going to be good." Fletcher rubbed his hands together. Glad he found this hilarious. But he didn't know how determined I was to be on their good side. Rick could tell me to clean the grout with a toothbrush, and I'd happily oblige.

"Sure." I led the way to the bedroom and bathroom I'd claimed as my own. Rick was right behind me with Fletcher on his heels.

Fletcher scowled at the made bed.

When I turned on the light to the bathroom, Rick looked around with an appreciative eye, and Fletcher's scowl deepened. "What the hell, man? It looks like you haven't been in here at all," he grumbled, and this time I did laugh.

"I study people for a living, Reed." I propped a shoulder against the wall. "It wasn't hard to tell that fingerprints and all forms of DNA are unwelcome in this house. Smart. If you ever need to leave in a hurry, your cleaning standards will make the exit process much quicker."

Rick lit up under the light praise. Fletcher looked like he sucked on a soured lemon rind.

"If you have any tips, I'm happy to follow them. Just show me what you want. I'm also happy to help you with the cleaning today. Can't say I'll be as good at it as you, but I'm not too bad."

Huffing the whole way, Fletcher went to the toilet and lifted the seat to check underneath. "Unbelievable," he muttered to himself.

Rick and I grinned at each other.

"He's just aggravated because he needed this lesson multiple times," Rick clapped a hand on Fletcher's shoulder. "He's messy by nature, but he's learning."

Scratching at his forehead, Fletcher flipped us off. He tried to hold his ire while we laughed, but he ended up joining us. This *was* comical.

After our laughter died, the conversation lulled. I could

have filled it with inane chatter and ass-kissing, but they'd see through my game right away. I'd rather show them with actions that I was here to stay and on their side.

"So, you and Drew are finally knocking boots." Fletcher hopped up on the bathroom counter as he pinned me with his gaze.

Well, shit. I didn't realize they'd be so direct. At least not Fletcher, the man of many words.

"Heard that, did you?" I kept my expression neutral. They weren't giving anything away, and I needed to know how to play this.

"I'm surprised it took that long. Vienna's wanted you for a while."

Rick was my kind of guy. He didn't mince words and dealt in truth. It helped that it was exactly what I wanted to hear.

"Is that so?" I swiped my thumb over my bottom lip to hide my glee.

"Big Guy is doing you a favor," Fletcher pointed out. "But I'm not. I've read your jacket, inside and out. I know who you've dated, who you just screwed, and who you screwed over."

I inclined my head. "I've never had a long-term relationship." Not even Krystle. We'd been far more partners-and-co-workers with benefits, no matter what label she'd slapped on herself. "Never said I had."

"No," Rick said with a nod as he glanced over the bedroom. "Before you made the bed, did you strip the sheets and covers from last night?"

"I did," I said, stepping out of the bathroom and moving to the closet. "I sacked it up because I wasn't sure if you had rules about using the washer and dryer."

Fletcher sneezed the words "suck-up." But I ignored him, because I was gracious like that. Besides, I was in a grand fucking mood and I wasn't going to ruin it before—

"Wait," I said, snapping a look from Fletcher to Rick and then back again. "Vienna went on errands—*alone*?"

Rick picked up the bag of linens, then motioned to my stack of dirty clothes, also resting on top of another laundry bag. "Bring those into the hall. Fletcher, your room is next. I'll go over the cleaning protocol there, Cash."

"Seriously?" Fletcher protested.

"Why are you complaining?" I asked him. "He's going to have me clean your bathroom."

"Oh, good point." With a grin, Fletcher clapped me on the shoulder. "And to answer your earlier question, Drew chose to go on her own. She did give us timeframes on when she'd be back and that she'd check-in. Today is not a special errand, but a general errand."

So today, she wasn't going after a target. I turned that over in my head. "Did she say who she was going to meet?

Was it this "Uncle David"? Dammit, one of us should be there.

"No," Rick said as he pushed open the door to Fletcher's bathroom. The white towels hanging on the wall were hung with an almost OCD fastidiousness. Rick would approve. He inspected the shower, then the toilet. When he lifted the lid, then the seat, Fletcher groaned.

Two yellow marks.

I tsked. "If you have gloves, I'll take care of it."

Rick passed me a set without a second word, then moved to the side like he intended to watch me work.

"We should know who she's meeting with." I kept my tone even, reasonable, and planted my flag firmly on the side of logic. There was a possessiveness threading through me that was none of those things, and until I knew what to do with it…

"Why?" Instead of just shutting me down, Rick studied me intently.

I wasn't the only one surprised. Fletcher flat out gawked

at him as he leaned against the door frame, arms folded. Visible in the mirror, he didn't even make an attempt to disguise his reaction.

"Because," I said, after spraying the bleach against the rim and ignoring the burn of it hitting my nostrils. "She told me it was her 'Uncle David' who found her father."

Rick frowned. "Why would that be important?"

"She never saw the body," I continued, and that yanked all of Fletcher's attention to me.

"What?"

"She never saw the body. The minute I pressed on that point, offering to interview him for her, she grew very agitated and combative."

"It might have been your approach," Fletcher said, though he seemed more distracted than annoyed. "She's only mentioned him to me once. I'm assuming if she calls him uncle, he's family or close enough to be family."

"Agreed," I used the scrub brush to not only remove the evidence of urine, but to wipe the whole bowl down, even under the rim. "That makes his involvement suspect because she cannot be a fair judge of someone that close to her."

"Explain." Again, Rick wasn't demanding, but he was trying to understand.

Straightening, I turned so I could include them both in my line of sight. "One, *he* found the body. Two, *he* disposed of the body because he didn't want Vienna to see his corpse. Three, *he* informed her after it was done so she couldn't even protest and see him *before* the disposal was finished."

"Huh," Fletcher raked a hand through his hair, gathering the mass up and back where he tightened it into a pseudo-man-bun. I'd give him credit, he could rock the hippie look. "That's shady as fuck."

"My point," I said with a shrug. "He might be one hundred percent trustworthy. She could be absolutely right about that. She has, at every turn, demonstrated a remarkably canny intelligence and been a sharp judge of character."

"Except the reporter," Rick murmured.

"To be fair," I offered. "Sandra Jane was a difficult read, and based on what we found at her public house, I wouldn't have labeled her a threat either."

"But you didn't like how devoid of anything personal it was," Fletcher pointed out, but I didn't need the boost to my ego. I'd done my job. But there had been little to work with. Maybe if we'd had more, we could have gotten to her sooner.

"I'm not questioning what Vienna believes," I clarified. "She's a brilliant woman, no doubt exists within me on that front. Based on what I know of the Judge, she would have to be because while there have been subtle changes to the Judge's M.O. in the last year, she's still left *nothing* that could convert into finding her. She isn't her father. But she doesn't have to be."

"What do you suggest we do?" Rick asked finally, and I met the Big Guy's concerned gaze. "I trust her."

"So do I," I assured him, and the minute I said those three words, that fact settled in my bones. "I trust her, and I trust what she says. She hasn't lied to me even when she had every reason to lie. She kept her answers vague or just didn't answer me."

Or she flipped the questions back at me. Her mind was sharp and her wit even sharper. Everything about her was intoxicating, and having tasted both her mind *and* her body now?

Yeah, she was the one.

"But to help her, I'm going to have to pull apart the investigation into her father's murder. We don't generally let victim's families get involved in cases because they bring their own biases and preconceptions with them."

"Not to mention it would be really fucking shitty?" Fletcher said.

"It would. It has been for her. She's hurting. I don't like that."

While neither man said anything, they glanced at each other. They didn't like it any more than I did. Turning back to the bathroom, I wiped the rest of it down with the bleach wipes and made sure I'd gotten every surface—even the ones that looked clean.

"I don't get you," Fletcher said when I'd finished. "You finally get her in bed and instead of sucking up to us or trying to bull your way into our relationship—you're talking about her dad and about her."

"You're going to agree to me being in her life or not. Nothing I say to you now will change it. Last night, neither of you interrupted—even when we got a little aggressive."

"If she didn't want you touching her, she would have broken your hand," Rick said. "But I would appreciate fewer bruises and bite marks."

"Noted. If she tells me the same thing, I'll adjust. But she certainly wasn't complaining last night."

"Or this morning," Fletcher muttered. "But I'm with the Big Guy, cause damn, what the hell did you do to her?"

I grinned. "Made her scream." Then my smile faded. "But my sex life with her is not your business unless she invites you into it. Just like how often you and the Big guy fuck her stupid isn't any of mine. I've seen the bruises you both leave, and I've seen her walk the next day. What matters is *her*."

"Agreed," Rick said sternly. "Fletcher…"

"Fuck me, I can't believe I'm asking this," Fletcher said. "What do you need from us?"

I thought they'd never ask.

VIENNA

THE DUCKS BRIMMED with effervescent energy as they stepped on each other to gobble up chunks of bread. They were cutthroat little things, fighting for each torn piece as soon as it left my fingers.

Discreetly, I wiped my face, smudging the dirt I'd smeared over my cheek and the tip of my nose.

Today, Uncle David and I were meeting in the park close to the city. It wasn't my favorite place to meet. But no one ever paid attention to dirty people in the park.

Funny how that worked. People actively avoided looking me in the eye when they assumed I was homeless. It was probably one of the better disguises for keeping our privacy in public. Like this state of life was catching. Or as if they could pretend there wasn't a problem if they ignored it.

I'd been on this same bench for an hour, and no one had even attempted to sit on the other side.

Across the park, a tall, elderly man with a ratty beard and holey shirt sauntered toward me. His mouth twitched to the side as his hands alternated between rubbing together and fidgeting with his clothes.

I had to work to suppress my grin.

Daddy had never cared for disguises. He'd use them if necessary, but he had never been a chameleon like Uncle

David. But Daddy had urged me to learn everything I could, understanding the importance of blending in with the masses.

"Hey, Ladybug," he hacked out a cough as he perched on the end of the bench, moving his legs side to side. To anyone who glanced our way, they'd see someone in-between hits of their drug of choice.

"Uncle David," I murmured, not glancing at him.

The ducks didn't even pay him any mind.

"You've been lax on keeping in touch. I've been worried about you." The mild disappointment grated more than I expected.

"I got caught up in some things that needed my immediate attention. But you'll be glad to know SJ isn't an issue anymore."

He grinned, leaned over, and sloppily slapped my shoulder. "I know. I've seen the news reports and even checked out the scene after you texted me."

I couldn't share in his enthusiasm.

"Let this go," I told her. "Your life is not worth his crimes. Don't let your father destroy you too." I hadn't wanted to take her life, not when I understood her motive.

"No, I have to find him—I have to make him pay. I will never stop…"

She forced my hand anyway.

I flinched as the ghost of a shot echoed inside my mind.

"What did she have that she thought was so groundbreaking?"

What evidence.

"Surprisingly, not a damn thing. The books were all but useless. Nothing that would lead her to the truth. She just excelled at using smoke and mirrors to make a compelling argument and hopefully draw out the worm."

And she'd caught one. I'd been stupid enough to let her

catch me, and if I hadn't been as well trained as I was, I could have lost Rick and Fletcher forever.

All because of her thirst to find her father's killer. Something I understood very well.

"Shit. No one would ever have suspected that. Not with the way she carried on in front of the cameras. I thought for sure she had something…" he muttered. Then he twisted and held out a grimy hand. "Give me some bread?"

"She put on a good game," I agreed, giving him a few moldy slices.

"I take it you have the books?"

"Of course," I nearly scoffed. He'd never questioned me like this before and it was starting to irritate me.

"Good. That's good. How have your other jobs been going? Anything I can help you with? You know, I used to be the right-hand man for your dad." He buffed his dirty nails over his shirt.

A child started crying in the distance as the mother rushed over to him, bending down to wipe his tears away with the hem of her shirt.

I'd made sure we weren't close to the playground, but unfortunately, I couldn't get away from all the families in the park. The little boy's gaze strayed our way, until the mother took his chin and tipped his face up for a kiss to the forehead. Then they started walking toward the lake.

"I'm good. If I need anything, I'll let you know." Tearing up the end piece, I wadded up the cheap plastic between my hands. "Why did you want to meet today? Just to ask about SJ?"

"Do I need to have a reason?" He turned his head just enough to look at me from the corner of his eyes. "You're like family to me. I wanted to make sure you were okay after what happened. The scene was clean. But you went dark for several days, and that isn't like you."

I nodded.

Uncle David wouldn't really know if that was normal or not if I hadn't let him know the general timeframe of when I was going to scope out her place.

"As you can see, I'm perfectly fine. I've already worked a small number of jobs since then."

He chuckled, the deep rasp scratching over my skin. "Your dad would be proud, Ladybug. You're cut from the exact same cloth. Intelligent, resourceful, and a moral compass that never strays. You did a great job, by the way."

"What do you mean?" I stuffed the plastic between my thighs.

"I told you, I checked out the scene myself. The place was immaculate. No one would ever know she had any connection there. And the photograph? Nice touch."

It took real effort not to give in to my body's reaction and whip my head toward Uncle David.

"I try," I murmured, but my mind was already a thousand miles away.

One of the answers to my problems couldn't have been right under my nose without my knowledge? Could it?

Daddy had always taught me to be two steps ahead, but since Sandra Jane, it felt like there was so much I didn't know.

And so much that Daddy purposely hadn't shared.

The one thing that was certain, I'd be making another stop before I went home.

———

Uncle David seemed almost reluctant to let me leave. If anything, he was so thrilled with the Sandra Jane job that he wanted me to join him for a couple of jobs he had lined up. He knew better, of course, Daddy and I didn't work with others.

"That was *before*, Ladybug," he pressed me, and I kept my chin tucked and my shoulders down. Turtling was something victims did; they closed down and pulled inward. They needed to shield themselves. The body language gave him the impression that I couldn't talk about this.

"Maybe a little more time," he said abruptly, rubbing my arm. "Trust me when I say it's easier to just rip the band-aid off."

"You always say that," I murmured, keeping my focus on the ducks.

"And I'm always right."

Was he? I hadn't really thought about that. As much as I wanted to hurry him along, I also didn't want to tip my hand about anything.

"Call me soon," he instructed when I just grew quieter and quieter. It used to help to see Uncle David. I felt—closer to Daddy somehow. This time? It was just painful. A reminder of what had been taken from me. I hadn't lost him. No, that indicated misplacing him.

That, I hadn't done.

"I will," I promised, squeezing his hand when he gripped mine. But he let me go almost immediately and I got to my feet to shuffle away. I'd picked up the grocery cart on my way into the park.

It took time to wander my way out, shuffling along with no seeming direction in mind. The fun part was I paused to pick some random items along the way, mostly trash, but it let me look behind me.

Uncle David was gone. Of course, he could be anyone— but he had no reason to follow me. The paranoia irritated me. Didn't make me hurry, though. Eventually, I left the park and walked down the block to the box store and behind it, where Colleen sat finishing her meal.

"You took a while," she said, almost springing to her feet. Her clothes were genuinely dirty and her face dusty with pollen. She'd slept in the park, I'd bet, probably under a tree. "I finished my food. All of it."

"I'm glad," I said as I surrendered the cart back to her. "I probably owe you for the extra time, huh?"

She snuffled a little, then rubbed at her nose before she glanced at her cart and me. "Yeah, I had to wait. You know they don't like it when I'm out here during the day."

"True, but you had a shopping bag *with* a receipt."

Receipts were important.

She gave me a toothy grin, the yellowing a testament to her smoking, but they were in remarkably good shape for a woman living on the streets. Then again, sometimes I thought Colleen lived out here cause she wanted to and preferred it to what society expected.

Not my place to judge.

"How about a pair of new shoes, another meal, and fifty dollars?"

Her eyes narrowed. "That's way too much. What did you do with my cart?"

As much of a hurry as I'd been in, this haggling was one of the best parts of talking to Colleen. "It's what I need you to do…"

It took some tough negotiations, and she talked me into adding a coat and a milkshake to the deal before I was done. Her part of the deal was to act as a lookout for me while I wiped off and brushed off the clothes I'd worn for the park.

Then she waited while I went into the store. I found half of what I needed there, but I'd have to go elsewhere for the rest. Colleen slurped happily on her shake and seemed *very* pleased with the socks I'd added to the new walking shoes for her.

I left before she discovered the extra food and the additional hundred I tucked in the pocket of the coat. She really did have her own code of honor, and I'd been late bringing her cart back.

The time spent in the box store was longer than I wished, but I'd picked this area for the meet with Uncle David because it was far away from where we usually got together. I also didn't want to risk Cash following me. Or worse, if Cash encouraged the boys to follow me.

I'd texted Rick before I turned off my phone. I would turn it back on as soon as I was away from here. For now, I pulled out my other burner and sent a message asking for a meeting.

The accountant and I didn't have occasion for face-to-face encounters, but he'd asked about coming to dinner for his payment. Dinner at the house with the boys required me clearing him. So, how about dinner in private first?

His swift responses and unhesitating affirmative were admirable, as was his understanding. The place he suggested for the meeting was very public but also over ninety minutes away.

I needed at least another two hours to gather items to get ready. No going home beforehand. The guys could *not* attend this meeting.

It'd be cutting it close, especially since I still needed to stop at a couple of other stores on the way. I'd make it.

It was only after I'd picked up a new dress, some cosmetics, and the right heels that I booked a hotel near the restaurant online.

The new system was wonderful, check-in, pay, and use your phone as your key. You never had to see anyone. Having an ID just for these types of occasions was a good thing. Daddy preferred cash for everything, but the world was moving away from that.

We had to move with it or risk being caught unawares.

Once I got to my room, I left my purchases on the bed and threw myself through a shower. The heat on my muscles was excellent, considering how sore Cash had left me. I'd managed to ignore it most of the day, but the bite marks had required some consideration in my dress choice.

My thighs burned and my cunt ached, but all of it in a kind of sensual way that left a lazy tug of pleasure in my belly. I couldn't risk thinking about them right now. Another reason to meet Uncle David this far away.

Fletcher and Rick would not get his approval, but Cash might make him act. I doubted he would ever trust a former FBI agent. I struggled with it still, and at the same time, I *wanted* to believe him.

The dress was a pale champagne shade and matched my hair. Light cosmetics, a blow-dry for my damp hair, and a pair of red shoes that would be far more memorable than I would be, and I was ready.

Cleaning behind myself as I got ready meant I left few traces behind, and I'd only touched the surfaces in the room itself with plastic. The bathroom wiped down neatly.

Not that there was any crime committed here, but one could never be too careful.

I turned the phone on long enough to send Rick a message that my errands had taken longer than expected. I would be missing dinner. But I was all right. If I would be any later than ten, I would message again.

Disappointment seemed to echo from his response, but I might have been projecting. All he'd asked was did I want him to keep something warm for me.

Yes, I'd told him. You.

Then I'd turned the phone off, lest I get too sentimental. Neither Rick nor Fletcher had objected to my time with Cash. They'd merely tucked me in between them, though Fletcher had scowled at the bite marks. I told him to hush, I'd enjoyed the pain in the midst of the pleasure.

It certainly wasn't a lie. Hours later, the bruises only served as a reminder, and my body softened at the idea. Once again, I packed those lust-filled thoughts away. I needed to focus.

An hour later, I followed the maître d' as he led me to a private alcove of the exclusive little French restaurant. "Ratio" rose with a smile at my arrival.

"Vienna," he said as warmly as any friend, then greeted me with a kiss against each cheek. "Let me." The command was directed to the maître d', who withdrew promptly while the accountant pulled out my chair for me. "You look lovely, I feel underdressed."

The light jest fell flat with me, considering he was dressed quite nicely. "Do you need a compliment?" I asked. "Or do you object to getting straight to business?"

A faint frown touched his brow as he filled a wine glass for me. He hadn't asked, nor had I told him, my preferences—but the white bore a label that was definitely one of my favorites. It slotted another piece of information so neatly that anticipation threatened to make me careless.

"Well, business, of course, if you require it. We are safe to talk here—within reason." His smile was quick and genuine. It softened his blue eyes and added a hint of mischief to them. "What can I do for you now, Vienna?" He adjusted his eyeglasses before picking up his wine glass.

"First, I have to thank you for doing such an excellent job at the cabin. The cleanup was impeccable."

He inclined his head. "I didn't expect you to go back."

"Then why did you leave the photograph?" I covered my own eagerness with a sip of the wine.

A long breath escaped him. "It was inevitable that you would discover sooner or later."

My gut clenched. The dull thud of my pulse was almost a sickening beat. "I should have thought you wanted me to know. Why else leave it?"

"Habits," he said with a shrug. "Also, when they took note of her disappearance, I didn't want anything to point back to you. The photograph has never been a part of your modus operandi."

"No," I said slowly. "It hasn't. How?" I studied him because nothing about him fit what I'd imagined the Vanisher to be.

Nothing.

This man—I knew this man. Maybe not well, but we'd done business with him for years. Daddy knew him. How could he…?

"Simple, people see what they want to." He gave me an indulgent look. "Even you. To be fair, you haven't seen as much of me as I have of you. Thackery—"

He hesitated and my heart slammed to a halt. It was like the whole world was suspended. Then it lurched into motion again. "Did you do it?" I demanded, no longer content to play this game. At his frown, I added in an even voice that would not carry from the privacy of our table, "Did you kill my father?"

"No." Despite the swift denial, he lasered his gaze onto mine. "What I actually did was…"

RICK

I WAS PROUD OF MYSELF.

Vienna was only six hours later than she was supposed to be, and I managed to hold my shit together. Fletcher and, surprisingly, Cash had helped out in a big way.

They'd both done their part for cleaning day, albeit Fletcher did so with a slight frown. He wasn't a fan of cleaning. Maybe if I hid little shots of coffee around the house, he'd be better motivated. I'd just have to use the decaf in most of them, so he didn't bounce off the walls.

"No, you're supposed to only count the tens, kings, and aces." Cash took a very small stack of cards away from Fletcher and exaggeratedly counted the tens and kings. There were no aces in Fletcher's stack. "You have thirty points."

"Why do I have to count my stack? Is that you flexing on me since your stack is much larger?" The ire in Fletcher's tone was so strong, I almost smiled. We'd learned something new about him tonight.

He was a sore loser.

Cash rolled his eyes. "It's not a flex. It's common in the game because you can count your cards quicker. There are only two-hundred-and-fifty points. I'll know how much I have when you and Rick count your points. Simple math, Reed."

"Sounds like you're trying to flex," he muttered as he tossed his cards in the middle.

"Rick, what do you have?" Cash glanced at me.

"Forty."

"So, I have one-eighty. See? That's why you count yours first." Stacking up the cards, he deftly split the deck and shuffled them a few times. "My deal."

After our cleaning was done, I'd made a nice dinner of beer brats and sauerkraut. Which they both seemed to appreciate. Then Cash roped us into a game of pinochle.

Neither had said anything, but I didn't believe they liked me standing at the window, and they were trying to take my mind off of Vienna's return. But what they didn't realize was that it soothed me to watch for her.

I'd given in, and let Cash teach me. We'd been playing for the last hour or so, and even as I was picking up the rules faster than Fletcher, it had been a good time all around.

The garage door opened, and I was up and out of my seat before either man could stop me. Fletcher was right on my heels when I opened the door to the garage, and Cash was crowding behind him.

"Is this what we do? We wait for Vienna and greet her at the door?"

I almost glanced back. Was he being a smart ass? Or was that a genuine question? Without seeing his face, I wasn't sure, except I had no desire to look at him when Vienna was getting out of her car.

Her long, toned leg appeared, then her other leg.

In sexy high heel shoes.

As she unfurled from the seat, all grace and sensuous movement, I frowned even as she smiled at us. Blood rushed to my dick as I mentally ran through her departure this morning.

She hadn't planned on being out long, and when she left, she had been dressed in cheap, worn, and dirty clothes. I didn't like this. Not at all. With her extended time and extreme change of wardrobe, it meant something unexpected happened.

I wish she had taken me with her. No one was there to watch her back. As much of a good face I put on for Vienna and Fletcher, my worry for her continued to gnaw at my self-control.

"Vienna," I breathed as she climbed the few short steps to the laundry room. I moved to the side for her to pass, but before she could get too far inside, I tucked a loose curl behind her ear and dropped a kiss on her upturned face.

She slid her arms around my waist, and I exhaled as I returned her embrace. Breathing came so much easier when I had her in my arms. Vienna squeezed my middle, breathing in my scent like she'd missed me as much as I had missed her.

I doubted that was possible, but I savored the thought all the same.

Releasing her, I gave her a gentle push toward Fletcher as I shut and locked the door. He would never voice it, but Fletcher needed her just as much as I did.

She gave him his own hug and kiss, and he happily hummed the entire time.

Cash, ever the watcher, waited until she stepped out of Fletcher's hold. The way his gaze swept her from head to toe, he must not have liked her wardrobe change either. If he had learned anything, he'd keep his abrasive personality to himself. When he was worked up, he tended not to have any kind of filter, and usually, filterless Cash rubbed Vienna the wrong way.

He stepped forward, probably intending to claim his own kiss since they had progressed past the dance where they exchanged sharp barbs and hot looks.

He pulled up short when her expression blanked.

"I was going to collect my own greeting, but you're

looking at me like you don't know me." Cash straightened up to his full height.

Vienna shook her head as if she needed to dislodge some inconvenient thoughts. "Sorry." She didn't add any more, and when Cash made no other moves to approach her, I placed my hand on the small of her back—her bare back—and guided her around both men and into the main part of the house.

"Have you eaten?" I asked softly.

"I have," she sighed like her day had been too long.

There was always so much pulling at her attention between me, Fletcher, Cash, finding her father's killer, and her work, that she needed more rest. Which I'd suggested on more than one occasion, and she never listened.

With the exception of the family day. That was a start.

Still, I couldn't hold my tongue. "Why was there an outfit change? Did anything go wrong?"

She stopped by the island and started to bend down to take off her shoes.

Stopping her with a hand on her arm, I bent down and slid my thumb in the side of the sharp red heels, slipping them off her feet. She groaned when her bare foot hit the cool tile.

Lifting one of her feet onto my knee, I pushed my thumbs into the tender flesh of her arch. She moaned, long and low. I gave the same attention to her other foot.

Fletcher adjusted his crotch and I shook my head at him. When I turned my attention back to her, she was smiling down at me.

Touching her fingertips to my hair, she finally answered me. "I had dinner wi—"

Then Cash showed how stupid he was as he cut her off.

"Wait, wait, wait. You left on an important errand—without backup—got delayed, all so you could get dressed up and have dinner with someone? A man?" Cash fired off as he came around the island, his shins pressing against my back.

I stood, forcing him to back away from Vienna.

The skin around Vienna's beautiful tawny eyes pinched as she narrowed her gaze on him.

"Man, I think you should probably check your tone," Fletcher offered a smart piece of advice.

"What?" Cash's voice sharpened on that one word. "You're kidding me, right? I get you're all a unit. An unconventional one. But aren't you at least a little angry that she came back dressed like sin and smelling of expensive perfume? There's literally only one reason a woman dresses like that."

I turned and shoved at his chest, jerking my head to the side in a clear warning.

His nostrils flared as he breathed out. "Look, I'm not saying she was fucking around. I'm just trying to point out that something very different from what you explained to me happened. Without backup. And most likely with another man."

I didn't want his words to get to me. I really didn't. There was truth to it. A woman, especially a brilliant woman like Vienna, played up her image for her surroundings, and she was dressed like she was at a party, club, or some other place where she tried to attract a target of the typical male variety.

But there was one thing that Cash didn't understand.

Vienna knew what she was doing. She was good at it. Excelled in survival, blending, and self-defense. And more than anything, I trusted her even when I ached to protect her. Especially after what happened with Sandra Jane.

The cords in Cash's neck stood out as he struggled to control his breathing. He seemed confused, angry. Frustrated.

"Vienna can take care of herself." Fletcher stepped up next to me.

"You're missing the big picture because you're staring at

one tiny fucking tree. Just put me out of my misery, all right? Who were you with?" He locked his gaze over my shoulder.

Stepping around Fletcher, Vienna patted his arm, as if she was thankful for his help but didn't need it.

"A mutual friend," she said. The strange expression she'd had when she looked at Cash earlier flashed over her face again.

Cash stiffened. "Fucking Ratio."

"You saw the blue-eyed fox?" Fletcher swung his head. "Really?" Then just as abruptly, he shook his head and glared at Cash. "Stop interrogating her. That's not how this works."

"No, that's not how you two work. It is how *I* work." Not once did he take his gaze off. "How the fuck do you know him? And *why* would you go see him without us—dressed like that? Is he a target now?"

It was like he flipped from one topic to the next, to the next. Not all of his questions were unreasonable—his tone, however, threatened to make me angry on her behalf.

"How do you know him?"

"He's an informant," Cash stated. "He washes money for dirty people, and occasionally, he—"

The abrupt silence from him and the fact that his clenched fists relaxed even as the vein in his forehead seemed to slowly vanish told me he'd answered his own question.

"Ah, look at that, you're thinking again." Vienna ran her fingers over my hand before leaving me to face off with Cash. "That was a rather irrational reaction from an investigator…" She walked her fingers up his chest like taking steps. "I might just be one of the dirty people he washes money for—"

It was Cash's turn to cut off Vienna, slamming his mouth down on her like a man on a mission. There was definitely anger in that kiss. Anger. Demand. And possession. The fact she pushed up on her toes to meet the kiss and fisted his shirt rather than push him away kept me in place.

When it went on for another full minute, Fletcher cleared

his throat. Vienna drew back, and Cash lifted his head, but he didn't look like a man who'd just kissed her. The frown tightening his forehead only deepened.

"You're not a dirty person," he finally said. "I had no idea he knew you."

"That just tells me he honors his promises and he's trustworthy," she answered, before she cleaned the corners of his mouth. There was a hint of pink there, her lipstick having smudged. "It also tells me that you have your own secrets, Mr. Morgan, or you wouldn't be quite so worked up about mine."

The stare-off between them crackled. Fletcher was right, fighting and sex brought it out in them—a kind of rage only the other one could answer. But she'd had a long day and she didn't *need* his rage right now.

"I'm going up to take a bath," she said eventually. "Think I could get a glass of wine?"

The last she directed at me, and I nodded. "Of course, I'll bring it right up."

"Thank you." She gave Fletcher another kiss before she slipped out of the kitchen. Cash stared after her. His expression was a mess of conflicting emotions.

"I'm gonna go do some research," Fletcher said, still eyeing Cash. Like our former federal agent, Fletcher wore a frown. Disapproval and sympathy also seemed to be warring across his face. "You know…probably better. I'll be up later."

Then he left us alone. I debated having words with Cash right now, but I didn't want Vienna to wait. After pouring her a glass of wine, I glanced at where Cash still stood, his expression thunderous.

We'd had an entire discussion about his concerns surrounding Vienna and her father's death. He needed a phone to make some calls and he wanted to retrace his steps. While I wouldn't sign off on giving him a phone until Vienna had said yes, I did agree to advocating for him *with* Vienna.

Since I was having second thoughts on that front currently, I tabled that discussion for the next day. I left him to sulk or sort out his thoughts while I carried the wine up to her room.

Music drifted out, a soft kind of bluesy music I'd never heard her listen to before. Tapping on the bathroom door before I opened it, I said, "It's me."

Vienna leaned back in the tub, one leg braced on the side, as though hooked there to keep her from sinking under the bubbly, colorful water.

The scents of vanilla and amber filled the air with just a hint of honeysuckle. I did like these bombs. We needed to find more of them for her. With her hair piled up on her head and her face bare of any cosmetics, she looked young and...

"Tell me how I can help," I said as I moved to sit on the edge of the tub and held out her wine glass.

"Nothing yet," she said, somehow finding a smile. The melancholy wreathing her wrenched at my heart.

"But soon?"

"I hope so," she admitted. "I need to think through this evening—the whole day, really."

Troubled and upset. "Vienna," I said, brushing my fingers along her damp leg. Beyond the earlier bite marks and bruises left from her night with Cash, there were no new signs of injuries on her. "I wouldn't normally ask—but did something bad happen with the accountant? Horatio?"

She shook her head. "Not bad—per se. Just...I saw Uncle David today."

I nodded. "He said something that upset you?" She'd told me a little about him, but not enough. I'd heard him on the phone with her once too. Beyond the fact that he was her uncle, I didn't know much about him.

"It's hard to explain, but—Uncle David knew my father. They were—they were close, and he's been my uncle for as long as I can remember."

But there was something bothering her.

"Before, I liked seeing him because it made me feel closer to Daddy."

The lost note in her voice just made me want to beat the whole world back and make them leave her alone.

"Today was different." She took another drink of the wine. "Different in a way I can't put my finger on, and then… then I needed to speak to the accountant. You have nothing to worry about from him."

While I didn't need to hear her say that, I appreciated it. "I trust you," I promised. "You only surprised me because you came back differently than you left."

"He chose a very nice restaurant for dinner. I had to look the part."

Dinner. "You paid him for the cleanup." He'd asked for dinner. "I thought he wanted to come here." Then I shook my head. "Of course, you wouldn't bring him here without being more certain of him. You're too protective of our space."

Ours. I liked the sound of it.

"Exactly. Thank you for trusting me."

"Thank you for coming home." Bracing my hands on the sides of the tub, I leaned down to kiss her. She returned the affection almost gently. It was aching in its sweetness and I brushed a second kiss to her forehead. "Soak, relax, enjoy your wine and the music."

"Do you like it?"

I canted my head. "I do. I've never heard it before."

"Something Horatio said," she murmured. "Reminded me of how much I used to like this. Daddy never did. Thought it was too sad. Better to go for straight jazz."

"I don't think it's sad." I gave it a bit of thought as I met her inquisitive eyes. "I think it's powerful and complicated. It's also beautiful. Like you."

A light dawned in her eyes and her lips turned up. "You always say the right things."

"No," I disagreed. "I don't. But I learn, and I know you appreciate honesty."

"So do you."

I grinned at her smile. "We are a good match."

"Yes," she said with another smile. "We are. Rick—about Cash…"

"Does he make you happy?" I knew the answer to this. I'd known it before she got there herself.

"When he isn't making me crazy."

"I think he will always make you a little crazy," I confessed. "He likes control."

"I know." She looked at her wine glass. "But can I trust him?"

"Only you can answer that." I trusted that he wanted her, that he was willing to bend and break the rules for her, and that he would do anything—including kill—to stay with her. I also believed he would mow down anything in his path, but I didn't want him to bull his way through her too. "I trust him with your safety. But I'm not sure I trust him with your heart."

Another kiss to her forehead, and I stood.

"I'll be back up in a little while. You need time to think."

"Maybe popcorn and a movie later?"

"I'd like that."

Leaving her, I closed the bedroom so she could continue having privacy and went downstairs. The door to Fletcher's study was closed, but Cash was exactly where I left him—standing in the kitchen, just glaring.

As soon as he spotted me, he said, "Did she say anything about what he wanted—"

"Stop," I told him. "Enough. Vienna will tell us what we need to know. You can stay. You can even be in her bed if that's where she wants you. But you don't get to question her like that again. Do you understand?"

"Or what?"

"Or I will put you in that cell, and I will leave you there until you learn better manners. You care about her. Act like it. What you were doing *wasn't* helping. You don't trust her."

"She doesn't trust *me*," he countered.

"You want her to trust you, then give her trust. Do as she has asked. You claim to have studied her father and everything about her. You say you're a profiler. You get people. Why do you keep treating her like a criminal? Or worse—like a possession?"

Shock blew across his face. Maybe he hadn't seen it. But he didn't get that excuse anymore.

"I'm going to make brownies," I said. "She likes them when she's sad. She might come down for a movie later, and we'll have popcorn then too."

It wasn't until I had the batter mixed that Cash finally said, "What can I do?"

That was better.

FLETCHER

YUP, I was absolutely hiding out in my lair while Cash made enemies and got into trouble. Cash seemed like the kind of guy to take other good men down with him just from being in close proximity.

No, thank you.

I preferred to stay in Drew's good graces.

To make the most of my time, I pulled up Dion's server. I'd already combed over it and collected all the essential details. It would have been reckless of me to wait. But a fresh set of eyes once a period of time had passed was always a good idea.

I'd been up for hours when I'd gone through it originally.

At the time, I'd been in the dark about a lot of things regarding Drew's overall goal of finding her father's killer. Now, with all my current knowledge, something might jump out at me.

Clicking on the Thackery folder, I shivered as I looked into the man's dead eyes.

Drew loved him. Idolized him even, and I was sure he had been a great dad. He had to have been with the way she missed him. But he was not someone I would have ever wanted to be left alone with.

Just a look from this man would have me pissing my pants and confessing every single crime I'd committed, all the way back to that pack of gum I stole in kindergarten.

Nope, I couldn't look at his photo anymore. And to be honest, I wasn't all fired up to look at sexualized photos of Drew when she was younger either.

I left that folder and started clicking through the others Dion had amassed. There was one on Noel Warrick, the woman Vienna had tested my skills on.

Ah, what did we have here?

A bunch of sub-folders were laid out under her name, each labeled with what I assumed was the last name.

One caught my eye.

Robert Schaffer. Police Commissioner two states over.

Shit, why was his name familiar?

Twisting in my chair, I switched to my other monitor and performed a basic internet search, looking for any mentions in the news.

Several articles praising his hard work and dedication to the good fight against crime were listed, then there were a few ten or so pages into the search that were forums instead of articles.

Interesting.

He'd taken in several girls over the years who had been saved from the sex trafficking ring. One girl he'd taken in at the age of thirteen, Monica, had accused him of raping her multiple times.

There were thumbnails of pictures, but I couldn't open them. I couldn't. My stomach wasn't strong enough for whatever might be in those images. Instead, I stuck to the black and white details.

Some of the girls ran away. Some were committed to rehab and never left there alive. There was one young girl still in his care.

In Dion's folder were testimonies, video footage, and email communication, all connecting Robert to Noel and her operations.

Hell, I turned my head to the side and squinted at the

screen, as if seeing less of it would make the man more palatable.

But it didn't work.

Shifting gears before my stomach rolled, I put together a current sleeve on the man. His employment record, list of properties, known associates, and work calendar. Robert was a busy man, both in the community and in private.

How had the media never connected him with that bitch? They were college friends. Stayed in touch throughout their careers.

From the email communication, he was a smuggling point for her. And the girls he took in? Ah fuck, I was going to be sick.

They were payments to him. And as a widowed public hero with no children, no one questioned him. Ever.

A few weeks ago, he'd given an interview about a drug ring his officers had shut down. That was why his name was familiar. His interview had played right before one of Sandra Jane's.

One thing was very, very clear.

This man had to die.

A knock at the door pulled me out of my dark thoughts as Drew stuck her head in. It was the middle of the day, but I'd had the blinds pulled down, hiding from the world. The cool glow of the electronics washed her skin in blue tones as if it were midnight instead.

"Hey," she said through a smile. "You've been in here practically since last night. It's not like you to be up before everyone else."

I hadn't woken up before Rick, but he had pulled Drew closer to him as I snuck out of bed in the wee hours of the morning. She'd slept through my departure, surprising the fuck out of me.

Even on my quietest days, I was still a raging bull when it came to Drew's sensitive hearing. She must have been tired.

My sexy death angel wasn't immune to stress, but I was glad to see Rick take such good care of her.

Me?

I was about to make her happy in an entirely different way.

"I have a present for you." I grinned, attempting to hide the horror creeping along the edges of my mind. "Come here," I said, holding my arm up for her to hopefully sit on my lap.

To my delight, that was exactly what she did.

Drew closed the door, and when she got close, she perched that perky, sweet ass right over my dick. This made the last hour a nonissue as I buried my nose in her hair, enjoying her clean, fresh scent.

Chuckling, she turned her face to nuzzle my temple. "What's this present?"

"Well, my sexy death angel, any plans today or tomorrow?"

"No…" She pulled back, her brows furrowed in question.

"Good, because I found a dickhead that needs to die." I opened the file with everything I'd toggled together on Robert Schaffer. Dion's file was great, and I had copied a lot of his documents and data over to my drive, but I had my own specific system and a particular way to organize the data.

She took the mouse from me, scrolling through the documents and photos I'd been too chicken shit to look at.

I was content to loop my arms around her waist and press my forehead against her shoulder. Drew was so soft, yet strong. Having her in my lap was like having my very own killer stuffy. I squeezed her to me just because I could.

After several minutes, she pressed back against me and I loosened my hold.

"Wow."

"Yeah," I agreed. "Fucking wow."

"You want this to be my next target?" She glanced at me,

then moved her attention back to the screen where Robert's headshot was from the most recent article touting him as a community hero.

His graying hair was swept back from his face, and he had a stern look that said he was a professional just doing his job. But no one saw what was underneath the mask.

"I think he needs to be. He has a girl in his house right now. She deserves to be free of that *monster*." Shit, I was more fired up over this than I realized.

"You're right. She doesn't deserve this." Her gaze strayed toward the other monitor where Monica's accusation sat at the top of a forum. No one ever took her seriously because she'd been in and out of rehab. The only reason he hadn't taken care of her was probably because she'd gone off the radar a few years ago, prior to the forum post dates.

"I'll get Rick and take him with me."

"I want to go too," I growled, scowling at Robert.

"Really?" Surprise flitted over her features. "I didn't think that was your thing after the last time."

Shaking my head, I shifted, and the chair creaked. "I'm invested. I want to see that mother fucker pay…preferably without blood, but I can look away if I need to."

One side of her mouth slowly tipped up. "Okay. But if Rick wants to go, we'll have to take Cash too."

I huffed out a laugh. "Why not? Make it a family affair."

"Family affair," Drew said with a laugh, twisting in my lap in just a delightful grind of pressure against my dick. I was pretty sure she said something else, but then she nuzzled her way across my lips. Kissing Drew was like gripping a live wire. The current charged through you, making all the hair on your body stand up. Then you touch her with your tongue, and if you were really lucky, she'd curve her tongue around yours.

The surge at the contact was just mind-blowing. I threaded my fingers into her hair as she ran her hands over my chest. It took me a minute to realize what she was doing, but then her palm glided over my bare abs. Fuck, kissing Drew was hot. Touching her. I needed to see—I cracked my eyes open and looked right into the ugly mug of Robert Schaffer.

I stiffened as revulsion crawled through me. It was like he was watching me with her, and he did not—

The screen went dark, and I dropped my gaze to Vienna, who stretched over and turned off the other screen. "My sweet little pincushion," she whispered in that soft voice. So much about her was soft. I cupped her breast through the shirt, and her nipple beaded tight at the contact. "That's it. Touch me. See me. No more looking at him."

"I didn't want him looking at you." It came out a growl, then her mouth fused to mine. She chased the piercing on my tongue like it was her personal mission. I'd never been so grateful for the damn thing as I had been the day she came all over my tongue. Oh, that was a thought, but before I could put a plan to action, she slid out of my lap and pulled her mouth from mine. I groaned. "Drew."

"I'm here," she said, and without the screens on, the room had gone dark with only little bits of light. Her top floated past me and all I encountered was warm skin. Wrapping an arm around her, I dragged her back to my lap and locked my lips around one of those delectable nipples. The flesh pebbled even more as I teased my piercing against it. Warm metal. Hot flesh.

My dick ached for relief and the shorts I had on weren't doing much for me anyway. Drew fisted my hair, and I scraped my teeth over her nipple. She seemed to like a little pain, and the moan she released seemed to confirm that. Fuck, probably not something I needed to figure out right now, but I definitely wanted to explore this later.

With a tug, she pulled my head back and I released her nipple with a little pop. "Fuck, Drew…"

"Hush," she commanded, then stroked her fingers over my face as light as a feather being teased over my flesh. Once again, she slid out of my lap. Instead of standing—she went to her knees. All the blood in my body fled into my cock a split second before she gave my shorts a tug.

I lifted my hips as she dragged them down. The relief as she freed my dick lasted for scant seconds before she wrapped a silky hot hand around my base.

"Fuck," I groaned and reached for her, but she pushed my hand away then gripped them and put them on her head. "What are you doing?"

"You can hold my hair, or you can hold the chair. But you will not hold anything else…" That was the sum total of her explanation before she fisted my cock again. The slick wetness of her mouth wrapped around my tip and I forgot how to breathe. I gripped her hair but refused to tug it. No, then she swallowed down around my dick and I was in her throat.

Blood pounded away in my cock as I fought against the urge to thrust. I didn't even pull her back or push her down. She lifted her head, tongue tracing all along my base to the tip. When I rested only against her lips, she traced the piercings themselves. I'd pierce the rest of my dick if she liked it that much. I'd pierce fucking—oh damn, she swallowed around me again, and I swore my brain just went offline.

It was all hot heat, deep pulls of suction, the caress of her tongue and then I was rocking in and out of her throat. She dug her fingers into my thighs and then around to my hips.

"I'm going to come, Drew," I warned her, just in case she needed to pull off. Not all women—she hummed. She. Fucking. Hummed.

My balls dragged up so tight I thought they'd been reclaimed by the rest of me before I came in one hot release after another. Nose buried against my abdomen, she held on until I finished pumping. Sweat dripped down my chest as I panted. Then I remembered to let go of her hair as she slowly released my cock.

That was… "Drew." I couldn't seem to form another syllable. Drew really was the perfect one, though.

"Yes, my sweet little pincushion?" The roughness in her voice was a fresh, tingling caress through my whole system. "Do you feel better?"

I did. I really did. "I want…" Words. I wanted words. Right, she was done sucking my dick, so I hauled her upwards as I staggered out of the chair. Thankfully, I stepped right out of the leg of one side of the shorts, or I'd probably have fallen on my face. As it was, Drew helped me as I moved her into my chair and then went to my knees.

Oh, she'd already taken off her shorts. Good Drew. "So good…" I murmured as I pulled her legs over my shoulders. The scent of her filled my nostrils, and I swore I could already taste her on my tongue.

It took me a little longer to make her cry out and come, but I was devoted to the effort. I paid particular attention to her clit until she stiffened and that rush of dampness flooded out of her. Making a woman squirt, definitely an achievement. Making Drew squirt? A goal for the rest of my life. When she'd had enough of my tongue on her clit, she wrestled me down onto the floor. Then my cock was buried in her cunt and my mind just whited out.

It wasn't until Rick knocked on the door about dinner a couple of hours later that I remembered other people in the house. The light from the hall slanted over us, where we were sprawled on the carpet in the dark.

I'd probably have to clean up the DNA later.

Worth it.

VIENNA

"POLICE COMMISSIONER, mid-sixties, retired cop, Detective-grade, jacket full of commendations and civilian awards," Cash recited the information from the packet that Fletcher had put together. "Widowed. No children. No other family."

"No, the last was a niece, but she died two years ago. Overdose." Fletcher's tone said he blamed Schaffer for that too. "The niece's parents died in some kind of boating accident. Not a lot of details other than the husband was probably the pilot of the boat and alcohol was involved."

Cash pinched the bridge of his nose. We'd driven most of the night then taken a nap in a hotel—all four of us in one room—that had been interesting. Cash had his bed, and Rick and Fletcher slept on the other queen with me. However, Cash had taken the bed closest to the door, a spot I would normally have taken, while Rick took the edge of the second bed closer to the door so we could put Fletcher the farthest away.

Four hours of sleep, followed by coffee with lunch from a diner nearby, and then we'd settled in to plan.

"This is not your usual type of case," Cash said, then

waved a hand when I raised my brows. "I mean, it is, but I thought you did more legwork before you went in."

"Normally, I would, but there's a girl there." I motioned to the picture of the house. Police Commissioner was an appointed position. One he'd held for nearly a decade. In addition to a significant salary, he also had personal security in the form of two detectives and one uniformed officer during his day. "We need to get inside, take care of him, and get her out."

Anything else was non-negotiable. Fletcher had been implacable on this point. My distraction the day before had helped. It had definitely let him sleep. But he'd worked through a chunk of the drive, pulling schematics and other details.

He'd also found out about the security company that provided the alarm system for the property. His absolute glee over it had been one of the few things to lift his spirits since he'd reviewed the victim profiles with Cash.

"Agreed," Cash said. Surprise fluttered through me and I met his gaze. Since my return from meeting with Horatio and Cash's initial anger over it, he'd been in a better frame of mind. He'd apologized without apologizing, then said we needed to learn to trust each other. So he would wait until I was ready to tell him.

That might be a while. The revelation that not only was Horatio the Vanisher, but he'd been looking after me for Daddy—or at least that was why he'd started tracking me—continued to play on repeat in the back of my head. I didn't understand it fully. How could I explain it? And that he was the Vanisher in addition to being the accountant?

No one else in the Network was aware, Horatio had told me. No one except Daddy. He trusted me with the information.

I hadn't fully processed what that all meant. Yet. I needed to lay it all out to digest. That would have to wait until later.

For now, Fletcher needed this job done, and this man needed to die for his crimes.

Cash flicked a look at Fletcher and then back to me. A second wave of surprise crashed into affection at that concern. He saw it too. Saw it and understood why this needed to happen sooner rather than later.

For the girl. And for Fletcher.

"What's our plan?" Was he trying to meet me on my terms?

"This is what I'm thinking," I began as I studied him. "There are four of us; the house is located on about six and a half acres. The property is fully fenced, and there's an electric current running through portions of it. Intermittent current, about a dozen cameras on key entries and exits, and a second-generation internal alarm system from Kingston Security."

"So, it should be a cakewalk."

The sarcasm entertained me. "Not quite, but close. Fletcher?"

"Kingston Security has a few flaws in their system. One is the fact that it's on a dedicated network, which means the system has to call out when a certain set of circumstances are met. Because it requires those circumstances—"

"There's a delay." Cash began to smile.

"Precisely. To get in, we go over the fence. Then wait exactly two minutes, don't move, don't breathe, don't piss." Fletcher tapped something on his digital pad showing the radius of the various cameras. Only two overlapped. "Once we clear that hurdle, then we move straight to the house, don't slow down, just get to the building and under the purview of the cameras."

"Motion-sensitive?" Cash surmised, then nodded. "Another sixty to ninety-second clock before it alerts on the movement. This is sloppy security…"

"Yes and no," Fletcher said with a shrug. "If you don't know how it works, you look for the redundancies to try and shut it down, but if you cut power or anything shifts in a pattern across each of these things—automatic alert."

Complex and yet simple. You truly had to understand how the system worked. Fletcher not only understood it, he'd hacked it before. So, he knew what *not* to do.

"Once we're inside, Fletcher will disable internal security. Rick—you need to take care of any physical security. I don't expect him to have private guards in his home. Men who hide the kind of dirty secrets he has are not going to want anyone to see what they have *or* what they are doing."

Rick nodded, and Fletcher gave me a thumbs up.

"Am I with you?" Cash asked.

"Where do you think you'll be most useful?"

Pleasure flared in his eyes. "Finding the girl. Because if I find this guy, I'm just going to kill him. You want something special for him."

It was my turn to smile. Cash finally seemed to understand. Truly. "Yes. You're going to need a weapon in case we run into trouble. Rick—you're with Fletcher once you've cleared security. I'll get the commissioner. Cash, you get the girl. Once we have her, Rick, I need you to get her out as swiftly as possible. She may not want to cooperate, and we'll have to deal with that when we get there. If at any time I call this, you stop what you're doing and walk away, understood?"

All three stared at me in varying forms of mutiny but nodded. Eventually.

A few hours later, I had to debate whether I needed to call it before we'd even gotten inside. Our target was not only *not* alone, but I recognized the man who arrived just as we came over the fence.

"Is that—" Fletcher started, and I jerked my head to the side in a sharp warning.

So, Fletcher recognized him too. Although, I doubted Fletcher recognized him for the same reason I did.

John Baddu. Known in the network as the Street Sweeper. He used his position as a medical examiner to clear up potential autopsy issues. When Reuben wasn't available, Daddy had used him a time or two.

Bodies would be transported to the morgue, and he'd write them up with a natural cause of death. Or, if the cause was clearly murder, he'd skew the evidence left on the body.

A very useful connection.

But Daddy had never liked him. Once, we'd heard a rumor that he enjoyed his autopsies a little too much, and we'd never used him again. He'd also gone on Daddy's radar, except he was pushed to the bottom of our target list since he dealt in corpses.

However, if he was here, in a state he wasn't licensed in, with a known contact of Noel's, there might be more truth to the rumors than I realized. And part of me dreaded learning the truth that was sure to come out by the end of the night.

One by one, we quickly dropped over the wall. We landed soundly, except for Fletcher, who lost his balance and fell onto his back right in a pile of rustling leaves.

"Sorry!" He whispered, much louder than he should have. In fact, he shouldn't have made any sounds at all. Seemed like I needed to add that tip to my pre-job lecture next time.

I glanced around, waiting for the telltale sign of approaching guards, but none came. The only noise left out here were the crickets and the whistle of a slight breeze. Robert's day guards must have left before John Baddu showed up.

Cash pinched the bridge of his nose as Rick pulled Fletcher to his feet and quietly wiped the dirt from Fletcher's ass. The last action pulled an incredulous look from Cash.

In any other situation, I would have laughed, but with the noise Fletcher just made, we needed to be extra vigilant. Fletcher tapped his watch, checking the time. We had thirty seconds left before we needed to be sprinting toward the house.

He held up five fingers, counting down slowly. When he reached zero, we dashed toward the back where the main keypad was located.

I was in the lead, Fletcher right behind me as Cash and Rick took up the rear. When we hit the back wall, we stayed just out of the halo of light cast from the light over the back door. Rick passed out latex gloves for us to tug on.

He'd ordered booties, but for a job where we needed to be stealthy, we'd have to take the risk of shoe prints and cleanup on our way out.

We waited a beat as Fletcher pointed out two cameras located on the house exactly where they were supposed to be. They were covered by black-tinted plastic to hide the swivel of the camera, but the red light was visible inside. When the camera turned toward us, we could see the light. When it shifted over the other side of the yard, we couldn't make it out.

Fletcher's hand went up again, and when all fingers were down, we ran to the door. I pulled my lock kit from my belt when the door opened.

A pudgy, middle-aged man with an unlit cigarette hanging out of his mouth almost crashed into me.

Not allowing for a loss of time, I stepped to the side, gripped his shirt, and assisted his descent down the stairs. I caught the door with my foot before it slammed shut.

He made a garbled sound as Cash plucked the cigarette out of his mouth, grabbing the back of his neck to push him toward Rick. Cash pocketed the cigarette as Rick snapped his neck and laid him down behind the covered grill.

The entire exchange was less than fifteen seconds.

I stuffed the kit back in the band of my utility belt and surveyed the rooms inside to ensure no one was watching. Good. All clear.

Motioning to Fletcher, I shifted to let him bypass me. He pulled out his phone, tapping a series of codes into the keypad as we entered the house. Rick shut the door and covered Fletcher's back while Cash pointed to the stairs that led to the second floor.

From our reconnaissance, Meredith's room was right next to Robert's bedroom.

I nodded, and he disappeared while Fletcher finished disabling the system. With two beeps, Fletcher's body relaxed, and he took in a long, silent breath. He gave me a thumbs up to let me know we were good.

We'd operated like a well-oiled machine, getting inside the house in under five minutes without tripping the alarm. Now for the most important part, finding the commissioner and ridding the world of one more monster.

Rick pulled out his gun with the silencer attached as he tapped Fletcher on the shoulder. He nodded to me and led Fletcher through the house to clear any potential security threats.

Once they were gone, I headed toward the other door that led to the basement. Several of the testimonies we'd found and reviewed mentioned a bedroom in the basement where Robert liked to take his victims. With the Street Sweeper here, that was most likely where they'd be.

But I needed to go in quietly and determine if the Street Sweeper also needed to die today.

I moved down the stairs on the balls of my feet. By never placing my entire foot on the stair, I limited the noise.

Turned out, I didn't need to worry. The basement must have been soundproofed because soft, forties, big band music drifted up accompanied by casual conversation that was completely blocked out when the door was closed.

Glasses clinked together, and mature male laughter overtook the music for a few notes. With each step I took and the closer I came, it seemed more likely that today would be the Sweeper's last for breathing.

The walls and ceiling were concrete, with no plaster or decorations here—nothing like how the girls had described the basement room. At the bottom of the stairs, the concrete continued through the room lit only by a severe overhead lamp. It swung on the chain as if one of the men had knocked into it recently.

My blood boiled as I took in the center of the room. Under the lamp was a metal table, like something John would have worked with in the morgue. And on the table was a naked young woman, maybe even a girl in her mid to late teens. Her mouth was taped shut and her body strapped in by thin chains at her ankles, waist, and neck, with metal plates pinning her wrists to the table.

She whimpered as John approached, holding a crystal glass of amber liquid in his hand. He used his free hand to trace a finger between the valley of her small breasts.

He grinned over at Robert. "She's perfect. I can't believe you were able to find someone like her with Noel's operations in disarray."

Robert poured a few fingers of bourbon into his own expensive glass at the makeshift bar by the wall. "I told you I wouldn't have an issue securing a girl. Your tastes, while I appreciate them, are pretty basic. White, teenage female with brown hair and eyes. Even without Noel's staff, I would have been able to procure a girl for you. At the very least, the Curator would have been able to assist." He took a swallow of the liquid as he approached the table.

Cupping the girl's breast with a callous hand, he gave a squeeze. "What's your obsession with this look anyway? Have mommy issues or something?"

John sneered at Robert, knocking his hand away. "Hardly. This is the look of the girl who fucked me over in medical school. She made me fall in love with her, then broke my fucking heart."

"You have a heart?" Robert snickered.

Leveling him with a dry look, John set his glass down on the small table at his hip. On that same side table, he unwrapped a cloth package and arranged several tools inside in a neat row.

My stomach bottomed out as he picked up a shiny scalpel that glinted under the unforgiving light of the lamp. That poor girl. She had to be sweating under the light, afraid of the coming pain and whatever horrors John had planned for her.

But she'd never find out. I'd save her before it got to that.

"I did. Then Elena smashed it to smithereens and took the job I wanted."

"So, this is your revenge?" Robert chuckled as he walked a few paces away and dropped into a bent-up metal chair. It creaked under his weight but held firm.

Laughing, John pressed his hand flat against the girl's abdomen and started to lower the sharp tool toward her flesh. "No. I had my revenge with Elena. But I found I had a taste for the less respected side of my profession. Too bad I wasn't born in an era where no one reported missing girls of impoverished families." He paused. "Or when they could be sold to put food on the table for the rest of the family."

"Oh, I don't know, John. Times haven't changed that much." Robert adjusted his crotch as he watched the girl's trembling body.

"Brace yourself, pet. This will hurt," John said as the tip of his scalpel pressed against the soft flesh of her belly. She whimpered and cried behind the duct tape.

"It will hurt, although I don't believe the girl has anything to worry about." I stepped out of the shadows, aiming my gun at John.

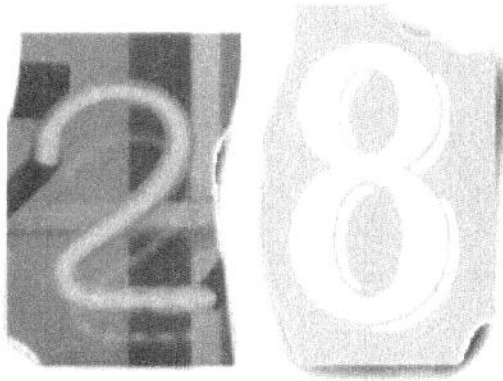

VIENNA

THE BLUEPRINT to the house showed the basement separated into two rooms. This one, and one more, with only one exit. Robert would have wanted to minimize the risk of the girls escaping him.

Which, ironically, would help in his demise.

Robert popped up from his chair as the scalpel clattered against the floor. At least the Sweeper recognized me.

"Jane?" John blurted out.

"Not quite. Although that was the name I went by at the time." I shifted the gun to Robert then back again.

"Who the hell are you? What are you doing here?" Robert blustered as he tried to rush toward me.

Because I had zero sympathies or respect for him, I lowered the gun and shot his foot. He screeched and hopped on his one good foot as blood leaked through his shoe.

"You crazy fucking bitch," he cried as he fell against the wall. "What the fuck are you doing here?" He screamed.

"John knows. I'll let him fill you in." And it would be an opportunity to see just what John thought he knew about Daddy and me.

The door opened at the top of the stairs, and Cash came jogging down. Out of the corner of my eye, I caught his slight shake of the head. He passed Robert for the door that led to the other room.

So she hadn't been in her bedroom upstairs. She also wasn't the girl on the table.

"What the fuck, John?" Robert yelled through blubbering tears. He tried to put his foot down on the ground but picked it back up as if any pressure was painful.

"Who am I, John?" I slowly moved toward the table. John held his hands up and shuffled back toward the bar.

"Jane, or that's who I know you as."

"And just who am I?" I needled, as I used one hand to grab the pliers and cut through the thin chains at her neck, waist, and ankles. We'd need either bolt cutters or a key for her wrists.

"I—I don't know," John stammered.

Cash came out of the room to the side with a thunderous expression on his face. He took a step toward Robert, but I stopped him.

"No, he doesn't get to die yet," I said. "Is the girl in the room?"

"Oh, she's in there. Covered in bruises and cuts. I need the keys to set her free." He approached Robert. "Don't worry. I won't kill him. Yet." He bared his teeth in a dark semblance of a smile.

Robert didn't fight as Cash searched his pockets, finding a small set of keys. When he turned away, he clocked Robert's chin with his elbow. "Oops."

More footsteps came down the stairs, and Fletcher and Rick appeared. Immediately, Rick ran to the table, whispering to the girl it would be okay as he gently pulled the tape from her mouth.

"Please. Please. I want to go home," she cried, and the terror in her voice twisted my heart and kicked up my thirst for blood. John and Robert's blood.

"I know. We'll make sure you get home," Rick assured her. Cash returned with a small girl, barely a preteen, crowding against his back. He tossed the set of keys to Rick, who went through each one until he unlocked the metal plates.

"Hold on," Cash said as he ducked back into the room. When he came back, he had a ratty comforter and wrapped it around the girl's body as the other girl, the one who had been forced to live with this monster, huddled against the wall in a dirty, stained t-shirt and pair of panties.

Robert and John watched the guys work with wide eyes. I was content to let them, not wanting to give too many secrets away in front of the girls. What they didn't know they couldn't recount later.

"I'll take them upstairs," Rick murmured and ushered the girls past an ashen-faced Fletcher.

Cash searched the two men for weapons. "They're clear," he said, and I tucked my gun back into its holster. For this portion of the job, I'd prefer to get my hands dirty.

"Now, where were we…" I kept my eye on them as I checked out the tools John had on the table. Outside of the brand-new scalpel, the rest of the tools were old, rusty, and appeared to be from at least a hundred years ago. "I didn't realize you were a collector, John." I adjusted the glove on my left hand before fingering the amputation knife, artificial leech, and ecraseur, a tool used to remove hemorrhoids and ovarian tumors back in the 1800s.

They were primitive surgical tools I was only aware of through my study of weapons. Daddy said if I was going to assist him, I needed to understand how all weapons worked, regardless of the profession they were attached to.

How poor would it be if you had a perfectly good weapon at your disposal and were overpowered by the monster because you didn't know how to use it?

That was probably one of the more understated lessons I'd used the most over the years. Especially when it came to extracting answers from targets.

"No one has told me who this fucking bitch is!" Spit

spewed from Robert's mouth as blood still dripped from his foot.

"You must have some idea who I am, John. No?"

"I know you and your father did the lord's work. You were noble in the jobs you took."

"What a fucking suck up," Cash muttered as he crossed his arms.

"Not quite, but close. Why do you think I'm here?" I picked up the rusted amputation knife. The edge of the blade was barely sharp enough to make a cut. What would John have used this for?

John's gaze snapped to Robert. "I think you're here for him." He lifted a shaking hand and pointed at Robert.

"You'd be correct. But, while you're here, I might as well make the most of my time with you. You have an association with Dr. Salinas, don't you?"

"No." He pressed his ass against the bar as he roughly shook his head. "I knew who he was, but I never actually worked with him."

"But you worked with Noel?" I moved my thumb across the blade. It didn't even snag on the latex.

John zipped his lips on that question but shot Robert a worried look. I hated when men used their wealth and strength over the poor and weak, but as soon as they were on the other side, they lost all their spine and pride.

Where was the fire that made them so cruel?

"Let me ask a different question, since you're tied so tightly into the network." He gulped, and I continued, "What do you know of The Judge?"

I was safe to give this asshole Daddy's name because very few people knew him as such. The hackers, Mart, and Uncle David were the only ones who knew his alias. Mart and Uncle David were trusted, but Daddy's reputation was so fierce, that we never had an issue with the hackers.

No, my issue with Dion had been an entirely different matter.

"I—um—I mean, he's been off the scene officially for at least six months or so."

I nodded, lowering my gaze so this prick wouldn't see my pain. He didn't deserve to see that glimpse of my humanity.

"Why do you think that is?"

John looked to Robert, to Cash as if he would have any answers, then his gaze settled back on me. "I don't know. He —He's shit. I don't know what you want me to say."

I shrugged one shoulder up as I motioned for him to get on the table. Robert could get his turn in a few minutes.

Normally, I'd have wanted to do more digging on John before taking care of him, but catching him in the act was all the proof I needed.

"Did you hear anything about why he stopped working so much in the public eye?"

John stayed pressed up against the bar as I approached him.

"Only tha—that he'd turned down some insanely lucrative jobs and the network wasn't happy with him."

I paused.

That was something I hadn't heard before. Daddy turned down jobs all the time. It was more accurate to say we didn't take jobs unless they were for transportation. So who would have been upset by that information?

"Who would that be in the network?" I touched the tip of the knife to his breast bone and dragged it down close to his groin. He whimpered, so similar to the sounds the girl had made. Did he even realize what he was doing?

"I don't know!" He leaned back over the counter to get away from me.

"No idea?" I slid the knife behind the buttons and popped them off one at a time.

"No! No one ever said. It was always mentioned as the

network as a whole. But you know those asses. Most of them only care about the money instead of the motive."

His saggy, hairy chest came into view as the shirt gaped open. "Well, if you have nothing else to tell me…" I pressed the dull edge against his stomach, just like he'd attempted to do a few minutes ago.

"Wait! Wait, wait, wait. The sex club owned by the Castillo family. They're a hotbed for Network gossip. If you want to know who the jobs were for, you'll find out there! That's where I heard it!"

I smiled. "That's good. I'm glad you remembered that. It's a place I'm very familiar with."

"You'll let me go then? You came for Robert, not me." A bead of sweat rolled over the wrinkles of his forehead.

Cash snorted.

"Why would I let you live when you're just as much of a monster as he is?" I glanced at Fletcher over my shoulder. "Do you want to go upstairs and wait?"

"No." His voice only wavered slightly. "I want to see that bastard die a painful death," he said as he nodded toward Robert.

"Okay, but go upstairs anytime you think you need to."

"Got it," he said. Fletcher still looked too pale, but I wanted to give him the opportunity to see this to the bitter end. I had to trust he'd leave when it became too much.

But maybe, seeing this through would help with his own nightmares.

With no warning, I sliced down John's chest. Unsurprisingly, the cut was jagged and more about pain than depth. Blood dribbled from the wound as John gripped the counter.

Fletcher gagged, and the sour stench of vomit filled the air.

"Really?" Cash asked drily.

I glanced back to check on Fletcher. He seemed okay for

the moment as he moved away from the pile of sick on the floor while clutching his stomach.

"I thought I could do it, but maybe I better go upstairs." He didn't even get a chance to turn away from us before Robert charged me.

He yelled in both rage and pain as he raised his fist.

Cash caught him around the waist and slung him against the wall.

"Like hell, I'm going to stand around waiting for my turn at that sadistic bitch's hands!" Robert screamed as he put weight on his injured foot and hobbled toward me again with as much strength as he could muster.

It was still no match for Cash.

He caught his throat in a tight grip, kicked his good foot out from underneath him, and using the hold on his neck, guided his fall and forced his face into the puke.

"That wasn't very nice, now was it," Cash tutted, turning the man over and smearing his face through the chunks.

"Oh god." Fletcher dry heaved at the wall as he tried to avoid looking at Robert.

"Was that necessary?" I asked Cash.

He shrugged. "The man's an asshole, and he shouldn't have spoken to you that way. But I haven't killed him." Cash gave me a pointed stare as if I should be praising him on his restraint.

It was commendable. And as Robert pushed himself up from the ground and attacked Cash, he continued to show his self-control as he systematically landed a series of kicks to his kneecaps, groin, and chest. With each kick, bones snapped, and Robert's yells of pain faded to a low, pathetic moan. He dropped to his knees before falling on his side to avoid whatever damage Cash had caused.

Then, like his temper had finally been unleashed, Cash tore into the man, landing so many kicks to the groin the man passed out.

All the while, John shut his eyes to avoid looking at the scene.

Fletcher scrambled up the stairs, heaving all the way as Cash snatched the artificial leech off the table and ripped Robert's pants open. The man was just regaining consciousness as Cash gripped his flaccid dick with his latex-covered hand and grinned into his face.

"Good. I wouldn't want you to miss the best part." Then he proceeded to stab him repeatedly with the needled tool.

Robert got a few punches in, and Cash's head snapped to the right, but he refused to let go or let up on his rhythm. "I saw her, you mother fucker. I saw how you had her strapped down in there. You don't deserve to live. Although if you did, I doubt your dick would be of any use now," he growled.

A small pool of blood gathered under Robert's ass as he slumped back against the wall. He'd passed out again, and from that level of pain, I doubted he'd wake up anytime soon.

"He's down. Go ahead and finish him. We need to get the girls out of here." I turned back to John.

In an intense burst of speed, the Sweeper dropped to the floor, grabbed the scalpel, and slit his own throat, slicing across the carotid artery.

Fuck. This hadn't gone to plan at all.

CASH

VIENNA WAS IN A MOOD. It was the only way to describe her current demeanor and expression—or lack of expression. From the moment "John" had sliced his own throat, spraying her in his blood, she'd gone almost deathly silent, communicating only as much as absolutely necessary.

Body disposal proved at least somewhat problematic. While I'd been tempted to ask her if she wanted to call *Ratio*, I kept that thought to myself. In my then frame of mind, I might have wanted to beat out of him how he knew her and what he wanted from her.

As it was, killing the dirty commissioner had actually fallen to me. A gift, really, one I enjoyed. It wasn't until much later, after we'd done the arduous work of re-staging the filthy scene and bagging the bodies for removal, that she said anything other than an instruction for what to do next.

"Thank you," she murmured. Exhaustion flickered over her face as she studied the basement, the blood smears we'd left as well as the open door to the cell where he'd kept his prisoners trapped. The only thing she'd done in there was to splash bleach around like someone too lazy to do an actual cleanup.

I got it. Forensics needed to find something. This was not a man who expected to be caught. The house offered a lot of evidence for his crimes. He'd kept records—fucking photo albums—and he had his very own dark room for developing the images.

In so many ways, he'd covered his ass, and what he couldn't do himself, he'd hired out for. He also provided a service for other depraved fucks. No, Robert Schaffer deserved a far harsher death than he'd gotten. But when the authorities came looking for him, and they would because he was a police commissioner, what they would find was the evidence of who he really was.

It would end up in a file somewhere. Some of this would make the news, although scrubbed in some ways. The rest would be shuttled off to the FBI, and eventually, it would make it into the jacket of unsolved's attributed to The Judge. Because the dick knuckle fit The Judge's pattern for eliminating the dark assholes who deserved it.

Stalking over to her, I ignored the blood still spattering her cheeks and sticking to her clothes. It was all over me too. We'd need to clean up before we left. Rick wanted to help, but she'd told him to stay with the girls. It shouldn't have surprised me that the man-mountain was a gentle and soothing presence for them.

Fletcher too.

Cupping her face, I pulled her wild golden gaze up to meet mine. The emptiness in them, as if all emotion had been bled from her, infuriated me. Dropping my face to hers, I locked my mouth on her parted lips. From the first brush, it was like a jolt went from me to her, and she wrapped her arms around my neck.

All teeth, tongue, and heat, she bit and licked back at me as I devoured her mouth. The blood in my body pounded south, and I ached to fuck into her again, but I wasn't doing it in this filthy fucking dungeon.

She deserved a hell of a lot more than that.

"We need to shower," she said when she dragged her mouth from mine. Naked.

I liked that plan.

Unfortunately, when she said shower, she meant an icy one down here with the drain in the floor.

Fine.

I got to see those gorgeous tits of hers as she sprayed the cold water over herself, and then I helped her wash and she did the same. No amount of clinical detachment kept me from enjoying my soapy hands on her body or hers on mine.

When my dick kept poking her in the ass, she finally turned and looked up at me. "You deserve a reward, Cash."

It was the first time she'd said my name in quite that tone, and I swore it blew a fucking switch in my brain. When she went to her knees on that stone floor, I wanted to tell her no. This wasn't the—she wrapped her mouth around my all too eager cock.

Fuck.

My.

Life.

I gripped her damp hair as she worked my length with that hot tongue and kept pulling me into her throat. When fire kindled in those eyes, I lost it. The moment her jaw relaxed, she gave me the barest of nods and I fucked her mouth like it was the only place I wanted to be.

The first rush of release turned my spine molten and my balls dragged up tight. But it was how she held me, massaging my thighs as she drained the tension right out of me, that undid me. When I pulled free from her lips, I was shaking, but the endorphins were flooding my system.

Wild grin in place, I dragged her to her feet and kissed the hell out of her. But she wouldn't let me do more. "I swallowed the DNA evidence. We don't want to leave any more down here."

Fuck, that was hot. "Later," I promised her and she merely quirked a smile before we got dressed in the clothes she'd brought in a bag and bagged up our discards. The bodies would need to come up too, but not yet.

The next few hours were spent getting the girls to someone who could help them. The authorities weren't even mentioned, and I didn't bring them up. Of course, Vienna knew people. What surprised me—maybe it shouldn't because I saw a lot of Vienna in the older woman—was that one of the people she contacted was Mart.

During the time we waited for her, I went through the house, using forensic countermeasures and cleaning up all evidence of our presence. Fletcher dealt with security, then green as he'd turned, fury had burned through the illness when he turned up the recordings.

So. Many. Recordings.

The evidence here would damn not only the commissioner but a lot of other powerful men and politicians. "Make copies of everything," I told him. "These are people who have the pull to shut this investigation down. We want to know if the authorities don't get them."

He spared me a look, then glanced at Vienna. She nodded and pride flared in my chest. This was the kind of work I'd been trying to do for years, unencumbered by politics or policy. Eliminate the bad guys, save their victims, and punish the rest.

Then it was time to go, the girls had been cleaned up, dressed, and were calm. Maybe too calm. But they listened to Rick, and that was the important part. Vienna and I moved behind all of them, eliminating traces of our presence on the way out.

Vienna drove while Rick sat in the back of the van with the girls. The fact they took such comfort from him shouldn't have surprised me. While he only had eyes for Vienna, these girls were the walking wounded and he was like a bear with cubs. His rumbling almost soothed them and I kept my eyes away.

Anytime I glanced, I swore those kids shrank in on themselves. Better to let them have their space. Mart hustled out with another woman, someone else Vienna seemed to know, but she didn't introduce us. The girls were reluctant but whatever Mart said to them got them moving as she hustled them over to her car.

After a few words, a hug, Mart, the girls, and the other woman were gone, leaving the four of us alone on this highway in the middle of fucking nowhere.

"She's a nurse," Vienna said even though I hadn't asked. "She works with trauma victims and helps relocate victims of domestic violence. She can help the girls get home, or she can move them into her network, and they will disappear somewhere safe."

"They know what we look like."

She nodded. "It doesn't matter. Trauma sharpens some memories and destroys others. But those girls have suffered enough. If they decide to turn me in…"

I got it. Somehow, I didn't think they would. We still had bodies to deal with, but that was just another drive to a funeral home and a cemetery. Money exchanged hands, the bodies vanished inside, and the older man who accepted the payment spoke to her in rapid Italian.

Was this some kind of mafia-linked business? I had questions—a lot of them.

"He's trustworthy," was all she said and I nodded. It was enough for now. "Rick? Can you drive?" Exhaustion seemed to weigh on her all at once. We rearranged with me in the back with her and Fletcher up front.

We drove the rest of the night and into the next morning. For the first time since they'd let me out of the cell—they didn't blindfold me or make me get into the trunk. Vienna was sound asleep, curled up in my arms. I offered to close my eyes, but Rick only shrugged.

So, I finally got a look at where she lived—an abandoned,

"incomplete" subdivision in the middle of nowhere. There was literally no one to see them come and go. It was—brilliant. Absolutely brilliant.

As much as I hated surrendering her when we got in, I let Rick take her up to the bed and tuck her in. Then I went to work cleaning up what we'd taken with us and handing off what needed to be destroyed to Rick.

I was part of the Judge.

It felt good.

Or it had, until a full day later, when Vienna strolled into a *sex club* dressed in an outfit that left me torn between fucking her right there or gouging out the eyes of anyone who looked like they wanted to do the same thing.

Maybe both.

"This isn't a good idea," she informed me when I took the lead.

"I got this," I told her. I had since they mentioned the Castillo cartel. I knew a guy. I just didn't realize the prick would be *here*. Made sense, though.

Moans were coming from the writhing bodies on stage where one woman had her face buried in the cunt of another. Behind the woman on her knees, a man railed her. He kept slapping her ass, the sound a harsh contrast to the wet pumps of his dick.

Yeah, that wasn't pretty.

I'd never been to this particular club, but it was set up very similar to one they ran just outside of DC. This level was the strip club. Hell, it was actually a sex club, but the strip club was the front.

Members-only, which was how they got away with some raunchy ass shit in the open.

The basement would be the gambling floor. Although, this place was a lot less classy than the establishment I'd been to.

My contact, or acquaintance really, was heading our way,

holding up who had to be one of the most beautiful men I'd ever seen—if heavily inebriated—by the scruff.

Through the smoke-filled crowd, he caught sight of me, nodded, and started heading our way.

"Who's that?" Fletcher stage whispered, which wasn't really a whisper at all. I'd have to work with him on subtlety.

"One of the unofficial sons of the cartel," I answered without taking my gaze off of Parker Adair, one of the mother fucking pillars of the Castillo family. An inch, maybe two, shorter than me, he was nothing to sneeze at either. With cruel eyes and a permanent smirk plastered on his face like he constantly laughed at everyone else, he had incited fear in my associates of the FBI. The lucky few who had been fortunate enough to meet him.

Fletcher whistled, and Rick quietly stepped closer to Vienna's back, as if he hoped she hadn't noticed how he protected her.

She noticed. Just like she noticed how I snaked out a hand to mold against the sweet curve of her ass. My dark saint made no outward signs of exasperation, but she let out a long-suffering sigh.

My lips twitched.

Reed, Rick, and I knew every single fucking pair of eyes were glued to said ass in her tiny skirt that nearly had her ass cheeks hanging out. *Nearly.*

Of course, we would do what we could to stake *our* claim.

Well, Rick might just be protective, but I'd argue to Vienna that he was just as possessive as I was. It made me look better.

"Morgan," Parker drawled, wearing his signature smirk as he stopped in front of me.

"Park." I nodded, placing just enough pressure on Vienna's ass so she took a step toward me. She didn't fight it and that made me extremely happy. It probably showed in my huge fucking grin.

"What brings you here? This isn't your typical scene." He canted his head, and his black eyes twinkled under the flashing club lights. "Aren't you supposed to be missing? I'm pretty sure my brother told me his favorite Fed was gone."

I shrugged, my smile shrinking into a grin. "Not missing. Just… reprioritized my life."

"And found better company, I see." His gaze skated over Fletcher and paused on Rick, most likely due to his emotionless vibe. If I hadn't seen Rick with Vienna or seen how he cared for us the way he did, I'd have pegged him for prime serial killer material myself.

I snickered. That was technically true for all of us now. With the exception of Reed. His stomach was a little too weak for true violence.

Then his dark gaze landed appreciatively on Vienna, and I stiffened. Theoretically, I shouldn't be worried. His eyes weren't blue. Not that I'd ever fucking admit that, but Fletcher was onto something with Vienna's type.

"Hmm, hello, pet. Have we met before?" he purred, and Reed growled in response. Good for him, showing some of his territorial side.

Vienna lifted one delicate shoulder. "Is this your club?"

Smiling, Parker let go of his companion, who started to slump sideways but caught himself. The man probably realized he was among top-tier predators. That tended to sober anyone up fast.

"You could say I have a vested interest in it, yes." He glanced at me, probably trying to figure out how much I'd shared with them.

"Assume they know what I know."

"Then you can say this is a branch of the family business."

"Though not your branch," I returned. "What brings you here?"

He huffed out a laugh. "Maikel is on the shit list at the moment, and I had to come deliver a message. I also had to collect this *pendejo*." Parker nodded at the man next to him. "I have big plans for him, and he can't deliver if he's wasted and in debt up to his ears. His brothers would be very unhappy with him," he said in a firm tone, more of a warning for his friend than us.

The man tried to smile, but it was a pained grimace instead as he ended up scrubbing a hand down his face. "Yeah, I get it. Just don't mention this to Lake. 'Kay? He'll have my ass in a sling."

Parker rolled his eyes and shifted his gaze back to me. "Don't think I missed your non-answer. Why are you here?"

Pandemonium broke out somewhere else in the club. It was muffled enough that it wasn't in the main room, but someone, a man, was throwing a tantrum and from the sounds of it, he was trashing whatever room he was in.

Park just smiled.

"I take it that's your doing?" I asked drily. Andre had always been the professional one. Serious, smart, and a fucking terror when he needed to be. But his brother? This man was off the charts wicked smart, and he played too much. His version of play usually got people tortured or killed.

I'd always liked the guy.

"If I have to leave the compound, I'm making it worth my while to be here." He cracked his neck on each side, wearing that insane grin the entire time. Yeah, he was my kind of guy.

"We're here to get some information. We've been told it's a hotbed of gossip here."

That sobered Parker up. "Only because Maikel is a lazy fuck who doesn't run a tight ship. Who are you looking for?"

"I think I see the person we should start with," Vienna said quietly, her gaze tracking an old man across the room.

He caught sight of Vienna and paled. Goddamn, I love the fear she struck in the shriveled-up hearts of men. I shifted behind her, pressing my raging erection into the small of her back.

Half expecting her to stiffen, I almost groaned when she ground against me.

A few tall, beautiful women walked up with eyes on Parker. Both looked like employees, wearing delicate chains attached to collars that hid nothing. They drank up Parker like he was a rock star and they wanted to drop and suck him off right here.

Not surprising given his well-known…proclivities.

The perky blonde woman slid her hand over his chest as she whispered something I couldn't catch over the music.

He caught her hand in a tight grip as he forced her away. "Sorry, love, I'm not on the market anymore. Spread the word," he said with a tight-lipped smile. The woman gasped in just the smallest amount of pain, or maybe surprise, as she stepped back into her friend.

I raised my brows. That shocked me. I didn't know him well, hardly at all, but he wasn't the settling down type.

"You're off the market?" I asked.

With the two women quickly retreating and the man next to him doing his best to appear like he wasn't hanging on his every word, Parker flashed us a devilish grin. "Enough to count."

"Does the lucky lady know that?"

He chuckled, and the sound was smooth like aged bourbon—everything most women loved. I squeezed Vienna's side to let her know not to get any ideas. And my dark saint rubbed her ass against me in punishment.

Fucking hell. If she wanted to talk to the old man, she needed to quit. Otherwise, I really would fuck her right here.

"No, but isn't that half the fun?" He winked and clapped his friend on the back. "I think it's time to get you home." He looked to me. "Try not to cause too much mayhem. I'd hate to have to come back."

He lightly bumped shoulders with me as he moved past.

Fletcher and Rick stared after them, as Vienna locked gazes with the man across the room. Like a deer caught in headlights, he was almost afraid to move.

Whistling, Fletcher tucked some hair behind his ear. "He's not much bigger than me—" sure if you don't count the forty or so pounds of hard muscle—"but he seems giant. He's like a tiger in a cage full of kittens."

"Like I said, that was a pillar of the Castillo Cartel," I repeated, because that explained everything. Someone like that, who grew up with those sharks, had to be dangerous to survive.

Vienna was already gone, floating between sex acts to reach the old man.

The music cut off, the lights turned on, and gasps filled the room.

That wasn't good. Whatever Park did was about to spill over into the club.

My long strides ate up the distance Vienna had put between us. I grabbed the man's arm and growled, "This way."

The harsh fluorescent lights had wet dicks flopping out and raccoon-faced women scrambling for some kind of coverage as a fight broke out in the corner. Yeah, whatever was happening in the back was spreading.

I steered the man toward the hallway labeled employees only, trusting that Vienna and the guys were on my heels. The hall had a few women stepping out of rooms, but when they saw us, they disappeared and shut the doors with a resounding snick of locks sliding home.

At the end, just before an exit, there was a bathroom. That looked like a great spot for an interrogation. And if Fletcher couldn't hold his dinner…well, he'd have a toilet nearby.

I loved how some jobs worked out perfectly.

Kicking the door open, I shoved the man in. Vienna was

after me, then Fletcher, and bringing up the rear, Rick locked us in.

"John Martin," Vienna crossed her arms. "I didn't think you'd be haunting the same spots so soon."

He straightened his tie, but there was nothing he could do to bring the color back to his face. "Yeah, well, I didn't think you'd be after me this quickly. I gave you what you wanted the last time," he grumbled. Sullen was never a good look on anyone. Especially anyone past the age of sixty.

She laughed. "You told me you were trying to put together a revenge game. I told you I'd let you live for now, but you were to report back to me if you heard anything about Red Death."

Red Death? I turned to glance at her. I hadn't heard this.

"Why do you think I'm here, dammit?" He snapped, and Rick took a step forward.

Holding up his hands, he backpedaled real damn quick. "Listen, I don't have any more information for you. Today is the first day I've been back, and people are being tighter-lipped than usual."

Vienna nodded like that was understandable. "So, no word on Red Death? Still no idea if it's a place or a person?"

He blew out a relieved breath as if he was past the danger of dying. "No. I've tapped every single contact I have and outside of the one I learned about it from, no one else has even heard of it. It's like the damned thing doesn't exist."

Vienna's eyes flickered. "Did you try the burner number again?"

"It's disconnected. Like it never was." Sweat started to bead around his hairline.

"What about Daddy? Did you ever hear anything about the Network being upset with him for passing on certain jobs?" She pulled a small stiletto blade from under the band of her skirt and caressed the edge with the pad of her thumb as her tawny eyes locked on him.

John Martin's words tumbled out in nervous succession. "Yes, I mean. There have been a few jobs punted his way and when he passed, people talked. But before you ask. I don't know where the jobs originated from."

"What were the jobs?"

"Shit, you're asking me things that happened a few years ago. Do you know how bad my memory is when it didn't affect my business?" He ran a hand through his thinning white hair.

"Try."

"Okay. Shit. I think there was one where a man was the target, but he ran a legit business. No crimes that Thackery would see as a reason for death. But word was, someone in the Network wanted to take over his business as a front, and he wouldn't sell."

"No idea who wanted the hit?" she asked conversationally, but I saw the way the skin tightened around her eyes. I almost stepped in, but Vienna wouldn't appreciate me butting into her investigation.

I'd pick my battles as long as she let me in all aspects of her mission. I could keep an unbiased eye on her and the evidence she collected.

"No. But I know the company!" He nearly shouted in trembling excitement. "It was Tremaine Enterprises."

"The gold mining company?" Fletcher asked, stepping forward.

John nodded. "That's all I know. Can I go now?"

Vienna studied him, then slowly nodded. "You can. However, the first order of your revenge game is to wipe Reuben's gambling debt."

He sputtered. "Do you know how much he owes? I'd either have to get the brothers' sign-off, or half a dozen investors."

"But you secured a location for the revenge game, did you not?"

"No! I've floated the idea around, and I think I found good partners for it, but there are no guarantees yet!"

"I have faith that you can make it happen. But Reuben's taken care of first. That's the price for you to live." She tightened her grip on the handle of her blade like she was fine with either option he picked, take care of Reuben…or not.

"Fine. Fine, okay. That's no skin off my nose. I'll make it work."

Rick stepped back and opened the door, and just when I was trying to figure out the best way to tell her I was familiar with Tremaine Enterprises and who the new owner was, she put away the blade and faced us.

"I'll be leaving at the end of the week for a day or two."

Why did I feel like it had something to do with that damned eye flicker?

VIENNA

AS SOON AS I was through the door, I sighed.

It was good to be back home. Right after we left the club, my brain started working overtime, running in multiple directions. Possibilities, people I needed to track down, the superficial satisfaction of getting one tiny step closer to finding Daddy's killer.

But now that I was back in my space, I wanted to push every wild and driving thought from my head and just *be*. Take a night for ourselves before I began the mad manhunt tomorrow.

I'd told the guys I would need a day or two at the end of the week, but I wasn't sure if I could make it that long.

"You said you wanted to rest tonight. That look on your face doesn't look like you're taking time for yourself," Rick admonished softly as he lined our shoes up on the rack.

Wrapping my arms around him, I buried my nose in his chest as Fletcher and Cash put their shoes up too. "I'm sorry, Rick. Before you all came into my life, there was no such thing as downtime. Sometimes, it's hard to turn it off."

"We'll help you." He kissed the top of my head, then set me gently away from him. "Go on up and take a bath. I'll bring you a glass of wine."

I hummed gratefully. "Just a small glass tonight."

He nodded.

When I turned, both Cash and Fletcher were nowhere to

be seen. Fletcher probably had a few things to take care of in the study. As for Cash, I had no idea where he went. That should bother me more than it did.

But some time over the last few weeks, I'd really started to trust him.

Even as he challenged me and set my blood on fire, I started to…need him. Very similarly to how I needed Rick or I needed Fletcher. Then again, so different.

The sound of running water reached my ears before I made it to the bathroom. Lavender-scented steam engulfed me as I opened the door. Fletcher straightened and gave me a quick, flirty grin.

"Your bath awaits, Drew." He stepped up to me, placing his hands on my waist and dropping a kiss to my upturned lips. He lingered long enough to start building that molten fire in my core, then he stepped away, too smug not to know the way his gentle touch and kisses affected me. "You'll get wine in a minute, but relax. If you don't, Rick won't be happy."

As tired as I was after the last twenty-four hours, my little pincushion was still able to pull a smile from me.

"Thank you," I murmured as I stripped and stepped into the steaming hot water. I turned to catch Fletcher, hoping I could entice him to join me, but he was already gone.

Well. I had to love how they took care of me, but they were missing one very important need I had at the moment.

The hot water lapped at my skin as I sunk down until it reached my chin. It soothed the aches on my sore body and was the perfect way to wash off the filth from a job taking down men like the commissioner and the Sweeper.

The door opened, and Cash walked in.

"Wow, I can't believe Rick let you bring the wine." One side of my mouth twisted up as I lifted a hand to take the half-full glass from him.

"We may have arm wrestled for it."

"Really?" I couldn't imagine Rick doing that at all.

He laughed and crouched next to the tub. "No. He offered to let me bring it up. I think that was his way of rewarding me for a job well done." Cash leaned forward like he was about to share some deep secret. "Between you and me, I'm more fond of your reward system."

I barked out a laugh, sloshing the water from my sudden movement. "I can drop a hint to Rick if that's your preferred reward…"

Grimacing, he shook his head. "No, that's quite all right. I love your rewards so much because they come from you."

"Mmhm." I took a sip of the wine, letting the cool liquid roll over my tongue. It was light and clean, the perfect way to end the night. Or start it, depending on if I got my way with one or two of the guys.

While Cash was here—

Shaking his head again, he gave me a rueful smile. "I love the way you're looking at me right now, my dark saint." He trailed a finger down my cheek. "But Rick was very strict in his instructions. You are to enjoy your bath, and if I'm not back downstairs in three minutes, he won't make my favorite breakfast anymore."

I almost commented on how cute it was that Rick made special meals for the guys, but I kept my thoughts to myself. I didn't want my teasing to change their relationship on any level. Maybe in a few months, I could give Cash a hard time.

Not Rick, however. He was too thoughtful to pick on that way.

Cash dropped his own consuming kiss on my lips, pushing his tongue in my mouth, dancing with mine. When he pulled back, I struggled to get my breath back.

"And on that note, I'm leaving." His hard cock straining against his pants told me how much he did not want to follow instructions.

I sighed as the door shut softly, leaving me alone. There

was always hope for when I got out. At least one of the guys would sleep with me. Fletcher joined us more often than not anymore.

There were soft sounds on the other side of the door, but no one came to join me. I was only slightly disappointed. Rick and Fletcher were probably exhausted and getting ready for bed, even if neither one would go to sleep until I was tucked between them.

Once the water started to chill, I let the drain out and grabbed the towel Fletcher had laid out for me. With my glass in hand and the towel tucked around my body, I opened the door to stop short.

Warm candlelight danced over the room as Rick stood shirtless at the foot of the bed with his arms crossed. Fletcher had stripped down to briefs and sprawled out on the bed with one arm behind his head. His cock thickened before my eyes.

Then there was Cash. He was also shirtless, but he had his arms propped on the dresser as he leaned into it. The gaze he cast at the guys wasn't excitement over a pending foursome. If I had to label it, it would be more of inconvenient irritation.

Rick smiled softly, and I saw what he was trying to do. I knew what I wanted.

But—I couldn't enjoy myself if not everyone wanted to be here.

"Gentlemen," I murmured. "This is a pleasant surprise." It was. I couldn't explain the adrenaline that pounded through me every single time a potential clue regarding my father's death dangled in front of me. When they were snatched away, it was worse.

"It was a long day," Rick said quietly. "It's been a long few days, and we thought you could use a little distraction."

I could use a little distraction. Rick had more than proven he would do whatever I needed or wanted, but he would also tell me what he needed. Fletcher was getting there. Sometimes, we both had to push each other, but we were willing to do that.

My gaze went from Rick to Fletcher, the wicked smile on his face said he was already making sensual plans. The heat those smiles ignited in my core was quick flaming, incendiary, and consuming. But my desire aside, the combination of candlelight, soft jazz, wine, and a hot bath with the promise of pleasure?

This was about more than just satisfying my baser desires and lust. If I were honest about it, it had been for a while.

"I appreciate that," I said slowly, not closing in on any of them. Instead, I drained the last of the wine. The smaller glass only helped to take the edge off. It definitely didn't relax my mind or the information I swore I was still rifling through, trying to figure out what it meant.

Why the revenge game? What job had my father turned down that incited Red Death's wrath? Had it been wrath? Was Red Death even a person? My conversation with Horatio on this subject had been less than enlightening. He wanted me to keep my distance from anything Red Death related, because too many roads led to Red Death, and until we knew which one we were on?

I understood his caution. It just didn't sit well with my need to find the person who took Daddy from me and punish them.

"But?" Fletcher said, sitting up. Concern flickered in his eyes. Blue eyes. They all had them, but they were all so different from each other. Those differences captivated me the way each man pulled at me.

Pulled and filled. More than just sexually. This was not a position I'd ever expected to find myself in.

"But not all of you want to be here," I said, setting the wine glass down on the dresser. Cash straightened at my nearness. His tousled hair fell over his forehead, making him look younger but in no way softer.

Rick and Fletcher had softer sides. Cash, I suspected, did not. He was all tense muscle, sharp wit, cutting mind, and demanding, damn near animalistic, sensuality. I'd gone from irritation to intrigue to indelible need for him.

But not like this… not forced.

"Worried about me, Dark Saint?" A growl underscored the words. There was that name again. Dark Saint. I'd been trying to ignore it since the first time the words fell from his lips. I wasn't a saint, but there was something wicked and altogether inviting about the reverence in his voice when he called me a dark saint.

A compulsion to become exactly that. I could lose myself in these men so utterly. I thought, maybe, it was already too late to extract myself from their lives.

Too late and I was too far gone. I didn't *want* to part from them. If Cash ended up betraying us—

I pushed that thought aside, the doubt creeping into my veins carrying its poison of fear. Losing Daddy had left a wound in my soul that was finally healing. Losing them might tear my soul in half.

Somehow, I doubted there would be any coming back from that.

"You don't want to share me with them." That wasn't a question. He'd made comments about understanding I already had relationships with them. That he got it was a package deal.

"I never said that," Cash countered, but his irritation remained a presence within the room. The rasp of it like sandpaper over my skin. "Rick over there said I was welcome to watch or to go. But it was your rules here, not mine."

Ah.

Understanding kindled within me.

Cash really, really liked control. Anticipation shivered through me. I liked it when he took control. All that violence he kept on a chain beneath his cool intellect and biting wit.

When he let it out, the beast of it was all-encompassing, and I was not ashamed at all to admit how fucking much I'd enjoyed his dominance-fueled pain-edging pleasure. The marks lingered for days after…

"So, you don't mind a foursome?" I canted my head, keeping my tone light. To be honest, I'd never had a three-some before Fletcher and Rick. I'd never allowed anyone to fuck my ass before Rick.

I'd never given *anyone* control over me or my body before these men. The thought of granting someone else the freedom with my body? It was anathema. But not these three men.

That realization brought with it the crystalized clarity that even Cash had earned that privilege. I enjoyed the push and the pull. I thrived in the promise of violence punctuating every single caress and kiss, but I *trusted* him.

I trusted them all.

Instead of blowing off my question, Cash studied me then straightened so that instead of keeping his back to Rick and Fletcher, he faced them. "Guys, don't do it for me."

Blunt and to the point.

"Aww, you're going to hurt my feelings," Fletcher said with just the right amount of drama. The twinkle in his eyes almost made me laugh. Almost. "Not to mention the big guy, right, Big Guy?"

Rick didn't roll his eyes, but he just gave a grunt of sound. If I hadn't caught the faint twitch of his lips, I wouldn't have seen the humor he suppressed. Fletcher was so good for him. They were so good for each other.

"You aren't remotely attracted to me," Cash said flatly, unmoved by Fletcher's teasing. With that, Cash looked at me. "I'll never say no to trying something if you want to. Just—I tend to be a greedy guy when I have my girl."

I rolled that over in my mind. He was right. When we were together, he possessed my body, my thoughts, the very air I breathed. It was a drugging experience that I loved.

But I didn't think he realized how it actually was between Fletcher, Rick, and me when we were together.

"What do you think we do when we're sexing it up with Drew?" Fletcher seemed to take pity on Cash, losing most of his smart-ass attitude. "It's not like I suck Rick's dick or vice versa. Every moment is about Drew. Her wants, her desires, her pleasure. Now, you would have to share, but as good as I am with my dick, I can admit that the experience can be more pleasurable for her when there are spare parts." Fletcher rolled his eyes like he couldn't believe he had to explain this.

Cash stiffened, then canted his head.

Rick stayed quiet, content to let Cash work this out on his own.

I was of the same mind. I'd answer any of his questions that he had, and tell him anything he wanted to know. But ultimately, being here or not was his choice.

He leveled those mesmerizing turquoise eyes on me. "What do you want?"

What *did* I want?

I'd been afraid to ask myself that question during their exchange. I did want all three of them together, connected to me during the most intimate act. But only if they were all as lost in the pleasure as I was.

Whether Cash was the one uncomfortable with the group act, or Rick or Fletcher with his presence didn't matter. Or I should say it all mattered equally.

"When I've been with both Fletcher and Rick, I've loved the closeness we had. I also love our individual time together. For us, I think both are important and necessary. Would I love for you to join us? Yes, I would. But only if that's what you want. I won't pressure you. I won't force you. A foursome is not a condition of your place with us." I held my breath as Cash rubbed his fingers over his forehead.

"I don't think I can just watch. As greedy as I am, I think that would be torture for me. That's not *who I am*."

Rick nodded. "Then you can participate. But if Vienna says stop, whatever you're doing, you stop."

I wanted to cover my mouth to hide the budding smile. I loved that Rick was protecting me like this. And I didn't doubt that Cash would stop if I demanded it, but that wasn't how our love-making worked.

It was wild, feral, and all-consuming.

With four of us, sex would require a bit more…coordination. But I was excited to experience all of us together, if Cash could go into it without reservations.

"No ass grabs. No tickling ball sacks or anything like that." He once again directed his comments to Rick and Fletcher.

This was good. He was setting his boundaries. Giving this thing between us a chance, for me.

The budding excitement unfurled deep in the pit of my stomach. My pussy pulsed in anticipation.

Rick gave one quick shake of his head. "That's not how this works anyway."

That was as good a confirmation as Cash was going to get.

Blowing out a hard breath, Cash stalked toward me, cupping the sides of my neck as his thumbs caressed my jawline.

"Fuck, you want this. I can see the desire heating those gorgeous fucking eyes of yours. They undo a man, you know that?" I didn't answer, and he didn't wait for me to. "All right, Dark Saint—"

There was that endearment again that felt like both possession and worship. I soaked in the meaning as he dipped his head to run his nose against mine.

"—I'll try this. For you. I can't make any promises for next time."

His gaze burned into me, seeming to enforce his words. Cash needed to know I was okay if this wasn't his thing.

Of course, I would be. But I wanted to make this an experience he enjoyed rather than just endured. I hoped the guys would be okay with it, and I trusted they would share if they weren't.

"Then this time, Cash…You call the shots."

His pupils flared as my words registered. He at least loved that.

"I'M CALLING THE SHOTS?" Cash asked, stroking his thumb against my pulse point. "And everyone listens?"

"I'm totally down with you calling the shots as long as you don't verify everything we say like ten times. She said you call the shots, man," Fletcher said. "So—like, call them."

The only one who said nothing was Rick. Cash transferred his gaze from me to my beautiful giant of a man. With his hands on my jaw and my throat, I couldn't look away from Cash. But I could read his expression, his eyes were intense and his lips compressed.

He seemed to search Rick for confirmation or denial. Or maybe he was just looking for what challenge Rick would present to my offer of ceding control. The lack of absolute hesitation in me should trouble me on some level.

A distant part of me seemed to be weighing each action I took. From the moment I broke Daddy's rules with Rick, I'd ventured across a line I couldn't—and in truth wouldn't—come back from. I was so far gone now, there was no hope for me.

But this was *exactly* where I wanted to be.

"Good," Cash said finally. Fletcher let out an impatient huff, but it was Rick's soft chuckle that fountained the delight within me. "Lose the towel, Dark Saint. You get nothing to hide that beautiful body from us while I'm in charge."

I didn't move away or attempt to withdraw. I just gave a little tug and the towel fell. It never hit the floor, whisked away by Rick. Cash tilted my head back, tracing his thumb under my jaw as he drank in the sight of me.

There were still marks from his teeth on one of my breasts. He licked his lips before dipping his head to press the gentlest of kisses there. It was so very much at odds with his more primal demands that it clogged my throat with emotion.

I swallowed back the hum of sound, then Cash delivered a stinging slap to my ass that forced the air out of me, and I snapped my gaze to his.

"Rule number one, don't hold back anything," he informed me with blazing eyes. My cunt clenched in anticipation as he rubbed in the heat to my burning cheek. "You want to scream, you scream. You want to moan, we get to hear it. Every single sound, whether it's their dicks fucking you or mine, we get them all. Understood?"

Fuck. "Yes," I said, licking my suddenly dry lips. Cash took this being in charge seriously. "You get all my sounds."

"Good," he murmured before dropping his lips to mine and delivering a bruising kiss that robbed me of my breath. His tongue demanded access, and I opened to him as he deepened it. This wasn't just a kiss of passion but one of possession—a stamp of ownership and demand.

Fuck me, I loved it.

A whimper of a moan escaped me when he dragged his head back and his eyes seemed to flare again at the sound. "Much better."

He glanced past me a moment, and though his expression never shifted, I swore the temperature in the room skyrocketed.

"Dark Saint, go suck off Fletcher. He's been a good boy and very helpful."

"Yes!" Fletcher let out a laugh.

"But don't let him come," Cash continued. "And I want this ass up in the air the whole time." By this ass, he definitely meant mine because he rubbed his hand over it. The grip he'd exerted at the club had been equally possessive and hot, but this was so much more than that.

Turning at his urging, I found Rick watching me with quiet pleasure in his eyes. I stroked my fingers over Rick's chest and up to his jaw as I passed him. He caught my hand and pressed a kiss to my palm before releasing me.

Fletcher was all eager smiles as I crawled onto the bed. He'd moved so his head was on the pillows. His beautifully curved and pierced cock waited for me, almost vibrating from the tension.

He'd already ditched his briefs, and I winked at him as I bent my head down to lick him from his base to his tip.

"Fuck. Yes." Fletcher let out a sigh.

"Rick," Cash said. "Does that ass of hers give you ideas?"

"Yes," Rick answered as I wrapped my mouth around Fletcher's tip. "I like her ass and her cunt. Both are sweet."

Being talked about in the third person was far more interesting than I thought. As I swallowed around Fletcher's cock, I wiggled my ass in invitation. A hand came down on the other cheek and it lit up, sending my cunt clenching. I sucked Fletcher all the way into my throat, and he cursed as his hips surged up. The force of his thrust could have gagged me, but I had a very strong reflex.

"Goddamn," Fletcher said, running his hand through my hair. "Do that again."

Did he mean me or—a second hand cracked against my left cheek, the one already blazing from earlier, and this time, a muffled moan escaped me.

"Goddamn, I bet her cunt tightens up perfectly if you do that while your dick is in her." Fletcher's eagerness made me smile as I went to work, sucking, licking, and swallowing his cock. They tasted so good, and I loved tracing his piercing, my sweet pincushion.

"It does," Rick declared, and then a cock thrust into me. It was so hurried and abrupt, I had no time to adjust to the size. I writhed, and a hand came down again as he kept pushing until I swore the pain was just there on the other side of the pleasure, right on the edge.

That was Rick, filling me to the brim. Rick, who stretched me so gloriously. Rick began to pump into me at a pace designed to throw me off, but then he'd deliver a stinging slap at odd intervals, and I was in heaven.

Every noise that spilled from the back of my throat pulled a similar one from Fletcher as he dug his fingers into my hair. We were both on a high that didn't have an end in sight.

As much as I enjoyed what Rick was doing to me, I enjoyed this act just as much. Bringing them pleasure with my mouth. Pleasing them in a way that so often made them lose control.

It was a power rush unlike any other.

But it was also about making them feel good. Wanted. Appreciated.

I forced Fletcher's cock to the back of my throat, his piercing rubbing against my tongue, and I swallowed. Letting up even while maintaining the suction, I lowered again. He shouted nonsensical expletives as he started directing my head with light pressure.

This was the high I craved.

Then he started to flex his hips and his dick grew harder. I lifted away with a pop of my mouth, saliva dripping from my lips to his cock. He groaned, tipping his head back as his fingers snagged on a tangle when he dropped his hands.

"God damn, Drew. That's better than any porno I've ever watched."

"He was about to come," I gasped as Rick landed another stinging slap to my ass, then soothed the spot as he continued to rail into me, his own soft grunts falling on my ears now that Fletcher had quieted down.

"Hmm, I saw that. Good girl." Cash swiped a tender hand down my back in warm approval.

I turned my head to catch a glimpse of him. His brilliant gaze locked on where Rick's cock entered my pussy over and over. The heat in his eyes ratcheted up the temperature by several degrees, pushing me closer to orgasm.

He was enjoying this. Enjoying watching Rick take me, even if he was conflicted by it, as the slight downward tilt to his mouth suggested.

Then he glanced at me. "You're close, aren't you? Let's see what I can do to help. Rick, don't come yet, but draw out her pleasure as long as you can." Cash licked his fingers and slid his hand between my stomach and the bed, and found my sensitive, engorged clit. He made small tight circles with just enough pressure that I tossed my head back on a loud scream, quaking with the power of my release.

"Shit," Rick muttered as he gripped my hips, pulling me back into his thrusts, and then he was gone.

I was left clenching and pulsing around nothing. I was both wrecked and left dissatisfied. Before I met the guys, something like this wouldn't have bothered me. In fact, I might have preferred it to avoid absolutely any chance of pregnancy, condoms or no. But with Rick, Fletcher, and Cash, I was left wanting in the worst possible way.

Resting my cheek against the bedspread, I caught my breath as so many hands caressed and grazed every inch of my body in butterfly light touches. It was soothing, sweet, but stoking that trembling fire from the emptiness they had left me with.

"Roll over, let us see you," Cash growled, with every bit of dominance in his voice.

I ungracefully twisted to my back and glanced up at the three hovering faces above me.

Fletcher was no longer at my head and was on his knees next to me. Some damp tendrils of hair stuck to the sides of his face, letting me know I'd pleased him. Rick, my beautiful Rick, was at the foot of the bed. His skin was flushed, and a light sheen of sweat glistened over his taut muscles. It was the best I'd ever seen him.

Then there was Cash standing beside the bed with his thighs pressed into the mattress. He was the only one who hadn't gotten any physical enjoyment yet, but the intensity in his face said his restraint wouldn't last much longer.

I couldn't wait.

"She's beautiful just fucked, isn't she?" Cash cupped my breast in his hand, testing the weight before pinching the nipple between his fingers. I sucked in a breath at the small bite of pain as my pussy clenched.

Rick and Fletcher murmured their agreements as they watched Cash slowly and methodically learn the dips and valleys of my body all over again.

"I think Vienna deserves a reward, wouldn't you say, boys?" Cash's dark grin did dirty, dirty things to my thoughts.

"Vienna absolutely deserves a reward." Rick cupped my feet, using his thumbs to press into my arches, eliciting a crude whine from my throat.

"I say we go with Drew's style of reward." Fletcher waggled his eyebrows, but neither man smiled. They were too mesmerized by my body and my face.

"That's a great idea," Cash agreed, then shifted Rick to the side. He grabbed the back of my knees and jerked me to the end of the bed and pushed my thighs up to my chest. Dropping to his knees, he blew cool air over my clit and I shivered. "Vienna, keep your eyes on Rick and Fletcher. Boys, show her how much you enjoy watching her getting eaten out."

Then he devoured my fucking pussy like it was his last

meal. My eyes rolled back in my head, and he stopped. Bastard.

"Uh-uh. Eyes on Rick and Fletcher. Every time you close your eyes, I'll stop."

Dragging my eyes open, I found Rick and Fletcher on either side of Cash, their hands slowly tugging at their hard, angry cocks. The hunger in their gazes nearly undid me, but I refused to let the pleasure pull me under.

Cash licked around my clit, then sucked it into his mouth for a few seconds before releasing it. Then he'd start all over again, with more pressure and teeth. He speared me with two fingers, curling up into my G-spot and then twisting his hand, so his knuckles rubbed along the sensitive lips.

I started to turn my head into my hand, then stopped. Cash noticed because he pulled away for the barest moments before murmuring *good girl*, then went back to his sweet torture.

Every time I was close, he backed off.

He seemed determined to drive me stark raving mad. Fisting the covers, I kept my eyes open, and it went against the rules of torture to let the sounds out, but I fucking did it. I groaned, moaned, and *whimpered* when he backed off again. My thighs trembled, but his hands were firm shackles keeping me in place.

"Cash," I pushed his name out, and he lifted his head up to stare at me with the same blazing hunger in his eyes that was written all over Rick and Fletcher. "I need…"

Eyebrows raised, he dared me with a slow smirk on his face. The fact he was damp with the evidence of my *need* all over his face just made his lips glisten in the candlelight. "What do you need, Dark Saint?"

He twisted his fingers inside me, curling them as though in invitation. I clamped down on him. Even as my inner muscles trembled and spasmed, I didn't want to let him go.

"All of you," I said, the broken note as close to begging as

I'd allow. But I had a feeling he could push—All at once, he moved, and then Rick, oh, my glorious Rick, pulled my legs up to his chest and he slammed into me.

The first thrust made me see stars, the second launched me as all the tension Cash had wound through me expanded. Hot tears spilled down my cheeks as Rick hugged my legs to his chest. Every push of his hips lifted me up off the bed, and I arched my back, fighting to keep my eyes open.

I swore I saw the thought go through Cash's mind a moment before the words came out of his mouth. "Can she handle anal?"

"Yes," Rick crooned in a voice that left me shaking for real.

"Swap then," Cash commanded. "Fletcher…"

"Oh, hell yes."

A flurry of motion had me flipped over as Rick pulled away, and then I was sinking down on Fletcher's pierced tip. I was so sensitive and still spasming that it had me shaking all over again. Slick fingers pushed into my ass. Trying to force those muscles to relax when Fletcher was helping me ride him, and another bone-shaking orgasm threatened, was no easy feat.

But my hand was in Fletcher's hair, Rick's lips were pressed against my throat, and I kept my gaze on Cash's the whole time.

When Rick swapped his fingers for his dick, I moaned. This was it—the perfect pinnacle of pain and pleasure. It was only made more perfect by the fact I had all three of them there.

A stream of invectives fell from Fletcher's lips, and I glanced down to collide my gaze with his. Then he whispered two words that tipped the balance.

"Love you," spilled from his lips as Rick sank all the way home.

Words Rick echoed against my ear, a pledge and a promise. "Love you."

I twisted and writhed between them as they found their rhythm. The pure force of them stretched me beyond what should be reasonable, and I wanted more.

I wanted…

"Dark Saint," Cash said, like he answered the desperate desire before I could give it voice. He was right there, his beautiful uncut length in his hand as he tangled his fingers in my hair. "Can you handle all of us?"

Can I? I didn't laugh. I didn't need to. This wasn't about humor, even if it was fun. It was about whether I could, and it was far more about what I needed. I licked my lips.

"That's my good girl," he whispered, fisting my hair. The moment he brushed his dick to my lips, I parted them and swallowed around him. "Sweet girl. That's it, fucking take us. Take every filthy fucking inch that you want."

When he used his hand to guide me, I let go. Let my muscles all relax. They had me—all of them. Fletcher's fingers bit into my hips as he lifted or held me steady while he thrust upward.

Rick's hand came down on my ass in a crack that sent hot washes of pleasure through me with his every stroke or left me craving more as he massaged in the heat.

Cash?

Cash held my gaze utterly captive as he began to fuck my mouth. The command came more silently than the others, but I loosened my jaw, relaxing it so he could thrust all the way into my throat. The salty bitterness of pre-cum swirled in my mouth. The room was thick with the scent of all of them.

They were everywhere, pounding into my skin, into my soul. I'd reveled in finding Rick, reveled in the discovery that he was as gentle as he was fierce. That he could care for me on such a deep level. Then Fletcher, oh my sweet pincushion who needed us to keep him safe, to keep the darkness away from him and who wielded his keen intellect with surgical precision.

Now Cash, the infuriating man who answered the darkness in my own soul. Who walked these same shadowy paths without remorse. I surrendered to all of them. The orgasm shattered me as I came, riding the waves of their relentless thrusts as they pushed me through one and into another.

Fletcher swore as he came, his whole body shaking, then Rick, but Cash held out, and when he finally came, I swallowed, determined to keep all of them in me.

Mine.

All mine.

"FUCK," I hissed as I threw the phone on the bed and it bounced to the end. Never had I allowed my emotions to bleed through on anything, but today it just couldn't be helped.

Ratio was the one who told John Martin about Red Death. He was the line I needed to start picking at to finally get answers, and he was out of the country on business for a while. Completely unavailable.

The man at least sent me a note.

My deepest apologies. I have important business in SA that will take me at least a few weeks. When I get back, let's grab dinner.

That was it.

"What's burned your biscuit today?" Fletcher flopped next to me and roped an arm around my shoulders.

He *loved* me.

I turned my head, and he nuzzled the soft skin just under my ear, then nipped playfully. Sinking into his embrace allowed me to gather my thoughts. Take a much-needed breather.

"What's wrong?" Cash stalked into my bedroom, freshly showered and rubbing a towel over his head.

I shamelessly took in his long, chiseled form. His body really was a work of art. Especially that ass...

"Okay, man, new house rule. No walking around in briefs

for you. It's an unfair advantage to the rest of us…Actually, Rick looks damn good in briefs too. It's unfair to me. I'm going to have to do hip thrusts to work on my ass curve, then I'll be wearing a thong around the house. Just wait. When I have a shaped ass, it's over for you bitches." Fletcher pointed a finger at a smirking Cash.

Since our foursome, Cash seemed to have a greater amount of patience for Fletcher's colorful comments. Was he even aware? From the satisfied glint in Fletcher's eyes, my little pincushion was.

I grinned like a lunatic because Fletcher just made my heart happy. Life would be soaked in tones of gray without him in it.

"Anyway, what's got you in a huff?" Cash stepped into the bathroom to drop the towel in the hamper and came back to perch on the end of the bed. The clean scent of soap wreathed off his fresh-from-a-steamy-shower body. Maybe I should have joined him.

"Something John Martin said. When we met with him a few months ago, he said he had only ever learned about Red Death from the Vanisher." I knew the Vanisher to be Horatio. The accountant. But I hadn't told them. Not yet. It wasn't my secret. When I'd met him for dinner, I'd been so stunned by the revelation, I hadn't asked him. Dammit. "I had planned to take a trip to see him—" Cash showed his displeasure at the sound of the Vanisher's name with a severe frown, "—but he's out of the country. Even if I tried to find his location and track him down, I doubt he would respond anymore. It was a very short blunt message."

Cash dropped his head, and I could see the wheel turning over in his mind. "Every case is a mystery. We might not need to speak to *him* right now. Not sure talking to anyone with that nom de guerre is a good idea. Tell me who Red Death is and why you think they're behind your father's death. Walk me through everything."

I nodded. The way Cash barreled his way into my life and business used to grate on my nerves. He was too heavy-handed at times. Unapologetic and callous. But now that I knew him a little better, I understood that was just the way his brain worked. He saw everything in puzzles and couldn't be bothered to soften his words for the sake of others.

That would be inefficient in his eyes.

And right then, I appreciated a second pair of eyes. Especially ones that were familiar with tracking and investigating.

"Let me grab my computer, then we can go over what I have." I hopped up and opened the secret door in my closet, grabbing my laptop from the shelf. When I came back to the bedroom, Cash and Fletcher were talking in hushed whispers that stopped when I appeared.

"Well, Drew. I have a few things I need to work on for other clients. Work calls." He planted a quick, wet kiss on my lips on his way to the door.

Cash had already taken his spot on my bed with his long legs stretched out before him. "Come on, Dark Saint." He patted the space next to him. "Critical thinking is my specialty, and I might have some insight you haven't thought of before."

I reclaimed my spot and opened the laptop. While waiting for me to go through the rigorous sign-in process, he hedged a question.

"Where did you learn of Red Death? Not from your Uncle David, right?"

Cutting my gaze to him in warning, he widened his eyes innocently. He knew how I felt about his feelings on the matter. To him, everyone was suspect. And I agreed…to an extent. When it wasn't someone who had supported Daddy and me all my life.

"Actually, no." I waited for the dark web to load. "I learned about Red Death when I went through Daddy's notes. Or what he had available in his room. The last target was Dr. Salinas, but I already ruled him out, as I told you before. However, there was one note that mentioned Red Death in his room. And when I went through the web, Daddy had built an entire folder around Red Death."

"So, you don't actually know that Red Death is responsible for his death?" Cash stared unblinking at the screen as I pulled up the folder.

"Absolutely? No. But this is the only thing that makes sense. This folder has folders and subfolders within. No real information, like he was building out the frame and was never able to fill it in." My voice caught as I thought of Daddy and all he'd never been able to finish. "I think it's a person Daddy was after. John Martin thought it might be a place, hence why he wanted to pay to use it for his revenge game. The Vanisher would know for sure," I sighed. Was he avoiding me on purpose? Did he know I spoke to John Martin? Or was it just a coincidence he was out of the country?

I didn't want to suspect him. He seemed genuine in his affection for Daddy and his motive for watching over me. I usually possessed solid judgment where character was concerned. There were no red flags from him. But like Cash said…everyone was suspect.

"What's that?" He pointed to the very last subfolder. It didn't even have a name, still listed as untitled. Clicking on it, it brought up a list of names that meant nothing to me.

Juan Rodriguez

Andrew McIntire

Gregory Lescheva

Cash froze next to me. "I know Gregory Lescheva. He's a consultant for the FBI."

I whipped toward him. "Is he dirty at all?"

He shook his head regretfully, as if he didn't want to stomp on this new lead. "No. He blurs a few lines here and there, but nothing that's out of the ordinary. I pushed way more boundaries than he did when I was on the force. Let's go through this from the top. You need to look at the evidence in a new light."

New light…

Light…

"Fuck!" I palmed my forehead. How was I so dense? Daddy didn't raise me to overlook things so easily.

I jumped up, racing around my room to put my laptop up and get dressed.

"What?" Cash yelled as he eyed me like I'd lost my damned mind. More like, I finally found it.

Stopping at the bed, I cupped his face with both hands and slammed my mouth on his. "Thank you. Now get dressed if you want to go with me."

He didn't ask where I was going or why. No questions at all. I didn't have time to bask in the trust he was slowly putting in me, but later.

Right then, I had somewhere I needed to be.

"Road trip?" Fletcher asked as I descended the stairs, dressed in comfortable clothes and a jacket. Rick was in the kitchen baking something. The smell was delicious.

"Just a short one," I told him as I opened the weapon's safe. Cash paused when I pulled it open from another door inside the closet beneath the stairs. His gun and holster were stored in there. I'd kept them there since we brought him home.

When I handed them to him, he gave them a brief look and then met my eyes. A lot of things had changed in the last few months. If he was going to be my partner, I needed him to be able to protect himself. He took the gun with a nod and then pulled the shoulder harness on. "I'll grab a jacket," he told me and pivoted to go back up the stairs.

"Drew?" Fletcher said, frowning as he watched Cash go, then glanced back at me. "Is this an errand or a business trip?"

How much danger were we facing? He wasn't alone in asking. Rick had come out of the kitchen, worry darkening his eyes.

So many distractions. These beautiful men were so distracting. Perfectly imperfect. Perfect for me. I finished putting on my own gun before reaching up to grip Fletcher's nape. He dipped his head swiftly into my kiss. It was fierce, hot, and altogether too brief.

"It's an errand only, I promise." Leaving Fletcher, I went to Rick. He cupped my face as I went to kiss him, his frown deepening as he studied me.

"You're upset."

"A little," I admitted. "More with myself than anything else, I promise. I need to check on this and I'm not going alone."

Cash descended the stairs right on cue. "I have her boys. Don't worry. No one is touching our girl."

I chuckled at that declaration. I didn't need them to protect me, even if I enjoyed the heat in his words when he said them. Rick and Fletcher, on the other hand, both relaxed. So, if that was what they needed, then so be it.

"Phone," Fletcher said, tossing one to Cash. "Keep it on. Our numbers are already programmed in."

"Got it," he said, sliding it into a pocket and then glancing at me.

"I gave you a gun," I pointed out. "You can have a phone."

Because trust had to start, and I did trust him. Even if unease prickled along my spine, that wasn't Cash, that was my own blindness.

Once we were in the car, Cash tilted his head to look at me. "Okay, what did you remember up there that has you arming up like we're going into a fight?"

While I'd assured Fletcher and Rick, my need for weapons hadn't escaped their notice. Then again, why should it? "I can't really explain it. I'm not playing vague on purpose—but the night you found me at the docks, Fletcher and I had gone to one of Daddy's storage units. I brought home all the files."

And I was an idiot.

"And?"

It was like he could hear me, though I didn't think he'd like the self-flagellation. I wasn't especially a fan. It wouldn't do us any good *now*.

"There wasn't that much in the files but I was too distracted—by Fletcher kissing me. By Rick at home. By hunting down a clue on who and what Red Death was, I forgot to do one crucial thing in that storage room. It's been there for months. It may be nothing."

"But you don't think it is." That wasn't a question. One I didn't really need to confirm as I kept the speedometer pegged at the speed limit on my race down the highway.

"I know it's not. This was Daddy. He would have left clues for me. Information no one could take *easily*."

That I hadn't even glanced at when I was there? Stupid. Stupid. Stupid.

"Talk to me, Vienna," Cash said, pulling me back to the present. "Tell me about your dad."

"Daddy?" That surprised me.

"Sometimes—victimology helps in these cases." The guarded way he said that sent ice plunging through my veins. I hated to think of Daddy as any kind of victim. But he was, right?

"Daddy has always hunted the monsters," I told him. "He's smart, self-educated, though I am pretty sure he also has a college degree or was close to one. He was my teacher as well as my father. Home schooled me. Found me different teachers when I needed them."

"Weapons. Self-defense. Combat," Cash ticked them off.

"Disguises. Camouflage. Espionage." Not that they'd called it that. Then I grinned at him. "Interrogation."

That got a laugh. "Pretty sure your dad could probably have taught you that, though I'm starting to wonder if he trained you like a profiler."

"Maybe," I said with a shrug. "It was never about listing off the skills; it was about developing the tools for what I needed when I needed them. I can do light maintenance on a car. I know how to handle body disposal. I can build a fake identity, but the digital age makes that harder."

"Hence, why you need someone like Fletcher."

"I need him for so much more than that." Light as it was, I was still chastising him.

Cash slid a hand over my thigh and squeezed it. "I know you need him for more than his skills. I meant that was how you met him."

"Yes."

"What about your mother?"

"What about her?" I glanced at him. "She's not a part of my life."

"At all?" He seemed surprised.

"Daddy got a woman pregnant," I told him in the same matter-of-fact tone he'd always used with me. "When she told him, she said it was more out of courtesy. She hadn't meant to, just an accident. Daddy asked her to have the baby, said he would take care of her until then, and after, he would raise me."

I used to add a little bit of fanciful romance to the tale when I was younger. But now? Now, I understood that Daddy had wanted me and the woman had agreed.

"She wasn't ready to raise a baby," I said softly. "Daddy promised it was never about not wanting me, she just didn't think she'd be a good mom. She trusted Daddy to take care of me, and after I was born, she stayed for a few months to breastfeed me, and then she left. Daddy took good care of her, so I know she didn't leave poor."

"I hate to ask this, but are you sure your mother left?"

"If you want to know did he kill her, remember how and why the Judge picks his victims. Then tell me, would he kill the woman who gave him me?"

"Fair," Cash conceded. "I'm guessing you don't have a name."

"No. I think Daddy would have told me if I had asked. But I always liked that he wanted me so much, he changed everything to make sure he could have me."

I always would.

By the time we reached the storage place, I was wound up again. My nerves kept me on edge. Once we were there, I went to the light in the center and unscrewed the bulb. I had to stand on my tiptoes. Cash took over, removing the bulb and then replacing it with a second one. After I closed the door, plunging us into the dark—then Cash turned on the light.

The purple-hue of the black light lit up the writing all over the walls. It was like his folders and sub folders. Only this was charts and timelines.

Names.

So many names.

"Vienna," Cash said slowly. "What was your father hunting?"

I didn't think it was a what. I thought it was a who.

A lot of them.

HOLY SHIT.

I knew the Judge had to possess a complicated mind. But I had no true idea. I stepped forward, lifting a hand to the wall, but I stopped just short of actually touching it. The cardinal rule of a scene, don't contaminate the evidence.

Even though I itched to touch the proof of his genius, he'd used UV ink. Here, in a public place, no one would ever think to test out a black light, except for his protégé. Someone he'd trained specifically to decode his work without ever writing it out.

Genius.

"This is a Venn diagram of sorts. But a really fucking complicated one." I moved back to join Vienna at her side. The neon glow of the ink sprawled out with names, codes, and dates. Some I recognized. Vaguely. Some I didn't. There were only a few places that intersected, with the exception of one.

The name in the exact center of the wall.

Gregory Lescheva.

Fucking hell. I had told Vienna that he wasn't dirty. But what had I told her? Everyone was suspect. Every fucking one. And I didn't see any validity to his name on that list because I'd worked with him before. I'd had beers with him after closing cases. Not often, but often enough that I thought I knew him.

Logically, just because his name was on the wall didn't mean he was guilty. But… Vienna was right. I knew how the Judge worked, and he would only be on this wall if he was fucking dirty somehow.

I glanced back at Vienna to see her fingers pressed to her lips as her eyes glistened. "Vienna?" I touched her elbow.

"This is the chain. He solved the entire chain, and he never told me he was even looking at the Network from this angle." Her voice was thick as she started walking the length of the floor to get a good look at all the names. "Terrance. Dion. Warrick. They're all here. Connected. Interconnected. This isn't a Venn diagram, Cash. It's a web. What if Red Death isn't a person but a network."

"A network within a network," I mused. But I couldn't look away from the name of my associate taunting me on the wall.

"A dirty, obscene network for the monsters. That's what Red Death is. Why so many in the Network have never heard of it. Dion had been lying, the bastard. He knew exactly what Red Death was." She laughed, the wet, bitter sound grating down my back.

"Lescheva is on this wall." I pointed to his name, trying to bring her back to me. She was spiraling. Vienna was blaming herself because she missed things. I saw it in surviving family members all the time, mostly in spouses. They would realize after their partner was dead that they didn't really know the person at all. But there were signs blaring them in the face that they overlooked.

How many opportunities had Vienna had to ask her father about his work? Probably too many to count.

And I was sure some of her raging emotions was fury that her father had kept so much from her.

But those were useless emotions. She needed to focus. Look at the evidence with a critical eye. And I was going to help her do that.

"Lescheva," I repeated. Then I pointed to the address written underneath. That wasn't his home, as far as I was aware. But it wasn't too far from here either. Maybe an hour's drive. Two if we hit traffic through the city.

"Hm?" She turned back around.

Good. That was good, my dark saint. Keep your attention on me.

"Lescheva is at the center. All connections lead back to him. We should start here. And lucky for us, I know him." I paused, making sure she was staying with me. "We need to start with this address. Where are the files you found here?"

Vienna's attention strayed to the wall, but she still answered me. "In the back. I made sure to grab them before we left."

"Then let's go. You drive. We need to stop and get a portable black light. I'll review the files on the way." I kept my words short. Clipped. She needed someone to take control of the situation, and that was me.

She nodded.

I took photos of every angle of the walls, making sure to capture everything. Then in a synchronized fashion, as if we'd been working together for years, we removed the black light bulbs, replaced them with the standard ones that were there before, and wiped traces of our visit away.

"I have a portable black light," Vienna commented as we made it back to the car. She opened the back, grabbed the box of files, and handed them off to me. Then, she removed the cover where the spare tire should be and pulled out a kit.

The files had been in with Fletcher for days. I recognized the box. As soon as I had it stored between my feet, I pulled them out one at a time. The kit was damn useful. The black-light was shaped perfectly for page reading.

Another trick to communicate with his daughter? A way to encode his messages? Were there black light notes in their home?

No, he wouldn't have done it there. That was why it was

here in a storage facility. Whatever her father had been doing, the hunt he'd been on, he'd done it *away* from her.

The GPS gave directions while I skimmed the pages. Not a lot of notes. A couple of cryptic references on some of the pages.

"Anything?" She didn't take her gaze from the road.

"No, there are some number and letter combinations, but nothing that makes sense to me."

"Five characters or twelve?"

"Two five and one twelve."

She nodded but didn't explain it. As much as it clawed at me to know, I left it.

For. The. Moment.

A few photos slipped out, and I frowned. The first two were no one I recognized, then there was one of Lescheva, though he looked a little rough like he'd been on a bender. The last one…

I stared at the last one hard. The guy's name was right there on the tip of my tongue. I knew him. Dammit, who was he?

Lescheva's name in a file. Lescheva's name on the wall. Lescheva's photo in the folder. Too many knots all following a string to the guy. Then there was this guy—dammit, what was his name? He'd been a friend of Pops or an informant.

Pretty sure he was more informant than friend, but Dad had liked him. It was going to give me a headache until I found the right thread to pull.

"Anything else in the file?"

"No," I said, tucking the photos back into place. "Just some pictures, more info on some of the names we saw on the wall. A few pictures. Apparently, he was zeroing in on Lescheva."

What the hell were you into, Old Man? Lescheva had also worked with my pops. I liked the guy, but if he'd aroused the

Judge's interest, there wasn't going to be much I could do for him.

She glanced at the open folder. Lescheva was on the top, but I pulled out the other picture again. Maybe he was linked through Lescheva and not just Pops?

It was all irritating the fuck out of me. I checked the GPS as she cut around town. That made sense, a direct route would put us right into traffic. We were going the longer way, but we'd get there.

I rubbed my thumb against my lower lip. "When we get there, I'll go in first…"

"No." She didn't snap or launch into an attack, she just shook her head decisively. "You shouldn't go in at all, the FBI is already looking for you."

I grimaced. "Lescheva knows that."

"What?"

"When I reached out to my contacts—before you took the phone away, he was who I was calling. Before you get pissed, I didn't say a word about you or the guys." I never would. "Lescheva is a consultant. He also knew Pops. So, he tends to try and look out for me, but I have my own way of doing things and he understands that too."

"That's why you want to go in first? Because he's a friend?"

"Partially," I said. "Partially, because I don't know what we're walking into. I don't know this address, but I don't really know where Lescheva hangs his hat. Why would I? Our relationship was more professional courtesy than anything else."

Except…

"I think he was hunting the Judge too, whether he realized he was on the Judge's trail or not." On her trail. Yeah, that was not going to work for me.

The sun was rapidly setting, and I swore it was like a

countdown clock ticked down the minutes the closer it got to the horizon. It was completely down by the time we pulled onto the street with the address. Without me saying a word, Vienna had already turned off the headlights.

"This is a lot more industrial than I expected." There were houses present, but most of them looked like they'd been abandoned. Or at least had fallen into disrepair.

"Old shoe factory," she said, motioning to the large building. "This town probably thrived on their business, it closed, and the people who could afford it moved."

And the people who couldn't? Or the people who wanted the cover? Abandoned homes in a dying town were as useful as Vienna's subdivision, except dying towns still had gossips.

Or at least they did in my experience.

"Go the rest of the way on foot?"

Without a word, she nodded then parked one street further over. We moved like we were sharing a brain. Maybe we were. The interior light of the car didn't come on when we opened the door. I checked my weapon and the kit before sliding them into my back pocket.

It had gloves in it as well as a set of lock picks. Vienna had her own, though. Still, I stayed with her as she made her way up the alley between the dilapidated houses. No exterior lights had come on, and there was only a faint sound that took me a second to identify.

At the edge of the property indicated by the address in the storage locker, I paused Vienna with a gentle touch to her arm. Fortunately, without exterior light, our eyes had adjusted. The fact there was a half-moon gave us some illumination.

"Listen," I whispered, barely moving my lips.

She tilted her head. I recognized the moment she picked up the sound of the motor. A generator. So not only was the house in use, there was a generator powering it. Vienna had something similar.

"Slow," I said and freed my gun. She nodded, doing much the same. We moved right up to the back door of the house, and I tested the door. It opened with one twist.

Okay, not locked. That *did not* bode well. Vienna slid ahead of me before I could say a word, and she was through the door. There were lights on, but no television or radio. No other sounds carried.

A faint hum from a refrigerator. Room by room, we cleared it. The place had a cluttered feel and a bit of a musty smell. Like age and disuse vied for dominance here.

Popping open the fridge, I scanned the contents. Vienna spared it a glance. The food was fresh, the milk unexpired, and there was takeout.

Nothing upstairs, but Vienna stared at the pantry door for the longest time. She was still there when I came back down.

Secret door?

When I went to it, she put a hand out to stop me, then pointed to the cord that followed the very edge of the floor and then up along the molding of the door frame.

An alarm.

I backtracked the cord to the wall, then put a hand over the box it was plugged into.

It was cold. No hum. Neither of us spoke aloud, even if we seemed alone. I curled my fingers to her, and she moved over to test the wall "plug" as well. It wasn't working.

With a nod, she went to the door and opened it. Dammit, I didn't want her going without me, but the interior was just a plain pantry.

Vienna pressed on a wall behind the shelves and the third panel opened another door. Music drifted up, and the sound had all the hair on my body standing up. Like a wraith, she descended the steps and I did not have her light feet, but I was right behind her.

Cells.

It was the first thing that hit me. Bars forming a cage of sorts. But it was definitely a cell.

It wasn't empty.

"Daddy?"

Vienna and the boys return in *Last Word,*
No loose ends. No mercy.

AFTERWORD

Let's chat…

I mean if you need a minute to process those last few lines, we can wait. But definitely, let's chat when you're ready.

Ready?

Great!

From the moment we wrote the first scene of Kill Song, Daddy has been a *presence* in these books. Thackery Drew raised his daughter to be capable, cool, competent, and very deadly. He also raised her with a compassionate heart. His loss is something that has been felt profoundly for us as the authors in every single word.

Vienna was so *alone* when she met Rick. A loneliness he began to help alleviate in her. Fletcher and Cash have certainly played their parts. Rick comforts her and backs her one hundred percent. Fletcher entertains her and reminds her to laugh. Cash pushes and challenges her. She needs them all. They filled in a very large gap she hadn't even realized was there even as they also helped assuage a loss they can never replace.

Is that Daddy in the cell? Is he alive? If he is—what does it mean?

You had to know we weren't going to answer that here, right? But we promise, answers are coming.

See you next time for the epic conclusion to the Cardinal Sins saga. Don't forget to order and leave a review!

We are so excited for what comes next. What about you?

ABOUT HEATHER LONG

I *love* books. Not just a little bit, but a lot. Books were my best friends when I was growing up. Books didn't care if I was new to a town or to a class. They were always there, my trustiest of companions. Until they turned on me and said I had to write them.

I can tell you that my own personal happily ever after included writing books. I've always said that an HEA is a work in progress. It's true in my marriage, my friendships, and in my career. I am constantly nurturing my muse as we dive into new tales, new tropes, new characters and more.

After seventeen years in Texas, we relocated to the Pacific Northwest in search of seasons, new experiences, and new geography. I can't wait to discover what life (and my muse) have in store for me.

Maybe writing was always my destiny and romance my fate. After all, my grandmother wasn't a fan of picture books and used to read me her Harlequin Romance novels.

Follow Heather & Sign up for her newsletter:
www.heatherlong.net
TikTok

ABOUT BLAKE BLESSING

Blake is a hyper asian ball of sunshine, and she cannot be contained in one box. Prone to random bouts of spinning or hyper-focusing, she's also equal parts goofy, ridiculous, and random. It's funny that she writes so much dark romance. Her goal is to provide stories about characters you can't help but root for through thought-provoking situations, even if they're a little—a lot—morally gray.

TikTok

ALSO BY HEATHER LONG

82nd Street Vandals

Savage Vandal

Vicious Rebel

Ruthless Traitor

Dirty Devil

Shamelessly Loyal (Novella)

Brutal Fighter

Dangerous Renegade

Merciless Spy

Reckless Thief

Fierce Dancer

Dirty Dancer

Bay Ridge Royals

Shamelessly Loyal (Novella)

Battle Lines

Deceptive Truce

Wicked Surrender

Violent Chaos

Desperate Victory

BLOOD Brothers

Burn

Lure

Own

Blue Ivy Prep

Problem Child

Mad Boys

Party Crashers

Money Shot

Bravo Team Wolf

When Danger Bites

Bitten Under Fire

Cardinal Sins

Kill Song

First Chorus

High Note

Last Word

Chance Monroe

Earth Witches Aren't Easy

Plan Witch from Out of Town

Bad Witch Rising

Fevered Hearts

Marshal of Hel Dorado

Brave are the Lonely

Micah & Mrs. Miller

A Fistful of Dreams

Raising Kane

Wanted: Fevered or Alive

Wild and Fevered

The Quick & The Fevered

A Man Called Wyatt

Going Royal

Some Like it Royal

Some Like it Scandalous

Some Like it Deadly

Some Like it Secret

Some Like it Easy

Heart of the Nebula

Queenmaker

Deal Breaker

Throne Taker

Lone Star Leathernecks

Semper Fi Cowboy

As You Were, Cowboy

Shackled Souls

Succubus Chained

Succubus Unchained

Succubus Blessed

Shackled Souls (Omnibus)

STANDALONES

Kiss of Fate (w / Blake Blessing)

Taste of Karma (w / Blake Blessing)

I'll Be Home… (w / Tate James)

Overexposed (w / Tate James)

Switchboard Duet

Talk to Me

Don't Let Go

Untouchable

Rules and Roses

Changes and Chocolates

Keys and Kisses

Whispers and Wishes

Hangovers and Holidays

Brazen and Breathless

Trials and Tiaras

Graduation and Gifts

Defiance and Dedication

Songs and Sweethearts

Legacy and Lovers

Farewells and Forever

Hellos and Happily Ever Afters

Wolves of Willow Bend

Wolf at Law

Wolf Bite

Caged Wolf

Wolf Claim

Wolf Next Door

Rogue Wolf

Bayou Wolf

Untamed Wolf

Wolf with Benefits

River Wolf

Single Wicked Wolf

Desert Wolf

Snow Wolf

Wolf on Board

Holly Jolly Wolf

Shadow Wolf

His Moonstruck Wolf

Thunder Wolf

Ghost Wolf

Outlaw Wolves

Wolf Unleashed

ALSO BY BLAKE BLESSING

The Collection

Snatched

Edged

Crazed

Bastard Brothers of Carnage Series

Addict

Convict

Killer

Psycho

Traitor

Mazza Series

Marks of the Mazza

Bonds of the Mazza

Secrets of the Mazza

War of the Mazza

Astrid Scott Series

Pretty Lies

Ugly Truths

Busted Dreams

Vivid Fears

Brittle Hope

Fragile Minds Duet

Fractured

Altered

Standalone RH Romance
Pin-up Girl

Standalone MF Romance
Full Glasses and Burju Shoes